ALTERNATIVE REMEDIES FOR LOSS

ALTERNATIVE REMEDIES FOR LOSS

JOANNA CANTOR

BLOOMSBURY PUBLISHING
NEW YORK · LONDON · OXFORD · NEW DELHI · SYDNEY

BLOOMSBURY PUBLISHING
Bloomsbury Publishing Inc.
1385 Broadway, New York, NY 10018, USA

BLOOMSBURY, BLOOMSBURY PUBLISHING, and the Diana logo are
trademarks of Bloomsbury Publishing Plc

First published in the United States 2018

Copyright © Joanna Cantor, 2018

All rights reserved. No part of this publication may be reproduced or transmitted in
any form or by any means, electronic or mechanical, including photocopying,
recording, or any information storage or retrieval system, without prior permission
in writing from the publishers.

Bloomsbury Publishing Plc does not have any control over, or responsibility for, any
third-party websites referred to or in this book. All internet addresses given in this
book were correct at the time of going to press. The author and publisher regret any
inconvenience caused if addresses have changed or sites have ceased to exist, but can
accept no responsibility for any such changes.

ISBN: HB: 978-1-63557-171-4; eBook: 978-1-63557-172-1

Library of Congress Cataloging-in-Publication Data is available

2 4 6 8 10 9 7 5 3 1

Typeset by Westchester Publishing Services
Printed and bound in the U.S.A. by Berryville Graphics Inc., Berryville, Virginia

To find out more about our authors and books visit www.bloomsbury.com
and sign up for our newsletters.

Bloomsbury books may be purchased for business or promotional use. For
information on bulk purchases please contact Macmillan Corporate and Premium
Sales Department at specialmarkets@macmillan.com.

For my parents.

Preface

"You must be new."

It was Olivia's third week at the production company, and she was standing outside of the office on Fifth Avenue. The man speaking to her was a client—she'd seen him arrive for a meeting earlier. He looked fortyish, and he was around her height, with a paunch. He was smoking a cigarette, and she had just returned from delivering a hard drive. He said his name was Geoffrey, but that everyone called him Geo.

It was a Tuesday night around seven, the first September in nearly two decades—as long as Olivia could remember—when she hadn't been in school. Days were still summerlike, but the light was changing quickly, and she could feel the crisp undertones of fall.

As they rode the elevator up, Geoffrey asked if she'd have a drink with him.

She told him she never knew what time she got to leave. Last night, she wasn't home until almost eleven.

"It doesn't seem that busy," he said. "I'll wait for you now."

There was something familiar in the way Geoffrey smiled at her that made Olivia queasy. He believed she would say yes, although he was close to twice her age and a stranger, and it was her impulse to thwart his expectation. But when she looked at him, she saw the possibility of seafood. There was nothing in her apartment besides black tea, a shriveled lemon, and a carton of milk she was afraid to open, even to pour down the drain.

She told him it was okay if he wanted to wait. He took a beer from the fridge in the kitchen and sat out front until a little before eight, when one of the editors asked Olivia what she was still doing there. Then she got her things and Geoffrey.

He led her to a Spanish place on Fifteenth Street she'd passed before on the way to the train. They sat at the bar, which was nearly full but subdued, and drank vodka martinis. The bartender who served them was older than Olivia but much younger than Geoffrey, and handsome, with wavy hair he tossed away from his pale green eyes. Olivia wanted to somehow telegraph to him that this was not a date—that she was there with Geoffrey only because—but there was nothing she could articulate, just a hot, restless anger. Her mother was dead.

Geoffrey told her to order whatever she wanted, so she ordered octopus and a potato omelet and clams with chorizo. The bartender set down a breadbasket and poured herbed oil on a white plate. Geoffrey asked her questions about her job and where she grew up and ignored the fact that she answered with a mouth full of bread.

Geoffrey worked for a large advertising firm. "A lot of golf," he told Olivia, with a smile that suggested this was likely to impress her. He barely touched the food when it came but ordered them another round of drinks.

He said he had separated from his wife six months before. She was living at their place in the Hudson Valley—a drag, he said, because it was beautiful there this time of year.

"So I'm stuck staying at a hotel while I'm still paying taxes on the house," he said. "Not the worst thing. I could get used to room service." When he laughed, the skin under his jaw wobbled.

Near the end of his second drink, Geoffrey excused himself to go to the bathroom. Olivia prepared to flee. Never mind that she might see Geoffrey again at the office. That awkwardness, existing as it did in the improbable future, was nothing compared to the trapped feeling that came from listening to him talk and made her regret the oily food she had just eaten so hungrily.

She reached for her purse, on a hook under the bar—a faded woven bag her mother had bought in Mexico before she was born—and stood up.

"Anything else?" the bartender said, leaning toward her.

"I'm just—" she began. He regarded her, calm and unhurried. His ethereal eyes surprised her again. She wished she had come alone to have a drink at the bar. Maybe she still would, another night.

"We'll take the check," Geoffrey said. She hadn't noticed his return. His thigh brushed heavily against hers as he took his seat. If he sensed that she'd been about to slip out, he didn't let on. The bartender brought the bill, and Geoffrey handed over a credit card without looking at it.

Then his hand was on her back, guiding her out through the crowded entrance. It was the first time Olivia had done this: come out of a New York restaurant with a man who had just paid for her meal, a man besides her father. It felt like an iconic moment in the movie of her life gone sour. She knew she should go home—it was just one regrettable night of drinks, nothing that couldn't be washed off. And yet something within her rebelled against a meek *goodnight* and a walk to the subway. Her mind felt like an overheating motor, chewing an inchoate, ludicrous plan.

Geoffrey hailed a taxi. "I'll drop you off," he said, and Olivia looked down at the sidewalk with a bare hint of a smile to indicate that this was what she'd been hoping for. They rode uptown in near silence. After ten blocks, he put his hand on her knee, and when she did not object, he began to stroke it lightly.

Geoffrey let her out of the cab and kissed her on the curb, clutching her lower back, his mouth boozy. He murmured something about a restaurant he wanted to take her to, next time.

"Would you like to come up for a drink?" Olivia said. Her mouth was dry and her palms were damp. She didn't want him in her apartment. And yet she needed to feel that she could make something happen.

Giddily, Geoffrey paid the driver. Olivia led him through the small lobby, avoiding the doorman's gaze. In the elevator, as he kissed her again with more confidence, it occurred to her that she didn't have anything to drink. The terrible milk came to mind, and she bit her lip to keep from laughing. Finding her mouth unavailable, Geoffrey kissed her neck.

In the apartment, she turned on as few lights as possible. She didn't want him seeing her life.

Geoffrey didn't seem to mind the absence of the promised drink. He propelled Olivia into the living room, kicking off his loafers while he made soft moaning noises. His tongue was a fish on land, muscular and desperate. "Not to be unoriginal," he said, "but you're a knockout."

She was the one to lead him to the bedroom, which was furnished like a mid-range chain hotel, with floral curtains that matched the bedspread and a large mahogany armoire. Light came through the windows from the street. The ancient clock radio on the nightstand reported that it was not yet eleven.

They were kneeling on the bed, both of their shirts off, when she said it: "It's a thousand dollars."

"Huh?" Geoffrey murmured. He was working the zipper of his jeans.

Olivia pressed her fingertips into his hairy chest, hard. "A thousand. For the night."

He pulled away, his drunken mouth gaping, his small eyes darting around the room.

Once she said the words, she felt calm. In the moment before he replied, everything constricted within her opened into vast, empty space.

"I thought," Geoffrey said softly.

Olivia felt a particular combination of elation and repulsion, a longing for everything that could not be. The room was too small to hold the way she felt. "What'd you think, Geoffrey?"

1.

On the flight to New Delhi, Olivia slept through landing and woke to announcements she didn't understand. She had the feeling of being dragged out of a different, preferable world, but she couldn't remember what she'd been dreaming. The air on the plane was warm and thick with bodies. Across the aisle, her brother Ty and his girlfriend, Christina, were checking seat-back pockets and peering into the crevices beneath the armrests.

"You missed breakfast," Ty said when he saw that Olivia was awake. "Not a tragedy. I think those were authentic Indian croissants."

"What I would give to be able to sleep like that on a plane," Christina said. It was the first time Olivia had seen Christina look even slightly disheveled. Her hair was tangled and she was still wearing a pink neck pillow.

"What's your secret?" Christina asked.

Olivia had taken two Xanax at the beginning of the flight and another one when she woke up somewhere over the Middle East. She wasn't sure how else anyone could expect to sleep on a plane. While she was considering her response, Ty retrieved her backpack from the overhead bin. Then they were moving slowly forward, and it was a game to take the smallest possible steps but remain in continuous motion, to pace herself exactly right.

They caught up with the others—Alec, the eldest, and his wife, Holly; Max, their father; and June, the woman Max was dating, whom Olivia did not plan to acknowledge. The pacing game ceased to amuse her. She rested her chin on Alec's arm and slipped into semi-dreams. There was drool on her chin, and then there was a uniformed man with a mustache, asking, "What is your business in this country?," and everyone was quick to say they were not there on business, which Olivia was fairly certain was not what he was asking, but either way, they got their stamps. And then they were at baggage claim, collecting the luggage—so much luggage, among the seven of them. Olivia wanted to curl up on top of one of the large suitcases, but by this point her brothers were heckling her, pushing her back and forth between them, determined to keep her awake.

Their guide appeared, holding a small sign that said HARRIS. He had been waiting for them at immigration, he explained hurriedly, but they must not have seen him. His name was Akosh. He was wearing a thin red tie, circles of sweat under his arms. Akosh brought them small plastic cups of tea, milky and sweet, because it was morning in India.

Outside the terminal, in heat that felt like a creature draped around their necks, they confronted an eight-lane circus of tour buses and jeeps and small green-and-yellow vehicles that looked like golf carts. Akosh tried to convince them to wait indoors while he fetched the drivers, but to her family's credit, no one retreated to the climate-controlled limbo of the airport.

All around Olivia, people seemed to be hustling in slow motion, their jerky movements suggesting speed Olivia did not see, though perhaps, still Xanaxed, her brain was slowing everything down. Several men crouched behind a tour bus, changing the tire, while cars lined up behind, honking rhythmically and incessantly. The smell—burning rubber, tropical sweat and incense, spices and urine, cows and their shit—was everywhere at once. Teenage boys, their yellowed shirts revealing triangles of hairless chest and stomach, rushed at her family, offering rides and trinkets, and Akosh spoke harshly to them in a guttural tongue, flipping them away with the backs of his fingers.

Alec's hands were on Olivia's shoulders. "We're going," he said, and Olivia saw that everyone else had followed Akosh into the rotary.

THEY HAD BEEN at dinner in the city when Max first proposed the trip. "I promised your mother I'd take her this year," he'd said. It would have been their thirty-fifth wedding anniversary. "Olivia thinks we should go anyway."

"I didn't say that." Olivia stabbed at a shrimp. It was Memorial Day, and the evening was warm, but the wait for an outdoor table had been over an hour, so they settled for sitting near the doors that opened onto the terrace. The restaurant was large and full of over-dressed groups cackling over shellfish platters. It seemed an odd choice for their small, somber gathering: Ty, Christina, and Max. Olivia's mother had died six weeks before.

"Olivia and I are going this summer," Max said. "I think the whole family should come."

Olivia hadn't realized this was an actual plan. It was true that the day before, Max had found her flipping through notes she'd made about the trip she and her mother had wanted to take. Max had leaned over Olivia's shoulder, studying her messy scrawl. "We should go," he'd said.

Ty glanced at Christina. "This summer could be tough. Christina has the bar at the end of July."

"August, then," Max said. "Before Olivia goes back to school."

"It's the monsoon," Olivia said. She was pretty sure that was true.

"There are cars. There are umbrellas."

Ty looked unconvinced.

"I've always wanted to go to India," Christina said softly, surprising them all.

"I thought you wanted to do something relaxing after the bar," Ty said. "Like the beach."

"I took an Indian history class in college," Christina said.

"I'll call the travel agent," Max said. "I think this could be good."

ON THE WAY to the hotel, Akosh reminded them of the itinerary: they would spend two nights in New Delhi, then travel to Agra to see the Taj Mahal. They'd tour Rajasthan for five days before returning home.

After they'd checked into the hotel, a splashy high-rise with dramatic flower arrangements and pools of water in the lobby, and after showers and a breakfast of omelets and coffee at one of the hotel's restaurants, Akosh herded the Harrises and Christina and June back into the jeeps for a shopping expedition. Shopping, he claimed, was a very good first-day activity: it defeated jetlag. "And you can dress like the local people," he told them.

Olivia didn't like the feeling that Akosh was being patronizing, though she could hardly blame him. Clearly they weren't going to blend in with the locals. She'd read about guides making deals with shopkeepers, receiving some sort of kickback when they brought tourists there. But when Akosh took them to the first store, which was large, with separate floors for men's, women's, and home goods, he didn't even go inside with them. He would take lunch, he explained, though it was only eleven, and collect them in an hour.

Max, Alec, and Ty had no real interest in outfitting themselves, but their presence seemed to rattle the other female customers, so they retreated downstairs to their own department, June in tow.

Back at the hotel, Olivia had tried to combat her grogginess with a couple of strong cups of coffee, and now she had the not unpleasant sensation that she was swimming on land. Her legs and arms were weightless, and there was a moment of surprise each time her sandaled feet made contact with the red tile floor. Christina was handing her clothes to try on that were the color of autumn leaves. They made her think of crayons, of that coveted color, burnt sienna.

Holly already had ten or twelve scarves draped over her arms. "For the girls," she explained. It was unclear whether she meant friends or employees. Holly was British and a model turned actress. Alec had met her in Los Angeles, where he was an agent. She was tall and thin and head-turningly stunning, with dark hair, nearly translucent skin, and light blue eyes. She was snobby but in a funny way, and the Harrises had been quickly won over, not least of all Olivia, who could recall with pleasure each time she and Holly had been mistaken for sisters.

Christina emerged from the dressing room in a lavender tunic and ballooning white pants. A saleswoman explained that these were the traditional salwar kameez outfits. To wear them properly, you added a dupatta, a long, wide scarf draped over your chest.

"Try some things on," Christina urged. Olivia liked the way she looked in the clothes Christina picked out for her. She stood in the fitting room wearing only a tunic, making what her mother had called her model faces—narrowing her cheeks and pouting out her lips.

"I love this," Holly gasped, and Olivia stepped around the curtain to see. Customers stared at her bare legs as Holly fondled a river of turquoise. Akosh had been right—they were entertained. Her mother would have loved this store for the colors alone. Olivia wanted to capture it somehow, but pulling out her camera here, while the other customers went about their business, didn't feel right.

When she came out again, wearing her own clothes and carrying the two outfits she had chosen, June had reemerged from the men's department. She was wearing a white silk jacket and standing in front of the three-way mirror. She adjusted the yellow scarf around her neck.

"That looks nice on you," Christina said.

Olivia made a mental note about Christina.

"Not very practical for this kind of trip," Holly said, glancing at Olivia. There was no need for any kind of jacket in India, except perhaps a waterproof poncho. Outside, the clouds were gathering. August was the middle of the monsoon, as Olivia had thought.

"It is late in the season," June said. She sounded disappointed. She turned sideways, still looking at herself in the mirror.

"Well, it's not exactly trendy," Holly said, relenting. "You'll wear it next year."

"Might as well stock up while my dad's paying," Olivia said.

June stiffened. Christina looked embarrassed too, as though she were implicated. Holly's eyes crinkled at the edges as they did when she was about to laugh.

June carefully removed the jacket, avoiding their gaze.

The men came back upstairs, carrying shopping bags and looking slightly uncomfortable.

"We talked each other into it," said Alec.

"This is going to be good," Holly said.

"Holly prefers me in a suit," Alec said, draping his arm around Christina, who seemed a little scandalized by Holly's sarcasm. "I'm the working stiff and she's the gorgeous actress, and she doesn't want anyone to forget it."

"Not true," said Holly. "I'm the one who got you to stop wearing Brooks Brothers on the weekend."

Olivia walked outside, leaving her bundle of Indian clothes behind. The clouds were very dark and a breeze raced through the humid air. She leaned back against the storefront and watched people pass. Stylishly dressed Indian women, some wearing saris and others in Western clothes, strolled along the covered walkway carrying shopping bags. There were men in suits and a smattering of foreigners as well. Three women walked by in burkas. Past the walkway and the road there was a grassy roundabout with a fountain in the center and children playing.

IT WAS ELEANOR Harris, Olivia's mother, who had wanted to go to India. She'd started practicing yoga around the time Olivia went to college, and as she became more serious about it, she began pestering Max to take her to its birthplace. But Max hadn't been interested in this more adventurous type of travel. To him, summers were for Europe or maybe Cape Cod, winters for the Caribbean. Finally, Eleanor said she would take Olivia, the year after Olivia graduated from college.

Last January, Eleanor's doctors had diagnosed the brain tumor: a high-grade, inoperable astrocytoma. In February, the first week her mother was really too sick to go out, it was Olivia who brought up the trip: *Where will we go, when we go to India?* They'd been lying in bed together, making fun of daytime television. Olivia pulled a map up on her laptop, and Eleanor, disinclined to mope, was immediately game.

They had looked at flights from New York and decided they would fly into New Delhi. The next day Olivia bought a few guidebooks, one with pictures and another with Bible-thin pages, and she read them, or tried to, while Eleanor looked at the pictures.

I want to see this, Eleanor would say, pointing at a picture of a temple or a statue of a Hindu deity. And Olivia would look it up in the guidebook and they would study the map and figure out how to get there. It was disconcerting to watch her mother, a high school English teacher with a formidable memory, begin to lose track of details, asking Olivia repeatedly where something was located. It was hard to know what was tumor and what was medication; by a few weeks after the diagnosis, Eleanor was taking painkillers, first just at bedtime and soon around the clock. Max set an alarm at night so she wouldn't miss a dose.

Olivia sent her family the itinerary she and her mother had sketched out. It included five nights at an ashram Eleanor had wanted to visit, so Olivia wasn't surprised when the travel agent steered them in a different direction—flying into New Delhi, but ditching the religious sites of Bodh Gaya, Varanasi, and Rishikesh in favor of Jodhpur and Jaipur, more popular tourist cities.

Still, negotiating with the travel agent had been a healthy distraction. Her mother had died in April, exceeding the three-month prognosis by only days. Olivia was in a kind of limbo until fall semester. She was splitting her time between her family home in Rye, New York, and the apartment her father had rented near Sloan Kettering, the cancer hospital in the city, under the apparently optimistic assumption that her mother would be undergoing months of treatment. Most people she knew either already had jobs in the city or were traveling, though at least Kelsey, her best friend, had been around. Kelsey had taken a year off before college, so by the time Olivia got home from India, she would be back in Colorado, finishing school.

OLIVIA PULLED OUT her camera just as the rain began to fall. Past the walkway, the drops were so big you could see them individually, or at least it seemed that way. She focused her camera on the roundabout and the kids and the fountain. The vehicles—cars and rickshaws—circling the roundabout interrupted the shot. She held the camera at chest level and tried to look nonchalant, and soon the passersby, fewer of them now and moving more quickly, walked in front of the camera too. The rain grew louder. The light was low and even, and she could picture how this was going to look, like a sort of mosaic, gray asphalt, green-and-yellow rickshaws, the intermittent green patch beyond, and darkness when people blocked the view. Everyone was seeking shelter from the rain in shops or flinging themselves into taxis. Soon there were fewer cars circling. She stood very still and kept filming. The children kept playing at the center of the roundabout. She saw one of them, a boy or a girl, she couldn't tell from this distance, extend their palms, face tilted toward the sky. When cars passed, they sent cascades of water up onto the stone walkway. Her feet were soaked.

Then Alec was beside her. "Getting anything good?" He was carrying several large shopping bags.

Holly was next to him, wrapped in a new shawl. "I threw the things you liked in with our stuff," she said.

Olivia turned off the camera. "Thanks. Where's everyone else?"

"Waiting inside for the drivers."

"June made such a spectacle of paying for that jacket herself," Holly said. "You'd have loved it."

"Try not to take this so seriously, kiddo," Alec said.

"Why not?"

"No one with good sense would have come on this trip," Holly said. "It doesn't speak well for her judgment."

"Men are swine," Alec said. "They're helpless without women."

"Bears with furniture," Holly agreed cheerfully.

"Dad screwed up, but he organized this trip for you," Alec said. "He thought it would be nice for you, to go on the trip you and Mom planned."

"This isn't the trip Mom and I planned." Eleanor and Olivia had wanted to stay at ashrams and hike in the Himalayan foothills. They had not envisioned luxury hotels that might as well have been in Europe. They certainly had not planned on June.

THEY'D BEEN EATING Chinese takeout in the kitchen, a week before they were leaving for India, when Max told Olivia that he'd invited a friend to join them on the trip.

"A friend?" Her mind jumped between her father's closest friends, men she'd known her whole life. She couldn't imagine any of them suddenly deciding to join the Harrises' trip to India.

"June. She and I—have been seeing a bit of each other."

"You mean dating?" Even as she said the words, she felt certain he would laugh and say, of course not, he was not dating, he had meant something else entirely.

Instead, Max merely looked embarrassed. "I suppose that's what you'd call it."

Still, it took Olivia moments to process. Her mother had died less than four months earlier, so recently that condolence letters were still arriving at the house on a near-daily basis. "How could you be dating?"

Max reached for a carton of food. "Your mother and I discussed it," he said. "She didn't want me to stay single forever. She wanted us all to be happy." He used his chopsticks to direct more beef with broccoli onto his plate.

"Forever is one thing," Olivia said. Numb disbelief was giving way to an animal sense of danger. "I thought this trip was supposed to be about Mom," she said. "To honor her." Her voice sounded small.

"Well, it's about the rest of us too. I thought I could use some company, while you kids are off having fun."

While she was wondering how to respond to this absurd explanation, Max ate a piece of broccoli.

"Mom just died," Olivia said, her voice rising. "We're not *supposed* to be having fun." It felt like a joke, or like her father was losing his mind. But as she grew outraged, and then unsuccessfully fought off tears, Max remained calm. It had been decided, he said, and though he was sorry she was upset, he had not been asking her opinion.

AKOSH RETURNED TO take them to the Lodi Gardens, which everyone liked well enough, but it was so hot and humid that after ten minutes of walking around, everyone but Olivia was camped out on benches in the shade, drinking bottled water and lethargically awaiting the return to the hotel.

Olivia forced herself to ignore the heat and walk around, mostly to get away from June. Though it hardly seemed possible, June's presence was worse than she'd imagined. Her hair, red and obviously dyed, was garish, and her clothing absurd—wide-legged white pants and a navy blouse with white anchors on it, appropriate for yachting in the Caribbean, coupled with waterproof Velcro sandals appropriate for catching frogs. Worse was her demeanor, which was determinedly sunny, as though she were either oblivious to what the Harrises were going through or believed it was her job to cheer them up.

The gardens, Akosh told them, contained a mosque and several tombs. In her film courses, Olivia had learned to look at the world in frames, noticing patterns in motion, color, and light, favoring composition over substance. There was so much more to look at in Delhi than there was at school or at home. But breaking these monuments down into components would feel presumptuous. This was a place with meaning and weight. It demanded narrative, and narrative was not her strong suit. She wondered if she would feel this way about all of India: not qualified to document it, even for the sake of art, or in this case, her thesis, for which she secretly hoped to find inspiration. She had only one semester left of college—she would have graduated in May, but she had dropped out in January when her mother was diagnosed. Her parents fought her over the decision initially, begging her to finish the year and graduate, but she was adamant. And she'd been right, especially given how little time her mother had had.

After a late lunch, they returned to the hotel. Olivia's room had polished wood floors, wood paneling, and a view that made Delhi look like a utopian parkland. Flipping through the channels, she found *Indiana Jones* dubbed in what she thought was Hindi. She watched for a few minutes before drifting off to sleep, still gripping the remote. She woke to the phone, which seemed to have been ringing endlessly in her dreams. It was Ty, calling to tell her to meet in the lobby for dinner in twenty minutes.

Stepping into hot water made her feel more like herself. The hotel shampoo smelled somehow Indian, spicy, though she couldn't identify the spice. She scrubbed and scrubbed her hair, feeling as though she were bathing herself in fragrant tea. She shaved her legs and got out feeling refreshed, but she must have cut her knee shaving, because a ribbon of blood twisted down her calf, spotting the white bath rug before she noticed. She found the source, applied toilet paper, and called the front desk for a bandage. She prepared a tip but hadn't thought to dress, so she opened the door in a hotel bathrobe, her long hair dripping. The man with the bandages smirked at her as he accepted the coins she gave him, which she thought were about a dollar but could also have been ten cents.

Olivia combed her hair and braided it down her back. In her new Indian outfit, a mustard-colored tunic that reached almost to her knees with the burnt sienna bloomer pants underneath, and her hair pulled back from her face, she barely recognized herself. She was pale in the bright bathroom lights and the circles under her eyes made her look older.

They were eating in another of the hotel restaurants that night, but everyone was waiting for her on sofas in the lobby. It turned out that Alec and Holly and Ty and Christina had met beforehand for cocktails. They were laughing about the weird drink names. Max and June sat next to each other, talking quietly.

Olivia had met June once before the trip. It had been Fourth of July weekend and she'd been at her parents' house. Max must have thought she was out with Kelsey, but she'd come home early and fallen asleep watching a movie in the den.

She'd awoken to voices and padded barefoot out into the living room. Max was there, talking with a woman Olivia had never seen before.

"Dad?" she said. She was disoriented from smoking pot earlier and from her nap and didn't know what time it was.

"Hi, honey. Meet June." Her father looked unmistakably guilty.

"What are you doing?" Olivia asked him, ignoring June, whose expression was startled if not downright fearful.

"I'm showing June the house," Max had said.

Olivia turned toward June. "Are you a real estate agent?" she demanded.

"No," June said questioningly, glancing at Max. "It's very nice to meet you, Olivia, but I should be going."

Olivia could tell she'd caught them doing something wrong, but she couldn't immediately process *what*. She was self-medicating fairly effectively that month. It was inconceivable to her that her father would be dating less than three months after her mother died. The truth was that Olivia hadn't thought about the encounter again for weeks, until her father had told her June would be coming to India.

THE RESTAURANT WAS pretty, with Chinese lanterns infusing the room with warm light and a large aquarium full of tropical fish. The menu was barely Indian—it was more like a trendy New York restaurant, with ingredients listed under each dish without verbiage: *Lime. Curry. Coconut. Ginger.* Holly and Christina were pleased, and thus Alec and Ty were too, and they ordered more cocktails. June was in a new outfit—a white miniskirt and lime green kitten heels. Olivia hoped the monsoon would return to wash her away.

She picked at her chicken, feeling like she was on her own subcontinent, while Max, June, and Ty discussed Manhattan real estate, and Alec, Holly, and Christina talked about exercise. The music was electronic and loud, and the restaurant was crowded—they had to raise their voices.

"You'll probably move to the city after you graduate, right, sweetie?" Max nearly yelled to Olivia.

"I guess." She hadn't thought much about it recently. Before her mom had gotten sick, she hoped to travel for a few months after graduation with her then-boyfriend, Pat. He wanted to take a year off before applying to graduate school. She wanted to take pictures of places she'd never been: the coast of Georgia, New Orleans, the sunflower fields and huge skies of the Midwest. She would have worked on her portfolio and her reel, and then in the fall tried to get a job in film. Pat wanted to move home to the suburbs of Boston for the year to save money. But film jobs were in New York and LA. Would Pat move to one of those places with her, or would they do long distance, or would they separate? Then Pat had broken up with her in December, rendering those negotiations moot.

Though she never would have given up the time with Eleanor, she wished she had already graduated and were staying in the city that fall. During the last surreal few months, Olivia had loved the anonymity she felt in Manhattan. At a time when she felt lonely even with her closest friends, walking around a crowded island of strangers, hiding behind large sunglasses, was a balm.

"Where will you live?" Ty said. "Brooklyn, probably." He laughed, as though the idea were slightly risqué, when really, his having lived only in Manhattan in his six years since college made him nearly an extinct species.

"Brooklyn is supposed to be very cool these days," June said.

"Maybe I'll live in Queens," Olivia said, just to end their happy forecasting of her mainstream future.

Christina chimed in from across the table. "Long Island City? There are some great restaurants over there."

"And you can take the water taxi," Ty said.

"I'd like to travel for a while."

They got the point and resumed their conversations, and then Olivia was alone again, and it was her fault. She asked Christina which exercise classes she should go to if she wanted good abs.

"You should try rock climbing," Christina said. "You're wiry, and it's a great way to meet cute guys."

"My daughter, Liza, goes to a rock-climbing gym," June said. "Olivia, she's exactly your age. She graduated from college in May."

Olivia knew from Max that June's husband had died a few years earlier and that she worked in human resources. It was hardly surprising that she had a daughter. But Olivia didn't like thinking about June's life beyond the confines of the trip.

Holly wrinkled her nose at the prospect of rock-climbing gyms. She swore by barre classes. "You lift micro weights for ages," she said.

Alec liked a class in LA that combined yoga with spinning. Soon they were all talking about exercise. Max played squash and racquetball and tennis. He had always been a runner, but he'd injured his hamstring a few months before and was relegated to swimming and the elliptical machine until he made a full recovery. Ty was the same—a serious runner with a love for racquet sports. June worked with a trainer twice a week.

Mom is dead, and we're in India. Why are we talking about this? Olivia wanted to scream. But she didn't know what they were supposed to be talking about, and maybe no one else did either, and that was why they were there, eating tiny, jewel-like dishes in a vast foreign city, struggling to make themselves heard.

Max tapped on his gin and tonic with a fork. "Thank you all for coming," he said formally.

Olivia glanced around the table—everyone, including June, was looking at him with the same bemusement she felt.

"It would mean a lot to your mom, I know, us all being here together."

Olivia sipped her drink, which was suddenly too sour, astringent. "She would certainly be surprised," she said. Faces twitched around the table. Her father said her name in a warning tone.

June touched Max's hand. "It's okay," she said. "This has been a really tough year."

Under the table, Olivia was tugging her cloth napkin between her fists. Her nails dug into her skin. "It hasn't been a year," she said quietly.

June's smile wavered at the edges but stayed in place. She nodded. No one spoke.

Olivia left the table.

BACK IN HER room, Olivia paged through the guidebook, looking for something to do. She wanted to see something so strange and captivating it would let her forget about her family for a few hours.

There was a knock at the door.

"Come on, get your things," Holly said briskly, when Olivia opened it. Alec was standing behind her. "We're going out."

Ty and Christina were waiting in the lobby. No one spoke in the cab. The bar they went to was in another hotel, just a few minutes away. It looked like a hotel bar in New York, with maroon velvet furniture and wood trim. Alec, Ty, and Olivia ordered Manhattans. Christina and Holly studied the cocktail list and ordered different drinks that looked the same when they arrived, decorated with fruit and umbrellas.

As soon as the Manhattans came, Olivia remembered that she didn't really like them. She'd made this mistake before, ordering a drink because her brothers did and then forcing it down.

"I fucked up," Ty said morosely.

"What do you mean?" Olivia asked.

"Dad called me a couple weeks ago, and said he was thinking of inviting this *friend*, this woman he'd met."

"And you told him it was okay?" Olivia said. Alec and Holly were nodding—they already knew.

"He asked me if I thought it was a crazy idea, and I said not crazy, exactly. I was trying to be nice. I didn't think he was really going to do it. But I told him people would be upset."

Olivia found it odd that Ty was referring to them, his family, as *people*. "I can't believe you didn't tell me," Olivia said. It was true that when she'd pitched a fit about June, Max had tuned her out. But it would have been different if she'd found out before it was already decided.

"I didn't think he would actually go through with it," Ty said again.

"He's never been alone," Holly mused.

"He's not alone. He has us."

From the looks her siblings exchanged, Olivia didn't get the sense they were too impressed by that argument. She jabbed the cocktail straw into the cherry at the bottom of her drink, trying to release some of its sweetness. "We have to get rid of her."

Alec laughed.

"I'm not joking," Olivia snapped. "If we do nothing—"

"She's flown to India, Liv," Ty said. "I don't like it either, but she's not likely to tuck tail because we're unfriendly."

"I think it's messed up," Alec said. "I'm with Liv." He reached out to squeeze her shoulder, and it was comforting, even though she knew Alec was just as likely to sympathize with Max the next day. He and Holly were nestled together on a love seat. They missed Eleanor too, but they had everything they needed.

"I'm not trying to defend her," Christina said softly, "but Max may not have told her how recently your mother passed."

Olivia had wondered the same thing. But she hated it when people said *passed*—it was an attempt to create ambiguity where there was none. "The obituary's online," she told Christina.

"What do you propose?" Ty said. "Refuse to speak to her? Booby-trap her room?"

"I'm game," said Alec.

"Alec, you literally wouldn't know how to be unfriendly to someone," Holly said. "You're a golden retriever."

It was true. Holly would happily play the stone-cold bitch, but as an in-law, she counted for less. And Ty—

"I'm not going to bend over backward being nice to her," Ty said. "Anyway, she's not here to bond with us."

A waiter in a white lab coat, his mustache expertly waxed and curled, came by to replenish their tray of puffed snacks. Alec and Ty ordered another round.

"He's sad and lonely," Christina said. "He isn't thinking clearly. This will pass." But Ty didn't look as convinced.

THE NEXT MORNING, the Harrises, Christina, and June visited the Jama Masjid, which Akosh told them was the most famous mosque in India. Though they dressed conservatively in their new Indian attire, the women were still required to wear plastic floral smocks over their clothes. By nine A.M. it was easily ninety degrees, and the smocks trapped the heat. Holly kept pointing out Indian women who were dressed the same way they were dressed, yet weren't wearing smocks.

They climbed the minaret in darkness, hands touching the cool stone walls as they found their footing. The narrow spiral staircase was crowded with children, whose slender bodies pressed up against theirs as they passed. At the top of the minaret, birds circled and called. The panoramic sprawl of Delhi lay beneath them.

After the mosque, they descended into the streets of Old Delhi. When Olivia emerged from the air-conditioned jeep, the smells were as encompassing as they had been the day before at the airport, but different—more pleasant—or else she was already growing used to them.

They were a large group clustered uneasily on a crowded street. Akosh led them, calling, "Single file, please!" over his shoulder. It was tempting to linger at every shop or stall they passed—the man selling incense, the jewelry store that proclaimed BEST PRICE in orange hand-painted letters. In front of some of the shops were shoe racks; the customers inside were barefoot, drinking glasses of tea.

Akosh stopped them just outside the gates of a turreted red palace. It was a Jain temple, he told them, that also housed a bird hospital. Olivia had learned about Jainism in a religion class she took freshman year. Jains swept the ground before each step, to avoid inadvertently killing insects.

Before their party could enter the temple, they had to take off their shoes and wash their feet. The heat was incredible. The edges of Olivia's bra were wet, as were the underarms of her tunic, but when she took off her shoes and stepped onto the stone platform surrounding the temple, she felt instantly cooled. The stone was worn smooth from the thousands, or maybe hundreds of thousands, of feet that had preceded her here, tourists and pilgrims. When she visited the cathedral in Florence with her parents as a teenager, the stories about the thousands of men who spent their entire lives building it had been nothing more than abstractions. But here it felt different—like she was connected to something timeless.

Inside the temple, Indian men knelt in prayer. Max and June were asking Akosh questions about Indian independence and partition. That afternoon they were planning to visit the parliament and Max was probably looking forward to that part of the day. Olivia saw a set of stairs and took it without waiting for the others. Her fingers grazed the bannister as she ascended, and again she felt that shiver of history, of the many layers of belief this place had absorbed.

The stairs brought her to a terrace that hugged one side of the temple. It faced the main street, Chadni Chowk, where they had been before. From this vantage point, the hubbub below seemed less chaotic. Olivia leaned against the railing and watched the dance of rickshaws, bicycles, and pedestrians, the warm hues of yellow and orange, red and beige. She closed her eyes and listened to the horns, the yells, and the quiet hum beneath everything, which she imagined was the humming of India itself.

After a few minutes, Ty and Christina came upstairs. "Crazy place," Ty said. He sipped from a bottle of water. He looked groggy, and Christina looked dazed. At home in New York, it was about one A.M. "Do you think we have to do the bird thing?" Ty said. "It sounds weird."

It *did* sound weird, Olivia thought, but they were there to do strange things. "I want to see it," she said.

Alec and Holly surfaced next, followed by Max and Akosh. Alec draped his arm around her shoulders. "Pretty amazing place, right?"

"It has this energy," Olivia said and immediately felt awkward. It wasn't the kind of thing a Harris said.

But Alec nodded. "It does." He cocked his head, as though listening. "It's like the building is emitting calm."

"Are you guys sure you're not just feeling the exhaustion of all the poor indentured servants who spent their lives building it?" Ty said.

Olivia made a face at him. "You don't know who built it."

"I do, actually," Ty said. "Indians built it."

"You think you're so funny," Christina said, coming away from the railing to take her place at Ty's side.

"You think I'm so funny," Ty said, wrapping his arm around her waist. "Or at least I hope you do."

BIRDS DO NOT smell good. This wasn't a surprise, but it also wasn't something Olivia had considered before visiting the Jain bird hospital. The bird smell was sharp and a little fishy, the kind of odor that made you feel unclean yourself. The hospital was designed for wounded game birds, but the Jains didn't discriminate. Akosh told them there were separate wings (he used that word, and it was hard to know if he was being playful) for different species: pigeon, parrot, chicken, sparrow.

"But birds of prey," Akosh said, holding up his finger in warning, "are seen strictly on an outpatient basis." Hawks and their ilk were not vegetarian, and thus could not be overnight residents.

Row upon row of cages held mangy injured birds. A bright green parrot, missing feathers and with one wing hanging at an unnatural angle, stared back at Olivia when she peered into its cage. Then it began to preen with vigor, sending feathers flying.

Holly wrapped her scarf around the lower half of her face, and Christina was discreetly cupping her hand over her nose, as though catching a sneeze. June, surprisingly, looked perfectly relaxed.

"This is insane," Ty murmured. "There are beggars missing legs on every corner, and they're rescuing pigeons."

Max stood still, arms crossed, waiting for the next thing. Her mother, Olivia thought, would have found this hilarious.

"Who funds the hospital?" June asked.

Akosh beamed. "It is funded entirely by donations. We paid an entrance fee, which goes toward the care of the birds."

Alec nudged Olivia. "Maybe they need an intern. You're not in a hurry to get back to school, are you?"

Max laughed loudly.

Olivia glared at him. "Actually, I'd love to stay in India for a while."

"Olivia still has one semester of school," Max needlessly reminded everyone. "That's why we're here now, instead of in the fall."

"I'm not sure if I'm going back," Olivia said.

Like magic, her family stood at attention. Until that moment, Olivia had assumed she'd slog through one last semester. Before Eleanor had gotten sick, Olivia loved college, though she hadn't thought of it in such simple terms. But her class had already graduated. Everything was different.

"You have to graduate," Max said.

"I don't *have* to. Lots of people don't finish college."

Her father leaned toward her, his calm expression of a few minutes ago gone. "People in this family do finish college. Especially people who've already completed seven-eighths of it."

"We'll see."

Behind her shoulder, a parrot chorused, *see, see, see.* Akosh had moved a polite distance away from them and was speaking quietly with one of the staff.

"Haven't we already paid for it anyway?" Max said. Olivia watched him realize he had not paid. "Didn't they send the forms?"

June looked nervous.

"Come out to LA," Alec said. "You can live with us and do a semester at USC."

"That's not going to happen," Max said, before Olivia could respond. "We'll talk about it later," he added, after glancing at June.

OLIVIA SKIPPED THE visit to the parliament in favor of a swim in the hotel pool and a nap. She'd hoped that an afternoon away from her family—and from June—would make her feel better. She had an email from Kelsey, who wanted to know what was happening. Kelsey hadn't believed June would really go. She'd been sure Max would rescind the invitation at the last minute, that somehow it would fall through. *She's here, and she's worn at least six outfits in two days*, Olivia wrote.

She awoke to knocking. She threw on her robe and peered through the peephole. It was her father, and she let him in.

"It was a very interesting afternoon," he said.

Olivia didn't say anything.

Max sat down at the desk. "We all miss Mom."

Olivia looked at him intently. "Do we?" She missed her mom in a way that felt like vertigo. Her father was a robot version of his former self.

"I'm not going to debate whether I should have invited June. She's here now, and we're all going to be civilized, including you."

"You wish you hadn't brought her," Olivia said with a rush of hope. If Max could admit he'd made a mistake, June would matter less.

"She's a nice woman, Olivia. It would behoove you to give her a chance."

Olivia looked away.

"The restaurant we're going to tonight is supposed to be great," Max said briskly, standing up. The matter had been resolved. "I'll see you downstairs in an hour."

Her anger was a poison that wouldn't stop spreading until it had infected every part of the trip. She'd read in the guidebook about a small night market and she decided to go. She wasn't going to tell anyone she was skipping dinner, but she ran into Christina, who was coming back from the gym, in the hallway.

"Tell them I'm not feeling well," she said. "Or don't. I really don't care."

Christina held Olivia's forearm. "I can't imagine how hard this must be."

Christina's highlighted hair was pulled back in a ponytail, tendrils escaping. Her cheeks were flushed and her forehead was dewy. She was wearing tiny running shorts that showed off her toned, doll-sized legs and a tank top with a built-in bra. Her phone, pink headphones still attached, was in her free hand. Picturing her jogging on a treadmill, listening to music or perhaps a podcast, about to shower and maybe have sex with Olivia's brother—it did not make Olivia feel any better. "Have a nice dinner," she said, pulling away from Christina's grasp.

THE CAB DRIVER seemed dubious when she told him where she was going, and the ride was longer than she'd estimated. From the outside, the market looked like a run-down shopping arcade, with people coming and going through an open doorway. Before she was inside, a guy no older than she, with a bare hint of a mustache, approached her and offered his services as a guide.

"What are you looking for?" he asked. "Gold, silver, silk? Silver bangles, maybe?"

When Olivia refused, the man made other suggestions, walking alongside her as she entered the market: *Gifts? Scarves? Earrings? Diamonds?* The last suggestion made her laugh aloud, and he became hopeful, but she looked studiously at the ground until he lost interest.

She stopped at a tea stall and bought a cup of chai from a wizened, nearly toothless man who was brewing it in a large aluminum pot. He gestured to the single plastic chair beside his makeshift stove. She sat, watching him as he dragged on a betel-leaf cigarette, stirring the tea to prevent a film from forming.

Her mother would have wanted to come to the night market. She would have drunk sweet, fragrant tea out of a glass with Olivia—she would have known, as Olivia did, that anything that boiled was clean.

All her life, Olivia had felt there was no one who existed principally for her. Her parents had each other; her brothers had each other, and then they had Holly and Christina. With Eleanor gone, Olivia saw her foolishness. When her mother had been alive, Olivia had never been lonely. Eleanor had tricked them both, Olivia and Max. She'd acted like Max was the center of her world, when really, it was Olivia.

With gestures and a few small coins, Olivia got a cigarette from the chai wallah. The wax match he struck for her burst jerkily into flames a beat late, throwing off tiny embers. She coughed when she inhaled, and he laughed.

"From America?"

"Yes."

"New York—Washington—Boston?"

"Los Angeles," she said, and then felt guilty for lying.

"Hollywood," he said. He had deep smile lines around his mouth and a playful glint in his brown eyes. Above the neckline of his tunic, his collarbone jutted out.

While the chai wallah was ladling tea into a glass for another customer, Olivia crushed the cigarette beneath her shoe and slipped away.

She moved from stall to stall, examining silver and jade rings. There was no gold, no silk, and certainly no diamonds that she could see. There weren't many people there, and—as another young man approached her, his smile slightly menacing—it occurred to her there was probably a reason for that. The market after sundown was not for respectable women buying fabric, and it was not for tourists either. Mostly the other patrons were boys and men, clustered around the stalls that sold snacks.

Olivia's new would-be salesman offered her better jewelry, the best silk, classy souvenirs, and low prices at a store nearby, and then, when she said no, he offered her hash. She paused before shaking her head, and he sensed her hesitation. He followed her past several more stalls, reciting names of other drugs in a loud whisper: cocaine, opium, ecstasy. Shopkeepers were watching the pair of them openly. Olivia averted her eyes.

"Stop," she said finally, turning toward the drug dealer so suddenly that he took a step back. Under her breath she added, "Hash, maybe."

His face opened into a wide smile. "Come, please, this way," he said, his tone now businesslike. He led Olivia past more stalls, toward a small side door on a different street. The night air was warm but fresher than the air inside the market. As her eyes adjusted to the dimly lit street, she saw men lounging together against the sides of buildings. A few cast sidelong glances at her and her drug dealer as they passed.

Her drug dealer turned and extended his hand. "Amrit," he said. "Come with me, very close." Soon he tapped on the window of a parked SUV. The window rolled down and Amrit spoke to whomever was inside.

"How much do you want?" he asked her.

"Just a little." She named a price she thought was about ten dollars.

He cocked his head and suggested twice that much. She fished money out of her pocket and handed him 800 rupees, slightly more than she'd said at first.

Amrit transferred the rupees to the person inside the car. The window rolled up, and he pressed a small plastic-wrapped lump into Olivia's palm. She closed her fist around it. She was already trying to figure out what her escape plan would be, but Amrit turned and walked briskly off into the night without another word. Olivia couldn't see anything through the dark car windows. It felt like the whole exchange had never happened.

Not sure what else to do, Olivia went back into the market. She was so jetlagged she might as well have been stoned already—she had no idea what time it was or how long she'd been away from the hotel. She wove her way through the market until she found the entrance she had come in. When she walked outside again, her cab driver was there waiting for her, leaning against his car and smoking a cigarette, as though this had been their plan all along.

SOMEONE WAS POUNDING on her door. The clock beside the bed said 4:35 A.M. and the phone was ringing. Olivia took it off the receiver. "Coming," she yelled. She was naked, and the room was air-conditioned to what felt like fifty degrees. She put on a robe, wondering whether there was a fire or some other emergency. But at the door was only Ty, dressed in a button-down and looking relieved to see her.

"You missed your wake-up call," he said. "We're supposed to leave in fifteen minutes. Everyone's at breakfast."

"It's so early."

"We decided yesterday, remember? Akosh says you have to leave for Agra before five or there's shitty traffic."

"Well, I don't want breakfast." Olivia glanced longingly back at her bed. She could almost remember what she had been dreaming.

"Just throw something on," Ty said. "Everyone's waiting for you."

Once he left, Olivia turned off the A/C, splashed water on her face, and pulled on yesterday's clothes, wrapping a shawl around herself.

The Harrises, Christina, and June were the only ones at break-fast, and everyone looked miserable. As soon as Olivia sat down, a waiter appeared, offering scrambled eggs and coffee, both of which she rejected.

"Banana?" Christina said, breaking off a piece of the one she'd just unpeeled. Olivia took it, and with this gesture, conversation resumed. Alec needed to talk to a client. Holly needed to talk to her agent, her mother, and her gynecologist. They were trying to calculate what time it was in Los Angeles and what time it was in London. India was off by half an hour from the rest of the world, a quirk that did not justify their inability to remember the time change. Ty told the times, while Christina, clearly a morning person, chirped to Max about how much she was looking forward to seeing the Taj Mahal, and Olivia ate her banana.

June yawned. "I was not ready to get out of bed this morning either," she said. She smiled at Olivia.

Before she could stop herself, Olivia pictured June and her father in bed, cuddling and burrowing as the alarm went off. June must have guessed what Olivia was thinking, because she blushed and looked away.

Akosh appeared a few minutes later to hurry them along. Everyone else's luggage was in the lobby already, so Olivia went back upstairs to get her things. Then she joined her family outside. It was dawn, and they were watching the two drivers pile their suitcases onto the roof racks of the jeeps. They had the procedure down: the older, larger driver, Devdas, hoisted or hurled the bags up to where Jay crouched to receive them. Then Devdas joined him on the roof, where they secured everything with bungee cords.

Olivia got into the first car with Alec and Holly. Before they even started driving, Alec was on the phone in the front seat and

Holly was on the phone next to her. They both spoke loudly, trying to be heard despite bad reception.

Olivia curled her legs up onto the seat and rolled her scarf into a ball. Outside the window, Delhi was gray in the early half-light. It didn't look exotic. It looked like any other dreary city, rousing reluctantly to another day.

She dozed, her head bouncing against the car door. She was aware of the lurchy clatter of the car and the Hindi music on the radio, and then she wasn't. She opened her eyes to bright daylight. The clock on the dashboard said 8:40, and Alec was still on the phone.

Holly was leaning back with her eyes closed, but she opened them as soon as Olivia stirred. "You slept through the whole ride," she said, sounding slightly resentful.

Olivia propped her elbow up against the windowsill so she could rest her head in her hand. It felt too heavy to hold. "What'd I miss?"

Holly sighed and sank back into her seat. "Nothing, really. Cows, et cetera. Shit roads."

Alec hung up. "You still feel like you're going to puke?" He reached back and held out a hand to Holly. She took it.

"Are you pregnant?" Olivia said. She saw Jay sit up straighter.

"Just carsick." But Olivia could tell from Holly's tone that she wasn't sure, that she was hoping she was pregnant. Holly had miscarried last fall—that's when the family found out she and Alec were trying. Olivia didn't understand why Holly wanted to have a baby now, just as her career was beginning to take off. Her mother had told her the baby thing hit you out of nowhere in your twenties or thirties—it had happened to her, it was happening to Holly, and it would happen to Olivia too someday. Olivia doubted this. She curled her legs into her chest again. She could still feel the hash she'd smoked the night before when she finally got home wrapping her like cashmere: a thin, sumptuous layer between her and everything else.

WHEN THEY ARRIVED in Agra, everyone wanted to see the Taj Mahal right away. But Akosh teased them, telling them it was best to see it first at sunrise, and they should wait until the next morning. That afternoon, they toured the red sandstone Agra Fort, which contained a lesser mahal. Olivia found that after just a few days in India, she had begun to turn quickly away from the beggars who approached her, as Akosh had advised them to do. She didn't know what it said about her and her family, that they were able to follow this instruction. She wondered if her mother's reaction would have been different.

On their way back to the jeeps, Olivia found herself walking beside Akosh.

"The fort was very nice," she said awkwardly. She wanted to somehow let him know that her skipping the parliament tour the day before had nothing to do with him.

He looked at her. "You are not enjoying the trip." His eyes held a gentle rebuke.

"I am," Olivia began. And then, under his continued gaze, she added, "Well, it's not your fault, or India's fault."

He laughed, and she looked down to hide her reddening face. How presumptuous, to assume Akosh would blame himself, let alone India.

"I do not think India is worried," Akosh said.

The others were ahead of them, waiting outside the jeeps, sipping water. But Akosh did not seem in a hurry. He'd abandoned the ties and slacks he'd worn in Delhi in favor of a polo shirt, khakis, and leather sandals.

"My mom died," Olivia said. "Four months ago."

Akosh nodded. Either he already knew or he just didn't know what to say.

"She died in April." Olivia soldiered on. "And my father brought that woman—June." Saying her name felt like a capitulation, and she wished she hadn't done it.

Akosh nodded again. "My father is sick," he said.

"What's wrong with him?" Olivia said.

"They do not know."

Akosh had told them that his family lived in Shimla, in the Himalayan foothills. He had moved to New Delhi to attend university and then a special training program to become a tour guide. But there was something about him mentioning his father that made Olivia realize he might be closer to her in age than she'd thought.

She resisted asking him more questions about his dad. Instead she said, "Is it nice where you're from?"

Akosh beamed. "Very nice, especially during summertime. In winter there's a lot of snow, but it's pretty." There were cathedrals there, he added, like in Europe. Olivia found this amazing.

"Why did you leave?" Olivia said.

"This is a good job," Akosh said. He watched Olivia absorb this.

"Are you going to go back?" she said. "To see your dad?"

"I would like to," Akosh said, but he was shaking his head no. She wanted to ask him more, but they were back at the jeeps.

IN THE MORNING, they left the hotel before sunrise. When they arrived at the Taj, the sun was just burning through the gray-blue haze, but the entrance was already crowded. Akosh doled out their tickets, and then they were pushing through a canal of archways into the light. People held cameras over their heads, photographing what they could not yet see.

And then Olivia did see it, at the end of a long reflecting pool, all that white marble, and its beauty was actually silencing. She and her family walked slowly through the gardens, stopping to remove their shoes as instructed, then continued up the steps to the platform surrounding the tomb. The day was already warm, the sun peeking over the horizon, but the marble beneath their feet retained the coolness of night.

Akosh set them free to wander, instructing them to meet back at the main entrance in an hour for a tour. After the first rotation around the mausoleum, the couples peeled off and Olivia was alone. She loved the way the marble felt under her feet, so dense and solid it was almost springy.

The temperature rose by the minute, and at first she blamed her wooziness on the bright sunlight. She paused to lean against the exterior of the tomb, pushing her braid out of the way so she could feel the cool marble against her neck. She sipped from a bottle of water Akosh had given her. But the water churned audibly in her stomach. She slid down the wall until she was sitting, and then even farther, curling up in the fetal position. She closed her eyes for a few moments. She wished someone would come and help her.

When she opened her eyes, she picked out Alec and Holly from a distance, sitting on a bench in the gardens, facing her. Didn't they see her? But then, she realized, it might not seem that strange to them: Olivia in a ball outside the mausoleum. She closed her eyes again, willing the appearance of Ty and Christina, or even Akosh. She could feel liquid running through her intestines, gathering force. She needed the bathroom, though she was afraid of what the bathroom would be like.

There was a hand on her shoulder and a voice asking if she was all right. Olivia opened her eyes and June's face came slowly into focus. She had been almost dreaming, surrounded by chanting water buffalo. In that moment, before June became June, Olivia saw her as if she were a stranger, merely a middle-aged woman, redheaded and with admittedly disarming hazel eyes, teeth stained from decades of coffee and red wine.

"I saw a sign for a bathroom back near the entrance," June said.

Olivia sat and June helped her to her feet. June led her down the steps, back to her sandals, and then along the garden path toward a vine-covered cluster of low buildings, chatting all the while, which was annoying but also provided a somewhat helpful distraction.

"Are you interested in Indian history?" June said. "Or architecture?"

"No," Olivia said automatically. "But being here makes me want to learn a little," she added, not willing to seem like a philistine. *Just breathe*, she told herself, amid the frenzy in her stomach.

"You're in luck," June chirped. "Because it's time to meet Akosh in a few minutes."

Olivia nodded, though she had no expectation that, once she found the toilets, she would ever be able to leave.

When they reached the bathroom, June gave the toilet wallah a few coins in exchange for a couple of sheets of plasticky pink toilet paper. She hesitated, then gave the woman a larger bill and took the whole roll, which she handed to Olivia.

Olivia went into the first stall. When she closed the door behind her, blocking the already dim light, she could barely make out where the toilet was, but she could feel her feet getting wet. She opened the door a crack to locate the white porcelain footrests, which were disturbingly speckled with what she told herself must be dirt. She cursed her choice of flip-flops.

"Doing okay?" June yelled.

She'd forgotten June would be waiting. "You can go," she called back as she squatted, holding her pants around her knees so they didn't fall into the toilet. "I'm fine," she added, just as the stream of liquid poured out of her, interrupted by a few loud pops of gas. She would have thought the physical anguish of the moment would have overpowered the embarrassment of having June within earshot, but it didn't, not completely. It was an effort to even stay upright, and there was nothing to hold on to. She tilted toward one wall, reached out her fingers, and found a precarious balance. She took deep breaths, breathing in her own shit because those were the only available breaths. She didn't know how long she'd have to stay like that.

2.

Olivia interviewed three times before they offered her the job. The last person she met was the producer, Amanda, who kneaded her temples as though in pain while she scanned Olivia's résumé. She asked how much of a time commitment the filmmaking class was.

"It's just Wednesday nights," Olivia said. "I can work weekends."

Amanda smiled faintly. "You can expect to work weekends."

The first week, Olivia worked sixty hours. The second, she worked seventy. Likely Productions didn't pay overtime, and Olivia didn't make enough to afford rent in any neighborhood she'd heard of, so she was still living in the apartment her father had rented near the hospital. People her age lived in Brooklyn, in places they shared with friends, or friends of friends, or strangers they met online. But Olivia could not imagine living with strangers. The people she knew in New York had figured out their living situations over the summer, when she still thought she'd be returning to Vassar in the fall.

Olivia mostly ran errands and kept the fridge stocked with upscale snacks. She loaded and logged footage for hours and sometimes delivered projects to clients on foot or by subway. Meetings were held in the office's bright, open kitchen, where clients were plied with craft beer and artisanal beef jerky.

The other runner, a pimply guy named Nick who was about her age, tried to be buddies with the editors and assistants and got yelled at constantly. Olivia didn't speak unless spoken to and got yelled at less. No one tried to befriend her. The only people who chatted with her were some of the clients, the male ones. They weren't intimidated by her the way guys in college had been. They might have thought she was hot, but they were advertising executives, men who ran things, and she was the one making cheese plates.

Since they'd returned from India, Olivia hadn't seen anyone in her family except her father. After Olivia had gotten sick at the Taj, they'd all gotten sick. They'd had to cut a town in Rajasthan from the itinerary to stay at the hotel and recover for an extra day. Olivia thought the trip had been a disaster, and she suspected her family agreed. But Ty began leaving her voicemails and sending texts. He and Christina wanted to hear about her job. They offered dinner at their apartment in the West Village or brunch on the weekend. She wasn't exactly avoiding them, but her hours were unpredictable.

Her father had been angry when she'd refused to go back to college—angry at her, and angry at himself for not making sure she had reenrolled months before.

"You'll go back in January," he'd said. "In the meantime, you'll get a job." He seemed to imagine she was going to live with him and work at Starbucks. But she'd called Alec, who had friends everywhere, and he'd gotten her the interview for the runner position at Likely. She'd written on her résumé that she'd graduated from Vassar in May. She didn't know if Alec had assumed she'd lie, or just hadn't thought about it.

"I have news," Ty said in his next voicemail, so Olivia called him back. But he said he didn't want to tell her over the phone. "Nothing bad," he promised, and she realized that was why she'd returned his call, because part of her was expecting cancer or some other terrifying thing, because now news could only be bad.

She met Ty and Christina on Saturday for brunch in the Village. She was a few minutes late to the restaurant, and they stood when she came in. Even after she greeted them, they kept standing there, smiling expectantly.

"What?" Olivia said.

Christina waggled her hand in front of Olivia's face. There was a diamond ring on her finger that hadn't been there before.

Olivia made what she hoped were polite exclamations. She asked when it had happened and Ty and Christina launched into the story, speaking over each other. It had been a week before, in the park along the river. Ty dragged Christina on an eight-mile run with him and popped the question, as he'd put it, at their favorite spot, a bench near the southern tip of the island where they often stopped to stretch. Ty said he had threaded the ring through his shoelace so it was on the inside of his sneaker. To retrieve it, he'd pretended he had a pebble in his shoe and taken the whole thing off.

"We were so sweaty," Christina said, her cheeks pink with pleasure.

"Did you run home?" Olivia asked. If she were ever proposed to, which she could not imagine, she would want the setup to be a bit sexier than running clothes and a favorite bench.

"We grabbed a cab," Ty said. He and Christina exchanged a private glance.

"Ty made a reservation at Nobu."

Olivia knew Nobu—they'd eaten there a few years before as a family, with Christina, when Ty graduated from law school—but it felt like all of this had some special significance she was missing.

"You have to make reservations a month in advance," Ty explained.

"Does Dad know?"

"We had dinner with him Tuesday. I called you, but I guess you were working late."

Tuesday—the night of Geoffrey. Her whole body had been shaking as he'd set all the cash he had, a little more than five hundred dollars, on the nightstand and reached for her, wounded, angry, and hornier than he'd been before. She didn't know what had made her do it. She'd never even had a one-night stand before. She'd only slept with three other people. But propositioning him had been electrifying, a stimulant that made the sex itself, which otherwise would have repulsed her, a kind of athletic exercise about which she had no strong personal feelings. Still, it was hard to believe it had really happened.

She asked to examine Christina's ring. It was a round diamond with tiny diamonds around it set in platinum. It was very sparkly, and she said so, and it felt like the first right thing she'd said.

Ty and Christina held hands at the table and asked Olivia what was new with her. She told them about work, the long hours and errands, the uptight producer and cool editors, how the office tried so hard to be casual even though everyone was clearly stressed out. She told them about the film class she was auditing at Hunter. She'd signed up for the class so she could begin working on her thesis, but she hadn't gotten out of work early enough to attend yet. Still, she had access to the editing lab, and she intended to begin cutting something from her India footage.

Ty and Christina listened without interrupting, four eyes trained on her.

"You've really landed on your feet," Ty said. "Well done."

Olivia was embarrassed by his parental tone, and she thought he was too, but she was also pleased. Though if her family knew about Geoffrey—well, she couldn't even let herself imagine it.

The food came—salmon benedict for her and Ty, a salad with chicken for Christina. The restaurant was busy and loud, with tables clustered too close together, and the waitress acted like she was doing them a favor every time she came by. But Ty and Christina didn't seem to notice. They praised their meals and asked Olivia several times if she liked hers.

It was a beautiful day, still warm enough for short sleeves, and after they finished eating Christina suggested a walk along Bleecker Street, which was lined with upscale shops. The sidewalk was crowded with people who looked like Ty and Christina: men in polo shirts and women carrying posh handbags. While Christina browsed in one store, Ty and Olivia waited outside, enjoying the sun.

"I think Dad feels bad," Ty said.

"About what?"

"Coming down on you so hard about school. He's impressed you got a job so fast. He's just not great at admitting he's wrong."

Olivia watched Christina's blond head bobbing as she bent to inspect items on the sale rack. She and Ty had met in law school three years before, during her first year and his last. Christina was from Philadelphia, but Olivia didn't know much about her family other than her younger sister, Erin, who was in medical school. Ty had mentioned once that Christina's parents had divorced messily when she was young.

"You should go out to see him some weekend," Ty said. "We'll all go."

"I was around all summer and he didn't seem to care," Olivia said. She hadn't seen her father since she'd gotten the job at Likely and gone out to Rye to pack as many clothes as she could fit in a suitcase.

Christina stood in the doorway of the shop, barefoot and wearing a blue silk dress. She motioned to Ty to come inside.

"Let's go admire her," Ty said.

THAT NIGHT, OLIVIA met up with her college friends Bridget and Laila at a bar in Williamsburg. She always had to go to them—asking people to venture to the Upper East Side was equivalent to asking them to come to Maine for a drink. People on the train were all dressed in different ways: shredded jeans, motorcycle jackets, pink hair, and tattoos, but also high-heeled ankle boots and wool harem pants, with the crotch hanging down to the knees. She felt too preppy in her one decent pair of jeans and a sweater. Even her mother's knee-high Frye boots, which she'd coveted since middle school, looked out of style.

Bedford Avenue was nearly as crowded as the train. Bridget and Laila had met for drinks earlier in the week, so they were caught up already on each other's new jobs. Bridget was an assistant at a travel guidebook, and Laila, an art major, was working at a gallery in Chelsea. Unbelievably, Bridget said she finished work around six most nights. She was living nearby with her college boyfriend, Kyle.

Bridget had grown up in New Canaan, Connecticut, where she'd been a field hockey and lacrosse star. She had perfect skin and thick brown hair that fell just past her shoulders. She didn't get too drunk or have passionate, illogical fights with Kyle the way Olivia had with Pat. Her smooth transition to New York after college only confirmed Olivia's view that Bridget was an alien creature. Someone like Bridget could easily have been boring, but she was smart and discerning and said really funny things sometimes. She was a good friend, all the more so once Olivia's mom had gotten sick—she'd stayed in touch throughout the spring and summer, leaving weekly voicemails, even if Olivia didn't call her back. Bridget had been the one, Olivia was almost certain, who made sure the rest of their friends attended Eleanor's memorial service and signed the condolence card.

Laila was Indian, from Mumbai. She was beautiful, with a musical British-Indian accent, and guys fell all over her. But she was also sunny and silly and fun to go out with. She hadn't been that interested in Olivia's trip to India after learning that Olivia did not make it to Mumbai or the south.

Of the three, Bridget was the only one who was doing anything substantial at work. She was editing the company's Toronto guide, which apparently was always given to the newbie, because it didn't sell well and couldn't be screwed up.

"How's the gallery?" Olivia asked Laila.

Laila's huge eyes brimmed with scandal. "André, the owner? He told me the other day that it'd be better if I wore skirts."

"What a creep," Bridget said.

"Maybe you should buy, like—" Olivia began.

"Yes!" Bridget said, immediately seeing where Olivia was going. "Like, a long Amish skirt."

"Or the ones the Orthodox women wear, that are sort of straight and go past the knee."

"Or a hoop skirt," Bridget said. "Or a corset."

Laila laughed with delight. "I need people to like me," she protested.

"Nobody cares what I wear," Olivia said. She hadn't thought to consider this a perk. "The editors dress like slobs." She was on the editing track; the production people were better dressed.

"I wear jeans on Fridays," Bridget said. She was sipping her vodka soda through a tiny straw—still, it was disappearing at a good clip.

"Is that a rule?" Olivia said. She wore jeans every day, usually the same pair she was wearing at the moment.

"I think you shouldn't wear them all the time or people won't take you seriously," Bridget said. "It's probably different everywhere, though. Should we get another?"

"Let's do a shot?" Laila said. "Tequila?"

"I probably have to work tomorrow," said Olivia. The editors, as usual, were scrambling to finish a cut.

They got a second round anyway: another vodka soda for Bridget, a whiskey and ginger ale for Olivia, and a shot and a beer for Laila. The bartender looked only a little older than they were, but she scowled at them as if they were gum on the bottom of her shoe, even though they tipped a dollar a drink.

Laila told them about the two guys she was dating—Kristof, an architect whom she literally met on the street, and Daniel, who came into the gallery her first week there. "What about you?" she asked Olivia. "Are you seeing anyone?"

"I've been working a lot," Olivia said.

"There's always cute guys at the bars around here," Laila said. "Even if it's late." She laughed. "Especially if it's late."

"Why would I want to meet a stranger late at night?" Olivia said. She felt stupid, then, when Laila shot Bridget a look—like they were going to have to explain to Olivia about sex.

"I was seeing someone this summer," she added. It was technically true. Before India, she'd been hanging out and hooking up with Brick, a pothead she'd gone to high school with who was now growing and selling his own supply. It was a relationship of convenience: there weren't many people she knew in Rye, Brick's schedule was flexible, and his work product was excellent. The trip to India had provided a natural break. Brick texted once or twice after she'd gotten back, but she had been staying in the city, and communication petered out.

"What does he do?" Bridget asked.

"He's in sales."

Laila and Bridget looked unimpressed.

There was no way she could tell her friends about Geoffrey, yet some part of her wanted to see their reactions. "This woman I work with did a crazy thing," she said. "A client asked her out for drinks, and she took him back to her apartment, and then she—she made him pay her."

Bridget and Laila stared at her. "This person works with you? At Likely?" Bridget said.

Olivia laughed, hoping they would join in. "Funny, right?"

"I don't think that's the word I'd use," Bridget said.

"Did she get fired?" asked Laila.

"Nobody knows," Olivia said. "She just told me."

Laila smoothed hair out of her face. "I'm sure she makes better money as a call girl than any of us."

"She's not a call girl," Olivia said, a bit too emphatically. "She'd never done it before. The guy was really lame and she just wanted—"

Now her friends were really looking at her strangely.

"I guess it was a pretty weird thing to do," she said.

By the time they finished their drinks, Laila was so busy scouring the bar for cute guys that she couldn't pay attention to what Olivia and Bridget were saying. Bridget was checking her phone more frequently, probably wondering where Kyle was, though she'd never admit it. Olivia said goodnight and made the long journey back to the Upper East Side.

IT WAS MID-OCTOBER when Olivia met Michel. By then, the days were shorter and less predictable; some were sunny and crisp, others chilly and damp. Michel came to Likely for a lunch meeting with two colleagues. He was good-looking in a European, metrosexual way: tall and thin, wearing skinny jeans. He had a mop of curly dark hair that looked well-conditioned and a French accent. Olivia didn't exactly make the first move, but she held his gaze for a bit too long when Amanda introduced them, and she touched his hand when she brought him an espresso.

Michel took her to a champagne bar that was a brisk ten-minute walk west of the office. They talked geography and education: He'd moved to New York from France for business school fourteen years earlier. His father was Israeli and he had family in both France and Israel, but Manhattan was home to him.

Michel asked Olivia where she went to school and how she'd gotten into film. He listened to her answers without a smile of recognition and didn't laugh at her jokes. But she could feel his eyes on her, even when she looked away.

He asked for the check abruptly while they were still sipping their champagne, complaining about the overhead lighting in the bar. Before Olivia could formulate a plan, he was on his feet, saying "I know a place we can eat." It wasn't a question.

Michel led her farther west into the Village, closer, she thought, to where Ty and Christina lived, though the streets around there confused her. An unmarked staircase led to a subterranean bistro where an old man played the saxophone. Michel's idea of eating turned out to be splitting the salmon tartare. He didn't ask her if she wanted anything else, and turned away the offered bread.

His apartment was right around the corner. It was as sleek and angular as Michel was, with gleaming hardwood floors, modern furniture, and a faint, pleasant aroma, maybe a scented candle or a nice shampoo. Michel poured them wine, put on jazz, and crumbled hash and tobacco into a paper. Olivia had a headache from drinking on a nearly empty stomach. She didn't know what she was doing there—had he even invited her, or had she just followed him like a stray? He wasn't *that* good-looking, she told herself, stealing glances at his profile.

Michel fiddled on his huge computer, answering emails, adjusting the volume of the music, and neglecting to share the spliff. She wondered if he'd forgotten her entirely. But she felt oddly passive, rooted to the spot she occupied on Michel's narrow gray couch.

Then Michel swiveled in his swivel chair. He stood up and pulled Olivia toward him. They danced, her sneakers squeaking on his polished floor. He kissed her neck, and then, lightly, her mouth.

"It's a thousand dollars," she said. She hadn't planned to say it, but she didn't like the way he was with her, how easily he'd seemed to forget she was there.

Michel stared at her, and for a moment she thought she saw something vulnerable in his expression. Then he laughed at her, lowering his hand to her waist. "Julia Roberts?"

She pulled away. He looked at her and saw that she was at least partially serious, and his expression turned cooler, though he was still smiling as he said "What a coincidence. Our rates are the same. It's also a thousand dollars to fuck me."

"No, thanks."

"Suit yourself." Michel walked away from her, into his tiny kitchen.

Olivia sank back onto the couch. She could hear him opening cabinets. He returned with a glass of water and sat down again at the computer, his back to her. Now she really should have left, but she stayed. She wanted a grilled cheese sandwich with bacon. She wanted somebody to make her a sandwich. She wanted to curl up on the couch, which wasn't even comfortable, and go to sleep.

Michel swiveled back toward her. "Don't let me keep you."

Olivia got to her feet, holding her coat over one arm. She left without looking back at him—at least she managed that—and walked down eight flights of stairs instead of waiting for the elevator. Outside, she pulled on the coat, an old one of her mother's. It was navy wool with toggles and a hood. It was raining lightly. The hood narrowed her field of vision and protected her from some fraction of the noise on Seventh Avenue. She walked east, looking for a train that would take her home. She stopped for a too-greasy slice of pizza on the way and ate it in the shop, which had lighting Michel would not have approved of. Her mother had been dead for six months.

AFTER HER FIRST month there, Olivia's days at Likely had become less electrifying, and the routine, the fact that people would have noticed had she not shown up, gave her a sense of purpose. She was sometimes yelled at by Amanda, who wanted Olivia to intuit her every need. But she also got to work with the editors, doing basic things like loading and logging footage. Tim, the editor Olivia worked with the most, was soft-spoken and smart. His assistant, Brian, who was a few years older than Olivia, was kind and funny and patient with her questions. Brian lived in Brooklyn and seemed like a potential friend. He had a girlfriend, who was in art school, and he talked about wanting a dog—that sounded to Olivia like the stage of life after the one she was in, but before Ty and Christina's.

Still, she was quickly realizing that film editing wasn't what she'd thought. The job was entirely about details—looking at a minute of footage frame by frame, trying something one way and then another, showing it to three people, and then going back and doing it all over again. In college, working on her own projects, she'd thought she liked that, but to be doing it on commercials and promotional pieces seemed mind-numbing, especially when she considered that some of these editors were in their *thirties*.

Plot was receding from Olivia's life. In the editing lab at Hunter, she would blur images from India until they were only colors and shapes. She wanted to tell the story of her mother's death, of what happened when cancer starved someone into pure, glowing essence.

For this, she chose the image of a sari she'd filmed drying on a line when they had stopped for tea on their way back to Delhi. She blurred the image until the pattern was no more than a trickle of gold at the edge of the frame, and she slowed the movement of the fabric so that it was like still water in the softest breeze. But she didn't know what came before or after that. A film, even a non-narrative film, should have a beginning, middle, and end, but she was stuck in ending.

The next time she went to the lab, she began again, with colors for everyone in her family: a mélange of ambers and greens for herself and her brothers, blue for Max, because of his eyes. But she wasn't interested in all this, the rest of them. So she narrowed the scope, starting with what her mother had been before she'd gotten sick. She used deep oranges and browns from the spice market, thinking of her mother as a nurturer, and the dark colors of the river, thinking of Eleanor's calmness and strength, and of how much she loved the water. It was a child's symbolism, but no one would know that— assuming anyone ever saw the film. She cut in part of the sunrise from the day after she'd gotten sick in Agra, when she had slept on and off for sixteen hours and then woke at dawn. Sunlight just before it hit the Yamuna River—sunlight hitting the river.

What she wanted was to create a film that would make people feel something they couldn't put into words, but everything seemed transparent to her, too obvious, and every time she left the lab she'd made the film shorter.

She spoke to Max on the phone for the first time in over a month. He had called a few times and left messages, which she had felt free to ignore. But it seemed Grinch-like to refuse to speak to him after the news of Ty's engagement. Their call was short. Max proposed lunch near her office during the week. He told her, when she said she couldn't plan on cutting out for an hour in the middle of the day, that it could be last minute. The following Friday, Amanda was out with a migraine and the office was quiet. Olivia emailed Max, and he told her to meet him at a sushi place near Union Square.

When she thought of her father, when she listened to a message he'd left her, a reel played in her head: him sitting next to June at a restaurant in India, that calm look on his face; him coming by her hotel room to tell her to be polite, all arrogant conviction that she would fall into line; his anger when he realized he couldn't make her go back to school. All he wanted, she thought bitterly, was to move on with his life. She was an annoyance to be dealt with.

But when she walked into the unassuming Japanese restaurant Max had selected and saw him sitting at the table, fiddling with his Blackberry as usual, the sense that she was preparing for battle dissipated. He was her father, a middle-aged, fiercely intelligent man with very blue eyes. He looked older and smaller sitting at the table than he did in her mind's eye. And he looked happy to see her, as if the tension between them hadn't mattered that much at all. He stood to greet her.

They both ordered chirashi specials and Max asked about work. He listened while she told him about her days, the errands and the small editing tasks, the rhythm of production.

"Do you want to be an editor?" Max said.

She told him what she had been realizing, that editing a feature film might be exciting, but editing commercials was monotonous.

"I think I might like producing more," she said, surprising herself. She hadn't thought that before, but when she said it, it seemed true. "I'm not sure why."

Max smiled. "Because then you would be the boss."

"The producer isn't really the boss," she told him. But she knew what he meant.

"Ty says you're taking a class at Hunter," Max said. A kimono-clad waitress brought their fish without looking at them. Another server refilled their mugs of green tea.

"I never get out of work in time to go," Olivia said. She sounded, she thought, like a much older person—a grown woman complaining about her busy schedule. "I've been using their film lab, though."

"What are you working on?"

Olivia couldn't bring herself to say that she was working on her thesis, or trying to. It would be an admission that she was thinking about going back to school. "Something about Mom," she said instead.

Max nodded. He submerged mackerel in soy sauce, avoiding her eyes. Olivia's anger returned.

"Don't you miss her?" she said. She couldn't stand that he wouldn't talk about it.

"Of course I do. But I'm a litigator, not a filmmaker," Max said. "There's less room for expression in my field."

She couldn't bring herself to ask him about June. Irrationally, she felt that acknowledging June would make her more real. Instead she asked Max about work. His face noticeably relaxed. He was a partner at a big firm in Midtown—one of the good ones, Olivia knew.

He began to tell her about the case he was working on, a big complicated takeover, and she struggled not to space out. There was so much fish left on her plate—tuna and yellowtail, scallops, some white fish she couldn't identify.

"So the associate came in," Max was saying. "This bright kid, a Harvard guy, Kenneth, and he handed me a stack of paper this big." He held his hands a foot apart, still holding his chopsticks between two fingers.

Olivia was feeling sleepy. Her father talking about work was almost a childhood lullaby. She sipped her lukewarm tea and bit into another piece of fish.

"It's thousands of pages of documents," Max said. "So I asked him, Kenneth, why are you showing this to me? And do you know what he said?"

Olivia shook her head.

"The opposing party sent it over. So I said, again, why are you showing this to me? And he said, because we aren't supposed to have these. They meant to send these to their lawyers. Can you believe it? Clowns."

Olivia tried to look like she knew what Max was talking about.

"The documents proved our point, which was that they had intentionally misrepresented the value of the company."

"That's great, Dad." There was no more fish on his tray. He had eaten it all.

Max could tell that she didn't get the joke. "Anyway, it's the same old grind," he said cheerfully. Olivia needed to get back to work, and he did too, so he got the check.

"You guys should all come out for the weekend," Max said as they parted. "It's the best time of year."

Olivia said something noncommittal. She couldn't imagine going if June were there, presiding over her parents' house. But maybe June was equivalent to a rebound relationship for Max, sort of the way Brick had been for her over the summer—just a warm body until he could face up to reality.

OLIVIA WORKED LATE Friday, helping Brian and Tim finish a cut and staying to have a beer with them. Spending time with them reminded her of hanging out with her brothers when she was a kid: she felt a little breathless, trying to simultaneously act cool and avoid calling attention to herself, since it seemed likely that her inclusion was merely an oversight. Tim caught a cab to go home to his wife, who was pregnant, and Olivia and Brian walked to the subway together, she headed uptown and he to Brooklyn.

"Fun weekend plans?" he asked her.

Christina was out of town, and Olivia had agreed to be Ty's date to a birthday party. "It's in Midtown," Olivia said, and she and Brian both wrinkled their noses.

"My girlfriend's print show is opening next week, so I think we're going to spend the weekend setting that up," Brian said.

"That's nice of you," Olivia said. She was waiting for some dry comment about him not really having a choice, but he just shrugged.

"What're her prints like?" Olivia asked.

"They're abstract," Brian said. "Lots of black and white, and then sometimes really bright colors. A lot of nature images from the woods near where she's from, but rearranged." He was smiling, clearly pleased to be talking about it. Olivia wanted, suddenly and rather badly, to be invited to the show. She was going to ask Brian more questions—where was his girlfriend from, how long had they been dating—but they were already at the station.

Saturday she slept in. Ty had said he wanted to see the apartment and would pick her up. She had the sense that the place smelled stale, so after she woke, she opened all the windows—it was a bright day with occasional gusts of wind—and emptied the fridge of its sinister contents. She took out the trash and then walked west to Third Avenue with the vague intention of finding something that would make the apartment seem better than it was: a characterless place with rental furniture. She bought a latte and a croissant from a French bakery she'd been eyeing on her morning walks to the subway and window-shopped as she passed shoes, lingerie, and fancy home goods. It was a neighborhood for older people, or at least richer people, but she had come to feel at home there. The croissant was out of a dream: still slightly warm, flakey on the outside and dense with butter at the center.

In the end, all she bought were a bunch of daisies and a bottle of bourbon so she could offer Ty a drink. She kept expecting work to call with some urgent errand, but it was a quiet day, a day completely to herself. In the afternoon, she went to the film lab. There she mostly wasted time, looking up sublets in Brooklyn and old cameras on eBay. But she liked being there; just stepping into the room, always quiet aside from the humming of computers, gave her a feeling of usefulness.

When she got home, she took a long soak in the bathtub and read a months-old magazine article about how dogs had and hadn't evolved from wolves. Several times she drained the cooling bath and refilled it with hot water. She stayed in too long and felt light-headed when she got out. She turbaned her hair in a towel and leaned against the sink, staring at her reflection. Her summer freckles had disappeared. She rubbed moisturizer into her skin, a rich French cream that had been her mother's, and put on some of Eleanor's Chanel perfume too.

Naked except for the towel holding her hair, she put on music and finished tidying the apartment. Earlier she had dumped the daisies in a plastic pitcher. She trimmed their ends and arranged them in an old coffee can, which was all she could find in the way of a vase. Once the apartment was clean, it was even more obvious how little in it was hers. The ragged coffee table books, on New York buildings and Madison Avenue fashion, whatever that was, had come with the place. Her clothes, when actually put away, fit in the bedroom closet and dresser with tons of room left over. She had a few books, her laptop, and her cameras—a digital SLR, an old medium-format film camera she rarely used, and her Canon. The bulk of her possessions, that random accumulation of old papers and photos and hair clips, outdated electronics, shoes that were out of style or needed new soles, textbooks and unmatched socks, were all back in Rye. She moved *Middlemarch*, which she had been struggling through since the summer, from the bedside to the coffee table. On the fridge there was a photo of the whole family from Max's fiftieth birthday seven years earlier, and another photo of Eleanor holding baby Olivia.

By the time Ty rang the buzzer, Olivia was dressed and wedging her feet into a pair of Eleanor's shoes—plum suede pumps that were at least half a size too small but irresistible.

Ty couldn't hide his distaste for the apartment. "Wall-to-wall carpet?" he said. "How did Dad find this place?"

"Quickly."

"It's probably not cheap, either," Ty said. "You should ask him to give you whatever he's paying for this. He helped me with rent my first couple years in the city."

"The only reason I'm here is that the lease goes through the end of January. Besides," Olivia added, suddenly protective of the apartment, "it's a good location."

"For what? The only thing it's near is hospitals." It was true that there was a sort of medical corridor running along Manhattan's East Side.

"There's grocery stores nearby, and drugstores. And this great bakery."

Ty laughed. "That's any neighborhood in New York. But as long as you like it."

Ty gave Olivia a pound of his and Christina's favorite coffee beans, already ground because he wasn't sure she had a grinder. He didn't want a drink—he wanted to get to the party. They took a cab to Midtown, getting mired in traffic on Fifty-Seventh Street.

Olivia asked Ty where Christina was.

"She had to be in Philly for work yesterday, so she stayed last night to visit her mom."

"You didn't want to go?"

"It's not like we have to do everything together," Ty said, and Olivia acknowledged that was true.

The party was in the back room of an industrial-sized bar. Men wore jackets and women laughed desperately. They wove their way to the bar, where Ty located the birthday boy, a baby-faced guy named Peter, and his girlfriend, Sabine. Peter was a friend of Ty's from law school. Sabine was pixie-like in ballet flats and a simple black dress, her dark hair cut short. She worked as a curator for the New Museum.

"How did you meet?" Olivia asked them once they'd introduced themselves. She was genuinely curious—how *did* people meet in this massive, busy city, outside of school and work?

"Online," Sabine said, sounding slightly sheepish.

"Have you tried it?" Peter asked. "Everyone we know is doing it these days."

"Not yet," Olivia said. "I just got here."

"Give it a year," Peter said. He draped his meaty arm around Sabine's thin shoulder.

Olivia wished she could keep talking to Sabine, who exuded cool, but more people joined their circle to greet Peter. People came to say hello to Ty too, asking after Christina. Seeing Ty through the eyes of the people who greeted him, especially the women, Olivia was aware of how handsome and well put together he was.

He was working long hours as an associate, but she knew he still worked out at least five days a week. He was a catch, and she found herself wishing disloyally that he were with someone like Sabine, someone who was in the arts and would introduce him—and Olivia—to things.

Olivia excused herself to use the bathroom, mostly because she wanted to walk through the room and scan the crowd. But it all looked the same—people at least five years older than she, standing in tight groups, clutching cocktails like life preservers and speaking over one another. This wasn't, she realized, like mingling at a college party. No one was going to talk to her without some kind of introduction.

It wasn't until she came out of the bathroom that she saw Michel. It was only his profile, but the jolt she felt made her certain it was him. He was across the room, tall enough to stand out, surrounded by women. She turned away quickly, even though he hadn't seen her, and rejoined Ty.

Olivia couldn't focus on the conversation Ty's acquaintances were having, although that might have been due to the fact that it was about renter's insurance. Ty looked bored too. Olivia kept turning her head, trying to track Michel's movements around the room, but she couldn't spot him.

"See someone you know?" Ty said.

"No. Maybe someone from work," Olivia said. She excused herself again to go look, though she knew she shouldn't. Her feet were killing her in the too-small pumps, which no one had noticed or commented on. The women at the party, almost to the person, were wearing short black boots.

Michel hadn't moved from his spot, though his companions had changed. She didn't know what she was doing. It would be embarrassing to run into Michel at all, let alone at a party she was at with her brother. But she didn't get to think about it for long—Michel turned his head toward someone who said hello, and then he was looking right at Olivia. They made eye contact and he smiled a big roguish grin. She quickly turned away. Moments later, he was beside her.

"Is it you?" She'd nearly forgotten the French accent, but there it was again. "My little hooker?"

Startled, she looked up at him and was met with an almost indecent smile.

"Buy you a drink?"

"The drinks are free." Olivia didn't even like this guy, but she was having some sort of reaction to him.

Michel's hand was on the back of her waist and he was guiding her through the crowd toward the bar. Olivia concentrated on not tripping over her feet in the horrendous, beautiful shoes. There were so many people—how did one guy have so many friends to invite to a birthday party?

Michel was apparently having the same thought. "These people aren't even his friends," he muttered.

"How do you know him?" Olivia said. She was embarrassed when she heard her prim voice, attempting to lead the conversation in a socially acceptable direction. She was terrified that Ty would appear and ask how they knew each other, and that Michel would somehow allude to the other night in front of him.

"His girlfriend, Sabine, used to work for me."

"She seems cool."

"She is very cool. She's also very hot," Michel said.

"How did she end up with Peter?" Olivia wondered if Michel and Sabine had ever been an item. She could picture it.

"She left to work in the arts. She needed to find some corporate bozo."

Olivia couldn't imagine Sabine was dating Peter for his money, but Michel spoke with authority. He probably thought she was familiar with this sort of arrangement, given the way that she'd propositioned him. It was an uncomfortable thought.

Michel waved Peter and Sabine away with the back of his hand. "Who knows if it'll last. She goes through phases. When I met her, her hair was blue. And before that, I think she was a yoga teacher."

Michel snapped his fingers to get the bartender's attention, a gesture the bartender received with appropriate dourness. Then he gestured to Olivia. She ordered champagne, and Michel asked for the same.

The bartender turned away and Michel said in a low voice, "I'm happy to run into you. I had a dream about you the other night."

Olivia's stomach tightened. She kept looking straight ahead at the bar.

"Don't you want to know what I dreamed?"

"You obviously want to tell me."

Michel touched her jaw, turning her face so that she was looking at him. "I dreamed I brutalized you," he said softly. "You put up a good fight at first, but then you were begging for it. You like it a little rough, don't you?" His smile was tender.

The bartender set down their glasses. Michel picked one up and handed it grandly to Olivia. "My lady," he said. And then he turned and walked away.

Olivia stood at the bar stupidly for another few moments, her toes curled inside her shoes. Then she began weaving back to where she thought Ty would be.

Ty was ready to leave. He told her Christina had caught the last train back from Philadelphia and was almost home. He looked surprised when Olivia told him she'd stay a little longer, but he told her to have fun and that maybe they'd see her next weekend.

Olivia found Michel talking with a pretty blond ten years older than she. She sidled up next to him and took his arm firmly, surprising both him and the blond.

"Darling, I'm ready to go," she said. Looking at his companion, she added, "I don't think we've met. I'm Michel's fiancée, Claudette." If she could surprise him, or make him laugh, she'd win this round.

The blond looked like she was about to choke. "I had no idea," she said to Michel. "Congratulations." Michel wrapped his arm around Olivia's waist.

They caught a cab downtown a few minutes later. Michel pulled Olivia onto his lap and she straddled him. They kissed, her head bumping on the roof of the cab.

Back at Michel's apartment, they had sex standing up. Later—she didn't know how much later—they did it again in the lofted bedroom. She liked this less well. His sheets were the softest she'd ever felt, and with his handsome face towering over her and the sexy, perfect lighting, it was harder to feel only what she wanted to feel.

When she woke in the night, Michel was sleeping on his stomach, one hand resting on her collarbone as though to prevent her escape. When she removed it, he turned and spooned her. His breathing was raspy and asthmatic, like a frightened animal. She couldn't sleep, but if she left, she didn't know if she'd ever be allowed to come back.

She woke again alone to bright sunlight. She threw on a T-shirt she found on the floor and drifted downstairs to the kitchen.

There was a note on the counter: *At the gym. Buy yourself break-fast.* Next to it was a hundred dollar bill. She stared at it for a moment, wondering if it was joke. Then she left it where it was, and went to retrieve her clothes from the living room floor. She washed her face with Michel's fragrant cleanser, and took the train uptown.

LATER THAT DAY, Christina called. She was in the neighborhood and wondered if Olivia was free. Olivia agreed to meet her at a coffee shop on Third Avenue.

Christina insisted on treating Olivia to her mocha. They sat at a small round table next to a gaggle of high school girls who were looking at one another's phones and shrieking. She and Christina exchanged eye rolls.

"What were you shopping for?" Olivia asked.

"Oh, we needed some new sheets, and Bloomingdale's was having a sale," Christina said. "I ended up finding some shoes too—or as my mother would say, they found me."

"Where's Ty?" Olivia asked.

"Work. He hasn't had a whole weekend off in—well, I can't even remember," Christina said. "Not that I'm complaining," she added. "He makes a lot more than I do." She blushed, apparently feeling that she'd overshared.

Christina told her they were considering a couple of weekends in June for the wedding. She named the dates, looking questioningly at Olivia. But June seemed so far off, Christina might as well have been asking about something five years away. "Of course I'll be there," she told Christina. "It's Ty's wedding."

"I also wanted to ask—you don't have to—but I would love it if you'd be a bridesmaid." The nervousness in Christina's voice made it instantly obvious to Olivia that this was why she had wanted to meet.

Alec and Holly's wedding had been over three years ago, just after Olivia's freshman year of college. The wedding had been in England, in a castle rented for the occasion. She'd been a little obsessed with Holly and had been thrilled when Holly asked her to be a bridesmaid. Mainly, the difference was that Eleanor had been alive, which had made the very fact of the wedding feel much more appropriate.

"Sure," Olivia said. "I mean, don't feel like you have to ask me, but of course I will if it's what you want."

To herself, she did not sound convincingly perky, but Christina looked relieved. "I'm so glad," she said. "I want Ty's family to be involved." It looked like there was something else she was going to say on that front, but then she changed tacks. "It's not going to be some massive group of girls," she said. "Just my sister, Erin—I think you'll like her, she's not much older than you—and then two of my friends, Heather, who I think you met once, and Lee Anne, who I grew up with."

"Or have more if you want," Olivia said. "It's your wedding."

"Erin's in med school in Boston, and Lee Anne lives in Philly," Christina rushed on. "So, no pressure of course, but if you wanted to come help me choose bridesmaids dresses, you could have a say. Obviously everything will look good on you, so *that* won't be the issue," she said, laughing. "But there are a couple places downtown I've heard have good ones, nothing too bridal."

Olivia agreed, thinking that she might find a way to get out of this closer to the time. "Where's the wedding going to be?" she asked.

Christina said they were looking at a few venues in the Hudson Valley next Saturday, assuming Ty could take the day off. "We're going to rent a car," she said. "You should come, if you're free."

Olivia said she'd probably have to work, and Christina didn't seem at all upset. Maybe she had only been being polite.

Olivia asked Christina whether she'd picked a wedding dress yet. After saying she didn't want to decide until they'd settled on a venue, Christina admitted that she had gone to one or two stores, just to get a feel for what was out there. She showed Olivia pictures and they huddled over her phone, blurring the line between themselves and the young patrons at the next table.

OLIVIA AND MICHEL fell into a sort of routine. It wasn't the kind where he took her to dinner. But she could rummage in his cabinets and find things to eat while he looked on with mild amusement. There was always champagne, and when they didn't finish the bottle, he threw it away. Mornings, he drank French press coffee with almond milk, too fatless and bitter for her. While he showered, she stole the guest chocolate from above the kitchen sink. And then he'd come out of the bathroom with toothpaste breath and call her Lady Godiva and they'd fuck again—on the couch, on the floor, once with her hip pressed into the counter so hard she had a bruise for ten days. He loved the bruise. The next time he saw her, he couldn't stop touching it. He pushed his thumb into it while he fucked her, even when she winced. He watched her face, waiting for her to tell him to stop, which she didn't, and he came early, with the look of a child having an accident.

They saw each other a couple of times a week, always at his place. One evening in early November—the days so short that by the time Olivia left work it felt like it had been night for as long as it had been day—Michel said he had presents for her. He'd ordered a bunch of lingerie online, or not exactly lingerie: a couple of lacy thongs, a camisole because he didn't know her bra size, and several pairs of metallic leggings. Apparently he had a thing for leggings.

Olivia modeled the thongs in the living room to instrumental jazz. Michel fiddled with the stereo, reaching out to stroke her hip.

"Perfect ass," he murmured appreciatively, as though he'd designed it himself. She stuck it out for him and then turned to face him, running her hands up her stomach and bare breasts. She was beginning to crave this alternate skin she wore for him. She was aware of the look on his face, hunger and a sort of cold admiration, and the chaotic music she couldn't follow. Michel disdained anything with a melody.

The leggings sagged on her and were not sexy, they agreed.

Later that night, Michel tried, not for the first time, to have sex without a condom.

"When I fuck other people," he said, "I'll use one."

"When you first met me, as far as you knew, I was a full-fledged prostitute. And you still didn't want to use one."

"Aren't you a full-fledged prostitute?" Michel had long, girlish eyelashes.

It was Friday. The dark blue sheet rippled like water under his pale skin. His tongue was in her mouth, on her neck, all over her. They looked good together—they were a sleek people. He would never marry her, though, because she wasn't Jewish. He did blow with his boss most weekends, but he cared about things like that.

"Can we order sushi?" she said, nudging him off her, the condom debate unresolved.

He called the place and demanded things. He looked sideways at her though those absurd lashes after each item for affirmation: salmon avocado, yellowtail jalapeno, seaweed salad.

"And tuna," she said several times. "I want white tuna."

"Come here, my little tuna," Michel said after he hung up.

When the buzzer rang, Michel answered the door in his white underpants, while Olivia lay in the loft, trying to touch the ceiling with her feet.

★   ★   ★

THE FOLLOWING WEEK, Olivia spoke with her father, and he brought up Thanksgiving. She'd been feeling nicely buffered by what she thought of as her secret affair with Michel. No one knew about him, really, except Kelsey, whom Olivia had told on the phone. The last time Olivia had gone out for drinks with Bridget and Laila, their flaunting of their own romances had bounced off her. She alluded to someone she'd met through work but refused to go into details. It wasn't because she thought they'd disapprove. Bridget might have, a little, but Laila would have been all glistening eyes and breathless questions. But the thing with Michel was only hers. She didn't want to share it—she didn't want anyone else's voice in her head while she was suspended in the snow-globe perfect world of Michel's apartment.

But Thanksgiving would be the first holiday without her mother. Thinking about it was a bumpy landing, especially after her father told her that Alec and Holly wouldn't be coming that year. June had offered to make dinner at the Rye house, along with her daughter, Liza. Ty and Christina would be there, and Max hoped Olivia would come too. Despite her father's even tone, Olivia could see he was bracing himself.

"I don't know if I'll get the day off," Olivia said. It was all she could think to say. She didn't want to leave her cocoon to fight with Max, but Thanksgiving in Rye presided over by June and this daughter of hers was unthinkable.

"That's ridiculous," Max said. "Of course you'll have the day."

"I remember plenty of times you worked on the holidays."

"A couple phone calls from the house is one thing. Besides, my salary was commensurate with my responsibilities."

Olivia remained noncommittal.

There was a pause, and then Max told her he'd received reenrollment forms that week from Vassar. "It's just one more semester," he said. "Maybe you can even get some sort of internship credit for your job and not have to take a full course load."

"I'm getting a lot more out of this job than I will out of a semester of college," Olivia told him. She was working hard. She wanted him to acknowledge that.

"I don't doubt it," Max said. He was still calm—she wondered if he'd practiced this conversation, maybe with June. "I've worked and I've been in school, as you know, and I've found work to be both more challenging and more rewarding. But you need a degree, sweetie, and the longer you put this off, the more disruptive it will be."

It was around eight, and she was walking from the subway to the film lab at Hunter. She hadn't once gotten out of work early enough to attend the class she'd signed up for, but she had been trying to use the lab a couple of times a week. Though Max was being kind, she found his tone, his very calmness, patronizing, and she got off the phone.

That night she stayed late at the film lab, tinkering. She had assembled about seven minutes of footage she liked, but there was nothing else from the India material worth using. The semester was two-thirds finished. She wasn't sure what she had accomplished— certainly not the beginning of a thesis. But she hoped she could ask the professor whose class she'd ostensibly audited to take a look and give her some feedback. She considered asking Brian at work to watch it, but she felt shy. The film, if you could even call it that, was abstract and non-narrative. She didn't know his taste besides the action movies they joked about at the office.

There wasn't phone reception in the lab, but when she emerged onto Lexington Avenue, she had a voicemail from Michel—incoherent, probably drunk.

She woke in the night to a heavy thump, like a person falling out of bed on the floor above her, and before she was fully awake, she thought, *It's Mom, Mom has fallen, Mom needs my help.* When she fell back to sleep, she dreamed that her mother was dead but still among them, charming and ineffectual—that being dead meant only that you were no longer taken seriously. She woke again to an orange sunrise. *Red sky at dawn . . .* but she couldn't remember the rest, only the brooding, anxious sentiment.

She dozed off again and overslept. She was out of clean clothes and didn't have time to shower. She rushed to work. She was half an hour late but the editors weren't in yet. She sat on a bar stool in the kitchen, the steam from a cup of coffee condensing on her face. It was the first day with a real chill, gloomy and damp.

Amanda clicked into the kitchen on her skinny heels. "What are you doing?" she said, when Olivia didn't immediately get to her feet.

"Waiting for Brian and Tim. I thought I'd have to take the Sirison piece over for them." They still delivered a hard copy when they finished a cut at Likely, though everything could be uploaded electronically. According to Amanda, it was this kind of detail—having a representative of their business show up to present the product—that distinguished them as a high-end boutique outlet. Brian and Tim, Olivia knew, thought it was a pretentious waste of time. Having been the delivery girl a number of times, Olivia agreed; it was usually the clients' assistants who received her, without ceremony.

"Brian took it up half an hour ago because you were late," Amanda said, grimly satisfied.

Amanda couldn't have been over five feet tall, and Olivia bet a size zero hung on her. She was always immaculately put together and pretty in a doll-like way, but her mouth was pinched and mean unless she was talking to clients. *Get laid, Amanda,* Olivia thought.

"Why are you still in front of my face?" Amanda said.

"Tell me what to do and I'll do it." Olivia got to her feet. She felt like she weighed a thousand pounds. She had the irrational fear that Amanda was about to slap her.

"Michel Zahavi and his team are coming for a lunch meeting at noon. His assistant just called and, like, announced it to me. I don't know what it's about. Go get lunch stuff. Something good— Saint Marie's or the Table. And get flowers," Amanda added, gesturing to the wilting lilies on the counter. "Those make me want to vomit."

Outside it was raining. They usually ordered lunch. Olivia couldn't tell if Amanda was just determined to find something to do with her on a slow morning or if she was honestly freaked out by this meeting and thought that special, expensive food would solve anything. Olivia bought an umbrella at the nearest bodega and got a receipt—Likely could pay for it.

She stopped at the bakery on the corner to buy a latte and an almond croissant. She played Michel's voicemail again, licking almond paste off her fingers, but she still couldn't make out what he was saying. It was loud in the background and it didn't sound like he was speaking into the phone. Maybe he had dialed her by accident. At the Table, Olivia chose things she thought Michel would like: fresh baguettes and house-cured salmon, sliced fillet of beef and horseradish, kale and grapefruit salad, Belgian beer, though she doubted he would drink at a lunch meeting. It felt funny, to be picking out a meal for her boyfriend—not that that was what Michel was—to please her boss.

By the time she walked back to Likely, the rain had slowed to a drizzle. Amanda stalked into the kitchen again as Olivia unpacked the provisions. She eyed Olivia's latte. Olivia ignored her and took cheeses out of the fridge to soften. She arranged the fish and meat on platters and refrigerated them. She sliced one baguette into rounds and left the other whole. By noon, she was at the computer in the interior office used by her fellow underlings, loading and logging footage.

She could almost feel Michel enter the office. She recognized his gait before she heard him speak. She stayed where she was. She felt nervous—she was afraid of being found out by her co-workers and embarrassed to have Michel see her at work, kowtowing to Amanda and everyone else. She could hear Amanda and Tim greet Michel and the people with him.

Brian was sitting next to her with headphones on, loading and logging too. The footage Olivia was watching was of a middle-aged couple doing yoga in a yellow, sundrenched room in a villa that, based on the wide shots of the surrounding countryside and the small European cars in the driveway, she guessed was in Italy. She put her headphones back on and light opera trickled in as the woman adjusted the man's hips in downward-facing dog, then bent to kiss his cheek. She wondered what this couple—the woman in her forties and the older man—were selling. Tuscan yoga retreats? Second marriages?

Brian nudged her. "Amanda's calling you."

Olivia let out a deep sigh and Brian laughed.

Amanda was in the doorway, tiny hands on tiny hips. "You have somewhere better to be, Olivia?"

"Sorry, I'm coming." Olivia stood up.

"Brian, you may as well come too, since you worked on this," Amanda said. They followed her back into the kitchen as she muttered under her breath.

Olivia and Brian were introduced to Michel and his colleagues, Melissa and Gary. Olivia greeted Michel as though she knew him slightly, in case anyone remembered that she'd met him before at the office. He completely ignored her. The food hadn't been touched, but Brian jumped right in, making himself a sandwich that included both salmon and steak. Michel watched, looking revolted.

"Can I get anyone a drink?" Olivia said, clapping her hands together idiotically as though she were hosting a tea party.

"Perrier," Michel said. "Lemon, not lime, no ice." Their eyes met. Where Olivia expected to find a glitter of humor, she was met with coldness.

"The same for me," Melissa said.

Neither of them thanked her when she set down their glasses, small lemon wedges balanced neatly on the rims. She shouldn't be angry with them for treating her like a waitress, she told herself. It wasn't as though she wanted Michel to acknowledge her and raise everyone's curiosity. But there was a feeling of outrage she could not stifle: Don't these people know who I am? Don't they know what my real life is going to be like?

She sat down and picked up a piece of baguette. They had been instructed to eat at meetings to make things look warm and friendly. *We want this to feel like a family to the clients*, Amanda's boss, Zack, had said in apparent earnestness, when Olivia met him.

There was the usual small talk about weather and traffic. Michel seemed edgy, and Tim must have sensed it too, because soon he asked Michel, in his low, soothing voice, "Is there anything in particular you'd like to cover today?"

"The work on the Attara piece was sloppy," Michel said. He was looking directly at Tim, his eyes so wide that Olivia briefly thought he was joking. "We weren't happy, and neither was the client."

Olivia hadn't worked on the Attara campaign, but it was a big project, she knew, something that had occupied Brian and Tim for months before she came to Likely. Attara was a hotel, or maybe a hotel chain.

Amanda looked almost relieved, as though she'd been expecting something worse. She seemed so stressed for someone who was still relatively young—around thirty, Olivia guessed. Brian was plowing through his giant sandwich.

"Okay," said Amanda, doing her best impression of a calm person. "We definitely want to hear about that. We're so glad you brought it to our attention."

"Can you be more specific?" Tim said.

Michel took a sip of no-ice Perrier. "The work was generic." His eyes darted around the room. Olivia wondered if he was high. "For these rates," Michel said, "it's appalling."

Tim and Brian exchanged quizzical looks. Then Brian took a huge bite of his sandwich. For a moment, a piece of salmon hung out of his mouth. He looked like a retriever. Olivia struggled not to laugh.

"Your employees clearly don't take their jobs seriously," Michel said, gesturing toward Olivia and Brian. "What are these people even doing here?"

Olivia finally looked at Michel. He stared back at her. She tried to make her eyes say, *This isn't funny. Please stop.* Warmth crept back into his expression, a hint of that vicious play. She imagined throwing a lemon at his high, pale forehead.

Amanda was looking back and forth between Olivia and Michel, and Olivia quickly looked away.

"We sometimes let our junior editors have lunch," Tim said mildly, soliciting a glare from Amanda and an inadvertent smile from Olivia, who was thrilled, even in the midst of this scene, to be referred to as a junior editor.

Amanda hopped to her feet. Her manicured hand slashed the air, dismissing the counter of food, and Brian and Olivia with it. "Should we watch the piece together, Michel? Let's see if we can pinpoint what the issue is."

"Issues," Michel snarled. "There are multiple issues."

"Great idea," Tim said, ignoring Michel. "Let's take a look. Is everyone finished eating?" No one besides Brian had eaten anything. Melissa reached for a couple of grapes.

Everyone stood up. As Tim led the group out of the kitchen, Michel lingered. "More Perrier?" he said too loudly. He gave Olivia a small, tentative smile.

Olivia turned to the fridge and pulled out the bottle. It was mostly empty—she poured him half a glass.

"Hi," he whispered.

Olivia shook her head at him.

Brian poked his head around the open doorway. "Coming, Michel?"

"In a moment."

"Go," Olivia whispered. "Please, go now." She turned away from him and began to clear the lunch things. A moment later, he left the room.

OLIVIA WAS ABLE to steer clear of Michel and his colleagues until they left—she tidied the kitchen, restocked toilet paper and paper towels in the bathroom, and even ordered office supplies from the archaic website where they sourced ballpoint pens and sticky notes. Later, Brian told her that in the end, it hadn't been all that dramatic. Michel had raised a few issues that were more or less legitimate and easy to fix.

"It would have been better if they'd said something earlier, but I'm guessing they didn't notice until the client pointed it out, which is probably why Michel was so pissed," Brian said. If he had noticed the weirdness between Michel and Olivia, he didn't let on.

Michel called Olivia before six and then at seven. He called again just as she was leaving the office at eight.

She picked up on the last ring. "What?"

"Hi, baby," he said cheerfully. "Will you have dinner with me?"

"What was that today? Were you trying to get me fired?"

As Olivia rounded the corner onto Fifth Avenue, Michel sprung into her field of vision. She stepped back in surprise.

"I was waiting for you," he said proudly. "Let's go home."

"You've never seen my home." Olivia strode ahead of him down the block, annoyed at herself for being even a little glad to see him. She wrapped her arms around her waist. She needed to get a heavier coat from Rye.

"Do you want me to see it? Should we go there?"

"Where the hell did you come from?"

Michel gestured behind them. "The brasserie."

It wasn't a brasserie. It was a crappy Irish pub. Usually she would have found his European flourish charming, but that night she didn't.

"I'll make you dinner."

"You're an asshole." And apparently a stalker, she noted.

"It had nothing to do with you." Michel hugged her sideways and planted little kisses on her temple. His breath was warm. "The work wasn't good."

She pulled away. "Why did you make it about me, then? I don't care if you fire Likely. But don't throw a tantrum and make eyes at me like it's all some game. I am totally disposable there." She struggled to control her voice, which was shaking. She hadn't thought she was that upset.

Michel was petting her hair. "I'll make it up to you," he said. "I'll call Tim and tell him you're the only reason to do business there at all."

Some people her age had boyfriends with whom they shared friends and hobbies, who helped them set up their art shows and cuddled with them on the weekends. Olivia looked into Michel's lined, handsome face.

"I bought groceries," he was saying. "I'm going to cook you a fish."

MICHEL CHECKED ON the salmon so many times it took forever. Olivia drank wine on the couch pants-less, watching Hitchcock on Michel's projector, rebuffing his advances. After they ate, they spooned on the sofa while the movie played on. Michel fell asleep and began his nightly rasp. He'd almost died as a kid, he told her once. His asthma was that bad. She was warm and full and she fell asleep too. When she woke, Michel was trying to lift her, to somehow carry her to the loft. Sleepily, they climbed the ladder. They lay on their sides and kissed, his stubble scratching her chin. She liked Michel best when he was sleepy. The rest of the time, he felt manic and too-many-limbed.

It rained all weekend, and Olivia felt sluggish and cozy, uninterested in leaving Michel's apartment except when tucked in beside him, under his stately umbrella. This was not good, she knew, but it was only one weekend.

Sunday afternoon was spent naked and high. They were supposed to be cleaning the apartment because Michel was in a tiff with his cleaning lady and had convinced Olivia to help him. Stoned, she liked cleaning, restoring order. The problem was Michel: stoned, as well as sober, he was primarily interested in sex. Soon the rubber gloves came off and they were fooling around on the couch, and then chatting. He couldn't stop touching her. At first it was flattering, but sometimes it felt more like she was being examined.

This mole is weird, he would say. *You should get it looked at.* Michel was a hypochondriac and went constantly to his internist, who did not take insurance and whom he referred to by her first name.

Michel only knew about Olivia's family in broad strokes but that day he began asking more about them. There was a hunger in the way he persisted in spite of her deflections.

"I don't think I'll go," Olivia said, when Michel asked what her family did for Thanksgiving, which was only ten days away. She'd avoided thinking about the holiday since speaking with her father. She couldn't imagine going. But not going would be a declaration of war. And wouldn't abandoning Max push him farther into June's arms? She tried to imagine Thanksgiving in the city with Michel, ordering Chinese food.

But Michel was appalled. Perhaps because his family was scattered around the world, he couldn't imagine skipping a holiday with them when it was as easy as boarding a commuter train.

"Things aren't good with my father," she told him.

"Does he hit you? Does he insult you to your face?"

Olivia admitted she had no such complaints.

"What's wrong with him, then?"

"Come with me," Olivia said. "See for yourself."

Even as the words left her mouth, she knew she was making a mistake. She wasn't being serious, but the invitation might not sound as absurd to Michel—a foreigner who'd already said he had no plans—as it did to her. The past few years he'd spent the holiday with a friend and his wife who had recently separated.

Michel asked whether she'd meant it, and it was her moment to back out. But that suburban politeness kicked in—she'd been brought up to believe that rescinding invitations was a mortal offense. Besides, if Michel were there, he would be the center of attention. There was a certain freedom in that.

"Company would be nice," she told him, ignoring the knots forming in her stomach. She told him her family wouldn't mind at all, but promised that she would call her father to be sure. What she actually did was email Max the Tuesday before Thanksgiving, once it was pretty clear that Michel wasn't going to back out, to tell him that she was coming and bringing a friend. He wrote back listing the train times, though the schedule was online—someone would pick her up at the station. But Michel wanted to drive.

THANKSGIVING DAY, MICHEL picked Olivia up at noon. The car waiting at the curb was a black Porsche. Michel got out of the car to open the door for Olivia. The interior was all leather and chrome, with that new-car smell.

"You can rent a Porsche?" she said. She wondered if he owned this car and hadn't bothered to mention it.

"Not through Hertz," he said, smiling. He told her there were services. A guy had brought the car right to his apartment an hour before.

Michel fiddled with the GPS and music on his phone, stopping only to sip from a cup of coffee while weaving through what little traffic there was on the Triborough Bridge. He refused to accept directions from Olivia. He was going seventy miles per hour, and then eighty. The big engine hummed. The car was low to the ground, and she could feel every wrinkle in the road. They barely spoke. Michel seemed more wound up than usual, and Olivia didn't want to further pull his attention away from the drive.

When they got off the highway in Rye, Olivia rolled her window down, though Michel complained about the cold. In fact, the day was bright and unseasonably warm, and she wanted to smell the Rye air, that hint of saltwater.

The house was not visible from the street, and it was easy to miss the driveway. They turned onto the dead-end road and then made the sharp left and they were there, parked behind the garage. Even from this angle, the house was impressive, with its peaked roof of skylights. Olivia found herself trying to see it through the eyes of a newcomer, waiting impatiently for Michel's reaction. But after she'd climbed out of the Porsche, swinging the heavy door shut behind her, Michel still sat inside, his head down, fidgeting with some gadget. She was wearing her mother's knee-high boots and the dark wool toggle coat. She'd even put on makeup, which felt like one more layer of protection between herself and the day.

The front door opened and Ty stuck his head out. His face registered surprise at the Porsche.

Michel extracted himself from the car with a slam. His curly hair alighted in the wind. His eyes were huge with mock alarm.

She walked toward Ty, Michel behind her. "This is my brother, Ty," she called to Michel. The space between the three of them was still too great for a proper introduction. She sped up her walk, hoping Michel would do the same.

"Dad said you were bringing a friend," Ty whispered as he kissed her cheek. "I thought he meant a girl. Who's this?"

"Michel Zahavi." Michel was next to Olivia, extending his hand to Ty.

"Come on in."

A short hallway led to the living room, which was large, with a sloped ceiling that went up twenty feet at its highest point. A wall of windows faced Long Island Sound to the east, just at the end of the lawn. There was opera music playing but the room was empty. Olivia tried to see the room as Michel might. Clouds over the Sound, though the day was sunny, created a sort of glowing light on the water. There was a grand piano that no one had played in years, several large, abstract oil paintings, and trim contemporary furniture. It was all quite exactly to Michel's taste. He fit in there, though no one else was likely to see it that way.

"People are in the kitchen," Ty said. "June's daughter is here."

"Who's June?" Michel said.

Ty raised his eyebrows at Olivia as if to say, *Did you meet this guy on the way here?*

"June is the woman my father's dating," Olivia said quietly to Michel. "I'm sure I mentioned her." Actually, it was likely she hadn't. She had been trying to see June as a phase, the way Michel was a phase. You didn't have to tell other people about such relationships.

They filed into the kitchen, where June was presiding over a stovetop of copper pots Olivia had never seen before. She set down her wooden spoon to come around the counter and hug Olivia. "I'm so glad you're here," she said, as though they were close. They hadn't seen each other since India. She introduced herself to Michel in the same friendly manner.

"It smells incredible in here," Michel said. He was right—Olivia's mouth was watering.

The back door opened and a laughing redhead about Olivia's age stepped inside with her arms full of firewood. She was wearing a Scandinavian wool sweater. Behind her, also in colorful wool and strangely jolly, was Max.

Max held his armful of wood carefully away from Olivia as he kissed her. "Olivia, meet June's daughter, Liza." He looked at Michel confusedly.

Liza's face was round and pink and freckled. She wasn't big, but she had an athletic, sturdy look to her.

Michel was nudging Olivia's arm and she remembered to introduce him. Max was rather curt, she'd thought, but Michel was clearly much older than she and she hadn't mentioned she was dating anyone.

"Is there somewhere I can put my jacket?" Michel asked. His accent was adorable—she hoped her family at least noticed that.

"Oh gosh, of course," June said, as though this was her job. "Honey, will you take their coats?" she said to Max.

It was strange to be treated like a guest in her own home. But she let her father take their coats.

Christina emerged from somewhere, to pull a magazine-perfect pie out of the oven.

"What time did you guys get out?" Olivia asked Ty and Christina.

"Eleven," Christina said. She looked pretty, in a navy silk blouse and sparkly earrings. Ty introduced her to Michel, and she gave Olivia a conspiratorial smile.

"We should have gotten a ride with you guys," Ty said.

"You should have," Michel said. "Why didn't you say something?" he asked Olivia.

"Why is everyone in the kitchen?" said June. "Go sit down, have a drink, relax. It won't be much longer."

Liza took a bottle of white wine out of the fridge and Olivia got glasses.

Christina stayed behind to help, but everyone else went into the living room. Ty and Michel located Max's scotch while Liza helped Max build a fire, something Olivia had never known her father to need or even permit help with in the past.

"Isn't it too warm for a fire?" she asked.

"We'll open a window," said Max.

Ty said something to Michel about football and they struck up a conversation of sorts, made painful, at least to Olivia, because it was obvious that Michel knew nothing about the sport.

Max straightened from the fire and poured himself a drink, taking ice from a silver bucket that someone, maybe June, had placed by the bar. Olivia remembered choosing the cranberry sweater Max was wearing as a Christmas gift with her mother, at least ten years ago. The tiny hole by the neckline was almost as familiar to her as the sweater itself.

There was a precision to the way things were laid out, flowered cocktail napkins beside a dish of smoked fish dip and crackers. It wasn't like past Thanksgivings, when everyone had been in pajamas, each responsible for preventing some side dish from burning. Eleanor had been a good cook but not a gourmet, and on a holiday when there was so much to keep track of, presentation tended to go out the window. Some years, the turkey had been a little dry. Once, for reasons Olivia couldn't remember—some fight about a canceled vacation or a business trip—Max had orchestrated the entire meal, with the help of Olivia and her brothers, while Eleanor lay on the couch in the den, watching Jane Austen adaptations on videocassette.

Olivia scooted closer to Michel so that Max could sit down. "So, Michel, how do you and Olivia know each other?" he said.

"Olivia and I work together," Michel said grandly.

"You're in film too?" Ty said.

"Michel's ad agency is a client of Likely's," Olivia said. "We met there but we don't work together. I'm only an assistant."

"Olivia is excellent at discerning still water from sparkling." Michel was joking, but the words hung in the air.

Max stood. "I'll see how June's getting along," he said, picking up his scotch, which had left a ring of condensation on the glass tabletop.

If Michel noticed that this interaction hadn't gone as well as it could have, he didn't let on. He ate a fish-dipped cracker and then turned to Ty and asked him what he did.

"So you work in film?" Liza said to Olivia, in a tone that suggested she had been told this but didn't really believe it.

"Yes."

"I work in publishing," Liza volunteered. "It's pretty much the same thing at our level, right? Lots of emails and errands?"

"I work on rough cuts," Olivia said. She scooted closer to Michel, to listen to his conversation with Ty. Michel was gamely asking her brother questions about his job—luckily he seemed to know more about corporate law than he did about football.

Soon June was calling them into the kitchen to supervise the carving of the turkey. Christina was in there with her, transferring dishes into serving bowls.

June stood over a large golden turkey. She looked satisfied and flushed from the heat of the kitchen. "Who wants to do the honors?" she said, brandishing a large carving knife.

"Why don't you go ahead?" Max said. At past Thanksgivings, he and Eleanor had taken turns carving at the table, bickering good-naturedly about who did a worse job.

"Ty, what about you?" June said.

"You're probably the only one who's any good at it," Ty told June.

June looked disappointed, but she turned her gaze to the bird and neatly amputated a drumstick, which she then transferred to the platter beside the carving board.

The rest of them ferried the other dishes to the table—Max with the Brussels sprouts, Christina with the sweet potato puree, Ty with the stuffing, and Liza with a gravy boat in one hand and salt and pepper in the other. All that was left for Olivia and Michel to carry was a big green salad and a small dish of cranberry sauce.

"We need more wine," Max said, as June set the turkey down at the head of the table.

"I thought you were going to let some breathe," said June.

"I'll get it," Olivia said.

"Get the pinot," Max called after her. "It doesn't need to breathe."

Michel accompanied Olivia to the basement, a cool, damp place where the Harrises stored wine, along with old sports equipment, Christmas ornaments, and outdoor furniture during the winter, during years when they remembered to bring it inside. Next to the racks of wine, Olivia saw a dusty fishbowl and several empty planters.

Michel picked up a bottle of champagne. "It's not chilled."

"They won't want that with dinner," Olivia said. "There's probably more white in the fridge." She took a bottle of pinot and a cabernet with a familiar label off the rack. She felt shy around Michel, as if it had been a long time since they'd been alone together, though it had barely been over an hour. It was more than that—in the presence of her family, Michel felt like a negligible stranger.

Michel set the champagne down with a clunk. "Did you even tell them I was coming?"

"I told my dad."

"*What* did you tell him?"

"That I was bringing a friend."

"You didn't tell them that we're seeing each other?"

Olivia laughed. "Are we seeing each other?"

He looked hurt.

"You know I haven't been talking to my family much. And we only met six weeks ago. Have you told your parents about me?"

Michel didn't respond. Olivia tried to move past him, carrying the bottles of wine by their necks.

Michel grabbed her waist and pulled her toward him. He put his nose against her nose. "Don't ignore me." He kissed her, hard.

"I'm not. I won't," she assured him. She didn't know what she'd been thinking, bringing him home.

★ ★ ★

MAX OPENED THE wine while people began dishing food to their plates.

"I tried to make everyone's favorites," June said. "The sweet potatoes are Christina's recipe, and I made the Brussels sprouts with chestnuts and bacon."

The Brussels sprouts did look familiar, but Olivia wasn't attached to any particular Thanksgiving dishes. She doubted Ty and Max were either.

"Is this your first American Thanksgiving?" June asked Michel, as everyone began to eat.

"Michel's lived in New York for fifteen years," Olivia said.

"Fourteen," Michel corrected. He took a bite of stuffing and immediately spit it into his hand. He dumped it back on his plate and began to dismantle it with his cutlery while the Harrises looked on with curiosity.

He found the offending morsel—an oyster.

"You're not allergic, are you?" June said.

"I don't eat shellfish," Michel said. "Or pork," he added, eyeing the sprouts.

"I'm so sorry," June said, looking chastened. "I didn't realize."

"How could you have?" Max said to June.

"And the Brussels sprouts have bacon in them," June said, clutching her forehead in distress.

Michel took a cleansing sip of wine. "It's no big deal," he said. "I can eat turkey and potatoes and salad—perfect."

"Olivia loves oysters," Max said.

"It's not like anyone eats oysters that often," Olivia said.

Max smirked.

For a few minutes, there was only the sound of cutlery on china, chewing, and swallowing.

"I'm afraid the turkey is a bit salty," June said.

"You see?" Liza said to Ty. Ty laughed.

"What?" said Olivia.

"I was telling Ty earlier," Liza said. "Mom is such a good cook, but she always finds fault with everything. Pretty soon she'll say the stuffing's dry, the pie is burnt, the vegetables are overcooked. You'll feel like you're eating airplane food."

"The pie isn't burnt," Christina said. "I made the pie."

Michel was smiling. "Actually my father does that too," he said. "But about my mother's cooking."

"She must love that," Liza said. They shared a laugh.

Ty shoveled food into his mouth, barely stopping to chew. It was understandable. Everything was delicious—the white meat wasn't dry, the sweet potatoes had been tempered with something so that they weren't too sweet, and the Brussels sprouts were so infused with butter and bacon fat that they nearly liquefied when you bit into them.

"So how exactly do you work with Olivia's company?" June asked Michel.

Michel launched into a description of what he did, how he liaised, as he liked to put it, between clients and creatives. He paused only to pour himself more pinot. He hadn't eaten much, and Olivia thought he might be getting a little drunk, which was unlike him. She dipped a bite of June's nearly professional turkey in gravy.

"Olivia's going to get tired of this soon," Max said, apropos of nothing. "She needs to go back to school."

"To film school?" Michel said, looking puzzled. Olivia had never actually told him she hadn't finish undergrad.

Max picked up on this immediately. "To Vassar. She didn't graduate yet. She has one more semester."

Michel looked unfazed. "I think it's not so important in her career," he said. "It's really about what you've worked on. And who you know," he added, laughing.

"That's your opinion," said Max.

"Of course it's my opinion."

They stared at each other for a moment, Max fierce, Michel cheerful.

"Liza graduated from Johns Hopkins this year," Max said, switching tracks. "She had a swimming scholarship."

"Partial," said Liza.

"And now she works at HarperCollins," said June, beaming. "For a very well-regarded publicity director."

Max set down his silverware and leaned back in his seat as if his point had been proven. *Her job isn't any better than mine!* Olivia wanted to scream. They were both assistants, for God's sake. At least in film, *some* people made money.

"I'm still living at home," Liza said, in response to another question from Christina. "Not for much longer, though."

"There's not much to do around here for people your age," June said.

"And you're selling the house," Liza said to her mother.

"Not immediately," June said quickly. "Maybe in the spring." But around the table, everyone stilled.

"June's neighborhood is very in demand," Max said.

Michel, who had been looking a little bored, perked up. He was obsessed with real estate. He wanted to buy something in the city but was always complaining about the insane prices.

"We weren't going to talk about this today," June said. It was her nervousness as much as anything that was making everyone pay attention. She fiddled with one of her gold earrings.

Max stood and walked around the table, refilling wineglasses, adding cabernet to everyone's pinot noir. No one seemed to notice.

Olivia sipped her mutt red. Something was happening that she was supposed to care about. Ty was looking at her—he was waiting for her to freak out and demand answers. But her brain felt a little soft around the edges from rich food and wine, and she had a certain reluctance to engage in another battle she likely had no control over. The stuffing was not only the best stuffing she'd ever had—it was the best thing she'd ever eaten, period. The thought gave her a stabbing sense of disloyalty, right below her rib cage. What right did she have to say anything? She slipped her socked foot up the bottom of Michel's trousers, and he put his hand on her thigh.

"So June would move in here?" Ty said in a strained voice.

How fitting, Olivia thought, that Ty should finally be rattled just when she was beginning to relax.

Max was standing behind June, his hands on her shoulders. "At least for now," he said. "Down the road, we might want something that can be both of ours."

June was clearing her throat loudly, urgently, but with the phrase *both of ours*, a phrase that could not possibly belong to Max, the damage was done. Olivia looked at Ty and then Christina. Ty's expression was stricken. Christina also looked panicked, which didn't make sense, until she said softly, "Ty and I thought we'd get married here next summer."

"We'd love that," June said quickly. "Of course you'll do that."

But June wasn't the one who was supposed to be answering. Max's face was blank, serene. "Of course," he repeated. It didn't even seem like he was listening.

Liza, the instigator of this unraveling, looked bored, as though this were old news to her. She was probably helping Max and June shop for their shared home.

Christina attempted to drag everyone back into some semblance of a conversation, asking Liza about neighborhoods and roommates. Olivia didn't understand why she kept engaging the enemy. Maybe because Christina was a relative newcomer to the family, she sympathized with June and Liza. Through the windows, though the light was fading, Olivia could still make out the Sound.

The Sound. That was what the Harrises always called it—what she was taught to call it as a child, years before she understood what the words meant. She still didn't know what made Long Island Sound a sound, rather than a bay or even a gulf. She thought maybe it was too big to be a bay. The constant refrain when she was a child was not to go down to the Sound alone. It was something she repeated to her dolls, playing in the yard by herself near the gate she wasn't to open: *You can't go near that Sound.* They could go when her mother came into the yard, ready to take a walk to feed the seagulls, because her mother understood that feeding stale bread to already fat birds was something a child needed.

Olivia kicked her heels softly into the leg of her chair. She would chain herself to the kitchen cabinets before she'd let Max sell this house. Ty and Christina looked as miserable as she felt. And Michel the real-estate maven was talking to Liza about apartments.

"There are still some deals downtown," he was saying. "I know a good broker."

"Brokers!" Liza said. "No one uses brokers. They charge you an extra month's rent."

"More than that, sometimes," said Christina, who definitely used brokers.

"You can negotiate," Michel said. "They find better places. My old studio was nineteen hundred dollars a month, in Chelsea."

"You call that a deal?" Liza said. "I have friends in Bushwick who pay five fifty."

"What is Bushwick?" Michel said, making a face. He squeezed Olivia's arm. It was another joke that no one was going to catch.

"It's past Williamsburg," said Ty authoritatively. Olivia was pretty sure he'd never been.

"I can't believe you use brokers," Liza said again.

"Michel makes a shitload of money," Olivia said, just to shut her up. "He doesn't need to not use brokers."

QUIETLY, THEY ATE pie—June's apple and Christina's pumpkin— no pecan, which had been her parents' favorite. The whipped cream, which June claimed to have over-whipped, was almost as thick as butter. Max dropped some into his coffee, and Olivia did too. Forks skidded on filling and scraped against empty plates.

"Mom, we never said what we were thankful for," said Liza, her mouth full.

Her daughter's tone was sarcastic, but June looked upset. "We usually go around the table," she said, looking at Max.

"Please."

Could they be serious? Olivia's head immediately filled with everything she was not thankful for. Michel looked like he was gearing up for another essay at dialectical victory.

June cleared her throat. "I'll start. I know this holiday can't be easy for the Harris family." She looked at Ty and Olivia. "It means a lot to me that you're all here, that we're sharing this meal. I'm thankful for that."

Ty, looking like he was being tortured, mumbled one long sentence about Christina and his job and the food. Christina spoke more clearly, if insipidly, about becoming part of the family.

And then everyone was looking at Olivia, waiting for what she would say.

But Max spoke before she could. "As June says, it's been quite a year." He looked sad and, at least for a moment, Olivia didn't feel quite so far away from him. Of course he didn't want to live alone. Her father was an animal, like she was, trying to stay warm, trying to avoid pain.

Max looked at Olivia, and raised his empty wineglass. "We're all doing okay."

"HOW ABOUT A walk?" June said, after the dishes had mostly been cleared. "It's not too cold. Then we can come back and play charades."

It seemed too obvious to point out that the Harrises did not play charades. Max, who played charades least of all, stood beside June in the kitchen doorway, his hand on her waist.

Ty declared himself too full and sleepy for a walk, and said that he and Christina would finish up the dishes. Liza was meeting up with friends who were home for the holiday weekend. June's face was brave at each of these rejections, and she was probably expecting Olivia to say no. But actually, fresh air was appealing, and there was no way Michel could drive them home yet, so Olivia and Michel and Max and June put on their coats and walked out the front door to the driveway. There, they stopped and looked at one another.

"Did you want to go on the road?" Max asked June. "There's not much of a shoulder."

Michel's hand was on the back of Olivia's neck. In the past she'd found this possessive gesture a little sexy, but that night it seemed more like he was trying to steady himself.

"Where do you usually go, when you take walks?" June said.

But Max didn't know—he didn't take walks at night. He ran a mile down the shoulderless road during the daytime, en route to the beach. "We can walk down to the water," he said, "but it's not very far."

"We should have done this at my house," June said. "Everyone in the neighborhood is out stretching their legs at this time of night."

They tramped back into the house and out the sliding doors in the kitchen. Olivia led Michel down the backyard to the gate near the Sound. No one had turned on the outdoor lights and it was dark once they got away from the house.

Though she walked quickly to put some distance between them and the other couple, she could hear her father and June.

"No one even cared about the food," June said.

"What are you talking about?" That was Max. Then, a few moments later, "Delicious. Stop fishing."

Michel did not appear to be eavesdropping. He was staring up at the sky, which was overcast, as though straining to make out the stars beyond the cloud cover. He tripped over a patch of uneven ground and caught himself against Olivia.

They did not talk. It felt like a journey to reach what was essentially the edge of her own backyard. Then Michel's eyes were on the water ahead. The lights of the city were visible in the distance, somehow larger and lonelier through the mist. Olivia felt a resurgence of the hopefulness of hours before—that Michel would like it, that he would be impressed. As though the water itself were hers to take pride in.

"Do you think he's really going to sell this place? The land alone—he'd make a fortune." Michel trailed off, perhaps imagining being the ruler of that kingdom.

Olivia nearly growled as she told him she didn't know. How could he not see that selling the house, the house her parents had built before she was born, was not something she wanted to talk about? They reached the gate and she felt for the latch. The metal was cold beneath her fingers. She couldn't hear her father and June anymore—maybe they'd gone back inside.

The land sloped downhill the last hundred feet to the water, ending at a retaining wall. Because the tide was out, they could sit on the wall, dangling their feet. The water lapped softly against rock, not far below. Olivia could feel the chill of the stone through her clothes.

From his jacket pocket, Michel pulled out a sleeve of tobacco she didn't know he'd brought. He began rolling a cigarette with his long, pale fingers. She wondered if he'd brought hash, but he didn't produce any. They were silent except for the rustling paper.

There was a breeze coming off the water, not strong, but it took him a few tries to light the cigarette, cupping one hand around it while he flicked the lighter. When he succeeded, smoke blew in Olivia's face. She waved it away, and then stood to move out of its path. Michel glared up at her.

"I don't want it on my clothes."

"You don't want Daddy to know you smoke."

"I *don't* smoke."

Michel threw the cigarette into the water.

"What the fuck?"

"Why did you invite me here, if you didn't want me?" His face was taut.

"You can't throw garbage in there. This is a natural body of water."

"If you don't want to do this anymore, that's fine." Michel got to his feet.

"If you weren't drunk, we'd be back in the city by now." It was true that she couldn't drive the rental Porsche, which had manual transmission. She'd never even driven in Manhattan. But she knew it wasn't a response.

Michel turned his back to her. She reached for him, wanting to make up, if only for the next few minutes. But when she touched him, he pulled away, and for a moment, she lost her balance.

Michel, hearing her inhalation, turned quickly toward her. Though she'd already caught herself, he dragged her away from the water as though rescuing her from certain death.

"Baby, be careful."

"I'm fine." She shook him off, annoyed all over again. "We could stand in that water."

"It's frigid."

"It's a cold shower."

"Why do you have to be so tough?"

Olivia had never thought of herself as tough. She saw her father's face, telling Michel that she loved oysters. "I only seem that way because you're being a baby."

"Why don't you go for a swim, then?"

They were facing each other, ready for combat. The moon had broken through the clouds and Michel's pale skin seemed to glow. Olivia remembered kneeling on the bed with Geoffrey, not knowing what the next scene would look like.

"Let's go inside."

Michel took her wrist. "I thought we were alike." He was too angry for the circumstance, for how long they'd known each other. She knew what he'd meant about their likeness, a coldness they showed to the world, but there on shore, certain in the knowledge that the house lights behind them would not be turned off until she was inside, she knew there was a part of her that was inaccessible to him, a locked-up safety. He couldn't see it, but he could feel its edges.

"We are alike," she told him.

OLIVIA HADN'T PLANNED to spend the night in Rye, but when Michel said he was ready to head back into the city, he didn't act like he expected her to come, and she didn't want to. She felt guilty and miserable and wondered if she should have used their fight as an opportunity to end things. She wished she had gotten in touch with friends to see who would be around, but the only person she spoke with regularly was Kelsey, who had gone to Michigan with her boyfriend for the holiday.

Everyone else was in the den. Christina's head was in Ty's lap and her eyes were closed. He petted her hair. Olivia curled into an available corner of couch. They were watching *Fargo*, which everyone had seen a million times, and soon Max and June peeled off for bed.

When it was just the three of them, Christina sat up, suddenly alert. "Who's Michel?" she asked. "He's good-looking."

Ty shot Christina a disapproving look. "How old is he?"

"He's—I don't know—a little older than you," Olivia said, though Michel was thirty-eight and Ty was ten years younger.

Ty looked dubious. "He looks older. Not that I'm claiming to be the fountain of youth."

Christina hit him in the chest playfully. "It's just a *fling*, Ty. Lighten up." She turned back to Olivia. "It is a fling, right?"

"Yes," said Olivia, though *fling* sounded more lighthearted than the thing with Michel felt. But then, she wasn't sure whatever it was with Michel had survived the holiday.

"My first year out of college—" Christina began.

"Hey, hey." Ty put his hands over his ears. "I don't think I want to hear about any of this, ladies."

"That's fine," Olivia said. "We really don't have to talk about it."

"Well, to change topics," Christina said. She pulled her legs under her and sat up straight. "I know it's still kind of far off, but you're going to get an email from Lee Anne soon about dates for the bachelorette party. She's thinking March or April."

"Okay," Olivia said. "Well, I mean, I basically have no plans, ever."

Ty and Christina laughed. "She's thinking something like South Beach if tickets aren't too pricey. Kind of a late-winter getaway. Or maybe," Christina added, seeing the look on Olivia's face, "just a fun weekend in the city."

When Christina stood up a few minutes later, stretching her arms overhead, to say goodnight, Ty lingered. "She doesn't have a lot of family," he told Olivia quietly. "I think it would mean a lot to her if you came. And it's probably going to be kind of pricey," he added. "But it's my treat. Just let me know what the tickets cost, or the hotel, or whatever they decide to do."

Olivia nodded, embarrassed. She'd never been to a bachelorette party before, and the idea wasn't especially appealing. But Ty and Christina were who she had now, and at least they were trying to be her family. Alec and Holly were across the country, and her father was re-creating his life without them.

Olivia finished the movie alone—the endless snow, the funny accents, the woodchopper. She caught the end of *Seven* with Brad Pitt and Gwyneth Paltrow on a different station—another oddly dark choice for Thanksgiving.

It was only when she turned off the TV and went down the hall to her bedroom that she realized how much she'd been dreading the moment. She hadn't been there since Labor Day. But after she flicked on the lights, she could see at a quick glance that nothing had been moved, nothing had been changed. The stuffed dog her brothers had bought at the hospital gift shop was still on her bed, a bottle of nail polish and the summer fiction issue of the *New Yorker* on the night table. Her books, and nobody else's, were stacked on the floor beside the bed.

The only additions she saw were a stack of mail on the desk— though she wasn't an alumna yet, Vassar was already soliciting donations—and next to it, a bag from Saks Fifth Avenue. Inside the bag were two sweaters of her mother's with a note on top: *These were at the cleaner. Thought you might like to have them. June.* One was a rich camel-colored cashmere V-neck. The other was black and closed with a belt. Their heft felt familiar in her hands. Instinctively she held them to her face, but they were odorless, sterile.

There was something else in the bag, wrapped in white tissue. Olivia lifted out a brown leather handbag. A slip of paper floated out with it. Olivia examined it—it was a gift receipt, with more of June's loopy handwriting. *Thought you might need something like this. Feel free to exchange.* The bag was ample, buttery, with a striped silk lining. Olivia knew by the label that it was expensive, but more than that, it was beautiful. The scent of the leather filled the air like a living thing. She'd never owned a bag like that—a grownup handbag, what women in New York City carried to work.

She hated that she liked the bag, not just because it was from June, but also because her mother would not have given her such a handbag. Her mother had not bought lavish things even for herself unless they were deeply on sale. It was too much to contemplate that evening. She put the leather bag back under the sweaters. She stripped out of her clothes and was asleep almost as soon as she crawled into bed.

3.

The first week of December, Olivia received an email from Max, sent to Alec and Ty too: *I'm trying to clear out Mom's study. Does anyone want anything in there?*

She called him when she left work. "You're just going to get rid of everything, aren't you?" she said when he picked up.

"I won't get rid of anything you want." There was a pause. "It's Olivia," he said to someone with him.

"Is June there?"

"We're on our way to a birthday thing in Greenwich for Davis Keller. You remember him?"

"Who has a birthday party for themselves when they're sixty?" Olivia snarled.

Max chuckled. "I agree with you, sweetie. Though his wife is throwing it."

She heard background noise, faint music. "Am I on speakerphone?"

"I'm driving."

"Take me off."

Max's voice came into focus. "Can I call you later?"

"We shouldn't be going through her stuff."

There was a pause. "I know. It doesn't feel right to me, either. But we have to try to begin."

"Is that what June says? Because she's moving in?" She was stopped outside the subway at Union Square. It was cold out but she barely felt it—that was the good thing about rage.

"Listen, why don't you come out this weekend? You can look through some of her things and tell me what to do with them. Maybe you'll find some photos we can frame."

Olivia was silent. Spending time out at the house with June and Max there as a couple—when it wasn't even a holiday—felt like tacit approval. But if she didn't go through her mother's things, would June be the one doing it?

"See if you can get Ty to come too," Max suggested. "At least think about it."

A COUPLE OF days later, on a cold, sunny afternoon, Olivia was there, sitting cross-legged on the floor of her mother's study, a lukewarm mug of coffee beside her. Ty hadn't wanted to come, though he had offered to look at anything Olivia thought he should see, meaning that she should do all the work.

Though the idea of the project was overwhelming, the study itself was orderly. Tax returns were filed chronologically. There were folders with warranties and receipts for major appliances, which Olivia tossed, knowing Max couldn't be bothered with them. Most had probably expired long ago. She found a collection of travel brochures, many fifteen years old, with outdated photographs of families on tropical beaches and skiing. The Harrises had never gone on any of these vacations: Telluride, Alta, Saint John, the Florida Keys. Olivia wondered whether her mother had wanted to—whether she had been disappointed when Max or the kids hadn't been enthusiastic, and she'd filed the brochures away, hoping to try again next year.

Another folder contained random school pictures of Olivia and her brothers. The best of these were memorialized in albums, but apparently Eleanor had hung on to some of the outtakes. Olivia's child self was skinny and long limbed, with a long snarl of brown hair. Her mother had been less interested in grooming by the time she came along (six years younger than Ty and nine younger than Alec, she'd been an afterthought at the very least—her parents would never admit that she'd been an accident). But the dresses were gorgeous, smocked and pleated. They seemed to belong on a different child, a tidier child. Always in these photos, Olivia's hands were in her lap, her smile close-lipped and sphinx-like. She remembered hating having her picture taken at school: the photographer, wearing a clown nose, would insultingly dangle stuffed toys near the camera. The snapshots of Olivia playing with her brothers were of a different girl entirely, a tomboy with scabbed knees, shrieking as she ran naked through the sprinklers.

Max dared to enter the study. He held out the coffeepot, offering a warm up. "How's it going?"

"There's nothing here," Olivia said. "You didn't need me to come do this." She had hoped to find more, something revelatory. Eleanor had lived in her study, grading papers, a cup of tea always at hand. But though the smell of the room and the objects on the desk—a clay paperweight made by Ty or Alec, a framed wedding photo of Eleanor and Max, a conch shell, and a piece of coral shaped like a dog—were as familiar to Olivia as the backs of her own hands, nothing essential of her mother was there.

Max sat at the desk chair. "It wasn't my idea," he said, looking past her, out the windows toward the Sound.

"June isn't an excuse. She can't make you do this." She didn't think they were talking about the study anymore.

Max said nothing. He watched her as she gathered stray photos into a pile.

"What?"

"Do you think you should see a therapist?"

The question was surprising enough to make her laugh. "Do you think *you* should?"

"Probably."

"Is this another June idea?"

Max sighed. "Your mother and I, we weren't big believers in—" He waved his hand in the air.

"Emotions?"

"Whatever. The point is, if you think it could be useful, I'm happy to pay for it. As long as the therapist doesn't tell you everything's my fault." He smiled weakly.

"I'll keep you posted," she said, getting up from the floor, and Max took the hint, and left her alone.

It was tempting to head back into the city, to leave the gloomy piles for Christmas, or for somebody else. She had plans with Michel that night, and she knew on an afternoon like this, he would be easy to find, bundled head to toe at galleries in Chelsea or else at home, working or catching up on the newspapers. Since Thanksgiving, they had been in a kind of limbo. Michel seemed wary of her and usually she had to seek him out. But, somewhat to her surprise, this dynamic had revived her flagging interest. She knew it couldn't last much longer. But a night with Michel, indulging in his brand of mild debauchery, could be the antidote to the heaviness of a day at home.

Yet there was a force keeping Olivia there, unsatisfied until she had opened every cabinet drawer and removed every folder. Dimly there was the idea that she might find something useful for her film, the film she was still trying to compose, in her mind as much as on screen, about her mother.

She found another cache of photos, these older: Eleanor as a child outside Boston, with her older sister, Vera. Both Eleanor and Max had grown up in the Boston area without a lot of money. Max and

Eleanor hadn't been the kind of parents who talked a lot about their childhoods or told stories about walking through five feet of snow to get to school. Olivia knew that Eleanor's father had been diagnosed with lung cancer when Eleanor was a teenager and had died the summer before she started college, when he was in his late forties. The following summer, she met Max.

Max had told Olivia once that Eleanor and her father had been very close and that his death had devastated her, though he hadn't used that word. Olivia knew that Eleanor's mother had pushed for aggressive treatment and Eleanor's father had died on the operating table during a risky surgery. But Eleanor had never mentioned her father's illness to Olivia—at least not that she could recall. She had told other stories about her father, happy ones: him taking her and Vera camping in Maine one summer, him sneaking her extra bowls of ice cream in bed when her mother wasn't looking. Sometimes she had mentioned him on his birthday, which was in March, the day before Olivia's.

In the bottom drawer was a folder labeled CORRESPONDENCE, which Olivia saved for last. It was crammed with a mélange of mail—everything from sappy Hallmark cards from long-dead aunts to letters Alec and Ty and Olivia had sent home from sleepaway camp, full of complaints and comic spelling. Like the folders of photos, there was a certain randomness: these couldn't be *all* the birthday cards and letters Eleanor had received since they built this house, so why this particular selection? Her mother hadn't been a pack rat, and Olivia wondered if this collection were her token gesture of nostalgia.

But Olivia couldn't help herself—she read the letters one by one, quickly losing track of time, until dusk. Her mouth tasted sour from the coffee she'd drunk hours before, and she had a headache. She rifled though the slim pile that remained.

At the bottom were several folded sheets of plain white paper. She smoothed open the first sheet and saw handwriting in inky blue:

E—

I'm still thinking of Amagansett, the morning light on the porch, the way your body feels in water. I am in awe of your strength. Here is what you asked for. Till next time.
—F

Olivia had goose bumps. *The way your body feels in water?* The cheesiness would have made her mother cringe—or laugh.

She opened the next sheet and a photo slid out. It was of her mother at the beach, wearing a swimsuit and holding a beer. She looked older than in the framed pictures around the house and the ones Olivia had been looking through all afternoon. The picture was recent, from sometime before Eleanor had gotten sick, but not long before. She was gazing at the camera, looking mischievous somehow, with laugh crinkles around a twisted mouth. Olivia recognized the expression not as her mother's but as her own.

"Find anything good?" It was Max, his head poking around the door.

Olivia startled. "No." Quickly, she folded the paper with the photo tucked inside. "Nothing. I need to get out of here."

"Will you stay for dinner?"

"I can't." She had no idea what time it was—it felt like it had been dark for hours. She was struck by an almost panicked feeling of needing to leave the room.

"Glass of wine? The next train isn't for half an hour, anyway," Max said, glancing at his watch.

"Sure."

They brought the bottle into the living room. Opera was playing as always—*Verdi*, Olivia thought.

"Where's June?"

"Errands."

They talked idly about Max's work at the firm. He was fifty-seven, and he said these days they were pushing the partners out at sixty, to make room for the young blood. He told her his hours were lightening—that many nights it was easy, for the first time in decades, to be home by seven. He was straining to be cheerful, but this saddened him, Olivia could tell. He'd been a lawyer—a titan of litigation, as a friend of her parents' once said—for more than thirty years. Without this career, without Eleanor, what would he be?

Growing up, Olivia had been aware that her father worked a lot, and his work had been treated with a degree of sanctity and deference that led her to believe it was important. They ate dinner after other families, at eight or eight thirty, and when Olivia thought of childhood afternoons, she thought mainly of hunger—waiting for dinner, restrained to a regimen of healthy snacks (apple slices or celery sticks) that wouldn't ruin her appetite. Endless homework at the kitchen table, waiting for Max to come home like a Pavlovian dog, while her brothers were busy playing sports or locked up in their bedrooms, too busy for her.

Sitting with her father, drinking the crisp white Burgundy her parents had been drinking for years, was not unlike a family evening in the old days, hearing a bit about office intrigue. But Olivia couldn't focus—she was wondering about the letter she hadn't read yet, the one accompanying the photo. Who was *F*?

Max asked how things were going at Likely.

Warily, wondering if he were going to bring up going back to school again, Olivia told him it was going okay. "My boss is tyrannical but it's almost stagey, you know? Like that's her thing, being a bitch. It usually has nothing to do with me. And the other people I work with are mostly cool."

Max nodded. "You'll learn, when you're in a position of power, that it's only okay to yell at people who are allowed to yell back."

"Meaning?"

"Your superiors. Your peers." He smiled. "Sometimes the client, though I wouldn't really recommend that. But not the secretaries, or the associates, or the—" he looked at her.

"Runner. I'm called a runner."

"Not the runners. Your boss—"

"Amanda."

"We'll see how far she makes it, yelling at twenty-two-year-olds. Oh, pretty far," he said, waving off Olivia's odd attempt to defend Amanda. "But at some point she'll run into someone higher up the food chain with a little class who doesn't tolerate that at all."

"It's the way the industry works. Everything's done in a rush. People yell."

Max raised his eyebrows. "What are you guys doing, defusing bombs? Everyone thinks they're in a rush."

June came in with groceries. She tried to hide her surprise at seeing Olivia still there. "Will you stay for dinner?"

Again, Olivia said she couldn't. It was after seven—she'd missed another train. She called Michel from the kitchen, wrapping the phone cord around her stomach before he picked up. Cell reception wasn't good that close to the water.

He finally answered, sounding both groggy and miffed. "Are you coming back?"

"I can."

"Don't put yourself out."

"What have you been doing all day?" *I have been sorting through my dead mother's things,* Olivia thought. *You have probably been smoking hash and playing with yourself.*

"I was reading."

She found that she needed to see him. "Take a shower," she said, wrapping the phone cord around herself a second time. "I can be there by eight thirty."

In the living room, Max and June talked quietly, fingers interlaced. The grocery bags sat on the floor, still packed. They looked up when she came in, dropped hands, smiled.

Max stood up. "I'm going to give you the Vassar forms," he said. "The deadline's coming up—it might be already passed, actually, but I'm guessing we can negotiate. It's your decision, and no one is saying you're not working hard—but please think about it."

Olivia took the envelope from him. "I need a ride to the station."

June's car was blocking Max's and they had to hurry to catch the seven twenty-eight, so June drove Olivia.

"It was good of you to come out today," June said in the car. "I know your father appreciates it."

"I didn't really do anything." The letters and photo were folded and stuffed in her purse—not the one June had bought for her, which was still in its bag, but an old one of Eleanor's. She'd left the study a mess, piles all over the floor.

"Still." June paused. "I just want you to know, your father isn't selling the house because of me."

A jolt went through Olivia's body. There it was—the acknowledgment that the house would be sold, as though it were a fact everyone had already accepted. The acknowledgment that she had no say. "He loves this house," she said. "He *built* it."

"He's not going to put it on the market right away."

Olivia hadn't thought Max was going to sell the house right away, so this was not consoling.

"Ty and Christina want to get married here. In the summer." June spoke slowly, almost fearfully, making Olivia mindful of what she was supposed to feel. A wedding at the house without her mother. Christina had mentioned it at Thanksgiving, but it was as though June thought redelivering this news—or making sure Olivia absorbed it—were her job. But at the moment, the wedding was the least of Olivia's concerns.

ON THE TRAIN, once she had secured a seat to herself, Olivia took the folded papers out of her bag. Then she replaced them. She felt something akin to dread at the prospect of reading more. She stalled, texting Michel what train she was on, telling him that she was hungry and that maybe they should meet at the good bistro on Tenth Street.

Finally, just past Pelham, she unfolded the second sheet, the one that contained the photo.

Ella—
You at the beach. Tuesday, my favorite day now. Counting the hours.
—F

That was it. Two letters and one fairly recent photo, all referencing the beach. She read the first one again, and then the second one again, and looked (again) at the back of the photo, but there was nothing more. She was pretty sure, though she could have kicked herself for not double- and triple-checking, that there had been no more letters like these in the pile. There'd been nothing left but a few birthday cards.

If these letters were from a lover, why would her mother have kept them—in a folder called *Correspondence*—even after she had gotten sick? Wouldn't she have burned them, or at the very least thrown them away? Could they have somehow been a joke made by a friend, a prank played by a student? But if her mother's high school students had sent her notes like these—*The way your body feels in water*—Eleanor wouldn't have found them funny.

AT THE BISTRO, Michel noticed her lack of focus. He asked questions: Was it hard going through her mother's things? Was she angry at her father for selling the house or dating June?

What Olivia had wanted was to order an extremely cold martini and the steak frites, to eavesdrop on people's first dates and split the crème brûlée. It felt weirder to talk to Michel about her family now that he knew some of them than it had when they'd first met. He would have found the love letters, as Olivia was already thinking of them, totally unrevelatory. He had the stereotypical Frenchman's attitude toward affairs: they were simply a fact of life, no more worthy of discussion than one's morning constitutional.

"There isn't much to say," she told Michel, annoyed when he persisted. "I went through old photographs. It was sad."

His feelings were hurt. So she asked him questions about his day—he had, as she'd guessed, been at the galleries—about work, about his friend Lucien, who had separated from his wife and was pining for her. It was easy to get him to talk about himself. But back at his place, he wasn't interested in her. He claimed he had emails to write, though it was Saturday, and fiddled on the computer while she lay up in the loft, flipping through far-off calamities in the *Economist*. Her mind returned nearly every moment to the letters, worrying them this way and that. Who had written them? Whom could she ask about them? She didn't want to show them to her family, nor could she imagine sharing them with friends—hers or her mother's. Though only a tiny sliver of her mind believed there could have been an affair, letting anyone else see the letters felt too disloyal.

The next day, Sunday, Amanda called and asked Olivia to come into work to help Tim and Brian, who were on a deadline. But when she got in half an hour later, after extracting herself from Michel's bed, Tim and Brian were surprised. They hadn't asked Amanda to call her, they said, but since she was there, maybe she could get them all a coffee, and maybe some egg sandwiches, and after that they could find something else for her to do.

They exchanged a collective eye roll about Amanda, but the truth was, it was nice to feel useful. On the coffee run, she called home. "Where's Mom's cell phone?" she said when Max picked up.

He didn't know. "It wasn't in the study?"

"I didn't see it."

Max put her on hold and checked a couple of places without luck. "Maybe your brothers know. Someone wanted it for something, maybe to invite people to the memorial, but I can't remember where it ended up." He didn't ask why she wanted it.

Olivia dropped the coffees and sandwiches off and tried Ty from the kitchen. He told her he thought he had it somewhere. "Dad gave it to me to get in touch with a few of her teacher friends about the funeral."

"Can I pick it up tonight?"

"If I can find it. Why do you need it?"

She told him she'd explain when she saw him, buying herself a few hours to think of something. He told her to come for an early dinner. The afternoon passed slowly. Tim asked her to weigh in on the closing sequence of the ad they were working on. Brian seemed tired, possibly hungover, and was quieter than usual. The holidays were approaching and spending a Sunday in the office probably felt even more dreary to them than usual, whereas other than tracking down her mother's cell phone, Olivia really had nothing better to be doing.

Later, she walked to Ty and Christina's apartment in a light snow flurry, the first of the year. Their place overlooked the West Side Highway and the Hudson River. Like Michel's, the apartment was decorated with modern, streamlined furnishings, but somehow, perhaps because they had moved in only a few months ago, the style felt more cookie-cutter, as though they had ordered everything from a single store. Which was not to say it wasn't a whole lot more attractive than her place uptown, with its heavy drapes and boxy, dusty furniture.

"This is so nice," Christina said, embracing her. "I love impromptu dinners. We should do this every Sunday."

Olivia refrained from pointing out that if they did it every week, it wouldn't be impromptu. After greeting her, Ty had returned to setting the table. There was something Olivia found touching about seeing her older brother lay out blue-striped linen napkins, pausing to straighten one before dumping both the fork and knife on it.

There was a chicken roasting, brown rice on the stove, a salad of frisée, goat cheese, and roasted squash, which Christina was gently tossing with vinaigrette. Music was playing, something with moody vocals.

Ty offered Olivia a drink: "A beer, I think we have some wine? We're just drinking water, we had a bit of a late night last night." When Olivia raised her eyebrows, Ty laughed. "It's all relative—we were out until, like, midnight—"

"Twelve forty-five," Christina corrected.

"Right. In other words, we're old."

Olivia shrugged. "I was probably asleep by twelve forty-five last night."

"You stayed in?"

Olivia wasn't sure she could classify Michel's as staying in. She straightened another napkin.

When the chicken was out of the oven, the skin golden and paper thin, the house filled with its scent. They sat to eat. Christina carved the chicken beautifully, removing the legs in pieces and somehow knowing exactly how to slice the white. Olivia wondered why she hadn't volunteered to carve the Thanksgiving turkey, and if she'd been annoyed that June had asked the men and not her.

The food, especially when eaten in bites that combined chicken, rice, and salad, was deeply comforting. It felt like exactly what one should eat on a Sunday.

Across the table, Ty kept eyeing his phone. "I'm sorry," he said, when he caught Olivia looking at him. "It's work." Christina didn't look thrilled, but she didn't say anything.

They chatted about Ty and Christina's move—they had been living on the Upper West Side while Christina finished law school, but they were both happy to be downtown.

Eleanor's phone was on the counter, charging.

"Why do you need it?" Ty asked again.

She had decided to mostly tell the truth, for lack of other convincing stories. "I found a couple notes in her study from someone who just signed *F*. I'm trying to figure out who they're from."

Ty frowned. "What do they say?"

"Nothing really. Something about a trip to the beach. It's probably someone she worked with—but I can't think of anyone whose name begins with *F*."

Christina looked intrigued. Ty asked to see the letters. Olivia said she didn't have them with her, though they were in her bag—she hadn't been back to her apartment since returning from Rye the night before.

"What are they, love letters?" Ty said.

Olivia forced a laugh. Part of her wanted Ty's help, but she couldn't include him until she knew what the letters were. "Come on. You've had her phone for months."

"But I wasn't snooping." Ty turned the phone on. "*F.* There's probably twenty people in here whose names begin with *F.*"

"Ty, let her have it," Christina said softly.

Ty handed over the phone without another word, though he still looked disapproving. Olivia slipped it into her bag as though it were nothing.

Conversation turned to Ty and Christina's wedding.

"We meant to talk to you about having it out in Rye," Ty said. "It just sort of slipped out at Thanksgiving. I hope it's okay. At the very least, it means Dad can't think about putting the house on the market till the summer."

Ty and Christina were both looking at Olivia, their expressions earnest.

"It's fine," she told them, and Ty looked satisfied.

But Christina persisted. "How are you feeling about everything? June and—the two of them maybe moving in together. How was it yesterday when you were out there?"

"They'd have to wait at least a year, wouldn't they?" Ty said.

"Well, it's not like we're doing anything about it," Olivia said.

"Your parents always seemed so reasonable to me," Christina said. "Maybe you guys should try talking to him. Maybe he doesn't realize how it's making everyone feel."

Ty laughed bitterly. "Max doesn't talk about feelings."

Olivia didn't know if they were just being nice or if Ty was really upset about June, but she had no appetite for the conversation. Her brothers could say what they wanted, but they still had families.

June eleventh, they told her, would be the date for the wedding.

"Will it be warm enough by then?" Olivia wondered. The past June had been rainy and cold.

"We're renting a tent," Ty said, "They can heat it if they need to."

"We figured it was better than waiting until later in the summer—it gets so muggy," Christina said.

"Christina wants June because that's when her favorite flowers are in bloom," Ty said.

"Peonies," Christina said, sounding embarrassed as well as pleased. "It's the end of their season, really, but hopefully we'll get lucky."

Christina seemed to be shrinking—she looked thinner to Olivia than she had been at Thanksgiving. Olivia thought she knew what peonies looked like—soft, messy. She tried to imagine planning her wedding around a flower, planning a wedding at all.

TY AND CHRISTINA sent her home with leftovers. Back in her apartment, Olivia cataloged the *F*s. She could exclude the women, if not based on the content of the notes, then based on the handwriting. There were three men she couldn't identify: *Fitz Glazer, Franco*, and *Frank*. There were no text messages with any of them on the phone.

Since Fitz was the only one with a last name, Olivia looked him up first. A Fitz Glazer worked at a prominent investment firm in the city. A photo showed a man approximately her father's age. The number in the phone was his work number. Olivia didn't know what her parents did with their money, but the name of this firm sounded familiar. It seemed likely that Fitz Glazer was their financial adviser. The idea of Eleanor receiving love letters from this graying financier, with his weak chin and fleshy cheeks, was revolting. But further internet stalking revealed that Fitz Glazer lived in Rye. Olivia wrote down his address, his email, and where he worked.

She moved onto Franco, who had a New York phone number. There was no last name, no other identifying information. She actually tried Googling *Franco Rye*, which, of course, did not turn up anything useful. Finally, around ten o'clock, fingers shaking, she dialed the number from her own phone. The call went straight to voicemail. "I am dust," a man's voice said. "At the ashram till spring. Send me an email. Peace." The voice had a drawling, laid-back quality, as if Franco were from the West Coast or someplace more relaxed.

Maybe Franco was someone Eleanor had known through yoga. She had made a few friends whom she'd attended classes with, though Olivia thought these had been women. Perhaps Franco was a yoga teacher—if he was at an ashram till spring, he had to be pretty serious about it.

Olivia got ready for bed. At eleven, she called Frank. A man barked hello on the second ring, and Olivia promptly hung up. She'd had no plan of what to say. Based on Frank's gruff, irritated voice, Olivia deemed him as unlikely to have been her mother's lover as Fitz or Franco. What was she doing? There was no reason to think that the letters had been written by one of these men. *F* could have been a nickname. And if Eleanor had been having an affair, would she have kept her lover listed in her phone under his real name, along with the tree man and school nurses?

The next day was cold and biting. Streets became wind tunnels. At the office, Olivia's coworkers were divided into camps: those with families, gearing up for the holidays with a kind of glowing bustle, and those like Amanda, who were single and thirtyish, and either returning solo to their parents' in Cleveland or Bethesda, or staying behind in the city. The second group became gloomier as the holidays approached.

Olivia felt unaffiliated. She was young enough that returning to Rye seemed normal, not like a sign of failure. Kelsey and some of her other friends from high school would be there. Brian wasn't going far from the city either. He was spending the holidays with his girlfriend's family in Massachusetts.

Technically Likely was only closed on Christmas and New Year's, but almost everyone was taking at least a few days off. Amanda asked Olivia accusingly what her holiday plans were. It was the first time in nearly two decades that the holidays did not mean a two- or three-week vacation from school. Given the way everything was, Olivia was just as happy not to be taking off weeks, but it was hard to imagine staying in the city the whole time. Her city friends—Laila and Bridget and a few others—would doubtlessly be with their families for the week between Christmas and New Year's. Michel was sticking around, but hibernating at his place for more than a day or so wasn't appealing.

So she asked Amanda when she was needed, and Amanda sighed in her Amanda way. "I'm not going out of town," she said. "I'll be here to cover any emergencies. So I guess you could plan on taking off the twenty-fourth, if you want. And probably the thirty-first, too. Unless something comes up."

Nothing was going to come up the week between Christmas and New Year's. As Max had said, they weren't exactly defusing bombs. But Christmas and New Year's fell on Fridays that year, giving Olivia at minimum two long weekends, with a three-day week in between, which was likely to be very slow.

"You'll end up being able to take the week," Brian told Olivia, when she asked him what he was doing.

"Are you going to?"

"Not officially. But Tim won't be around and I don't think anyone else will be either. Katie wants to stay in Massachusetts the whole time, maybe even go up to Stowe and ski. I'm going to email everyone the Sunday after Christmas and ask if I need to come in."

But if Olivia didn't work, she didn't get paid. She wondered if at Brian's level—only one promotion away, though it would take at least a year—there was paid vacation.

Olivia slogged through her work, but her mind was elsewhere—the holidays, whether June would be there every second if she spent time in Rye, Fritz, Franco and Frank. She emailed Ty and Alec: *Who are Franco and Frank on Mom's phone?* Nobody knew. She couldn't ask her father, because what if he didn't know either, and he started wondering? She wrote back to her brothers: *Is Fitz Glazer their financial adviser?*

Ty wrote back almost immediately, his irritation at her snooping evident even via email. *I don't know. What are you looking for? Ask Dad.*

But Alec responded later in the day saying he was pretty sure Fitz was their parents' financial adviser. Olivia was initially relieved, before realizing that this piece of information didn't prove anything one way or the other.

She avoided Michel in favor of sleuthing. She looked up all the yoga studios in Rye (there were five, and it was also possible that Eleanor went to a neighboring town). On all the studio websites, she looked for a teacher named Franco, with no luck. Two of the studios—Mala and Kriya—sounded familiar. She was annoyed at herself for not being certain where her mother had practiced yoga, but next time she was in Rye, she could go to the studios and ask around. She emailed Holly, who had sometimes gone to classes with Eleanor when she visited, but Holly didn't remember which studio it had been. Eleanor had friends who would know, but Olivia didn't want to ask them—yet.

For Frank, there was nothing to investigate, which made him the most suspicious. He could be anyone. Olivia tried looking up his phone number but got nowhere. She couldn't bring herself to phone him a second time.

Wednesday, Olivia emailed the two yoga studios, asking whether there was a teacher named Franco who had taught there in the last five years. She had wanted to call the studios, but at Mala, the phone rang and rang; at Kriya, there wasn't even a number listed.

Christina's friend Lee Anne emailed about Christina's bachelorette party. *It's time to give back to the friend who always does so much for us,* the email began, sounding to Olivia more like a call for end-of-year charitable donations than party planning. A few weekends were proposed in March and April. Locations were tossed out—the North Fork of Long Island, where, according to Lee Anne, it would still be chilly but they could go to wineries and otherwise *indulge,* Miami or Saint Thomas, if people were up for something *more exotic,* or even—if they wanted to be cultural—*London, which Christina loves!!!* Or, Lee Anne added in parentheses, a weekend on the town in New York, if that was all they could manage.

Within an hour, Olivia's inbox was flooded with responses from Christina's friends. Susan said April was too close to her due date. Heather expressed her enthusiasm for all of the dates and all of the destinations. Erin, Christina's sister, couldn't commit till the last minute because of medical school. One woman loved the idea of London; another said Miami was the only choice for that time of year. Olivia organized the emails to go directly into a folder so they would stop populating her inbox, making a mental note to check for the verdict in a few days.

By lunchtime the next day, a woman named Suzanne from Kriya had written back. *I'm the owner and we haven't had a Franco here, but I'll ask around. You aren't by any chance Eleanor Harris's daughter, are you? I know she had a daughter named Olivia. Please feel free to call me directly or stop by the studio.*

Suzanne left a number. Olivia's heart sped up as she read Suzanne's email. The prospect of meeting a stranger who had known Eleanor was thrilling in the way of a new romance. She hadn't realized that she hungered for this—learning something new about her mother, pumping a stranger for details. But it was more than that—it was almost as though everyone who'd known Eleanor had soaked up some quantity of her essence. The people she knew, like her family and her parents' friends, had already emitted the Eleanor they had stored. But a new person was an unexpected reservoir.

Olivia phoned Suzanne back on her way to meet Michel for dinner. "Thanks for your email," she said, when the call went to voicemail. "I am—this is—Eleanor Harris's daughter. I'm trying to track down someone I think she knew." She left her number.

Michel was pouting and pissy when she met him at the restaurant on his block. She was growing tired of the place, though she'd agreed to go. The drinks were good, but the food was average and Michel never ordered off the menu anyway—he was always asking for chicken or fish cooked without butter, steamed vegetables or salad on the side. Olivia wasn't interested in lean protein, and alternated between the steak tartare, which one couldn't eat multiple times a week, the too-salty Moroccan lamb burger, and the daily fish special, which—she had to yield to Michel on the point—was always prepared with an excess of butter.

"I'm not even late," Olivia said when Michel haughtily presented his cheek, rather than his lips, for a kiss. She was three minutes late, which didn't count.

"You're too busy for me," he said. He said it sarcastically, as though it couldn't possibly be that Olivia had actually been busy—as though she'd been dividing her time between shopping and nightclubs.

Olivia sipped from his drink and ordered one of her own, along with the lamb burger. Even with Michel annoyed at her, even though whatever it was between them was limping along exhaustedly, there was something comforting about sitting at the table across from him, enacting this dating ritual. So she asked him about his week, and he told her about work, and that Lucien's wife had filed for divorce, and Lucien was heartbroken.

"They're married but she's just calling it quits," Michel said indignantly, as though Lucien's cheating on Paulina with his assistant were not its own form of abandonment.

Olivia's phone was ringing. It was Suzanne. Olivia excused herself to take the call, ignoring Michel's look and the arriving food.

Even by the entrance, the restaurant was crowded, so Olivia stepped outside. Suzanne's voice was low and calming as she told Olivia she was so sorry for her loss. "I didn't know your mother well," Suzanne said. "But I got a really nice feeling about her. I'm so glad I got to meet her."

Olivia murmured her thanks. She felt foolish. This woman had known her mother slightly, had perhaps taught her yoga a couple of times. Olivia couldn't exactly interrogate her over the phone.

"The man you're looking for is named Franco?" Suzanne said.

"Yes. My mother mentioned him," Olivia lied. "I wanted to meet him."

"I can't think of anyone," Suzanne said. "But Eleanor took classes with several teachers here, and one of them may know who Franco is. I'm going to ask around."

Olivia thanked her.

Suzanne asked if Olivia would be home for the holidays. "Come by the studio if you have time," she said. "I'd love to say hello in person." There was a pause. "How are you doing?"

"Okay," said Olivia. She felt somehow that she was lying, that she was supposed to either be more upbeat or dramatically less so.

Back at the table, Olivia confronted her cooling burger and Michel. "Look, I'm sorry," she said. "It's family stuff. I'm trying to figure out some papers of my mom's."

Michel visibly relaxed, and Olivia felt annoyed—what had he suspected her of? The burger looked dangerously undercooked, and the fries were soggy, and so she ate Michel's steamed vegetables, the most appealing thing on the table.

They went back to Michel's place. She expected, even hoped, that he'd be all over her once the doors were closed. But even when she kissed him and tugged suggestively at his waistband, he pulled away. She didn't know why he wanted to see her at all, if he'd lost interest in the sex.

"What are you thinking about?" she asked him later. They were in bed in the loft, her teeth as clean as his natural toothpaste would allow, her skin newly hydrated with his moisturizer.

"Sex and money," he said. "That's all I ever think about."

She understood the insult—sex, but not with her. *This will be the last time I see him,* she told herself. *This will be at most the second-to-last time. The penultimate time,* she thought, triumphant at remembering the word. If it weren't so cold out, maybe she would have gone home right then.

She turned out the light and Michel cleared his throat. "What are your plans for next week?" he asked. "For Christmas."

"I don't know how much time I'll get off."

"They won't tell you?"

"Well, I'll go to Rye for some of it, at least."

"Who else will be there?"

"I don't know." Did Michel want to be invited? Impossible, she thought, after the last time. She rolled onto her belly and reached one arm under her pillow. Her fingers curled around the edge of the mattress. That was how she had begun to sleep: pinning herself down.

Michel reached under her shirt and traced patterns on her back. This was her favorite thing. He kissed her ear. His breath always smelled good. "Goodnight, baby," he said.

KELSEY CALLED THE next morning as Olivia was out on a coffee run. It was a week before Christmas and the city was frigid.

"I'm at the airport," Kelsey announced.

"In New York?"

"In Denver. I'll be home tonight." Kelsey wanted to know if Olivia would be in Rye that weekend. Olivia started to say no, and then thought about Suzanne and the yoga studio.

"Come to Katonah," Kelsey begged. "Spend the weekend with us. You don't even have to tell Max you're in town."

It was not unappealing. Olivia loved Kelsey's parents, Edward and Nina, and their warm, cluttered house in the woods. Olivia said she would think about it.

That night, for the first time, she went out for drinks with Brian and Tim and Jake, one of the other editors, at a bar near the office. Tim's wife was at home with their baby in Carroll Gardens. But Brian's girlfriend, Katie, came. She was petite, with bangs and a slightly hoarse voice that she kept apologizing about. Brian, usually so laid-back, couldn't keep his hands off her. They had been together almost two years, Olivia learned. Katie was in grad school at Pratt for painting as well as printmaking. She lived on the border of Clinton Hill and Bed-Stuy, Brooklyn neighborhoods that Olivia had heard of but not visited.

Brian lived in Park Slope. "He's the yuppie," Katie rasped, and Brian just smiled, his big hand wrapped around Katie's tiny triceps.

The jeans Katie was wearing cost two hundred dollars, Olivia noted, so she couldn't exactly *not* be a yuppie.

Olivia sipped her beer, feeling slightly ill. It would be nice, she thought, to have a real boyfriend, someone like Brian, who wanted her to come out and meet his friends. Brian and Katie were older than she, at least a little—she knew Brian was twenty-eight, Ty's age, but Katie looked younger. Maybe by the time she was their age, she would be in a relationship like theirs, something solid and wholesome.

They were at an almost divey Irish pub, a relic that had somehow survived in the sterile, posh environs of Union Square. The bar and stools were dull dark wood that felt greasy to the touch. There was a jukebox and Tom Petty was playing. Olivia and Jake and Tim played darts while Brian and Katie flirted at the bar.

"You're not bad," Jake said, after Olivia came in second. "Do you have brothers or something?"

"Two," Olivia said, though it was really Max more than Ty or Alec who had taught her bar sports. He loved playing pool and was good at anything that required a kind of Zen focus.

Jake was in some ways an older version of Brian—more L.L. Bean than hipster, but handsome in a scruffy way. He looked like he was in his early thirties, around the same age as Tim. Olivia had the idea that he was from the west somewhere, Portland or Denver, though she wasn't sure if she'd actually been told this or had made it up. In another life, he could have been a ranch hand. Kelsey would have had a huge crush on him.

Olivia peeled off when Tim did. On her way to the train, she saw that Michel had texted. There was no thrill, even briefly, when she saw his message. A dirty, unpleasant feeling replaced it—a similar feeling to that of remembering some mistake she'd made in childhood, a hurt she'd never apologized for.

Saturday morning she took the train to Katonah. She'd texted Kelsey the night before, and Kelsey had responded with exclamation points, but it was Kelsey's father, Edward, who was there to greet Olivia at the station. He stepped out of their ancient Volvo wagon to give Olivia a hug.

"Kelsey's still sleeping," he told her. He was shaking his head, but fondness for his only child seeped through his disapproval. "The time change, you know."

It was noon. Olivia was instantly annoyed—that Kelsey had implored her to come so early, and then hadn't even bothered to wake up. The time change was only two hours—it wasn't as though Kelsey had just returned from Japan. But her irritation quickly dissipated over bland, comfortable chatter with Edward in the car. Kelsey was Kelsey: maybe it was a relief that, of all the things that had changed in the last year, she wasn't one of them.

Edward Grant was an architect. He and Kelsey's mother, Nina, had met later in life, in their midthirties—it was a second marriage for them both. In and out of their house constantly while she was growing up, Olivia had noticed a giddiness to their relationship that her own parents did not display. They'd known each other for less than two years when Kelsey was born; they were still discovering each other.

The Grants had sold their house in Rye and built their dream home in Katonah when Kelsey left for college. It was an upside-down house—the upstairs mostly glass surrounded by trees; the downstairs, where the bedrooms were, cozy and cabin-like. Olivia could smell Nina's buttermilk pancakes the moment Edward opened the door. The first one to greet her was the Grants' old black lab, Ulysses. He was the third in a series of Grant black labs named Ulysses. Olivia crouched down to say hello, scratching him under the chin. Ulysses, too stately to lick, touched his cold black nose to hers.

Kelsey was sitting at the kitchen table in huge pajama pants and a worn wife beater that showed nipple, talking to her mom. She smelled faintly: BO, American Spirits, lavender. She hugged Olivia ferociously and kissed her neck and cheeks. "Thank God." Behind her, Nina was smiling, waiting for a hug of her own.

They ate the incredible pancakes with thick, smoked bacon and maple syrup on all of it. Kelsey would commit to only one pancake and one slice of bacon at a time, but worked her way through four of each. She had a couple of pounds of perennial baby fat around her stomach, which didn't stop her from being petite and generally regarded as hot, but it drove her crazy and she was always on some diet, trying to eliminate carbs or meat or fat.

Kelsey regaled everyone with stories from school. She and her friends had gone camping and it snowed; she barely finished her final for Music History of Africa before she had to catch the flight home. That was why, she explained to Olivia, she had been so tired and needed to sleep in: because she'd gotten an extension till five P.M. on Friday, but her flight was at ten A.M. on Friday, and so she stayed up all night. Drew, her boyfriend, was there too, she told them proudly, in her tiny bedroom, trying to finish his philosophy paper ("Isn't there a *library*?" Nina said).

"Anyway, it all got done," Kelsey said. "But now I'm afraid I'm getting sick. My throat feels all scratchy."

Olivia inched her chair away from Kelsey's and everyone laughed.

After they ate, Kelsey and Olivia left Kelsey's parents in their sunny kitchen and retreated downstairs to Kelsey's lair, a large bedroom with wood floors and indigo walls that induced sleep and sloth. Kelsey showered. Olivia lay on the bed flipping through an old magazine. From the windows, you could see Nina's painting studio, built a short distance from the house. Olivia's parents had expressed a rather disapproving attitude about the Grants' professions.

Nina had inherited some money—not a fortune as far as Olivia knew, but enough so that she could be a painter and an art therapist and Edward could be a not-that-prominent architect, and they could still afford nice vacations and fancy summer enrichment programs for Kelsey while Olivia stacked and unstacked lounge chairs at the beach club the way Alec and Ty had before her, because her parents thought it was good for her. *Wouldn't it be nice to build a house with someone else's money?* Olivia remembered her mother saying when (perhaps not coincidentally after Nina's mother died) the Grants had built their house. As though the Harrises' house was somehow less indulgent because Max had earned the money himself.

Kelsey came out of the bathroom with a billow of steam from the shower. She puttered, combing through her tangled hair, piling dirty laundry from her suitcase on the floor.

"Close your eyes, your Christmas present is in here," Kelsey ordered and Olivia obeyed, hugging her knees into her chest. The room smelled familiar: the smell of Kelsey. Olivia wondered what her own bedroom smelled like to other people—what the smell she carried with her, without being able to sense it, was.

Olivia answered Kelsey's questions about work—tedious but not bad. "The Michel thing, I think it's over, or it needs to be over," she said. Ignoring the look of relief on Kelsey's face (Kelsey, reasonably enough, had not approved of Michel), she continued. "My dad—I don't know. It's like he's in a trance. He doesn't seem sad, and he's just this puppet, doing whatever June wants."

Kelsey perched on the edge of the bed. "Has he said anything else about selling the house?"

"No. But he had me go out there last weekend to go through my mom's stuff."

"Oh God." Kelsey's eyes were wide with indignation. "It's only been, what, six months?"

"Eight."

"Still."

"It's not like he made me do it."

"I don't get it," Kelsey said. "Your parents were such a unit."

Hearing Kelsey say what she herself had thought uncountable times only made things worse. "I don't think this means they weren't a unit," Olivia said. "It's just—he doesn't—"

"He doesn't know how to deal. Maybe you should talk to him," Kelsey suggested. "Tell him how this is making you feel. Maybe he's just so upset that he isn't thinking straight."

It was a version of what Christina had said a few weeks ago, and Olivia wanted to believe it. But since she'd found the letters, everything had become more complicated, in ways she was afraid to articulate, even to herself.

The day was a sort of cocoon. They watched old movies on TV with Kelsey's parents, and were drinking wine by the afternoon. The three women made dinner together—spaghetti with homemade meatballs. Soon after they ate, Edward and Nina retired to their suite-like bedroom, leaving the girls. Kelsey had obtained a couple of Nina's Klonopin and gave Olivia one and they lay on the couch with *Sleepless in Seattle* on low, chatting about guys and nothing in particular. Olivia hadn't taken a Xanax in months, though she still had a little emergency stash. She'd forgotten how nice it was to float, to feel physically removed from one's worries, as though everything that had once mattered were on the other side of a velvet wall.

On Sunday, toward the end of another fabulous Nina breakfast, Olivia mentioned that she wanted to go to yoga. She tried to say it casually. She had seen on Kriya's schedule that Suzanne taught a noon class.

Kelsey looked at her strangely. "I thought you hated yoga."

"I've never done it," Olivia said. But she knew what Kelsey was talking about. Kelsey had raved to her about yoga, which she took at college, and Olivia always pooh-poohed it. In her admittedly limited experience—she'd taken maybe two classes in her life—she'd found yoga boring. She'd played field hockey till college and was generally athletic, though she didn't exercise much anymore, but she hadn't seen the point of all that slow stretching.

Because Kelsey and Nina were still looking at her with curiosity, Olivia admitted, "It's the studio my mom went to. I got in touch with this woman who used to teach her."

Both faces transformed, Nina's with understanding and Kelsey's with excitement. "This is so great," Kelsey said. "You're going to love yoga, if you can just be open-minded about it."

Olivia had no interest in loving yoga. But she didn't correct Kelsey. She borrowed leggings and a T-shirt, and they set off together to the studio in Rye in Nina's old station wagon.

THE FEW STUDIOS Olivia had been to before were heavy with incense, sweat, or some pungent combination of the two. But Kriya was clean and relatively odorless, at least in the reception area. When she and Kelsey gave their names at the front desk, it turned out the woman they were speaking with was Suzanne herself. She also was not what Olivia had been expecting. She had spiky dark hair and appeared to be in her late forties. Tattoos flanked her muscular arms, and she was clad in black. She came out from behind her desk to give Olivia a hug.

"Your mom was—is—a wonderful woman," she said. Kelsey murmured her assent, though Suzanne had not acknowledged her yet. "She was so funny. And strong." She looked quizzically at Olivia. "We met before, you know. I was at the memorial service."

"It was a blur," Kelsey said protectively, though she hadn't been there.

"Of course it was." A bell above the front door rang as more students entered. "You'll take a class, right?" Suzanne said. "I'll give you both guest passes. And then we can chat."

The class they were staying for was called Vinyasa + Yin and it was ninety minutes long. The studio, which was large, with abundant natural light, was already nearly wall-to-wall with mats. Most of the yogis were women in their thirties and forties, though some were older, and there were a decent number of men. When Olivia and Kelsey hesitated, unsure where to put down their mats, people got to their feet and made space in two neighboring rows without being asked.

There was a buzz of happy chatter in the room, which didn't cease when Suzanne came in. She squeezed a few people's hands as she made her way to a simple altar near the back wall, where there were fresh daisies in a vase. A few moments after she sat down, the studio erupted in three long oms.

They began with a few poses that were vaguely familiar to Olivia. But quickly, she was out of her depth. They were on one foot and one hand—then on one foot and no hands. They held lunges for so long that Olivia's quads shook visibly. She was sweating, though the trim blond to her right was not. Kelsey, who had always been comically unathletic, moved seamlessly. She peeked back at Olivia from warrior two to mouth *She's awesome.*

As Olivia struggled not to fall out of a preposterous twisted lunge, Suzanne came over. She clamped Olivia's back leg with her own and then put her hands on either side of Olivia's rib cage and spun her chest up toward the ceiling. "Breathe," she said quietly, and Olivia drew in a huge, gasping breath.

She kept thinking the class was nearly over, only to realize they still had to do the entire sequence on the left side. But just when she was resigned to her fate, Suzanne lowered the blinds and put them in pigeon pose and told them she was going to leave them there for five minutes. This, apparently, was yin yoga—holding stretches for a very long time.

Since her mother's death, Olivia had found a perverse comfort in the fact that the worst had already happened. Nothing she could do, no mistake she could make, could compete with losing her mom. But the letters were a threat to that paltry sense of security: maybe things could be even worse than she'd thought.

She couldn't feel the toes of her right foot, which she was guessing was not the desired effect of yin yoga. She shifted and her hip cracked audibly.

"Let go," Suzanne said. "Let go again."

In front of her, Kelsey let out a bedroom sigh, and something snapped back to place in Olivia's brain. That was what she needed to do: to honor Eleanor by not going on some wild-goose chase. Her mother had not been having an affair. She had some private papers she'd forgotten to get rid of. And the photo—let it go. It was none of her business. It was actually that simple. What else could she let go of?

They lay on the floor in corpse pose, bolsters under their knees. Everyone's breathing quieted. There was a melodic chanting on in the background that, under different circumstances, Olivia could imagine hating. She fell almost instantly into a skimming dream state. Someone—it must have been Suzanne—was lifting her head, tugging gently on the back of her neck, massaging her shoulders with a musky oil. She wanted it to never end, though it was over in seconds. She wanted to stay lying on the floor in the warm room forever.

After class, Olivia felt ebullient and calm, happy to have come and happy to go. She approached Suzanne to thank her for the free class, but Suzanne gestured for her to wait while she spoke to other students. So Olivia went out into the lobby, where Kelsey was pawing through racks of luxury knits.

Suzanne found them a few minutes later. Olivia told her she'd enjoyed the class, which felt true in spite of the fact that she'd wanted to flee for most of it.

"I'm glad," Suzanne said. "Listen, I think I may know who Franco is. Franco Damiani, he used to teach at another studio in town. He's not there now. But Krista—another person your mom knew—she knows Franco, and she thinks your mom did too. She gave me his email."

"Who's Franco?" Kelsey said.

Neither Olivia nor Suzanne answered.

"Thanks," Olivia said slowly. "It's okay. I just wanted to know—so that's how he knew my mom. From teaching yoga."

"Possibly," Suzanne said. "I'll give you the email address. You can ask him."

"I don't need it."

Suzanne looked surprised. "Well, if you change your mind, you know how to find me. Do you live out here now?"

"In the city."

"And your father?"

"He's still here." *For now*, she almost added.

She smiled sadly. "First Christmas. Can't be easy."

"It hasn't happened yet."

Suzanne laughed. "Fair enough." She gave Olivia another quick, forceful hug. "Come back anytime. And let me know if you want that email address."

"What was that all about?" Kelsey asked as they walked out of the studio.

"I found some letters in my mom's study and I was trying to figure out who wrote them. I thought it might have been that person Franco. But it wasn't."

"What did they say?"

The photo of her mother in a swimsuit holding a beer flashed through her head. She waved Kelsey off. "Nothing. It was silly."

Kelsey eyed Olivia. She wasn't buying it. But Olivia said nothing more. Eleanor Harris had been a wife, a mother of three, a high school English teacher, a practitioner of yoga. If the letters had been some big secret, she would not have stored them in the folder with the camp letters and the old holiday cards. They were not a puzzle to be solved.

THE REST OF the weekend at Kelsey's was a blur of comfort food and fires and old movies. Olivia took the train back to the city with Edward on Monday morning. She slept the whole way in, pinned in the middle seat between Edward and another businessman, her head jerking upright at each station stop. She bought a coffee at Grand Central and was in the office by nine fifteen. Amanda, Brian, and Jake were standing around in the kitchen, talking about a TV show they all watched. Amanda actually solicited Olivia's opinion, only to scoff when Olivia admitted she hadn't seen it.

It was the first day of winter and the city was deeply in holiday mode—there wasn't much to do at Likely. Olivia hadn't heard back from Michel, though she'd texted him Friday that she was going to Kelsey's for the weekend. *Let it go,* she told herself, but was unsure in this instance how her new mantra applied. Let go of Michel? Or of worrying about Michel? What if letting go meant being less resistant to Michel, inviting him to Christmas at the last minute?

But that wasn't the answer. Christmas would be her and Max, Ty and Christina, probably at some restaurant, maybe going to the movies or opening presents after dinner—Holly's family had decided to visit Holly and Alec in LA. On the twenty-sixth, she might go to Greenwich with Kelsey and Nina, who always hit up the sales. She didn't owe Michel anything.

Tuesday was as quiet as Monday. Amanda and Jake found her things to do: sorting and reorganizing old files, scanning and then shredding ancient contracts they would never need but wanted records of. After work she went to the film lab, anxious to do something more to her movie before her access expired at the end of the year. She reviewed her footage: under eight minutes from the trip to India, mostly totally abstract, with one sped-up sunrise and a few shots of birds on wires in different cities. It wasn't the beginning of a thesis—it wasn't the beginning of anything. It was the closing montage to a story she hadn't told, because she didn't know how to tell it. Or maybe it just was what it was—seven minutes and forty-three seconds of color and movement and light.

A few weeks away had given her fresh eyes. She changed the order of a few cuts and ended up staying late, tinkering. The short walk to her apartment was freezing. When she got home, she ran a hot bath and soaked until she was fully warm and sleepy. She remembered that the lease was up on the apartment at the end of January. She would have to think of something to do. Maybe she should ask Brian, she thought. He might have friends who needed roommates, or would at least know where in Brooklyn she should look. Her life in the city had begun to acquire a sort of solidity to it. She'd get her degree at some point, she supposed—she'd look into transferring. She could probably take a few credits at one of the city schools and still get a Vassar degree.

Her mind landed briefly back on the letters she'd found in her mother's study. She'd look again, she resolved, when she was back in Rye. She'd make sure she hadn't missed anything, and maybe she'd even find a way to ask Max if he knew Frank—the man on Eleanor's phone whom Olivia had not yet identified.

BY WEDNESDAY THE twenty-third, Olivia and Jake and Brian and Amanda were the only people in the office. Jake was going on a ten-day vacation—almost unheard of at Likely, from what Olivia could tell—so he and Brian were working on a project that wasn't due till mid-January.

"When are you going to Massachusetts?" Olivia asked Brian.

"I'm not."

"I thought you said you were going to Katie's."

"I'm probably going to have to work," Brian snapped, right in front of Jake.

Brian left the room a few minutes later, and Jake said quietly, "He and Katie broke up over the weekend."

"Really? But they were so . . . at the bar . . ." Olivia trailed off, embarrassed to admit she'd been studying them.

Jake shrugged. "I know. Brian's the best," he added. "You should cheer him up." He waggled his eyebrows at her suggestively.

A year ago, Olivia had been home from school, following her mother around the house like a puppy. Alec and Holly had been home and the house had been bustling with gift-wrapping and ornaments and good smells. She didn't think she could cheer anyone up.

But she found herself trying, smiling and joking with Brian when they passed each other in the halls. And when Jake announced they had finished and even Amanda was ready to call it quits till the following week, it was Olivia who asked if anyone wanted to go for a drink.

Jake had things to do. Amanda said she had to run an errand. "You two go to Molly's," she said, referring to the pub they'd been to the week before. "I'll swing by if I can."

It was only four o'clock, but it was nearly dark out. Olivia found it comforting, though, that the darkest day of the year was technically behind them. She was reminding Brian of this as she layered on clothes in the lobby—a cashmere sweater of Eleanor's and a thick wool scarf Ty and Christina had given her for Christmas last year, followed by Eleanor's wool toggle coat, which really wasn't warm enough, even with the sweater under it, but which she'd kept wearing through the fall. She put on the special iPhone gloves Michel had bought her. Brian had on a down parka that looked like it was from the same era as the wool toggle coat.

No one at work knew about her mother. No one at work knew anything about her family, and she didn't realize what a huge relief that had been until Brian asked her, as they pushed open the glass doors into the wind, about her holiday plans.

"I'll go home," she said. "I guess in the morning. Rye."

"Who'll be there?"

"My dad," Olivia began.

Michel was suddenly standing before them, in his fashionable black coat with the fur hood, glowering at her.

"Michel?" Brian said. Olivia was disconcerted until she remembered that Michel was a client.

Michel ignored Brian. He probably didn't even remember Brian. He and Olivia stared at each other. She felt as though she'd been caught doing something wrong. But she hadn't done anything, she reminded herself. She didn't even think she'd failed to return a call.

"You didn't have a meeting, did you?" Brian finally asked. "Everyone's pretty much cleared out." He glanced up at the building behind them. Olivia admired his calmness, his reasonable, friendly tone.

"Just passing through," Michel said. He cinched some cord and his hood drew tight around his face. He took long strides past them, toward Fifth Avenue.

Brian and Olivia walked in the other direction, toward Molly's. "Weird," Brian said. He glanced sideways at Olivia, but said nothing else.

At the pub, Olivia ordered a beer. She felt shaky, exhilarated or terrified, something that was too extreme for the circumstance. She excused herself and stepped outside to call Michel. The phone rang and rang, and she left him a message, which she'd never done before. *I'm sorry that was awkward. I was headed to a work thing. I'll be home later—call me back.* She could end this officially, she thought. That was what adults did.

Her phone rang the moment she stepped back inside.

"Where are you?"

She named the pub.

"Come over," Michel said savagely.

"I can't. I'm not going to."

"What's wrong, baby?" Michel said, changing tones. "You've been ignoring me for days."

"Nothing. It's just—" She could barely hear herself over the music. She stepped outside again. "I think this has run its course, don't you?"

There was a strangled pause, in which she realized she had been far too cavalier.

"I'm sorry," she said. "Maybe it's just—" *The holidays*, she was thinking. *My mother.* And yet she didn't want to make excuses and be forgiven. She didn't want to be standing in the cold, outside the bar with the lights and the music, talking to him. She wasn't his baby.

While she hesitated, Michel hung up.

Swiftly, she shook off her guilt. They hadn't been a real couple. She had never expected Michel to not see other people. He was nearly twenty years older than she and rarely pretended to have much of an interest in her beyond the physical, though the physical had come to entail cuddling as well as sex. She shouldn't have needed to spell out to him that it was over. It would have been cleaner, though, to end things at Thanksgiving, when he'd given her the chance.

At the bar, Brian was buying them shots of whiskey.

"This is a bad idea," she said, after draining hers.

When Brian laughed, his eyes became slits and wrinkles.

They played darts and drank beer. There was a slightly off-kilter joy to being young in the city, out of work early, and wholly unaccountable on a day when most people had somewhere to be. They shared the space with a group of international students and some middle-aged career patrons who huddled quietly over their drinks. They, the five o'clock occupants of Molly's, were a crowd who did not fit in, and Olivia had that by then familiar feeling that the world had ended, and yet life carried on.

It was easy to talk to Brian—about movies, about people they worked with, and eventually, on their second beers, about relationships—the ones they had just ended. Katie had broken up with him, he told her, the Sunday before.

"Was it out of the blue?" Olivia asked, remembering again how cuddly they had seemed Friday night.

"Not really. We fought a lot. She's in this different stage: art school and being sort of, you know, image conscious. She likes to go to all the new places." Brian smiled in what might have been embarrassment. "I just want to relax on the weekends."

"But you didn't want it to end." Olivia took the last sip of her beer, a dark, milkshake-like stout.

"Who ever wants anything to end?"

Olivia said there had been someone—someone, she told Brian, she'd met soon after moving to the city—who wasn't really right for her.

"He wasn't on the tenure track," she said, borrowing the expression from her mother, who had used it once about a college girlfriend of Ty's.

"But you're so young," Brian said, a little wistfully. "You're probably not even looking for anything serious."

That was true, she admitted.

"I'm not either," Brian declared. "Not anymore." He suggested another round, but to her own surprise, Olivia begged off. There was a version of herself who would have stayed to see where the night went and arrived in Rye late the next day, hungover and without Christmas gifts for anyone, and gotten away with it. But a different self prevailed that evening. She wanted to retain the lightness between her and Brian. Besides, work was the one place where she felt normal. She didn't want to ruin it, the way she had risked doing with Michel. She had expected Brian to somehow know that Michel was the man she was referring to, and she was relieved that he had not.

The city felt emptier and emptier. She and Brian hugged goodbye, and he headed south to Brooklyn, while she walked up Fifth, wondering what she could buy her family for Christmas. The fight with Michel felt like it had happened months before, though she was only a short walk from his place.

She bought herself a bag of chestnuts from a vendor on the corner and walked to the R train on Twenty-Third. She took the train to Fifty-Ninth and Lex—Bloomingdale's. The store was a madhouse (this was where everyone left in the city was apparently gathering) but the drinks had inoculated her. For Christina and Ty, she bought special smartphone gloves like the ones Michel had given her, with metallic pads on the thumb and forefinger—forest green for Ty and black with faux-fur trim for Christina. She was going to buy her father a pair too, but she spied a shearling hat with earmuffs. She couldn't really imagine Max wearing it, but she tried it on and it was so warm and soft. Maybe he would wear it if she bought it for him.

Thus Christmas shopping for the downsized version of her family that would be assembling the next day, including navigating the frenetic store and waiting in line behind squabbling teenage girls, took twenty-five minutes. It was only seven thirty when she got home. She called the house as she began throwing things in a tote bag. Her father answered.

"Ty's on the train now," he said.

"Should I wait till morning?" She stopped packing and sat down on the edge of the bed. She should have called earlier—she didn't want to spend the night in the apartment.

"No, no, come on out. Let me know which train you get on. Someone will pick you up." There was a pause. "Is it just you?"

She told him it was.

"Okay, honey. See you soon."

JUNE AND LIZA were skiing, so at least it was only the Harrises and Christina over Christmas. They spent the twenty-fourth lounging. Ty and Christina did some last-minute shopping for Christina's family, whom they were visiting over New Year's. Olivia dressed warmly and went running for the first time in nearly a year. For dinner, they picked up takeout from an Italian restaurant in town.

Alec and Holly called after dinner with news: Holly was pregnant, due in July. Alec sounded ecstatic, and Holly more measured, nervous. They were a little shy of the twelve-week mark, but had decided to break the news to their families over Christmas.

When they got off the phone, Max and Ty looked as sad as Olivia felt. The arrival of this baby, the first of a generation, made Eleanor's absence all the more impossible to ignore.

Quietly, Christina said how wonderful it was, a summer baby.

"Although," she added, "This may mean they can't come to our wedding."

No one had thought about that yet. Holly's due date, they calculated, was five weeks after the wedding, so it was still possible she could fly, but barely. Olivia didn't say it, but Holly didn't seem the type to travel across the country thirty-five weeks pregnant, especially after a previous miscarriage.

"We could probably change the date, right?" Ty said to Christina. "It's going to be here so it's not like there's a venue involved. We could wait until September."

Christina, looking stricken, murmured something about deposits.

Max didn't think they needed to postpone. Even if Holly couldn't make it, Alec would fly in for a night. "There will be plenty of chances for everyone to celebrate together."

When Olivia was growing up, they had opened most of the presents Christmas Eve. Her parents had wanted credit for the larger gifts. To Santa were relegated stocking stuffers: alarm clocks, chocolates, socks, and gadgets much like the ones that could be found at museum gift shops. But that year there were so few presents that they saved the whole affair for Christmas morning.

Ty and Christina fussed over the gloves. They both claimed, repeatedly, that they'd been wanting to buy a pair and that Olivia was a genius for having thought of it. Max didn't say as much about the hat, but he tried it on and remarked at its warmth, clearly pleased.

The main thing was just not to think about the year before, Olivia reminded herself, as she opened the soft green sweater Ty and

Christina had given her. Holly had sent a black clutch with long suede fringe and a gift certificate for a pedicure at a spa in SoHo. Max distributed checks, smiling apologetically. There were a few gifts under the tree from family friends: coasters and notecards, a fancy wine opener and a tiny wallet, distributed seemingly at random between Ty, Christina, and Olivia.

Those same family friends, the Vincents, lived a mile away and had a big Christmas lunch every year. It was mostly made up of their family: three children, grandchildren, and assorted uncles and cousins. Max and Eleanor had often stopped by for a glass of wine in past years—Alec, Ty, and Olivia had turned up their noses. They'd preferred Christmas at home, with only their own family.

But that year, with their family down to a group of four, Max had accepted Marjorie Vincent's invitation. No one acknowledged the slight humiliation of attending a party they had long shunned. They rode together in Max's car, Christina and Olivia in the back. The large colonial house was warm and fragrant: spiked hot cider, baked ham, browning butter and sugar. There were Christmas carols playing. Christina shone, bantering gracefully with people she barely knew, her diamond ring flashing and attracting praise.

Olivia drank a mug of spiked cider and then another one. Every time her mind flicked back to last year—Kelsey's family stopping by with their famous eggnog, Eleanor's strange fatigue, which they had attributed to holiday stress, although Eleanor had never been stressed by a holiday—she repeated her *Let It Go* mantra. She applied the same mantra to a drunken uncle who leered at her, a toddler who tricycled into her shins. Talking with the Vincents, even the kids, who were roughly Alec and Ty's ages, would have been excruciating, she thought clinically, were it not for her detached attitude. Carla, Dan, and Trip, all married, all with corporate jobs, thought they were being friendly by grilling her: How was her job? Where did she live in the city? Was she thinking about graduate school?

When the meal was finally over, Olivia helped herself to a plate of tiny desserts—lemon square, fig bar, pecan brownie—and collapsed on the couch next to Christina. She had no idea what time it was or how long they'd been there. "Where's Ty?"

"Marjorie had a niece she wanted him to meet," Christina said drily.

"Oh God. Is she still trying to set him up with people—in front of you?" Marjorie had long been trying to entice Ty with some extended family member.

"I think I'm safe," Christina said. "I saw the niece."

Olivia laughed. She had never heard Christina be even a little mean before. It made Olivia like her more. "Is she awful?"

"She's, like, forty. She looks like a cat person."

"Do you think we can leave soon?"

"Someone just has to make the move."

Max found them on the couch. He was already wearing the hat Olivia had given him and jingling his keys. "Shall we set a limit on how much fun we can have today, ladies?"

They found Ty on the porch in his coat, taking a work call. Max clucked disapprovingly as he herded them to the car.

"It's Christmas Day," he said, when Ty finally hung up. "Sometimes you just have to say no."

"I'll say no too, when I'm a senior partner," Ty said, annoyed.

They went to the movies in the neighboring town. By the time they got home, it was a respectable hour to retreat to their rooms, declaring an end to the holiday. Olivia had a text from Brian, who was in Connecticut with his family, wishing her a merry Christmas.

★　★　★

THE NEXT DAY was sunny and nearly fifty degrees. Olivia spent the morning picking through the Greenwich sales with Nina and Kelsey. Kelsey and Nina bought two bags full of clothes and shoes at Saks. Olivia bought one sweater, still expensive at 40 percent off, and Nina bought her a fancy lip gloss she tried on *Just because*. She had decided that day to use the handbag June had left in her room over a month before, and Kelsey and Nina both commented on it, touching the soft brown leather. Olivia's old wallet, a woven-cloth item she'd had since high school, looked dingy in comparison, so when they stopped at a smaller boutique on Greenwich Avenue, Olivia bought herself a new red leather one.

Ty and Christina had gone to a spinning class and were lounging back at the house. They were going over possible honeymoon destinations, scrolling through pictures of African safaris and South Pacific islands. Olivia made a ham sandwich and sat with them. Planning a blowout vacation: that was something she could get behind.

"We could do a safari and stop in Europe on the way, to get over jetlag," Christina suggested.

"Hmmm," said Ty, a noise Olivia knew he made when he was about to disagree. "But wouldn't we want to go to Cape Town or Johannesburg? It's easy to get to Europe another time."

Christina looked disappointed but nodded.

She was easy to get along with, Olivia thought. Ty was too—maybe that was part of what attracted them to each other. They would have a life without a lot of drama. "But Europe could be fun," she pointed out, though if it were her, she'd choose the most exotic thing possible.

"How much time would you want to spend at the beach?" Ty asked Christina.

Olivia remembered that she had never checked on all those messages about Christina's bachelorette party. Quietly, she fetched her laptop and joined them, scrolling through the thread. The consensus seemed to be the first weekend in April, in Miami. Lee Anne and Erin had both written privately to Olivia, asking if that date worked for her. Guiltily she wrote back, apologizing for the delay and saying that sounded great.

Ty got up, saying he was going to take a nap.

"Working?" Christina asked Olivia.

"No." She paused. "Is your bachelorette party supposed to be a surprise?" She'd noticed Christina wasn't on the emails.

Christina laughed. "Not really. I know where it's going to be, it's not like I'm going to be put in a car and blindfolded, but they're going to keep restaurants and whatever else a surprise."

"Well, I'm just writing back to them now—I got busy at work and sort of forgot," Olivia admitted. "But I'm in. It'll be great."

Christina beamed, making Olivia feel even guiltier. "That's so sweet of you," she said. *Sweet* was not something Olivia was used to being called. "I know it might not be your favorite way to spend time, with a bunch of women you don't know."

"It'll be nice to meet some new people," Olivia told her.

SUNDAY NIGHT SHE returned to her apartment. It should have been a relief that the first Christmas without her mother was behind her, but it felt like the opposite. With every year, she supposed, Eleanor's absence would feel less dramatic to everyone else. But every month that passed increased the distance between Olivia and Eleanor in a way that felt spatial, and Olivia was certain that more time would only make her miss her mother more.

A few people were back in the office—Tim, Brian, Amanda, the other assistant, Nick, and some of the assistant producers. But there weren't any client meetings and there was the not unpleasant feeling of being in it together with the others who were not off skiing or on the beach somewhere. Brian suggested they get drinks again, but Olivia was cool. He'd just broken up with someone he'd been serious with, and he was the closest thing to a friend she had at work. Besides, he wasn't even really good-looking—he had a bit of a beer belly and a broad baby face—though Olivia couldn't deny that she found something appealing about him. He didn't have Michel's stylishness or Pat's mountain-man appeal. But he had eyes whose color seemed to change with the light, and curly, soft-looking light brown hair that reminded her of a little boy. He had a nice smile and big hands that looked goofy typing on a keyboard or a phone. His voice was unexpectedly deep.

Instead of flirting with Brian, Olivia emailed Suzanne and asked her to recommend a yoga studio in the city. Suzanne wrote back right away with the names of a few places, and Olivia went that same night to a candlelit flow class near Union Square. She didn't like the teacher, who called herself Shanti, as much as she had liked Suzanne. Shanti was in her twenties and said things like *Lift your arms to the sky* when what she actually meant was *Lift your arms in the direction of, but nowhere near, the ceiling.* But she liked the class anyway. She liked that, unlike in Suzanne's class, they didn't sit in pigeon pose for an eternity and she liked, weirdly, sweating in a warm room full of people. She stayed warm the whole way home.

Her mind flickered to Michel a few times that week. He had been part of her routine in the fall and she expected to miss him, but it felt like thinking of something you ate that had made you sick—her mind recoiled. But she missed, if not Michel himself, the space he had occupied, and some of his accouterments: his tasteful apartment, his weird music and snacks. If she was going to be single for any length of time, she was going to need to get better at feeding herself.

Kelsey called on Wednesday to talk about New Year's plans. Before Christmas, she had said that she and Olivia should spend the holiday weekend in Katonah, being old grumps. High school friends were home in Rye and there would probably be a smattering of house parties to choose from. But plans had changed, and she'd called to propose they spend New Year's Eve in the city.

"Some high school people, you remember that girl Sloane, and Oscar, say they're renting hotel rooms," she said. "I don't know who's going to be at home, actually. It sounds like everyone's either in the city or away."

Amanda came into the kitchen before she'd responded to Kelsey, and she got off the phone quickly. "Is there anything I can do?" she said to Amanda quickly. Lately Amanda had seemed to be warming up to her slightly and Olivia didn't want to backtrack.

"No, you're fine," Amanda said slowly. If Olivia was not mistaken, Amanda was giving her a once-over. Olivia looked down, half expecting her pants to be missing, but if anything, she was dressed a little more nicely than usual, in the sweater Ty and Christina had given her with the purse from June still slung over her shoulder.

Amanda kept looking at her, so Olivia retreated to the interior office, where she opened old files, pretending to work. There was nothing to do. She hoped business was only slowing down because of the holidays. Maybe Amanda was wondering if they really needed Olivia.

Brian came back from lunch and joined her. They were the only two in the office besides Amanda. Brian seemed in no hurry to leave either. He was online shopping, picking over sale merchandise. Olivia cleaned up the desktop, renaming and organizing files.

Amanda stuck her head in at four. "I'm heading out."

Olivia and Brian got to their feet to do the same.

"So I'm off tomorrow?" Olivia said.

Again, Amanda was looking at her curiously. "Yes. Yes, enjoy the long weekend. See you in the New Year," she added, a false brightness in her voice.

"She was being extra weird to me today," Olivia told Brian after Amanda left.

"The holidays are tough for aliens," Brian said. "Makes them miss their home planet."

They took the elevator together and Olivia was hoping Brian would suggest a drink, but he was busy texting someone and barely even noticed when she said goodbye. Maybe he was getting back together with Katie, she thought.

In the wake of Christmas, at the onset of another four-day weekend, the prospect of the uptown apartment was especially bleak. Olivia stopped at a grocery story on Third Avenue. She barely knew what to buy: pasta, tomato sauce, a package of prewashed spinach leaves. She bought a bottle of cheap red wine at the corner liquor store.

When she got back to the apartment, with groceries that would not make any meal she felt like eating, she poured herself a glass of wine and called Kelsey back.

"Let's rage," she said when Kelsey answered.

KELSEY GOT THERE around noon on New Year's Eve. She scanned the living room. "You've been living here this whole time?" she said, her voice carefully diplomatic.

"You saw it over the summer." Olivia tried to see the room from Kelsey's eyes: though tidy, it had not actually been cleaned in months, and dust bunnies had collected along the walls. The too-large couch—some sort of imitation leather—dominated the room. The curtains were maroon for some reason, and even when open, prevented much light from entering the room.

Kelsey walked to the windows and put her nose against the glass. "There's a little park across the street."

"Saint Catherine's."

"Do you ever go in it?"

"I'm not that far from Central Park," Olivia said. She had never been in Saint Catherine's, but she was ashamed to admit it.

Kelsey had brought pot. They rolled a joint and got inspired—or rather, Kelsey was inspired and coaxed Olivia along—to revive the apartment. Kelsey unearthed a vacuum cleaner Olivia hadn't known existed and made quick work of the dusty floors. She even found an attachment that let her attack the couch and the curtains.

Olivia donned rubber gloves and cleaned the kitchen and bathroom. She put on music and they danced whenever they passed each other in the apartment. When Olivia came back into the living room, Kelsey had removed the curtains entirely—the rods and heavy fabric lay in a heap on the floor. Kelsey was standing on a chair, spraying the windows with cleaner. Light streamed in.

Olivia burst out laughing. She couldn't believe she hadn't thought to do that, just take the ugly curtains down, in all those months. She helped Kelsey bundle up the fabric and they stashed the whole mess in the hall closet, where the vacuum had come from.

They opened the windows to get rid of the smell of cleaning products. Kelsey surveyed the living room. "Let's paint it!"

"I think the lease is up in a month." She'd kept intending, and forgetting, to figure out where she was going to live starting in February.

"Well, it looks much better," Kelsey declared. "I think we should have a New Year's party."

"No one's going to want to come to a New Year's party all the way up here," Olivia said. She wasn't surprised that there'd been a hidden agenda behind Kelsey's cleaning spree.

"Olivia. Most of our friends are in the suburbs right now drinking their parents' gin and eating leftovers and basically dying of boredom. They will absolutely come to a party, any party. And it's easy to get here on the train."

Kelsey was right, Olivia realized. It wasn't that their friends wouldn't come. The truth was she was embarrassed by the apartment—both its relative grandiosity, compared to the places other people her age lived, and its utter lack of coolness. "What if I don't want to have a party?"

Kelsey stood in the newly bright living room, her hands on her hips and her pale hair in a high bun. Her cheeks flushed with the afternoon's exertions. "Tough."

Kelsey made calls, cleaning out the fridge with her free hand, while Olivia tidied up her bedroom. She had to admit, it was energizing to put the apartment in some kind of order, and anyway, there were a million excuses she could give about why she lived there: it belonged to a relative; she was house-sitting; or even the truth—that her father had rented it but wasn't using it. Kelsey exclaimed as she discovered things in the fridge, a moldy yogurt or a completely brown and shriveled lime that had been hiding in the butter compartment.

"Sloane and Amber are coming," Kelsey announced. "And those guys, Brick and everyone."

"Brick?" Olivia said with mild interest.

"That isn't weird, is it?" Kelsey said. "I forgot until this second that you guys had a thing."

"I pretty much did too," Olivia said. She hadn't spoken to Brick in months.

"It's fun to have someone to kiss at New Year's," Kelsey said. "Isn't there anyone you'd like to invite?"

Olivia thought of Brian, and shook her head.

"I can *tell* you're thinking about someone," Kelsey said. "You must tell me."

Olivia told Kelsey a little about Brian, emphasizing the reasons that he was off-limits. Kelsey looked displeased when she mentioned that Brian's art-school girlfriend had just broken up with him.

"Maybe you'll meet someone new tonight," Kelsey said. They were in the bedroom, and she picked up the corner of Olivia's synthetic comforter. "Can't we buy you a new bedspread at least?" she said with disdain. "This looks like somewhere you'd bring a prostitute."

Olivia thought of that night with Geoffrey, three months before. She still had the money he had given her—she'd wondered why he'd been carrying so much cash—tucked into an old running shoe in her closet. Queasiness about the encounter had prevented her from spending it. When she remembered the night she'd met Michel, how she'd propositioned him too and he'd rejected her, she felt even weirder. She didn't know who the person was who'd done those things. Did everyone feel that way—that their past actions, even from just a few months before, were the doings of a stranger? She didn't think so.

And yet she had saved the money, because in addition to making her feel uneasy, it also made her a little proud. Maybe it was time to move on, she thought, to *let it go*. While Kelsey was in the bathroom, she put the bills from the shoe in her wallet.

They went out to buy supplies for the party: vodka and cranberry juice and seltzer, limes, plastic cups, a token bag of pretzels. They came home and ordered sushi and made a drink.

"At least it looks like a *clean* chain-hotel suite," Olivia said.

Kelsey laughed. "I didn't mean to hurt your feelings," she said. "You have your own place. I'm still in college—I'm happy to be able to hang out here."

People came as Kelsey predicted, toting six-packs and cheap magnums of wine. The girls had decided to pretend that Olivia was, in fact, house-sitting, to make it seem imperative that the place not be trashed.

The girls came earlier, Sloane and Amber and a few others who'd been friends of Kelsey's but not really Olivia's. Laila was visiting her family but Bridget came with Kyle, tan from Christmas with her family in Saint Lucia.

Olivia had a pleasant buzz going by the time Brick and some of the other guys came. Brick was friendly and had brought with him a tiny girl named Chloe who looked like she was still in high school. Olivia was mostly relieved when Brick slapped her five and pulled her into an easy hug, though there was a flickering wistfulness at no longer being the object of his desire.

Brick and his entourage brought better things than wine. Olivia took an oxy and did a bump of ketamine, and when someone put on electronic music, the night stepped off into a sort of underwater profundity.

But drugs had a funny way of looping her back on herself. After the first flood of euphoria, she felt a hollow in her stomach, a homesickness for last summer, when grief itself had been the most powerful drug.

She lay on her back on the bedspread. Her throat was tight from dragging on someone's cigarette, but the soreness was just there, it didn't translate into pain, and she wondered if that was how all pain was, truly open to interpretation, not inherently good or bad. She was still pondering this as Lucas, the boy with the oxy, leaned over her and jammed his tongue into her mouth. Surprised, she kissed him back for a moment, almost reflexively, and then placed a hand on his chest and pushed him away.

"Olivia Harris." His eyes were slits like envelopes.

"That's me." She wanted to be doing something else, she thought, feeling more bored than anything. She wasn't sure how she had ended up in the bedroom or how long Lucas had been there. The party was loud in the living room.

"The girl I could never get in high school, and it turns out, it's so easy." She heard the rattling of pills, the prescription bottle in Lucas's pocket. He was shaking it.

"We didn't go to high school together." She'd just met him that night, she was almost positive.

The envelope eyes opened.

"Did we? I thought you were Brick's friend," she said.

"Brick's friend—from high school. God, you're wasted. I sat behind you in American history junior year."

Olivia sat up cross-legged on the bed. "Really," she said. She thought he was full of shit. "Who was the teacher?"

"Nancy Jenkins." Lucas was standing now—they were apparently having some sort of confrontation. She realized that the bedroom door was closed, that Lucas must have closed it, thinking— thinking whatever he had been thinking. She felt hot, then cold. The K had worn off, and with it, that feeling of interconnectivity. Her throat was actually sore. And Lucas needed to get out of her bedroom.

But he didn't want to hook up with her, she saw, though that might have been his original design. He just wanted to be recognized—for her to tell him that she remembered sitting in front of him in Mrs. Jenkins's American History, that she had only forgotten because she was so high on the drugs he gave her, and the drugs other people had given her.

"I was in that class," she said. "I don't remember you being there. I guess because I was facing forward." She got to her feet nimbly, in a way that felt somehow yogic, and walked past him out of the room, leaving him standing there with, she imagined, his mouth hanging open.

Hours passed. She was dozing on the couch with her head in the lap of a college friend of Kelsey's, and people were talking about going up to the roof. Olivia said there was no roof, and people laughed. Every building had a roof, they said, and she wanted to go there too, but someone—the guy, or Kelsey, or somebody else, was telling her to wait a while, rest, come up later. And then she opened her eyes and the lights were still on but the apartment looked empty, and then she saw, on the floor beside the couch she was lying on, that Kelsey was there, her bra dangling out one arm of her tank top, next to a sleeping guy Olivia had definitely never seen before, in Mrs. Jenkins's class or elsewhere.

NEW YEAR'S DAY, after they finished reconstructing the apartment ("Why did you make us clean it all up yesterday if we were just going to do that?" Olivia asked crossly, extracting a cigarette butt from between the couch cushions) as well as the night (Olivia agreed with Kelsey that if Kelsey didn't remember making out with the guy she woke up next to, it almost definitely hadn't happened), they went to brunch at Bridget and Kyle's place in Brooklyn. Olivia texted Brick, who'd said he was staying in the city, to get some pot, but he didn't write back. After a restorative Bloody Mary, she called him.

"Why'd you diss my boy Lucas?" he said when he picked up.

"I didn't—" she said automatically, and then remembered the bedroom, the history class. "Fuck," she said out loud.

"That was rude."

His confrontational tone startled her. She'd forgotten how little she knew these people. Brick, whom she'd only befriended after high school, running into each other at the town beach club, had done a year or so of community college, but he was a real drug dealer now. She knew nothing about Lucas. Sober, she thought she remembered him—slightly—from high school after all, but she couldn't tell if it was just her brain creating a memory of what it had learned to be true.

"I'm sorry," she said, feeling trapped, rather than apologetic. Brick had said the night before she should call him anytime if she needed a hookup.

There was noise in the background—Brick too was at some sort of New Year's Day gathering. He made an irritated grunt. "Whatever. Don't hit me up for a while." He hung up before she could respond.

"Is he coming?" said Kelsey.

"No."

Kelsey looked disappointed. Olivia told her what had happened the night before with Lucas.

"You trampled the heart of a thug," Kelsey said. "Nice work, Liv."

"You can do what you want," Olivia said. "But I'm going home."

They walked to the train. As they waited on the platform, Kelsey said, "I was only teasing. He shouldn't have tried to make out with you—what a jerk."

Olivia nodded. She found that she was holding back tears. It was a new year, but everything felt terrible, and she didn't even have the superficial comfort of Michel.

Kelsey's expressiveness was usually endearing, but now her face was too much of a mirror, dramatizing Olivia's unhappiness. She hugged Olivia, breathing warm air on her neck.

Back in the apartment, Olivia told Kelsey the whole story about the letters from *F* she'd found in her mother's desk. She hadn't even been thinking about the letters until the long train ride uptown. But in her hungover misery, she felt the need to be confessional.

Kelsey's eyes were huge. But she was a loyal friend, convincing when she told Olivia that it must be some old silly thing. "*F* could be someone she knew in *college*," she said.

They were curled on the couch, their feet tucked under them and their knees touching. Olivia almost mentioned the photo of Eleanor in a swimsuit, which seemed to date the letters in the recent past. The way the papers were all mixed up in the folder, the photo could have belonged somewhere else. But the letters were on white printer paper in ballpoint pen. They didn't look old.

OLIVIA SPENT THE weekend recuperating in Katonah with the Grants. When she entered the lobby at Likely Monday morning, Amanda was waiting for her. She had the same weird look on her face she'd had before New Year's.

I'm going to get fired, Olivia thought, *and Amanda knew it last week, but she didn't want to ruin my holiday—because somehow she's much nicer than I thought.* Though she didn't know why she was about to be fired, she noticed that the prospect made her feel much worse than she would have expected.

Amanda's voice asking Olivia to step into the rarely used conference room was a dim inevitability. Nearly everything at Likely took place in the open. This was the room where deals were negotiated and sometimes called off. Tim was already seated at the table— he did not look up when Olivia and Amanda came in. Zack, Amanda's boss, was there too, as well as a woman Olivia had never seen before.

"This is Janet, our attorney," Amanda said.

Janet smiled a grim, closed-mouth smile. She was probably only forty but dressed like an older woman. She was wearing frameless glasses and after acknowledging Olivia she quickly returned her gaze to the legal pad in front of her.

Olivia was told to sit down. She was given a glass of water, something that had never happened at work before. She had the flickering thought that maybe she was reading it wrong, they were going to give her a promotion, or ask her to rat someone else out— hell, maybe they were going to ask her to run the whole company and needed the lawyer present.

"Okay, Olivia," said Amanda. She blew out her lips. "First of all, I'm really sorry this is happening. And I also want to let you know, you don't have to say anything."

Olivia took a sip of water.

"One of our clients has made an accusation." Amanda looked down at the notepad in front of her, unnecessarily. "He's accused you of propositioning him . . . of soliciting money for sex."

Olivia imagined she could hear the blood draining from her head, while at the same time, her paltry breakfast (coffee, leftover Christmas cookies) was on the rise. She opened her mouth and then closed it. Then she forced herself to look around the table. Tim was still looking down, but he was red to his ears. Zack was looking straight ahead, in the direction of Janet. Janet was making a show of writing something on her legal pad.

Only Amanda looked at Olivia. "You'll soon learn, if you haven't already, that people are fucking crazy."

Janet stiffened.

"We have no idea if this person is telling the truth, or part of the truth, or even if you spent any time with him out of the office. And if it were a less important client, we'd accept a denial from you and tell him to go to hell or press charges. I don't actually know if you can press charges for that. But it's not a client we can throw away. And he's asked that we let you go."

Janet cleared her throat.

Amanda continued. "If you categorically say that this is false," she said, referring to notes, and Olivia wondered what the purpose of the word *categorically* was in that sentence, if perhaps it wasn't a bit redundant, "if you would swear before a judge that none of this happened, we can't fire you."

"But either way, you'll lose the business," Olivia said.

Tim jerked his head up. "This is such bullshit," he said.

Amid the nightmare unfolding around the conference table, Olivia thought, *Tim likes me. He really likes me!*

"So what we have to ask," Amanda said, "is what do you want to do? If you say it's not true—" She looked helplessly at Zack and Janet.

"If we terminate you unjustly, you can sue us," Zack said calmly. "But in that case you'll have to prove that these accusations are false. Alternatively, you could resign, and Amanda will be happy to write you a letter of recommendation."

Saying I was very good at making cheese plates.

"And not a word of this gets breathed outside of this room," Amanda said. "We'll tell people whatever you want."

"Why is Tim here?" Olivia said.

"Because he's the one the client called."

She hadn't thought it possible, but her humiliation actually increased—Michel telling Tim, of all mild-mannered Midwesterners, that Olivia propositioned him. Tim defending her, or perhaps too shocked to say anything at all.

"Can I think about it?" Her voice sounded foreign to her, robotic.

"You're entitled to think about it and to contact an attorney." Amanda was blushing as she added, "Legally, we just can't let you back into the office until we know how this will proceed."

"I have to stay in this room?"

"We can't let potentially hostile employees back into the workplace," Janet droned. "You're free to leave the premises, of course, and contact us when you've—"

"You think I'm going to start shooting people? Over *this* job?" Olivia's voice was shaking, and her cheeks were hot, but she wasn't going to let them get away with this final insult. "You pay me fifteen dollars an hour to run errands. I'd be better off working at Whole Foods. They have health insurance."

Tim let out a single syllable of laughter. Amanda's head was in her hands. "Olivia."

Contact an attorney. She felt slightly hysterical when the lawyers who came to mind were her father, Ty, and Christina. She was enough of a lawyer's child to know that the deal they were offering was bad, but they were giving her the chance to amputate this mistake and walk away. The job was over for her. There was no way she could stay, no matter what kind of negotiation ensued. Even if she could get Michel to take it all back, she'd always be the girl who was possibly a prostitute. The fact that she hadn't asked them the name of the client was probably a sign of her guilt.

"I'll quit," she said quietly, and she could feel shoulders relax around the table.

Conveniently, there was a letter of resignation prepared for her to sign. There was no severance pay, because she was leaving by choice. But as a courtesy, Janet said, she was to be paid for the rest of the day, and allowed, under supervision, to gather her things, of which there were none.

Brian blundered into the lobby, just starting his day as she was leaving. He asked her what had happened but she waved him off. And then she was walking uptown in a light snow, all the way from Sixteenth Street to the Flatiron District and then Midtown, ignoring the buzzing of her phone and the blister forming on her right heel from yet another pair of her mother's too-small boots.

She wanted to not be able to believe Michel did this. She entertained the possibility that it could have been Geoffrey, angry and lonely over the holidays, seeking retribution.

But it was all too easy to see Michel working himself up and calling Tim, not thinking about anything except his wounded pride. She'd spent several months sleeping with a man who thought that a fair punishment for breaking up with him was being humiliated and losing her job.

"No more fucking men," she yelled abruptly on Fifty-First and Fifth, drawing terrified glances from a family of Japanese tourists. She walked on.

What would her mother say? The thought of her mother knowing about any of this made her cry, huge tears of self-pity that froze on her cheeks.

Back at the apartment, she curled in a ball on the couch. She pulled a blanket over herself and closed her eyes, trying to make herself feel invisible, the way she did when she was upset as a child.

But it wasn't working—she was too caffeinated and she couldn't turn off her brain.

The best plan she could think of, in terms of finding quick occupation and avoiding having to tell her family what had happened, was to go back to school, to Vassar, that semester. Within minutes she was on the phone with the registrar's office, where a dull and unsympathetic assistant told her it was too late to transfer.

"But I'm not transferring," she kept saying. Apparently because of the haphazard way she'd dropped out the previous January, various paperwork was necessary. The administrator said she'd put the forms in the mail, and asked Olivia's address.

"Like the postal mail?" Olivia said. "You can't email them to me?"

"No," the woman said with finality, as though this were Olivia's last in a series of unreasonable demands.

Transferring to Hunter was a better idea, but they told her the deadline for applications was in September.

"We do make exceptions when we can," the woman there said. "But I know for a fact we're full."

How could they be full, Olivia wondered, when she wasn't even asking for housing? She made a quick list of other city colleges—Columbia, Barnard, NYU, the City University system, which she didn't know anything about other than that Hunter was a part of it.

Answers on the phone, when she was able to get through, were the same: she was welcome to take a class or two, they would gladly accept her money, but actually *transferring*, with the intention of earning a degree, was more complicated.

When Olivia stopped making phone calls, she sank into the couch with self-loathing. She ignored two texts and even a call from Brian, but when Michel phoned in the late afternoon, she was so astonished that she answered.

"Baby."

"Are you fucking kidding me?"

"I'm sorry. I was pissed off."

"You're *sorry*?"

"It was going to be too hard to work there, with you. I should have just fired them, but Tim pressed me for a reason—I didn't plan it."

"You didn't plan it?" She was stupidly repeating Michel's words back to him.

"I can help you find another job. A better job. I know—"

Olivia hung up.

★ ★ ★

KELSEY WAS ALREADY gone, out west for a ski trip before her last semester began. Olivia couldn't help thinking that if she'd been fired before the holidays, she could have gone skiing too, rather than being stuck in Manhattan with literally nothing to do for the rest of her life.

She made pasta for dinner, which she undercooked and had no appetite for anyway. She tried to watch an episode of a TV show people at Likely had talked about, but she couldn't concentrate. She remembered her stash of Xanax from the summer and took one, which helped a little with the whirring, unpleasant feeling. She called Kelsey, but went straight to voicemail.

What had seemed in the morning like a light flurry had stealthily become a heavy snowfall. She stood at the window, drinking sharp red wine left over from their New Year's party out of a coffee mug. In the streetlight, she could make out the precise way in which the snow piled atop the thin branches of a tree below, coating the top of each thin branch and then rising into a triangular peak.

She had to figure out what to tell her father. Maybe Vassar would let her work on her thesis remotely, even if she couldn't reenroll. She could tell Max she was taking the spring to complete her thesis, and then get her degree after summer session.

The thesis she had planned during her last semester at Vassar—a silent film that exposed the dark underbelly of the corporation that provided the school's food—seemed like a joke a year later. Her fall work at Hunter on the India footage was the only thing she had interest in, really, something that focused on her mother, but she didn't know how to package it. She didn't think the film had to be feature length, but it couldn't be seven minutes of scarves and spices and sunrises.

Before she fell into a restless sleep, she emailed her old adviser, Terrance. When she searched for his name in her inbox, she found the last two emails he had sent her, almost a year before. In the first, after she'd missed a scheduled meeting, he'd asked if she was okay. Ten days later, in early February, he expressed sympathy about her mother's illness—he'd found out, though not from Olivia—and asked her to please keep him up to date.

Olivia hadn't responded to either email and felt guilty, writing to him so long later and only because she needed something. She liked Terrance—he was younger than many of the professors, laid back yet erudite.

She explained her predicament, trying to be brief: She'd been working in New York but she wanted to finish her degree. Vassar wouldn't take her back that semester, but could she work with him on her thesis that spring?

She woke early the next day and forced herself out in the cold to go running. She barely made it two miles and she was wearing the wrong clothes—sweatpants that let the wind blow right through them and an old parka that was warm to the point of suffocating— but for a few minutes, standing in a hot shower, she felt what must have been a runner's high. All seemed possible. She could get a grant to go work on her thesis somewhere exotic, or she could contact Alec about a job in Los Angeles, or even maybe transfer to UCLA or USC as Alec had suggested the summer before—maybe out west, they weren't so uptight about transfer deadlines.

By ten A.M., the burst of enthusiasm had subsided. It was Tuesday morning and she had no place to be. It was hard to fathom that she'd spent last spring and summer like this, with no order to her days, reading and napping and smoking some pot. She tried Kelsey again and left a message, read the news online, drafted a scathing email to Michel, deleted it, and finally located a yoga studio nearby that had a new-student special.

The noon yoga class was made up entirely of women, all of whom were older than Olivia, some by only a few years and some by several decades. They did not look like women who were hurrying to the class from a lunch break, but rather women whose entire afternoons were a series of lovely appointments. The instructor did not shy away from mentioning love handles and bikini bods, but the class still finished on a quasi-spiritual note, with a few moments of sitting in meditation, and Olivia left the studio feeling better. She stopped on the way home to pick up a carton of soup, but the positive mood evaporated again once she was back in the apartment. It wasn't even two in the afternoon, she was exhausted from exercise, and still had nothing to do for the rest of her life.

Later in the afternoon, Terrance wrote back, asking Olivia to call him. She did, immediately. He couldn't have been kinder or more gracious about her sudden reappearance, telling her how sorry he was about her mother.

Terrance told her he'd already spoken to the head of the art department, who'd spoken to the dean. If she could file her thesis by May, not only would they accept it, they'd let her walk in graduation. That was, assuming she enrolled immediately in the thesis course, which essentially meant paying Vassar for him to work with her.

"Sorry about that," he added, sounding embarrassed. "I'd be happy to do it for free, but they have their policies. Technically, thesis is a class, because you get credit for it."

"Of course," Olivia said, trying to sound as though the money were nothing. She'd hoped to execute this plan without having to present Max with a bill.

She would then need just two courses to graduate; as she'd guessed, the easiest thing would be to take them over summer session, but she could also speak to the registrar about transferring credits from another school.

"I'm teaching history of Italian film over the summer," Terrance added shyly.

He didn't sound surprised when Olivia said she wanted to scrap the thesis she'd proposed before. He said he'd email her the current requirements when they got off the phone. "You do have to follow them closely," he warned. The student films were reviewed by a committee, and could be rejected for being too long or too short. And if the thesis was good, he added, it could be a doorway to something else.

Olivia promised that she'd follow the rules.

SHE GOT THROUGH the week somehow, through a combination of running and yoga classes and TV interspersed with internet rabbit holes. Twice she picked up the phone to call Ty, and then put it back down—she still hadn't come up with a good story. She could, she supposed, simply say she'd been laid off. But strangely, pride held her back. Though telling the truth was impossible, she didn't want everyone to think she had merely been dispensable.

Kelsey finally called her back Wednesday night. She was horrified and sympathetic, and did not even ask what had happened. Quickly and cheerily, she moved on to Olivia's impending return to college.

"I don't know how I'm going to tell my dad," Olivia said, struggling with annoyance. Did Kelsey find it so totally unsurprising that Olivia had been fired?

"Just tell him you want to go back to school," Kelsey said. "He'll be thrilled."

But Olivia didn't think it would be that simple. Max would be glad she was going back to school, but he would wonder at her sudden change of mind, when the job at Likely was supposedly going so well, and when it was too late to reenroll at Vassar for the semester. Even if she thought of a credible way to explain it, it would still feel like a failure. Which, of course, it was, she reminded herself.

She emailed Max and told him she'd like to come out and see him over the weekend. He suggested lunch at the house on Saturday and actually asked if she'd prefer it to be just the two of them. She told him it was fine if June came. A buffer in this instance could be helpful.

June had made quiche and salad and was nearly bursting with good cheer. She told Olivia about skiing in Vail over the holidays with Liza—it snowed every night, the fresh powder was waist high.

Max looked happy to see her but also wary. He probably suspected that this impromptu visit was more than a gesture of goodwill.

"I want to go back to school," Olivia announced soon after they sat down to lunch.

Max actually clapped his hands together. "Terrific. When?"

She explained to them what she'd found out—that she couldn't go back to Vassar for the semester, but she could work on her thesis and go to summer session. They'd let her walk in graduation, she added, hoping this ceremonial tidbit would be a selling point for Max.

"That's a great plan," Max said.

He looked happier than Olivia had seen him in some time. She swallowed mounting guilt and continued, telling him the tuition price for the thesis tutorial with Terrance and the summer session. "It's actually a little less than paying for a full semester."

Max waved away the mention of money. "It's no problem. The lease is almost up on that apartment you're in," he added. "But I'm sure by now, since you know the city, you can find something better."

"I wouldn't necessarily have to stay in the city, to work on the thesis," Olivia said cautiously. "I was thinking I might travel."

Max looked puzzled. "What about your job?"

So he hadn't gotten it. Olivia looked down, and then forced herself to look up, trying not to sound defensive. "I'll be working on the thesis full time," she said. "I don't think I'll be able to work at Likely too."

Max frowned, doing math in his head. "That doesn't seem very efficient. Why not just keep working until summer—and then take the classes and finish the thesis at the same time?"

"Then I couldn't walk in graduation," she said, feeling ridiculous. No one in her family would believe for a moment that she'd care about walking in graduation. "Besides, I want to make the thesis really good. It could be the doorway to other things," she added, quoting Terrance.

"Weren't you working on it already at Hunter last fall?" said June.

"Sort of, but that's the thing—I could never make it to that class because of work," said Olivia, thankful to be tossed the opportunity to strengthen her case.

Max took it all in. "There's plenty of time for everything," he said. "Stay at work till the fall, then go back to school. If you quit your job after four months, it'll be a blip on your résumé you have to explain. If you stay there for a year, or most of a year, it'll look substantive. It'll count for something." Max took a bite of quiche. It had been decided.

"Well, I can't stay till the fall, as it turns out," Olivia said, trying to keep the panic out of her voice.

"Why not?" Max said. All four eyes looked at her—her father's blue, June's hazel.

"It's not working out."

"That boss of yours still being a pill?" Max smiled. "It's good for you, sweetie. And maybe it'll be easier, knowing there's an expiration date in sight." He picked up his fork, held a bite to his mouth, paused. "Quit a month or two early, if you want. I'll help you out, or you can live at home. You can get a head start on your thesis."

"I was fired," Olivia said.

"Fired?" Max said.

"Actually, they let me resign."

"What happened?" June's tone was sympathetic.

"They found out I hadn't graduated." Olivia hadn't planned this. She'd been provoked into it, and in the moment, it seemed like yet another way to convince Max that the only thing she was good for was finishing college.

"You didn't tell them you hadn't graduated?" Max said. "You told me you did."

"I don't remember saying that," Olivia said.

"You lied to them?"

"I put Vassar on my résumé—which wasn't a lie."

"Did you put a graduation year?"

"Yes."

"When you hadn't graduated?"

"Yes," said Olivia.

Max stood up, ignoring June's hand, which was on his arm. "Explain to me how that isn't lying."

June looked like she'd been slapped. *He's not mad at* you, Olivia wanted to tell her.

"Why didn't you just go back to school last fall when I told you to?"

Olivia was quickly realizing she could have thought of a dozen better things to tell her father. She was fired unfairly for screwing something up. She was fired because her boss had it in for her. There were financial problems at Likely and she'd been let go. If he only knew the real reason. He wouldn't be angry then—he'd be speechless.

But confronting Max's anger had always been energizing as well as intimidating. She stood up too.

"It was all a little much for me. Mom dying, you—" She glanced at June and stopped talking. Dragging June into it wasn't going to fix anything.

"I needed some time," she said instead, more calmly. "And now you're getting what you want—I'm going back to school."

"And you just expect me to support you between now and when you actually get your degree," Max said.

"I never said that." She'd been hoping for it, though. Her bank account was in the triple digits.

"You're spoiled," Max said. "Your brothers aren't spoiled, but you are. We did something wrong."

Olivia let his words wash over her. "I can think of a thing or two."

Max let out a highly exasperated noise and strode out of the room, toward his study.

June offered a small smile.

Olivia looked down at her plate, where there was still most of a piece of quiche. She sat down and took a bite.

"He'll cool off," June said.

"So you don't think I'm totally stupid?"

"You made a mistake. But you were at a difficult moment, and your impulse was to get a job and support yourself. A demanding job, and you were doing well at it, weren't you, until this happened?"

"My dad thought it was a waste of time." Olivia felt the warmth of June's quietly offered praise.

"It's between you two. But I don't see it that way."

"He thought I should have stayed in school when my mom got sick. They both thought that."

June's expression was almost one of annoyance. "Well, of course you didn't do that."

MAX STAYED OUT of sight as Olivia and June cleared the table. Olivia remembered that Suzanne taught at Kriya on Saturday afternoons. From the yoga studio, it was a long but doable walk to the train station.

"Max, come say goodbye," June called with forced cheer when she and Olivia were ready to go.

Max emerged from his study, his finger holding his place in whatever tome he was reading. He pecked her cheek, his body tense. "We'll make a plan," he said. "You can always move back in for a few months if you need to."

Moving back into the Rye house with her father and June was a horrifying possibility Olivia had not yet considered. She nodded, unable to look at him.

She was early for Suzanne's class and wearing the wrong clothes. She flipped through the racks of stretchy pants and tops for sale, but nothing was under seventy dollars. She sat and looked at a book on the chakras, about opposing energies moving up and down the body. She could not envision her pragmatic mother reading such a book, let alone taking it seriously.

Suzanne arrived just as the previous class was letting out. She greeted Olivia with a hug and did not seem as surprised to see her as Olivia herself was surprised to be there. "Are you changing before class?" she asked, nodding at Olivia's jeans and sweater.

"They're all I have with me. It was a spur-of-the-moment thing." She hoped Suzanne wouldn't ask her to buy one of the yoga outfits.

Suzanne pulled a cardboard box from under the front desk. "Lost and found. I bet you can find something."

Olivia found some leggings and a large T-shirt that were a slight improvement, though they didn't smell that clean.

She'd attended four other yoga classes since she'd first been to Suzanne's and found that she was able to slip into the rhythm of the class with less confusion and more pleasure. The class started off slowly compared to the weird Upper East Side power yoga she'd been attending the week before, but midway through, she was dropping sweat onto her sticky mat in warrior three and it felt like every muscle in her body was shaking. She couldn't breathe as slowly as Suzanne instructed them to, but she liked the challenge of trying to slow her breath down.

The class was less crowded than it had been the first time—maybe people were still away on vacation—and Suzanne came to adjust her several times.

When they settled into what Suzanne called a restorative twist, Olivia began thinking again about the mysterious *F* who had brought her to the studio in the first place. The reasons that she'd dropped the investigation were hard to recall. Because she'd thought it was none of her business? Because her mother couldn't possibly have been having an affair?

Well, so what if Eleanor had been having an affair, Olivia thought. Look how quickly Max had moved on—maybe none of it had been as it seemed. She had plenty of time on her hands, and no reason not to email Franco. Maybe they would become friends. Maybe it would be good for her thesis. She didn't know what she wanted to make a film about, but she knew she wanted it to be about her mother in some way. Shouldn't she try to meet people who knew Eleanor, especially the ones she didn't know anything about?

Let your body be heavy, said Suzanne. But Olivia didn't want to be any heavier—she wanted to drift off, to be carried away. She felt weighed down by several lifetimes' worth of mistakes and miscalculations. The mantra going through her head constantly the last week was *Fuck*.

Some part of her had been insisting, all through the past year, and especially with Brick over the summer and then Geoffrey and

Michel, that this wasn't who she really was. That if her mother hadn't died, she would be living a different, more upright life.

But maybe, she thought, as they switched sides, she was exactly the same person she'd always been. Maybe this was who she was: someone who thought it was a fun game, in the moment, to sleep with a dorky rich guy for money, and try it again on a better-looking guy. To cheat her way into a job she didn't really deserve. Maybe she had no moral compass. She touched the hollow place below her sternum—the place such a compass would occupy, if she had one.

After class, she told Suzanne she'd decided she wanted to get in touch with Franco after all.

4.

Olivia was curled on the upper berth, hugging her backpack, which provided at least a symbolic shield from the men below, who sat watching her as openly as if they were at the movies and she were on-screen. The train rattled and squeaked in a four-beat rhythm. Her teeth were fuzzy and her eyes dry. It was just past sunrise, and she was approaching the end of a nearly thirty-six-hour journey from New York to New Delhi and then from Delhi by train to Gaya.

She'd opted for the "sleeper" class carriage, which she soon realized was deceptively named. There had been no sleeping so far, though she'd been on the train for more than twelve hours. There'd been a little dozing on the lower berth; when she'd opened her eyes, three men were actually sitting beside her, watching her from a distance of ten inches. She'd gasped, and they'd politely moved a few inches farther away from her. The other bunks nearby were empty. Wordlessly she'd heaved her backpack onto an upper one. She climbed the ladder and curled around her pack, eyes open.

She chose sleeper because it was much cheaper than the air-conditioned carriages, and she hadn't thought she cared that much about A/C. But the air around her smelled like sweat and shit. The shit was coming from the toilet nearby, predictably enough, but it also seemed to be coming from outside the train, from the air that blew in the unscreened windows as they moved east through the country. They were passing through swampland, farmland. It was morning now, her second morning back in India.

A current of excitement ran through her. Thank God for private schools and their ridiculous funding systems. Once she had promised Vassar (in the form of a check from her father) that she'd be completing her thesis and returning for summer session, it was a relatively simple matter to apply for and get a research grant for her thesis. It was funny, if you looked at it a certain way: the easiest path to her father's money was through an educational institution that took a large cut. She'd spent most of January scurrying around collecting letters of recommendation and filling out applications, and in return, was awarded enough money to cover three weeks of travel in India, including airfare.

She'd spent a lot of February on Ty and Christina's couch. They'd been nice to her, much nicer than they'd needed to be, somehow making her feel that it was not only okay but actually sort of fun for them to have a kid sister around. They both worked long hours, but Christina's day started and ended earlier. Most nights she'd go to the gym after work, and Olivia began meeting her there—Christina had procured a seemingly limitless number of guest passes. Christina would usually take a class—Pilates or yoga or spinning. Sometimes Olivia would join her, or else she'd run on the treadmill and then do a few yoga poses in the stretching area.

On the way home, they'd pick up something for dinner—Christina made dinner almost every night, though it was often something simple like a big salad with take-out chicken mixed in. When Ty couldn't be home in time for even a nine o'clock dinner, it would just be Olivia and Christina eating together. Christina looked exhausted after her eleven-hour workdays and the gym and yet she politely made conversation, trying harder than Olivia did to find common ground or asking Olivia questions about growing up and her family. Olivia, who even after an infinitely lazier day lacked the energy to reciprocate, promised herself that the next night, she'd make plans so that Christina could do whatever she wanted when she came home from work instead of interviewing her fiancé's sister.

But Olivia didn't have that many people to go out with in the city, nor did she have an influx of cash. A few times during that month, she invited Bridget and Laila to meet her at art openings or movie premieres she knew would be free. Twice she met up with Brian for a beer.

She told Brian what she'd told her father—that she'd lied about graduating from college, and Likely had found out. He didn't ask a lot of questions, which suggested to her that he knew she wasn't telling him the whole story, or even part of the story, but he was too polite to call her out. She was sorry to have to lie to him—lying created distance, and the last thing she wanted after the past year was to feel more disconnected.

Brian told her people at work missed her, and then they talked about other things: her thesis—a portrait of her mother—and the trip she was organizing; Brian's roommate, who was getting, Brian believed, far too involved in a cultish self-help group; the prevalence of new high-end Mexican places in the city, and how none of them (according to Brian) were as good as their cheap counterparts.

Max was still mad at her. He thought it was ridiculous that she was returning to India; he justly used it as evidence of how much she wasted the last trip, which he persisted in calling her idea. Her brothers thought it was weird too. They didn't like the idea of her traveling in India by herself. *Why don't you do your thesis about Italy?* Ty had said. *Mom loved Italy.*

Only Kelsey knew about the search for Franco. The plan had started with an email to Franco early in January, sent under the name

Alexandra Sage. *You probably don't remember me*, the email began. *I took your class a few years back in Westchester. I'm recently widowed* (Olivia wasn't sure where that came from, but it felt right) *and looking to get back into yoga. Are you still teaching? Where can I find you?*

It had been almost a week before Franco wrote back. *Nice to hear from you, Alexandra. I'm in Bodh Gaya, studying with Swami Satchananda for the spring. Not sure what will come next, but I may return to the NY area. I will keep you posted!*

Alexandra didn't write back. Olivia researched. The center where the swami taught sounded familiar, and when she looked it up, she remembered why. This was the ashram her mother had wanted to go to when they had planned their imaginary trip to India. Bodh Gaya was a famous pilgrimage town, where the Buddha was said to have attained enlightenment under a tree.

The moment Olivia saw the ashram's website, which looked like it had been designed at least ten years ago, she knew: *I have to go back to India. I have to go back to India, and meet Franco Damiani.*

When you knew what you wanted, everything became simpler, more streamlined. There was no doubt that Eleanor had known Franco, had somehow been influenced by him. The ashram did not seem to be famous, though it was mentioned as being *legit* and *uncorrupted* on various user forums. The Franco from Eleanor's phone said he was in India—the Franco Suzanne had put her in touch with was at an ashram in India Eleanor had intended to visit. Clearly, they were the same person.

The ashram's website said to apply at least six months, or preferably a year, in advance by writing. It did not say what an application should consist of, though it did list the cost of a four-week stay, which was thirty-two thousand rupees, or a little more than five hundred dollars. There was a telephone number, which she didn't call, and a mailing address, which she did not write to. Instead she figured out the closest airport.

INDIA. THE TRAIN stopped in the apparent middle of nowhere. Her audience detrained for a stretch and a smoke. These breaks in the journey had been happening at regular intervals, and though smoking was tacitly permitted between the train cars, there seemed to be something extra-appealing about doing it while standing on solid ground. A stroll didn't sound bad to Olivia, either, but the logistics involved (if she took her large backpack with her, would someone snag her bunk? If she left it, would it be stolen?) were too much for her to weed through on such little sleep.

She did stand and walk onto the platform between cars. From there she could check on her backpack every two seconds, but still get an unobstructed view of the countryside, if that's what it was called there, they were passing through. The smells and colors were familiar, as if from a dream. She leaned against the metal door-frame. Even when stopped, the train rattled and vibrated against her back.

Then they were moving again, and with each rotation of the wheels there was for an instant the sensation of falling forward. They were passing through more swampland or maybe lowlands—she wasn't sure of the correct name for the endless grasses, a green so electric the color seemed likely to bleed if you touched it. They passed through a small station—cement platform, signs in Hindi, vendors with baskets of tea and biscuits, watching the train roll through without stopping.

A chai wallah was making his way down the car. Olivia bought a plastic cup of tea and a package of biscuits. The familiarity of the spiced milky tea made the interlude between the previous August and that moment on the train nothing but a long night's sleep. She climbed carefully back onto her berth and ripped open the packet of chocolate biscuits with her teeth. After she'd finished, she took out her camera, and positioned it between the bars over the open windows. She filmed the green, water-buffalo-speckled motion, one lone road threaded through.

SHE ARRIVED AT the ashram just before nine on Saturday morning, the first Saturday in March. She buzzed at the wood gate and was ushered along a gravel path that edged a large courtyard to a small reception area. It was already warm, and the man at the desk waved flies away, unperturbed. The large fan standing beside his desk seemed to spin once per minute, and the man told her in simple but clear English that she could not be admitted to the ashram without a reservation, there were no exceptions, and he was sorry.

He recommended that Olivia go into town, where there were plenty of places to stay, and get some rest. "India has many good ashrams," he said. He regarded her calmly. He was in his fifties at least and small, with striking cheekbones. She could find no angle from which to attack his argument.

A gong was sounded and people clad in white filed into the courtyard silently.

"The yogis," the man said.

Olivia nodded and smiled. This was a thing her mother had taught her, about getting what you want: be nice, but don't go anywhere.

"They are ready for breakfast," he said. He laughed at some private joke about yoga or breakfast that he didn't share with Olivia. Then he returned to his newspaper.

Olivia sat down in the one other chair and folded her hands in her lap.

"I suppose there is no harm if you join the students for breakfast," the man said. "Perhaps they can give you a recommendation."

Olivia thanked him profusely, left her backpack propped against the wall, and followed his directions. On the other side of the courtyard, obscured from view by a cluster of trees in the middle, she found a buffet and picnic tables. She took a metal bowl off a rack. A young Indian woman dressed in a green sari served her a large ladle of porridge, which Olivia dressed with slivered almonds, pomegranate seeds, and jam. She filled a metal cup with tea from a canister and sat herself at an empty spot at one of the tables. No one was speaking, and she wondered how exactly she was supposed to ask for recommendations, not that she intended to do so.

She ate. She realized there was a piece of masking tape on her cup that said *Heather* in permanent marker, and began to suspect she'd stolen someone's bowl, as well. She was conspicuous among the yogis in her tea-stained yellow T-shirt and jeans. But no one was looking at her.

A middle-aged man stood and rang a small brass bell and everyone began to speak. The people at her table greeted her with *namastes*, offering her little bows. They were a man and two women, who appeared to be about ten years older than Olivia.

The man extended a hand. "Brandon."

"Olivia."

Brandon had a pleasant, open face with bright green eyes that reminded her of Ty's. An unexpected pang of homesickness for Ty and Christina's clean, quiet apartment hit the back of her throat, registering initially as thirst.

The women at the table were named Jenny and Sylvie. She told them her plight. "Do they ever make exceptions?"

They didn't know. Brandon said he didn't think all the rooms were full at the moment. "But the ashram is big on procedure," he added with an exaggerated eye roll. Almost everyone stayed for at least two months, he told her, and rebooked for the following year before they left to avoid the hassle of mailing in their application.

It was Brandon's second time there, Jenny's third, and Sylvie's first. Brandon and Jenny were yoga teachers, though they did other things as well. Brandon was a theater actor turned yoga teacher turned massage therapist. Jenny taught kids with learning disabilities, and Sylvie was a writer.

To enlist their sympathy, Olivia told them about her mother's desire to come there and the film she'd received funding to make. She didn't tell them it was her college thesis project, hoping they might think she was slightly older and thus more worthy of their time than she actually was. And she didn't say anything about Franco.

"What are you going to do if you don't get in?" Sylvie asked with genuine concern, and Olivia realized how she must look—like a bratty kid who'd just flown around the world, expecting the rules to be bent for her. So she began babbling—there were other places her mother had wanted to visit, the ashram was just part of a whole tour, the deadline for the project was May, so she thought, since she was going to be in India anyway, that she would at least try to visit the ashram.

After all, what was the big deal? she thought. *Why on earth would you need to book six months in advance to visit an ashram in the middle of nowhere?*

Jenny looked dubious. Brandon drummed his fingers on the table. "Let me see what I can do."

★   ★   ★

BRANDON TALKED TO Chris, and Chris conferred with Elisa, and Elisa and Chris spoke to Ragit, and then Chris, a tall, whip-thin blond man with a tidy beard, approached the dining area where Olivia alone remained, watching little green lizards on a rock in front of her eat a leisurely breakfast of spiders and flies, to tell her that she could stay. Chris did not sound pleased to deliver this news. She didn't know whether he was sorry the rules had been bent for her, or simply too evolved to view this turn of events as either positive or negative. She also didn't understand the hierarchy—who Chris was, who had made the decision.

Chris told her there was a double room available for the next two weeks. After that, he said, they would try to work something else out. He was assuming she planned to stay at least a month. She didn't correct him, though her flight home was in three weeks, and she wanted to visit Goa after two weeks at the ashram. Instead she thanked him with what she hoped was appropriate deference and went back to reception for her backpack. The man there, whom Chris referred to as Samir, did not look at her as he showed her to her room.

The rooms were up a flight of stairs from the courtyard, along an outdoor corridor. Olivia's faced outward, into a swamp behind the ashram, and was closest to the bathroom, Samir pointed out with pleasure. There were holes in the screens on the door and window that had been neatly repaired with wire. Inside were two twin beds with mosquito nets and two small sets of wooden shelves. A handmade broom leaned against one corner; a single light bulb dangled from the ceiling. There was a stack of lavender sheets on each bed. Samir handed her a padlock for the door.

Olivia thought of unpacking; of going out to buy water; of looking for Brandon, or someone, to ask what the schedule was. And then she set down her backpack, lay on the mattress closer to the window, hugged the bundle of sheets, and fell asleep.

EACH DAY BEGAN with meditation and chanting at five, then asana (the term everyone at the ashram used for yoga) from six to eight. Then there was an hour to be endured before breakfast, which was spent waiting in line to take a short, deliciously cool shower, and, at least for Olivia, retreating to bed to lie wet and naked beneath the sheet, inhaling a packet of biscuits.

After breakfast, students divided into groups for classes: breathing, yoga sutras, beginning Sanskrit. Some were learning to play a strange yogic instrument called the harmonium. No one told Olivia what she should do, where she belonged. The first few mornings she napped and read, alternating Wilkie Collins's *The Woman in White* with Desikachar's *The Heart of Yoga*, which Suzanne had recommended.

There were about forty students in residence, mostly Westerners and a handful of Indians, and three Indian teachers: the swami, his daughter, and her husband, one of the swami's first disciples. During the morning asana period, the swami called out the names of the poses, and the daughter and son-in-law walked around the room, adjusting people. They barely touched Olivia. She didn't know if this was because she was an outsider, unwelcome despite having been admitted, or because her form was so appalling they didn't know where to begin.

The first few days, she was sore in places she'd barely known existed—the bottom tips of her shoulder blades, ribbons of muscle that ran between her ribs. It felt like her insides, her organs themselves were straining. And Franco was not there.

Opinions on his whereabouts differed, but the consensus, among Brandon, Jenny, and Sylvie, was that he would be back soon. No one could say exactly when he had left, but it was a day or two or three before she'd arrived. Brandon thought Franco had needed to sort out his visa to extend his stay. The place was a drama mill, and her new companions were eager to know her business with Franco, but she kept it simple: *I think he knew my mother.*

Afternoons, she wandered through town with her camera, searching for something she could not name, something that would justify her presence in Bodh Gaya, her return to India. She filmed in the small market and near the gates of the main temple, aware that she was shooting nothing more than stock footage of India (Spices! Water buffalo! Barefoot children with tangled hair!). To escape self-condemnation, she once again zoomed in on images to the point at which they became unrecognizable: jars of cloves and cardamom pods so close up they were nothing more than slightly out-of-focus textured browns. Her craving for abstraction, for metaphor, was almost physical, but she could not will herself to construct meaning from her surroundings. And meanwhile, every time she took out her camera, everyone within a fifty-foot radius stopped what they were doing to watch her. She'd brought the Indian clothes she'd bought last summer with her, and tried to dress respectfully in the small town, keeping her hair neatly braided, but once she was holding the camera it was no use—she might as well have been a blond in a bikini. The street kids lined up to get in front of the camera, and when she filmed them, they demanded coins for starring in her movie.

Back at the ashram, she had to choose between hiding away in her hot, smelly room (proximity to the toilets did not turn out to be a good thing, and she understood that Samir had been gloating) or sitting in some public space where she could not help feeling observed and like a misfit, reading either her mystery novel or her introductory yoga text while the rest of them faithfully copied Sanskrit characters into the colorful school notebooks that were for sale in town. Some people were even reading the sutras in Sanskrit, Brandon told her.

So it was a relief when, on her third afternoon in town, she found a small, empty garden to sit and read in. She was quickly getting used to the heat, which wasn't as overpowering as it had been in August, and she was conscious that she was missing early March winter weather at home.

She was alone in the park for about half an hour before some of the local kids found her. There were three boys and a tiny girl with a runny nose, a little sister. They were eating small fruits, which they stored in their pockets. They stood before her eating the fruits, dropping the peels and spitting the pits onto the ground.

The tallest boy, who was maybe eleven, pointed to her feet, clad in leather sandals, and then to their own bare feet. "Shoes," he said.

Olivia smiled faintly and pretended to return to reading.

The boys spoke to her urgently in Hindi, scattering in the words *shoes*, *please*, and *money*, their voices growing louder as she continued to stare blindly down at her book.

She looked up at them again and bowed, something she had seen others from the ashram do: *I acknowledge you, and your lack of shoes.*

They looked at her scornfully and continued to chatter.

"Shoes," she said, finally. "You need shoes." She reached into her bag. She knew she was making a mistake from the way their eyes grew large—despite their persistence, they had not expected to succeed.

She took a five-hundred-rupee note out of her wallet, less than ten dollars. "Four pairs of shoes," she said. She pointed at the children, one by one.

The oldest nodded and took the note, and the three boys turned away from her and ran toward the street. Only the little girl stood there, watching Olivia.

One of the boys turned back to retrieve the child. "Thank you," he said, taking the little girl's hand.

She read a few pages, and relief at being alone in the garden again gradually overtook her uneasiness.

Then children began to arrive. First there were three, then seven, then quickly too many to count, their voices low as they approached her. Most of them were barefoot; a few wore ratty plastic sandals.

They clustered around her. "Shoes," they said.

She stood up, fighting to remain calm. Some of the children looked angry. One boy who couldn't have been older than eight tugged on her shirt.

"I'm sorry," she said. She pushed her way around them and headed toward the street.

The kids followed her, their feet quiet on the dirt path. "Shoes," they said, and "Five hundred rupees." They held out their hands so she had to physically push them out of the way to continue.

It was less than a ten-minute walk back to the ashram. Rickshaw drivers pulled up alongside her offering their services, but nonsensically, she didn't want to make further displays of wealth. She hurried along the dirt road, avoiding water buffalo, sweating, swearing under her breath, thronged by children. Every shopkeeper and marketing woman stopped to watch her.

When she was nearly halfway back to the ashram, she stopped in her tracks. She put her hands on her hips and straightened to her full height. She was tallish for a woman in America, and she was definitely tall for a woman in India.

"Enough," she said loudly. She thrust an arm out from beneath her dupatta, pointing toward town. A few of them stepped back, startled by the force of her movement. "Leave me," she said. They stood, watching her. "Go home," she nearly shouted, almost succeeding in keeping the tremor out of her voice.

She began to walk again, willing herself to be slow, to be stately. A few kids continued to follow her. She took long strides. When one of the persistent children tugged at her scarf, she whirled around again and took off her sunglasses and the straggling remainder stopped in their tracks.

The sun had set and there was a crescent moon rising behind the children, though the sky was still a hazy blue. She was using the trick she had learned in elementary school when she had stage fright—look at the exit sign in the back of the auditorium and the audience will think you're looking right at them. If she looked into the eyes of the children, she believed that the force of their gaze and the righteousness of their anger would simply obliterate her.

It worked. They turned away from her, the crazy, mean, blue-eyed witch. Some of them held hands as they walked back toward the village. A few broke into a run. She stood still, watching them go. She stood there so long she began to believe she could actually see the moon rising, and in the busy village, she was entirely alone.

OLIVIA STUMBLED HER way into the routine of the place. Brandon adopted her; ten years younger, she became the pet of him and his cohort, someone for them to educate. Jenny and Sylvie were college friends. Jenny lived in Boston. She was on a semester-long sabbatical from the charter school where she taught. She wore her brown hair cut short in a style that seemed studiously low maintenance (she was also one of the few women at the ashram who wore lipstick, Olivia had noticed, which undercut the breezy vibe a bit).

Sylvie, who was from New York, was blond and pretty and the quietest of the three. She had published a novel and was working on a collection of stories. She was somewhat newer to yoga, though not as new as Olivia.

The blatant sexism of the ashram surprised Olivia. It was a given that men were better at asana (which she learned meant the physical practice of yoga, as opposed to the philosophical and religious parts), their bodies more adept at "floating" through vinyasas. All the important historical teachers she heard mentioned were men, and even though female students outnumbered male at the ashram, none of the women were awarded the same respect as Chris or Ragit, who were the most senior.

Olivia's attempts to "float back" from uttanasana to chatturanga were comical veering toward dangerous. Whenever possible, one of the teachers rushed over to demonstrate, yet again, that she should step back, not jump; that she should skip chatturanga; that she should move to the wall before attempting a headstand. But Olivia was stubborn and frustrated. There were men and women in their sixties at the ashram who'd mastered this, and she had once been an excellent field hockey player. She wanted to be allowed to try. So when the teachers weren't watching, she planted her palms beside her feet, bent her knees, and thud-thudded back into chatturanga, which resembled a belly flop a bit less with each passing day.

The teachers loved to say "Close the earthly door. Open the heavenly gate." This mystified Olivia. She thought it had to do with the chakras, but then Brandon explained that the bandhas, which Olivia had never heard of before, were also involved. Mula bandha, the root lock, was the most important one—you kept it closed so that energy didn't flow out of your body through the genitals.

"For women, it's basically doing a Kegel," Sylvie told her.

Olivia nodded, trying to look as though she knew what a Kegel was.

"Like you're trying to stop peeing in the middle," Jenny said.

Olivia asked Brandon what it was for men.

"Between your balls and your asshole."

BY THE END of the week, Olivia's arms had grown stronger but there were twinges in her shoulders. She was still sore between every rib, her hamstrings felt strained, and even the soles of her feet were tender. There was still no sign of Franco.

Saturday night Brandon-Jenny-Sylvie invited her to eat with them at the nicer restaurant on the other side of town. It was in a sterile hotel, the food served in stainless-steel dishes; it more or less resembled one of the midrange Indian restaurants Olivia had been to at home. Alcohol was not served, but Jenny spoke to a young boy, who seemed to be present for this purpose, and he returned twenty minutes later with a bottle of gin. Olivia could not look at a child without wondering if he had witnessed her shoe crime. But the boy was well dressed, with lace-up shoes, and delivered the gin politely to Jenny, accepting his tip with thanks.

They drank gin and tonics, Brandon making jokes about the colonial days. Olivia felt uncomfortable in the mostly empty, air-conditioned room filled with obsequious waiters and wondered why they didn't just drink gin at the small restaurant across from the ashram where they ate every other night. But her new friends, who had been there for several months, were buoyed by the change in surroundings. Jenny and Sylvie in particular were chattier than they'd been before. This was their Saturday-night ritual, she learned, though some weekends were spent traveling to other towns and cities.

They ate palak paneer and chicken tikka, the first meat Olivia had eaten since she'd been in India. Yogis at the ashram were expected to be vegetarian and she was surprised to see the rules broken without comment by Brandon-Jenny-Sylvie, who seemed more or less devoted to the practice. But then, why should she be surprised? she thought. Yogis were still people, full of contradictions and generally willing to justify what they wanted.

Jenny was trying and failing to forget about a guy back in Boston. Olivia gathered he was an ex, or that it was one of those nebulous, ongoing affairs.

"Now that I'm here," Jenny said, "he's getting in touch almost every day. When I lived ten blocks away, he was always working."

"He's in marketing," Brandon told Olivia, his tone suggesting that that explained everything.

Sylvie made a face at Brandon. "Marketing's not so bad. Try dating a writer."

"Everyone in Boston is obsessed with sports," Jenny complained, splashing more gin in everyone's glass. "Red Sox, Patriots—"

"Didn't you grow up there?" Brandon said.

"As if you know anything about sports in Cleveland." Jenny passed around the ice, which was melting in a porcelain soup bowl and which Olivia had used with trepidation in her first drink.

Brandon flexed his bicep. "Everyone wants to date writers," he told Sylvie. "Everyone wants to be in the next book."

"What about you, Olivia?" Sylvie asked. "Are you seeing anyone?"

"I was seeing this older guy over the winter," Olivia said. "He was—" She paused, unsure how to characterize Michel. Brandon handed her a cigarette and she took a drag. They had finished eating and were splitting two cigarettes between the four of them. "Sort of sexy," she said, "and also sort of terrible." She was tempted to tell them that Michel had gotten her fired from her job—they seemed like an audience who would appreciate a villain—but she wasn't sure she'd want to answer the questions this might raise.

"I'll cheers to that," Brandon said, raising his glass. "Sounds like every guy I've ever dated." Brandon hadn't talked about his love life in front of Olivia. Sylvie had mentioned that he'd been living with someone in San Francisco, but it had ended over the winter.

Jenny was nodding. "Not that you asked for my advice, but the older men are, the more bad habits they've learned. And you're young, so there's no reason you shouldn't date people in their twenties. Hell," she added, stubbing out her cigarette, "there's no reason I shouldn't either."

"So that's your new plan?" Sylvie teased Jenny. "Go young?"

"It's worth a try."

Sneaking a few cigarettes a week seemed to be part of her compatriots' rebellion against the ashram, like the gin and the chicken. Brandon-Jenny-Sylvie had a decade on her, but they didn't seem much older. In one way it put her at ease, but it was also disconcerting. She planned to have a lot more figured out when she was in her thirties.

OLIVIA HAD BROUGHT her laptop but the ashram didn't have internet—in fact, she hadn't even seen anyone there using a personal computer. In town there was an internet café, and on the Tuesday of her second week she went there. She bought a soda in a glass bottle and sat in one of the cubicles sipping it, feeling completely, and not unpleasantly, divorced from contemporary life. Next to her, teenage boys with trace mustaches played computer games.

She had an email from everyone in her family, one from her adviser, Terrance, three from Kelsey, and one from Brian. She began with Brian's. It was short—a joke about work, a question about how her film was going. Her film. She'd been staying afloat by following the schedule, letting the physical practice of yoga tire her out and not thinking much beyond the end of the day. And that's what she told Brian. *Re the film*, she concluded, *I don't know what I'm doing. I thought I would get here and just know it when I saw it. Stupid.*

Kelsey wanted a progress report, and she was also updating Olivia about guy drama, both her own and her friends'. Ty and Alec and even Holly and Christina wanted to know how it was going, and Max, too, sent a short email: *Hi Sweetie, I hope you are having a good time over there. Can't wait to see what you make of it. XOXO Dad*

Her father had never expressed eagerness to see her photos or films before. It must have been one of the oddities of email, or maybe June was influencing him. Max wasn't a great typist, and sometimes the emails he'd sent Olivia in college had her mother's electronic fingerprints all over them.

The connection was painfully slow, and during the time it took Olivia to simply open and read this collection of messages, the modem had to be restarted twice. So she wrote a message back, copying her entire family and Kelsey, trying to answer everyone's questions: *The ashram is great. Some of the people are nice and I have dinner with them. Small poor quiet town. I gave kids money for shoes and nearly started a riot. Really sore from yoga but I'm improving. The movie is going OK. Slow computer. More later. Love, Olivia.*

★   ★   ★

Since the incident with the shoes the week before, she'd found a back way in and out of town, longer but less trafficked, and she walked it slowly that afternoon. She was growing resigned to the fact that Franco might not come back anytime soon. She was also considering extending her stay in India, not because of Franco exactly, but because if she left the ashram Sunday, as she'd planned to, she would have accomplished nothing. While she was there, she might as well learn yoga. She'd been making progress, and that morning had been rewarded with an assist in parivritta trikonasana, revolved triangle. The thin hands of the female teacher made Olivia's spine inches longer.

And she had to figure out her movie, though that continued to feel fairly hopeless. She'd thought she could escape the blocked feeling by changing locations, that India would inspire her, and maybe it would have, if she hadn't been trying to make a film about her mother. But when she walked around with her camera, she was mostly aware that she, Olivia, was there, and her mother wasn't. She'd seen India twice in the eleven months since Eleanor died—and her mother hadn't seen it at all.

She wondered what the India was that Eleanor had imagined, and why she had wanted to come. She tried to imagine her mother in this town, living in the ashram, waiting in line for a cold shower and practicing asana for two hours every morning, learning Sanskrit or how to play the harmonium. She couldn't see it. Either there was a lot she hadn't known about her mother, or there was a lot her mother hadn't known about the ashram. Eleanor hadn't been a princess, but the ashram accommodations were pretty rustic. If you slept under the mosquito net, it was hot—and the power went out most nights, killing the ceiling fan. Olivia had abandoned the mosquito net after the first night, but she was getting bitten by all sorts of things, and could only hope her malaria medicine was working. The smell of the toilet pervaded the residential area. The food was bland, and she'd had an upset stomach after the hotel dinner Saturday night.

Maybe, she thought, she should leave on schedule and go somewhere else, to Goa as she'd planned, or even the mysterious Andaman Islands. She could lie in a hammock somewhere, read all day, gain back some of the weight she could tell she was losing, and surely come up with something to film. Maybe the trick was not to imagine Eleanor in India but to simply find pieces of India that reminded her of her mother, as she had tried to do last fall at Hunter. She wondered if it was too late to abandon the idea of making the thesis about her mother and focus on something else entirely.

Wednesday afternoon she hired a rickshaw to take her out of town, to a well-known market where she could buy some gifts. She'd promised Kelsey silver bangles and she wanted to find something for Terrance, as a thank you.

Upon first glance, the market was unimpressive, a huddle of tarp-covered stalls on a dusty lot. But inside, it was nicer than the shops in town. In a silk stall, a beautifully dressed Indian woman demanded to examine bolt after bolt of colorful cloth. The fabrics she rejected she flipped away with the back of her hand and the shop boys carefully replaced them on the shelves. The silks were organized by color. Almost all of them had a pattern.

The silks the woman liked underwent an additional test: she placed each bolt on the counter, struck a match, and held it to the edge of the fabric. An instant later she licked her fingers and extinguished the flame. Olivia couldn't believe this was allowed, but the shop boys watched passively, and the man who seemed to be the owner looked on, calm and smug.

As the owner was cutting lengths of the three fabrics the woman had selected—they must have passed the match test—a wind rushed into the stall, blowing a green-and-gold fabric over her head. For an instant the contours of the woman's face, her mouth open in surprise, was visible through the fabric. She laughed, a brilliant, sparkling sound, and clawed the cloth off her face, and it felt as though they were all united—the owner, the boys, the woman, and even, Olivia imagined, herself, standing outside the shop and watching. Of all the moments since she'd been back in India, this was one she wished she'd filmed, but though she had her camera with her, in its bag, partially hidden under her scarf, there had been no way to pull it out without ruining the very scene she wanted to capture.

On the ride back to the ashram, silver bangles tucked safely in her camera bag and packages at her feet containing silk for a sari and a few small statues of the Buddha and Ganesha, she saw a building she hadn't noticed before. There were girls in uniform playing outside, which was probably why she noticed it; she had not seen schoolgirls out much, only the street kids, most of whom were male. The building was nondescript, dusty concrete, with a sign that said GIRLS' PLACE in English, as well as a longer name in Hindi.

Olivia asked the driver to stop. "What is this?" she asked him, pointing at Girls' Place. He shrugged, either because he didn't know or couldn't explain it in English.

She asked the driver to wait and descended from the rickshaw, leaving her packages.

The girls noticed her as she approached, but most of them did not stop playing. They were all wearing plaid knee-length skirts and white blouses. The door to the building was open. She walked inside and once her eyes adjusted to the dimmer light, saw that she was standing in front of a reception desk. The woman behind the desk was Indian, but like the girls, she was dressed in a simple Western outfit.

"Can I help you?" the woman said, with a proper British accent.

"I was just wondering—what is this place?"

"It's a girls' school," the woman said. "Most of the students here are street urchins, or the children of prostitutes. Otherwise, they would not go to school." She said this matter-of-factly—she had probably explained it to foreigners before.

Olivia learned that the school was funded by an international charity as well as donations. During the few minutes she chatted with the woman at reception, who went by Jane and turned out to be the history teacher, she saw several Western women more or less her age walk by. Jane said they were volunteer teachers, English girls on their gap years. Olivia found herself hoping Jane would ask her questions about herself, even ask her to volunteer, but instead Jane handed her a pamphlet about the school and the charity, concluding their conversation. It was only when Olivia was halfway out the door that Jane called "You're welcome to visit again."

BY THE TIME she got back to the ashram, everyone was at dinner. She put her loot away in her room and went to the restaurant across the street where her friends ate most nights. It was one in a row of nearly identical restaurants, but each clique at the ashram had its regular spot.

Brandon looked giddy when she walked in, and Jenny and Sylvie were regarding her with unusual interest, too.

After she ordered her customary dish of vegetable rice topped with an egg, Brandon leaned toward her. "He's back."

It took a moment to register. "Franco?"

"Uh-huh. He got back right after you left this afternoon."

It was her twelfth day at the ashram, more than two weeks since she'd left New York. This was it—the man she'd come to find. "Where is he now?"

"Usually his crew eats here," Brandon said. "He could be here any minute."

But Franco didn't come to the restaurant that night, though Sylvie lingered with Olivia, drinking cup after cup of lemon-ginger-honey tea. Sylvie admitted to Olivia that she was at the ashram mostly to do research for her next book. "I like yoga," she said, "But not enough to fly all the way here just to study it." She told Olivia that she wanted to write about the culture at an ashram. Meanwhile, she got to practice yoga and spent a lot of the day writing in a quiet place. "It's actually a perfect writing retreat."

Back at the ashram, Olivia couldn't sleep. It was hot, as usual, and her mind was busy with weird fantasies about Franco and her mother, anticipating what he would tell her. Meditation had made her more aware of the absurd narratives her mind spun nearly every minute, which often took her far into the future. Franco would reveal that he had been madly in love with her mother, but she had been unattainable, professing her love for her husband and children but offering him her friendship nonetheless. Franco had come to India to get over his grief and didn't even know that Eleanor had died. She, Olivia, would be forced to deliver the news. Franco would tell her that Eleanor was a brilliant yogini, among the most naturally talented he ever saw—until he met Olivia, of course. Franco would fall in love with her, too, and she would have to gently reject him, telling him he was in love with her mother's memory.

Disgusted with these saccharine scenes, Olivia ascended to the roof of the ashram, the bedsheet she'd wrapped around herself trailing behind her. Outside, the temperature was comfortable, a smooth transition between air and skin. The moon was nearly full, the stars plainly visible. She lay on her back on the concrete roof, the sheet spooled around her, staring up at the sky. "Where are you, Mom?" she whispered. But she felt like she was asking the question before an imaginary audience, trying to convince them, and herself, that her mother was listening.

SHE TRIED TO pick Franco out the next morning during asana, but they all had their regular spots, and with forty-odd people in the room, she couldn't see everyone. Brandon pointed him out at breakfast, whispering his name in her ear and pointing even before silence had been broken. She paused for an instant before she looked where he was pointing, aware that it was the last moment of not knowing what Franco looked like. Then she turned toward the buffet, where Franco was filling his bowl.

At first she could only see the back of him—tallish, strong, sinewy arms, white T-shirt—more or less like all of the guys there. Then he turned around. Franco was hot. Heart-flutteringly, blush-inducingly good-looking: gray eyes, a five-day beard, and a jawline like a blade. He didn't look older than forty—he looked Michel's age. He caught her staring, and she quickly turned back to her porridge, feeling her face heat.

After the bell rang, Brandon offered to introduce her. But Olivia balked. She hadn't planned, after all this time, what she would say when she met. In the story in her head, he would see her and immediately know who she was. But in reality, this was not likely—especially because, since she'd already been caught staring, she was too shy to plant herself in front of him for inspection.

Instead she trailed him at a distance through the day, sitting in the back of the pranayama class while he sat cross-legged in front. As she practiced alternate-nostril breathing, she could glimpse the back of his neck between other people's shoulders. His brown hair was flecked with gray and curled at his neck. She could see the veins on the back of his tan arms.

She continued to observe him at lunch. The table was crowded around him—she had the sense that he was popular at the ashram, that he drew people in. Some of those people were women. He was flanked by two, a blond Californian waif named Pearl, and Gretel, a German woman around Eleanor's age, who was a kickass yogini.

"Why don't you just go introduce yourself?" Brandon said, his patience with Olivia's half-presence at their table wearing thin.

"She's sniffing it out," said Sylvie. "Determining the angle of approach."

Olivia was still learning the social rules of the ashram. She'd been lucky to have been taken in by Brandon, because she didn't think she'd have gotten along well with many of the other groups. On the surface, everyone was polite, friendly, even loving. She could have certainly sat down with her morning bowl of gruel at any table and been welcomed with equanimity. But no one asked her questions, and the few times she'd tried to make conversation with Pearl and a few others who looked closer to her in age, asking them how long they'd been practicing yoga and where they were from, the answers they gave were monosyllabic.

"It's really a spiritual retreat," Sylvie had explained later. "Everyone has their friends but it's expected that you're allowed to sort of turn on and off—people can just suddenly feel like being silent. Everyone stays in their comfort zone, big-time."

Franco did not seem to be the silent type. Olivia wandered back to the buffet, pretending to be interested in seconds, in order to come closer to him. The women on either side of him regarded him adoringly. His face was open and relaxed, his smile easy. Up close he looked a little older, maybe midforties. He was telling a story about border crossing. Chris was among the others at the table, and for the first time, Olivia saw him smile too.

Chris was the alpha dog, the one Westerner who'd been allowed to remain in residence since the previous summer. Olivia had learned his role was that of a sort of guest liaison—an apparently coveted position that he had been awarded after three years of annual visits. Olivia deduced that Chris had earned this position based on his asana practice, not his people skills, but he did take the responsibilities seriously: he'd stopped to ask Olivia if she was settling in okay and tell her she was welcome to attend any of the morning seminars (he actually called them that) if she chose.

TRYING TO BOTH stalk and avoid Franco, combined with her bad night of sleep, left her exhausted, and she napped and read all afternoon. At dinner that night, Franco was at their restaurant as Brandon predicted. She didn't want to approach him in front of other people, but she sat where she could see him, bracing herself to speak to him at the end of the meal.

She didn't need to. He came over to their table as the food was being served. He greeted Brandon by name and the women with hellos. He looked right at Olivia. "I don't think we've met," Franco said.

She considered, confusedly, telling him her name was Alexandra Sage, the pseudonym she'd used to contact him in January. But then she told him her name was Olivia.

He looked at her for a long moment, still holding her hand. "Olivia Harris?" he said quietly.

She nodded, scared.

"Eleanor's daughter."

She nodded again, with more confidence.

He pushed air out through his lips. "Wow." He sat down, straddling the bench seat beside her. His face was less than two feet from hers. She could see sunburned skin peeling where his T-shirt hung away from his collarbone. In the dwindling light, his eyes were no color at all. In the background, Brandon-Jenny-Sylvie made feeble efforts to resume a conversation.

Franco ran his hands through his hair, giving off the impression of a hero at the end of a long battle. Then he smiled at her, a brilliant, white-toothed smile. "It's about time we met."

THEY WALKED TO the main temple and sat on stone steps in front of the Buddha, near the pond with the fat white fish that tourists fed. It was probably no later than eight P.M., but it was later than Olivia had been walking around town since she'd arrived. At that hour, the temple grounds were occupied by teenage boys, who traveled in twos and threes.

"She died last April," Olivia told Franco. It may not have been the best icebreaker.

"You think I don't know that?" he said savagely.

In that moment, Olivia knew he'd slept with her mother. It was no longer a question she needed to ask. Dumbstruck, she was silent.

Franco stood, hands in his pockets, and whistled a four-note tune. He seemed angry, which she had not been expecting. She hadn't even asked him for anything yet.

"How'd you find me?" he said eventually.

"I was cleaning out her study. I found some letters."

He looked like he was struggling to remember. That he could have forgotten was unbearable. "They were both about the beach. Meeting at the beach. Amagansett. There was a photo—she was drinking a beer."

Franco smiled. "She kept those." He tilted his head back and stroked the stubble on his neck. Then he dropped his chin and looked at Olivia. "I haven't said this yet, but I am so sorry. She was a wonderful woman. I can only imagine how hard it's been." They were pat things to say, but he said them as though he really meant them, and forgetting everything else for a moment, hearing that he'd known her mother, and that he thought she was wonderful, was enough to make Olivia's eyes sting.

But Franco wasn't finished. "I can understand your curiosity, finding those letters," he said. "But your mother never would have wanted you—any of you—to waste your time digging around, when it came to me. She loved you guys so much. This wasn't some sordid thing."

Of course she loved us so much, Olivia thought. She couldn't believe that Franco thought that was his news to deliver, and that he wasn't even trying to cover up the affair or apologize for it. Even more alarmingly, Franco seemed to think that after coming all this way, Olivia could be dismissed simply because her mother wouldn't have wanted her to investigate. Who did he think she was?

Yet she suspected it would be wise to take a subtle approach. So she nodded and gave Franco a little smile, and asked him how he had met Eleanor.

Franco told her he first met Eleanor in a breath workshop three years before that his friend Krista had been teaching. "She had this loud, mannish laugh," he said. "And she was so direct. She said flat-out when people were introducing themselves that she thought pranayama was a bunch of bullshit but she was willing to be proved wrong."

Olivia waited.

"She was talking to Krista, asking questions after the workshop. I went over to say thanks and Krista introduced us. Told your mother I was a bodyworker, and a teacher, and she—your mother—asked for my card."

Gross. Olivia could see it all too clearly—this handsome man, more than ten years younger than her mother, with his hands all over her, telling her about pressure points in her lower back. At least, she could see Franco doing this. She couldn't see her mother falling for it.

Franco was waiting for her to say something. Controlling her voice carefully, she asked, "So then she went to your classes? Or—?"

"She came to my class a few times. Our relationship developed." Seeing the look on Olivia's face, Franco added quickly, "That's not a euphemism."

Okay, Olivia thought. *He knows the word* euphemism.

"We became friends. We started having tea once a month or so, talking about meditation. She wanted to start a meditation practice, and I . . . I helped her with that."

"I'll bet you did." Olivia couldn't help it—it just slipped out.

Franco shook his head, as if scolding himself. "No. We're not going to talk about this. I'm sorry, but it's for the best."

Olivia bit the inside of her cheeks to keep from arguing. She was going to need a better strategy than simply demanding that he tell her everything.

"But listen," Franco continued. "I know I seem kind of freaked out right now, but it's really great to meet you. If I can help you in any way while you're here, I want to."

He began to walk back toward the entrance to the temple, and Olivia had no choice but to follow him. He asked how long she'd been there, and how long she planned to stay. She found out that he'd left the ashram the night before she'd arrived. He'd been visiting a friend, and he'd be staying for another six weeks, until the end of April.

Olivia remained vague on her own travel plans, telling Franco the date of her ticket home, but that she was thinking of extending the trip. She mentioned a project for school.

"How's your dad?" Franco said. "And your brothers?"

"They're—" She stopped. "Did you meet them, ever?"

"At the memorial service."

Olivia didn't remember Franco being at the memorial service, but she hadn't remembered Suzanne being there either. What she remembered from that day were near hallucinatory fragments—being very cold in the church and Holly taking her outside to stand in the sun as soon as the service was over, warming Olivia's hands between her own as though it were winter, not a beautiful spring day. People crying who had no right to be crying—distant cousins, colleagues, people Olivia didn't even recognize. Laughing with Holly about a red convertible in the parking lot. It had rained the night before. Who had decided to put the top down before coming to the funeral?

Franco hugged Olivia goodnight when they were back at the ashram. "We'll talk again," he promised. In his embrace, she could smell his armpits and his hair. *My mother had sex with this man*, she thought. It was going to take her a while to wrap her mind around that. Yet it felt good to hug him—it was the first time in her nearly three weeks in India that someone had touched her without the intention of correcting her form.

Back in her humid, foul-smelling room, Olivia sat down on the tile floor in the dark beside the bed. She took off her sandals, and then she threw one, hard, at the opposing wall. While Olivia had been at college, studying and partying and believing a set of things about her family, how much they had loved one another, all of them, but especially—it had sort of gone unspoken, it had been the premise of everything—Eleanor and Max, married for almost thirty-five years, while she had felt safe in the certainty that she had one of the better families it was possible to end up with, her mother had been not only growing a brain tumor but also sleeping with her hot gray-eyed yoga instructor.

She hadn't considered what it would feel like to have her suspicions confirmed. The ache she'd been carrying for eleven months was morphing into a new feeling, colder and possibly worse. Who had her mother been? Suddenly, she could no longer form a clear image in her mind of what Eleanor had even looked like. She had the photo Franco had taken with her, tucked inside a book, but she didn't want to take it out.

WITH FRANCO BACK, the calm routine at the ashram was shattered. She had a focus again: she needed to woo him, convince him to tell her everything that had happened. Maybe once she knew everything, there would be a way to understand what her mother had done. Chris had juggled things so that she could stay in her room one more week, but after that the ashram was full.

Brandon-Jenny-Sylvie wanted to know how the conversation with Franco had gone. She didn't know how to explain it without telling them the main thing, so she was vague: Franco knew her mother, but hadn't been very forthcoming. She would speak with him again. She was surprised when they didn't sense that she was holding back and pump her for details. Maybe some part of her had been hoping to be forced to tell them everything. But the ashram wasn't college. These people weren't here to become her bosom friends—their interest in her life was finite.

The exception to this might have been Franco himself, who, over the next few days, paid attention to Olivia's yoga practice. He began to position himself nearer to her in class, presumably so he could observe her. This made the two-hour class electrifying and stressful. Trying to impress him, Olivia became freshly aware of how bad she still was at yoga, especially the morning when, pushing herself to impress Franco, she toppled sideways out of a handstand, narrowly missing collision with the yogi next to her and landing loudly on the floor.

After class on Saturday, Franco offered to give her some pointers. He made her do certain poses in front of him and corrected her alignment. This annoyed her. She hadn't spent all this time tracking him down so that he could teach her yoga. It was also weird to have her dead mother's lover touching her.

"You're not bad, you know," he told her, sensing her frustration. "You're very flexible. You just have to bring it under control."

Jenny had said something similar a few days before—that Olivia's alignment wasn't perfect, but she was just "bendy." She'd said it with mild annoyance.

But Olivia hated stretching. She always had. In high school, when she had played varsity field hockey, she'd taken strategic water breaks when they stretched during practice. So it was funny to her when people said she was flexible: other than during sex, she had consciously avoided any sort of acrobatics for years.

To tolerate all the slow stretchiness of yoga, Olivia focused on the parts that were not about stretching but instead were about force. Pushing the outer edge of her foot into the ground, shifting her weight from her feet to her hands—these things she could do. *Gentle, gentle*, the teachers would say, sometimes touching the hinge of her jaw to show her she was clenching.

Franco offered to give her something called an ICP, an in-class personal, where he would assist her in every pose during class. Olivia repeated this offer back to Brandon-Jenny-Sylvie at lunch, acting suspicious of it. Without consciously deciding to, she had begun to report on Franco to her friends as though he were hitting on her.

But Brandon told Olivia to take Franco up on the ICP. "Sweetie, it's a thing he could charge a hundred and fifty dollars for in New

York," he said, his tone suggesting that Olivia, of all possible fools, did not deserve such an honor.

"It'll deepen your practice, for sure," Jenny said, the most sincere she'd been.

So Olivia told Franco she'd do it, and Monday morning, he crouched behind her as class began, lifting her rib cage up with his two hands even as they sat chanting. He pulled forcefully on her hips in downward-facing dog and supported her thighs in upward-facing dog. He stabilized her in half moon pose and she felt her rib cage grow huge, her spine unfurl. She hadn't realized that the instruction to *spin your heart toward the ceiling* in extended side angle was actually somewhat attainable.

Franco smelled like incense—everything at the ashram smelled like incense—and tangy sweat. Though Olivia kept trying to imagine otherwise, there was actually nothing that felt sexual about his assists. He handled her body as if she were a child or an animal—firmly, professionally, and with care, his love nonspecific. Had he touched her mother this way? Olivia wondered. Had he touched her this way when she was his student, and differently later on?

The teachers closed the wooden shutters in the practice room for sivasana. It was confusing, as though they were being told to go back to sleep. Outside, Olivia could hear birds. Franco picked up her legs and swung them back and forth, bringing her lower back to the ground. He lifted each arm to adjust her shoulder blades. He cupped her head in his hands and tugged gently, then placed her head back on the mat and rubbed her temples, tracing a pattern from her forehead to her ear, again and again. He kept doing this for whole minutes. When the bell gonged, she could hear the creak of him standing. He pushed down on her shoulders before he moved away.

★　★　★

OLIVIA'S PLANE TICKET home was in less than a week. She continued to sit with Brandon-Jenny-Sylvie. Sometimes Franco would stop by their table. They talked about yoga and India and the ashram, but never about her mother.

Brandon was growing tired of her preoccupation. "Whatever you need from this guy, just ask him," he told Olivia at lunch.

"I don't need anything from him."

"You're in India, babe. And you walk around with your head God knows where."

Olivia told her friends about visiting Girls' Place the week before.

"Are you going to volunteer there?" Jenny asked.

Olivia had been proud of simply noticing the school. She hadn't thought of volunteering. She had been thinking of her film, which was supposed to be a portrait of her mother. The thesis deadline was in six weeks, and she'd taken grant money to shoot something in India.

Her mother had been a teacher. Her mother had cared a lot about education, and the education of women. She would have liked the girls' school. If Olivia could film at the school, maybe it could be beneficial for Girls' Place too—maybe they could use footage or photos she took on their website, if they had one. Maybe she could help them build a website.

On Tuesday, she took a rickshaw to the school. Jane recognized her and welcomed her back. She listened to Olivia's proposal, nodding thoughtfully, then left Olivia in the dark lobby for nearly twenty minutes while she went to confer with the principal.

The principal, a woman in her fifties, came out to meet Olivia. She and Jane thanked Olivia for her offer, but said they preferred to have a longer relationship with anyone who worked with them. Olivia had mentioned that she'd be heading home before the end of the month. She would be welcome to volunteer—to read to the children in English.

"If you come back to India, let us know," Jane said. "I'm sure you would make a very good film. It's just too rushed."

Ashamed to have assumed she was bestowing some kind of favor on the school, Olivia agreed on the spot to read to the children.

Jane led Olivia into a classroom. About fifteen girls who looked to be ten or eleven years old sat at small desks, their posture excellent, as the teacher, an Indian woman who couldn't have been older than Olivia, stood at a chalkboard. The lesson was grammatical—the teacher was explaining something about the structure of sentences, subjects and objects. Olivia noticed that the girls' attention remained on the teacher, even after she and Jane entered the room, until the teacher stopped the lesson to acknowledge them. They all wore uniforms and their hair was neatly pulled back in braids or ponytails.

Jane introduced Olivia as a filmmaker from America.

"She is here to read with you, with Miss Arya's permission," Jane said. The girls looked intrigued. Olivia, feeling generally like a fraud, wondered what she was going to read.

But they had not expected her to come prepared. She was shown a selection of books, a few of which, like *Little House on the Prairie*, she recognized from her own childhood. She could, Miss Arya said, read anything she liked, but it might make the most sense if she read the next chapter of *Carry on, Mr. Bowditch*, the book they were reading in class, thus saving them time on that night's homework.

Olivia took her place at the front of the room. She began reading, aware of the dryness of her throat, which made her voice crack slightly. The last time she could remember reading out loud was a year or more ago, when she and her mother had been planning their trip. It wasn't that Eleanor couldn't read, but the drugs she'd been on—the painkillers—made her sleepy and unfocused. Sometimes she'd dozed while Olivia read from the guidebooks, and they'd both pretended not to notice.

The chapter she was reading was about a boy on a sailing expedition who seemed to have no family. She read two short chapters and then paused, looking at Miss Arya—Jane had left once the reading began—to know whether to continue. Miss Arya began clapping, and the girls followed suit. She came forward and took the book from Olivia. "Girls, can we thank Olivia for reading with us?"

"Thank you," the girls said in a chorus. They looked neither bored nor fascinated by her. They were simply expectant, ready for the next part of their day. It occurred to Olivia as she said goodbye to Jane in reception that they probably hadn't cared about her reading to the girls, who were clearly old enough to read to themselves. They asked her to read because she'd shown interest in being involved, and if they let her be involved, she might donate, which was probably the only way she could actually be of service.

After she left the school, Olivia went to a nearby café to try to change her plane tickets. She was scheduled to fly home on Saturday, but she imagined it would take at least that long to work on Franco, and then she still had to return to New Delhi, a day-long affair. And she hadn't given up on spending a week at the beach in Goa.

Really, there was nothing to rush home for, she thought, though something nagged at the corner of her mind. Getting to India had been expensive, but being there wasn't—she could stretch her grant money another week.

She was able to push back her flight home for ten days, till April sixth. She bought a ticket to Goa for her last week. That gave her almost a week in Bodh Gaya before she'd take an overnight train to Kolkata and fly south. She would finish filming in Goa, she resolved desperately: it was more touristy there, so it would be easier to walk around with a camera, and the environment was lush and beautiful, at least in pictures. She would film markets and beaches and jungle, if she could find any, and add it to what she already had, and go back to New York and edit it into something that would pass. She wrote briefly to her family, letting them know her change of plans and then hurried back to the ashram for evening meditation.

She asked Chris and he spoke with the teachers and told her she could shoot a morning of asana practice as long as she asked permission before filming anyone's face, and not to use the footage to make money, which by that point felt like a bad joke.

Really, she'd needed a deadline. With her ticket booked, she worked up the courage to approach Franco again. She found him at dinner the next night, not at their usual restaurant but at the one next door. She stood beside him awkwardly until he paused in his conversation with Elisa and Ragit and noticed her. When he did, his face was open and friendly. It was as though he'd already forgotten there was anything uncomfortable about the situation.

"I'll be leaving on Monday," she told him. "I was hoping we could talk again."

"Have you been to the Kali temple yet?"

She hadn't.

"You really should see it before you leave," he said. He proposed they go the next day, Thursday. "We can leave right after practice and make a day of it," he said.

That night in her room, Olivia read about Goa in her guidebook, the same one she'd bought the year before for her mother. Goa was considered an outlier, wealthy and liberal compared to much of India, with a large contingent of partying Europeans. Though that had been the attraction, Olivia felt surprisingly unexcited by this prospect. She liked the rhythm of being at the ashram, how calm she felt waking early to practice. She'd barely drunk the whole time she'd been there—she'd eaten meat once, at the hotel restaurant.

She found an ashram in Goa that was recommended by the guide. The teachers were Westerners but fairly authentic—the clientele was said to be a mix of Europeans with some Aussies and Americans. It was near a beach that was pretty and bohemian, nothing fancy.

The prospect of spending a day with Franco led to another largely sleepless night. She bolted out of sivasana at the end of practice to be first in line for the shower. Then she used the phone in reception, which cost ten rupees a minute, payable to Samir, to call the ashram in Goa. The connection was bad and she had to yell to make herself understood: she wanted a place there for five nights. The price was higher than she'd expected, much higher than the ashram where she was, but she thought she'd be able to scrape by on her grant money if she didn't go on any more shopping expeditions.

They left right after breakfast. Franco quickly negotiated a fare with one of the rickshaw drivers waiting outside the gates of the ashram. Olivia hid her embarrassment; the fare was less than what she'd paid the week before to go to the market, a much shorter distance. India might have seemed inexpensive to her, but she was still spending much more than someone who knew the ropes and a handful of Hindi phrases, and, perhaps, was male.

On the ride, Franco told her a little about the area. He'd first come in college, he said, more than twenty years before, though after that he hadn't returned for a decade.

When he'd come in college, he told her, Bodh Gaya had been much more off the beaten path. There'd been nowhere to stay besides the ashram and other places like it—the new hotel hadn't been built yet. All the food in town made the yogis sick, and it was difficult to get bottled water, so they'd often had to resort to iodine tablets, like backpackers.

"Everyone was living on beer and packaged biscuits," he said. "It was pathetic."

He told her he'd begun teaching yoga after he turned thirty. Before that, he'd been an aspiring actor. "I even modeled a couple of times," he said, "if you can believe it."

Olivia could.

He'd started teaching yoga thinking it would be a better day job than waiting tables. It turned out that it was almost as hard to make money teaching yoga as it was acting, and he'd had to keep waiting tables, but yoga became another passion project. By the time he was thirty-five, he'd been ready to let acting go.

"Without any regrets," he was quick to add. "It just wasn't my calling anymore. Who knows? I could get back to it someday."

Soon after that, he'd become a massage therapist. He studied qigong and taiji, and he had his eye on a Chinese medicine program, on acupuncture school, and weaving it all together. He made intersecting waves with his fingers when he spoke of weaving.

But those degrees would be expensive, and he was waiting for the right time. "You'll learn this," he said. "The path unfolds. Your job is to pay attention."

Olivia remembered her mother, the Thanksgiving before she'd died, telling her and Holly about life's way of carrying you off if you didn't have a plan. She didn't think her mother would have endorsed Franco's strategy, at least not when it came to her children. But clearly, there were things Olivia hadn't known about her mother.

Franco told Olivia about different styles of yoga he'd tried. Restorative yoga, he said, was good for the nervous system, and as he was becoming older he was becoming more interested in slowing things down. "It would've bored the shit out of me ten years ago," he admitted. He told her about the Kundalini snake, the wild sexual life force curled at the base of the spine.

Olivia rode with her dupatta covering her mouth and nose and sunglasses on, shielding herself from the dust that spewed up from the road, tugging her mouth free to ask Franco occasional questions. He laughed at her, saying she looked like a memsahib, a colonialist.

The temple was small and made of shiny black stone. It seemed to have rained recently there, though it hadn't at the ashram. Everywhere was the sound of dripping water—from the banyan trees that stood guarding the temple and from inside the temple, where water dripped from the ceiling and the open door. Inside there was a pool with petals floating in it, pink and yellow, some beginning to brown. Franco told her there was a big puja, a ritual, every morning, with a goat sacrifice once a week. Drops of goat blood were used to bless the doorway at sunrise.

Just inside the blessed doorway sat an old man, so still that Olivia didn't see him until her eyes adjusted to the darkness. By his feet was a tin of coins. When Franco and Olivia paid him, he held their coins between his palms and lifted his hands to his forehead in prayer, whether blessing the givers or the coins, Olivia didn't know. Other than the dripping water, the temple was silent. It felt like a cave, something natural, not something manmade. There were small shrines carved into the walls with images of the goddess, and a few candles, burning in liquid pools of wax.

There weren't many other visitors, just a few old men shuffling around outdoors who looked as though they might live at the temple, or at least hang out there a lot. Franco said they were sadhus, itinerant monk-like men, some of whom smoked a lot of ganja.

She had read about Kali in her guidebook the night before so that she would know something. Kali was described as the goddess of time, of change, of power, of creation and destruction—so pretty much everything. But the temple was not in the guidebook. She didn't know exactly why Franco had deemed it important that she see this small place during an off-hour, but she was glad to be there. It was unlike anywhere she'd been before.

She and Franco and the man by the door were the only people inside the temple. She took her camera out of her bag and looked at the temple keeper and held up the camera hesitantly. It felt like the least appropriate place to film she'd been so far, but she wanted to, and he nodded a minuscule assent.

She doubted anything would even show up, it was so dark in there, but it was the sound she wanted, the sound of the water dripping from different places and their bare-footed shuffling and nothing else.

She filmed outside the temple too—the sadhus and the banyan trees.

After a while they left the temple grounds and walked across the street to a restaurant, where they ordered sodas.

"So," Franco said.

"So."

"I've been thinking. Maybe there's a way for me to tell you a little more, without it feeling like a betrayal."

"Could I at least get the chronology?" Olivia said, resisting the urge to take her camera out again. "Like when things . . . started happening."

Franco squinted up at the sky.

"You met three years ago in the breath workshop," Olivia prompted.

"That's right."

"And you became friends, and you helped her with meditation." She continued quietly, afraid he would clam up again when she said the words out loud: "When did you start sleeping together?"

"About a year later, I think. In the spring."

"Two years ago?"

"That's right." Franco fidgeted uncomfortably in his plastic chair and sipped his soda.

Olivia sipped hers too before asking the next question. "And did it continue—the sleeping together—until she got sick?"

Franco looked puzzled. "Well, she was sick the whole time."

"Right. I guess I mean when she was diagnosed."

"The affair—if that's what you want to call it—lasted until the fall," he said. "I don't remember when exactly. We were close before it started, and we were friends after that part of it ended. Really, she was just a dear friend." The word *dear* sounded funny in his mouth, like he wasn't accustomed to using it, but was using it intentionally.

"A dear friend who was also a student, to whom you wrote love letters."

He smiled. "Maybe I was in love with her. Is that so awful?"

No, it was not so awful. If Olivia could forget about the sex, the betrayal, it was nice that her mother had had Franco's love, along with all of their love. But how Franco felt wasn't the question. "Listen," she said. "I'm trying to understand my mother. The version of her that I knew—" she stopped herself.

"Wouldn't have been sleeping with me," Franco said.

"I didn't even know yoga was that important to her," Olivia said.

He laughed. "I'm not sure the fact that we slept together says anything about her relationship to yoga."

"How did it start?" Olivia said. "Who started it?"

He hesitated. Then he began. He and Eleanor had been on one of their regular Tuesday tea dates. They had talked about meditation, about asana, but about other things too. He'd wanted her to try some herbs for insomnia. He'd offered to order some for her, and she asked if he had any that she could take that night. So they went to his apartment.

At his place, he'd offered to make her more tea, but she said she'd had enough tea, so then he offered her a scotch. They sat on the couch, drinking his cheap scotch—really it looked like Eleanor was just touching it to her mouth, the amount in the glass stayed the same. He drank his because he was nervous.

"Honestly, I'd never considered before that things were heading in this direction," he said. "I knew we had a connection, but it was one of those maybe-in-another-life things."

"So you're saying she seduced you?"

Franco looked absorbed in memories. Then he smiled. "I'm not accusing her of anything."

"She was much older."

"Eleven, twelve years," Franco said. "That's not that much."

Olivia wanted to know more, though she felt she shouldn't: who'd said what to whom, who'd made the first move. But she couldn't ask, and even if she could, Franco wouldn't tell her.

Instead she said, "Did she want to come to the ashram?"

"She wanted to go a lot of places."

"Did you two ever go anywhere together? Amagansett?"

"We went to Amagansett, just for a night. That was in the fall. And then Mexico."

"You went to Mexico?" Olivia tried to sound nonchalant.

Franco paused, picking up on the fact that this was a big piece of information. "You know she loved the beach."

The straw from his soda was between his teeth, and he was tugging on it. Whatever he was avoiding was growing larger.

Olivia pressed on. "For how long? What did she tell my dad?"

"A week or so. I think she told him she was going on a yoga retreat."

The trip to Mexico was difficult to fathom. Olivia had no memory of her mother going on a yoga retreat the fall before she died. Could Franco have been making this up? "You just went on a romantic getaway to Mexico?"

"I wouldn't call it that."

"What would you call it?"

"You remember she got those headaches," Franco said slowly.

The headaches. The ones that had been symptoms of the cancer, which Eleanor had minimized and ignored, along with fatigue, until January, three months before she died, when she'd had the first seizure, and they'd done a scan, and there was the tumor, its tentacles wrapping her mother's brain in a twisted embrace.

"There was a clinic in the Yucatan," Franco continued. "Holistic. We were—she was trying to treat them."

"God. I wish she had gone to the doctor." Olivia hadn't known her mother had been trying to alternatively treat the headaches.

Franco was silent.

"Everything could have been different. If they'd caught it earlier."

"You think?"

Maybe Franco was one of those people who believed in fate—or karma—or that chemotherapy and radiation were toxic and evil.

"At least we would have had more time."

"Time isn't always about quantity."

Time isn't always about quantity. How dare he. But Olivia didn't want to get sidetracked. "What did they do at the clinic?" she said. "For the headaches."

Franco pushed away from the plastic table. "Enough," he said. "I've already said more than I meant to."

"No," Olivia said. She stood too. The café owner hovered nearby. "You don't get to decide that." She had a horrible feeling that whatever Franco was holding back had nothing to do with an affair. Or that it was something that made everything worse. Maybe her mother had been planning to leave her father when they went to Mexico. She felt cold under the hot sun.

"Olivia, you know everything that matters. She got sick, and she died way too fucking young. It was—it is—a tragedy. And we were all powerless." Franco jammed his fingers in his back pockets and stared up at the hazy sky.

Olivia fished for rupees and dropped the notes on the table, so the owner would back off. "You don't get to decide," she said again, quietly. "You know why?"

He looked at her.

"Because you aren't part of this, not really. I'm her daughter." She tried to quell her rising voice. "I matter in this story, not you. And it's not fair, it's not right, that you know things that I don't." Her voice broke on *fair*, as she heard how childish and helpless she sounded.

"You didn't even see her after she was diagnosed," she added randomly, as if to prove Franco's negligibility.

Franco sat down again. The café owner discreetly collected the bills from the table.

"That's not true," he said. "I saw her when I could—but you were almost always there."

That stung—the possibility that while she'd thought she was being a good daughter, by her mother's side, her mother might have been wishing Franco the yoga hunk were there instead. She wanted to ask why he couldn't have just visited anyway, while she had been there, if he and her mother were really such good friends. But she sensed he was trying to throw her off the scent. She crossed her arms and stared down at him.

Franco sighed. "I can't believe this. Sit back down."

Olivia sat. "She knew she had cancer before." She hadn't known that she was going to say this or that she was even thinking it until the words came out her mouth. "That's the thing you've been trying not to tell me."

Franco nodded.

"She knew, or she suspected?"

"She knew."

Olivia's throat was dry and her soda was empty. She could feel her heartbeat in her stomach. "How long did she know?"

"A little while."

"How long?"

"I think she told me in May. She said she'd found out a few weeks before."

"Before you started sleeping together?" May was eight months before the Harrises found out Eleanor was sick, and nearly a year before she died.

"Right after. It was great pillow talk."

"What exactly did she know?" She was over-enunciating, the words like objects in her mouth that could possibly choke her.

"She'd been to the doctor." He spoke slowly, but with resolve. "She'd had a scan. She'd been given—pretty bad odds."

"What were the odds?"

"I don't know. I don't even think she told me. But it was clear to her that surgery and chemo weren't the way to go. She said her father died of lung cancer. That it was really too late by the time they caught it, but they put him through treatment anyway. She said it made things worse, harder on everyone, the false hope and then the way chemo fucks you up."

Behind Franco, in the street, a horse-drawn rickshaw was standing still, the driver gone to run an errand. The horse stood unattended, its bones clearly visible through its mangy brown coat, its ear twitching. Flies alit and hovered around an open sore on its neck. What Franco was telling her sounded like a joke. It was like something a character on a trashy TV show would do—get diagnosed with cancer and then hide it from her family. Only on a very bad TV show would this plot be tenable, the family failing to notice the cancer until the mom was actively dying. Olivia looked back at Franco, feeling like a producer rejecting a shoddy script. "Why would she tell you? And not us?"

"She said her family—you guys—would want her to get treated. She didn't want a long period of everyone being worried."

"So you helped her treat brain cancer with—herbs?"

"Not treat it. Manage symptoms. The clinic in Mexico, that was more about treatment."

"What did they do to her there?" The nauseating likelihood that Franco wasn't making this up began to assert itself. Speaking like a normal human felt as physically effortful as walking on a tightrope— every part of her body was involved.

"There were different modalities. There was a shaman—several different types of healers. Acupuncture. Chinese medicine. A lot of time to meditate."

Olivia took slow, deep breaths, the kind she'd been learning since she began practicing yoga. Yogic breathing: for when you find out a Mexican shaman knew your mother had cancer before you did.

Franco looked defiant, almost angry. "You see? You see why maybe it's okay not to know everything?"

Olivia felt clammy underneath her cotton tunic. She sat very still.

Franco was standing. He was running his hands through his hair, his face twisted. "Fuck," he whispered. Then, louder, "Fuck, fuck, fuck, fuck, fuck." He punched his forearm with his fist. Olivia felt disdain for his outburst. She crossed her arms and kneaded her elbows with her hands.

"I didn't want to fucking get in the middle of this!" Franco the yoga teacher shouted at Olivia.

Olivia focused on the places where her body was making contact with something—her feet on the ground, her butt in the plastic chair, her arms touching each other. She sat up very straight. "You should have thought about that a long time ago," she told Franco. "Before you slept with a married woman." A married dying woman.

Franco stalked off into the street. The horse rickshaw was no longer there, though she hadn't noticed the owner returning. A few men and children were hanging around watching the scene unfold. She wondered if they thought it was a lover's quarrel.

She reached across the table and took Franco's soda and drank from it with her own straw. The onlookers dispersed. Franco didn't return.

When she'd finished the soda, she got to her feet. If she didn't want to navigate her way back to the ashram by herself, she'd need to go with Franco.

Franco was waiting for her across from the temple, a rickshaw beside him. Once he saw her, he got in. She climbed in next to him. They didn't look at each other. He seemed to be engaged in some kind of lively internal dialogue that caused him to jerk his head and flinch occasionally.

She took out her camera and turned it on. "I'm going to film this," she said to Franco. He didn't respond. She filmed the road ahead of them and the back of the rickshaw wallah's head. The footage would be bumpy and unusable, probably. But she wanted it anyway.

After a few minutes Franco turned to face her. "I didn't know," he said. "I didn't know at first that she wasn't telling you guys, okay? Can you turn that thing off?"

She didn't turn it off. She shot the entire twenty minutes of the ride back to the ashram. Franco's face, his arms hugging his sides like Olivia's had been at the café. The landscape, brilliant green marshlands studded with field laborers and water buffalo. The dusty road. The rickshaw wallah—legs thin as a child's propelling them forward on a bicycle—who she only realized halfway through was the same man who'd brought them to the temple.

It was only two o'clock, hours to go before evening meditation. The yogis were dispersed and out of sight, napping or reading or doing whatever they did during the afternoon. Inside the temple gates, Olivia started for her room and Franco caught her arm. She whirled toward him.

He let go of her and took a step back. "Did anyone ever tell you you're kind of terrifying?"

"Yeah."

His laugh was forceful, brief. "Your mother was a smart lady. It's not like she had a death wish. I'm sure she would have gone with chemo or whatever it was if there was a real chance." He paused, trying to gauge her reaction. "Maybe she just had a gut feeling."

A gut feeling. Olivia remembered telling her parents she had a *gut feeling* she should go to school in Colorado with Kelsey instead of Vassar, and just how well they'd responded to that. In the Harris family, using the gut for really anything other than digestion was discouraged. She nodded at Franco and turned toward her room.

OLIVIA LAY ON her bed. The power was out, and without the fan, the room was hot and relentlessly still. Her mind ran along a tight loop: from Franco to the months her mother had spent on useless cancer treatment to learning about her mother's diagnosis in January and how meager the options had been to her mother's death. Then back to Franco—the person her mother had chosen to confide in. She lay there until she could not stand it anymore, and for some time after that, until her mind settled on one memory.

A month before she'd found out her mother was sick, on a Saturday in December, Olivia had woken at noon in her bed at school, naked, to find Pat fully dressed, sitting at her desk with a mug of coffee, his face paler than usual.

It had been so unnecessarily humiliating—being broken up with, after more than two years, while Pat was dressed and she was not.

After she'd argued with him—she was not too volatile, her reaction to seeing some random freshman sitting on his lap at a party the week before had been wholly proportional—and after she wrapped herself in a sarong, and gathered things in the room that belonged to him, and threw them in his direction, not necessarily caring if they hit him—and after he stood there in the doorway, silently, while she turned away—she'd called her mom.

"Oh, sweetie," her mom had said. "Shall I come up?"

Olivia nodded furiously, trying not to cry. Already, she was noticing additional items of Pat's (a sweater she'd borrowed last winter, a collection of Nabokov novels) that she hadn't seen in time to throw.

"Or do you want to be with your friends?" Eleanor asked.

She could hear her roommates prowling the hallway. They'd surely overheard at least some of what happened. But she wasn't ready to confirm their suspicions. It was a small school; breakups of long-established couples were newsworthy.

Olivia didn't know how her mother had planned to spend that Saturday, but she must have left Rye right away, because she arrived in a little over an hour. She took in the scene: her daughter, still wearing a sarong. The roommates meekly murmuring hello. The coffee and dining tables cluttered with books and beer bottles. Dishes in the kitchen sink, beginning to smell. "Home?" she said, jangling the car keys.

Olivia had thought about this later, guiltily—her mother, who'd been complaining vaguely of headaches, driving two and a half hours to pick her up when Olivia had her own car at school.

They spent the weekend together, Olivia and Eleanor. Max was in and out but Saturday night all three of them went out to dinner. Her parents didn't mention Pat or pump her for details, but that was their way. That Max didn't interrogate Olivia about her plans after graduation, as he'd been doing every time they spoke for the last few months, was, she knew, a concession to the breakup. Instead they talked about novels they'd read and movies they'd seen, and Eleanor announced that she was done waiting for Max to take her to India— she and Olivia would go next winter.

Sunday morning Eleanor went to yoga while Olivia slept in. They had a late breakfast together—scrambled eggs with feta and chives, buttery golden toast. In the afternoon, they watched *The Philadelphia Story*. Eleanor dozed off. She'd taken a nap the day before, too, when they'd gotten back from Poughkeepsie. *My mother's getting older,* Olivia thought. It felt adult, and also melodramatic, to even entertain the sentiment.

She left her mother sleeping on the couch in the den and wandered into her parents' bedroom. Her father was off somewhere, at the gym or running errands. Olivia curled up on the bed, facing the windows. It was overcast and the water was a surgical gray. There was a cozy hopelessness to being at home. The house was quiet, somehow quieter than it had been when she still lived there and her brothers were away at college. Her parents' regular life, the one that didn't revolve around their children, had a Spartan quality to it—the lack of snacks, the tidiness of the house.

Her mother was calling her. She came into the room and lay down next to Olivia. She rested her hand on Olivia's hip. "It's a moment in time, is all," she said.

"You'd already met Dad by now." Olivia was feeling for the wound as if it were anatomical, something she could palpate with her fingers. It was surprising and not heartening to realize she could let Pat go. There were other types of men she wanted to date—more sophisticated, taller ones. The blow to her ego might be the worst part. She wondered how her mother had felt when she'd been dating Max. Would she have been crushed if things had gone badly?

"It was different then." Eleanor rolled onto her back. Her body, still clad in yoga clothes, was like Olivia's—their tall, narrow frames and curved fingers, the way the veins protruded inside their elbow creases and on the backs of their hands. Everyone said Olivia looked more like Max, but as she gazed at her mother's bicep, she thought, *In thirty-three years, that will be my arm.*

"I didn't really have anyone else," Eleanor said. "Vera was already married, my mom—" She rolled her eyes.

"But I have you."

"And Dad. And Alec and Ty, and your friends."

"But someday I won't have you."

Olivia had gone over the conversation at least a dozen times after Eleanor was diagnosed. But she still didn't believe she'd been intuiting anything. She was just wallowing in her mother's attention.

Eleanor made a noise in the back of her throat, a *hmph.* "I'm not going anywhere."

Olivia touched Eleanor's hand. "Promise?"

There was a pause. Then her mom promised.

For the last year, there was an altar to Eleanor in Olivia's mind. Thinking of her mother was an antidote to whatever she didn't want to be dealing with, capable of making her feel chastened or vindicated, depending on the circumstance, but always somehow transported. In the midst of her ruminations, her mind went instinctively to that place, seeking comfort, and was met with emptiness. Her mother had known that weekend that she was sick. She had known over Christmas, when Holly had told them about her miscarriage, and she had comforted Holly, telling her there was plenty of time for babies. She had even known the summer before, while she and Max spent weekends with friends in the Hamptons and the Vineyard, putting off a family trip because of everyone's conflicting schedules. Eleanor had known—she had prepared, in her way. Why hadn't she thought her family deserved to do the same?

OLIVIA FELT LIKE a shell of herself those last few days at the ashram. She considered packing her bags and fleeing, taking the train to Kolkata early to lose herself in a throng of tourist hostels and bars until her flight south. But she stayed, going through the motions of yoga and meditation as well as she could. Her friends were getting ready to leave as well—it was the beginning of the real hot season in Northern India. Brandon was leaving a week after Olivia, stopping in Thailand, and then New York. He wasn't certain what his plans were after that.

"You can stay with me in New York," Olivia said, though she didn't know where she'd be living.

"Thanks, girl. I hope to have better options," Brandon said, but she could tell he was pleased she'd offered. She felt a pang of regret—that they had bonded and were separating, or perhaps that they had failed to bond more.

Franco greeted her warmly when they saw each other around the ashram, but he didn't solicit further conversation, and neither did she. He wasn't in their restaurant at night, and he was late to breakfast and lunch most days. But Sunday at lunch he came to her table. He remembered that she would be leaving the next day and asked what time. She told him first thing in the morning.

"Make sure to say goodbye before you go," he said. "I'll look for you at dinner."

Olivia spent the afternoon poking around the local shops with Sylvie, buying a few cheap souvenirs—colorful notebooks decorated with the Hindu deities, glittery Buddha stickers, a string of rose-wood prayer beads called a mala, which she would either keep for herself or give to Kelsey. They stopped at the internet café in town. When Olivia checked her email, there were a flurry of replies from her family about her extended trip. She opened Ty's.

You realize you're missing Christina's bachelorette party, right? Would have been nice if you'd discussed it with her first, but I assume it's too late to change your plans?

That was it, Olivia realized, her stomach clenching—the thing she'd been afraid she was forgetting. She hadn't thought about Christina's party in weeks. She went to the folder where she'd relegated the emails from Lee Anne and the others. There were dozens of emails she'd missed, the girls booking hotels and dinners and spa appointments. The gathering was the first weekend in April, and she'd be home a few days later.

She considered changing her ticket back. She could skip Goa—wasting the ticket and paying yet again to change her flight to New York. That was what she should do, and she went as far as looking up the number for the airline.

But she couldn't fathom being in Miami with Christina and her friends, her mind full of Franco and her mother as everyone got pedicures and drank cocktails and talked about the wedding. And those weekends were really about spending time with your girlfriends and probably gossiping about the groom, which would only be awkward if Olivia were there.

She scrutinized Ty's message for subtext. He was so mild mannered that he wouldn't have said anything unless he was upset. But really, all he was saying was that she should have discussed her plans with him and Christina first, which was certainly true. And if he knew what she had learned from Franco, he would understand why she wasn't feeling up to a weekend in Miami.

Instead of responding to Ty, she wrote to Christina. She apologized, but said her thesis had required that she extend her trip. She couldn't quite shake the guilty feeling, but she told herself that when she got back, she'd be a model bridesmaid—she had plenty of time to make it up to Christina.

BRANDON SUGGESTED THE hotel restaurant again as a send-off dinner for Olivia. Because she wouldn't be at their regular place across the street, she went to Franco's room beforehand to say goodbye.

The metal door behind the screen was closed, and Olivia hesitated before she knocked, wondering if he were asleep.

There was a delay before the door opened. Franco's face was flushed and he seemed slightly out of breath, as though he had been practicing in his room. He was shirtless.

"Olivia," he said. "What's up?" He looked at her as though she were a casual acquaintance, as though he couldn't imagine why she'd be stopping by.

"I'm headed to dinner," she heard herself saying. "I wanted to say goodbye."

He smelled a little like pot, or tobacco, or a combination of the two. He stepped forward to hug her.

"Goodbye," he said. "We'll keep in touch."

She peered over his shoulder into the cave-like room. There was someone else in there. It was that girl Pearl, sitting in bed, the sheet drawn up over her lap.

Olivia jerked away from Franco. Quickly he reached back and pulled the door closed behind him.

She stared at him in disbelief. "I guess this is a bad time," she said. "Sorry."

His face registered no embarrassment, no shame. "I didn't intend for you to see that."

"You really like all ages, don't you?" Olivia said. Pearl couldn't have been much older than she was.

"She's—" Franco began. "Never mind. I don't have to justify myself to you."

"That's good," said Olivia. "Because you couldn't possibly."

OLIVIA LEFT AT dawn the next morning, after a sad jumble of a dinner in which no one was paying attention to anyone else. The journey to Goa would be long, but she was relieved to be traveling again. Traveling, especially alone, was cathartic. There was so much to do and pay attention to—negotiating with drivers, managing the tickets and the passport and the visa. She couldn't escape her thoughts entirely, but it felt as though she got a head start, leaving them a few paces behind. She'd sprung for a second-class A/C train ticket to Kolkata. She hadn't been in air-conditioning yet on her trip except at the hotel restaurant and she felt like she was being refrigerated, but at least she had her own clean berth, and a nice family across from her, who insisted on sharing their homemade naan and curry. They expressed surprise that she, an unmarried young woman, was traveling alone, and from Gaya to Kolkata of all places.

"I'll be meeting my brothers in Goa," she told them, wanting to feel that she belonged to someone, that in the eyes of this family, she was not just some stray. And it worked—the husband and wife nodded their approval, and stopped asking her questions.

Goa was way more out there than she thought it would be, especially coming from the rural north. The town was full of hippies and carefully dressed bohemians; restaurants served chocolate-chip pancakes and falafel.

The yoga center was on the beach. Olivia was assigned a bamboo bungalow with a porch, at the edge of the jungle, the cheapest they'd had but still luxurious compared to the ashram. There was a queen-sized bed made up with crisp white sheets, and Olivia's private bathroom had hand soap and a little bottle of shampoo.

The afternoon Olivia arrived, after close to twenty-four hours of travel, and after the owner, Robin, an Australian who had moved to Goa with her Canadian husband ten years earlier, gave her a tour, Olivia put on a swimsuit and a sarong. She stood in the doorway of her bungalow. It was warm, and she could smell the ocean—and not the toilet. The tightness that had been in her chest since the visit to the Kali temple wasn't gone, but for the first time since then, it wasn't the only thing she felt. She could see a glimpse of the water between the trees. It was her twenty-third birthday.

Someone called out and she turned toward the sound. A man was standing on the porch of the next bungalow over. He was shirtless; as he walked over to introduce himself, she could see his six-pack, his sinewy arms.

His name was Will. He was English and just a few years older than she, taking a vacation from his job at a nonprofit in Chennai.

Like her, Will was a yoga newbie—*Thought I'd see what the hype was about,* he told her, in a storybook English accent. She almost laughed aloud as they strolled down toward the beach together, chatting. If she'd believed in God, she might have thought he was sending her Will as a peace offering.

Thus began a week that, despite what surrounded it, was truly delicious. Goa was a festival of sensual pleasures. After three weeks of rigorous asana at the ashram, the more varied classes at the center felt like dance parties, and though there were students far more advanced than Olivia, she didn't stick out as a neophyte.

Asana practice was in the morning in Goa as it had been at the ashram, but at a reasonable seven A.M., with a delicious breakfast—eggs, fresh bread, tropical fruit, even coffee—immediately after. Morning practice and breakfast constituted the entire formal schedule. Some people chose to study with Robin or her husband, Carl, later in the day, taking private lessons in asana, chanting, or the yoga sutras, but most of the guests were just enjoying a yoga-flavored holiday and spent their afternoons sunbathing, getting massages, or reading in hammocks under the palm fronds.

After breakfast, Olivia's mornings were spent afloat on the raft of Will's bed, a warm breeze coming through the open windows. The giddy tenderness of these hours was familiar to Olivia as if from another life—in college, she and Pat had lazed away mornings in bed, but in the last year it had not occurred to her that she might revisit this type of carefree lovemaking (because though love may not have actually been involved, there was no better word for what they were doing in that bungalow). As they drifted after sex, or between sex, Olivia could hear monkeys scrambling on the roof.

Will was interested in film—he fancied himself a bit of a cinematographer too, he confessed—and on their second day together, he inadvertently helped Olivia solve the thesis problem. When she told him she was trying to make a film about her mother, set in India, he mused, "Your mum never saw India."

"That's kind of the point," Olivia told him. She'd wanted to capture the part of her mother that wanted to see India. Now, thinking about her mother at all brought back the tight, winded feeling in her chest. She'd spent the past year trying to make sense of her mother's death, only to learn that she'd been working with faulty information.

"It's a shame she can't see your film, then. You could show it to her."

Of all the things that seemed *too bad* to Olivia at the moment, that her mother would never see her still-barely-existent thesis film did not rank. But, she reflected, as she took a drag from the spliff they were sharing, perhaps Will was onto something. Instead of trying to make a film about her mother—a notion that felt more preposterous by the day—why not make a portrait of India *for* her mother?

The new concept was no worse than the old: both relied primarily on the faculty taking pity on her. But the pretense of the film being for Eleanor rather than about her would let Olivia put her mother out of her mind as much as possible and shoot whatever she liked.

Will accompanied Olivia cheerfully on afternoon excursions around Goa, outfitting her with his comfortable male presence and unlimited hash. They went to markets and temples and beaches, where the local children swam in their clothes. They walked around the town, where hippieware was sold. There were lots of tourists with cameras in Goa, so Olivia felt less out of place using hers. She filmed more sunrises and sunsets.

By nightfall, she and Will would be at one of the local restaurants, where the offerings were more diverse and tastier than they had been in Bodh Gaya, drinking beer and playing Gin Rummy (if it was just the two of them) or 500 Rummy (if another traveler joined in). There were a few bars that played music at night, but they would retire to Will's bungalow by nine or ten o'clock.

Every night, Olivia would wake and return to her own bungalow. Will didn't spend the night in hers; they never discussed it. Olivia loved being near him when they were awake, loved the way he petted her even as he dozed off. But they would be together for a week, nothing more, and she preferred to keep those first moments of the day to herself, the other half of the bed still cool.

By coincidence, they left Goa the same day. Will was returning to Chennai and Olivia was beginning her three-flight journey back to New York. Will chivalrously offered to share a cab with Olivia, though his flight left two hours after hers.

The sun was just rising as they left the yoga center. Will put his arm around Olivia's shoulders and she rested her head on his chest. She didn't want to go back to New York, but she felt, in that moment, deeply at peace.

"I think I'll be coming to New York in the fall," Will said.

He was trying to be nice, but Olivia knew they wouldn't keep in touch. She wanted the moment to be free of false promises, crystalline in its empty pleasure.

"Shhhhh," she said, and he laughed softly—he understood.

5.

Olivia landed at Newark on a Wednesday with her backpack and a cheap plastic tote overflowing with souvenirs and dirty clothes. Released from Customs, she was borne through a canal of drivers bearing signs and families excitedly waiting for their person. She looked for the AirTrain, then stopped—she didn't know where she was going. She hadn't asked Ty and Christina if she could stay with them again, nor had she discussed her return with her father. She'd intended to find a sublet in the city, but hadn't begun looking yet. She called Bridget and left a sheepish message asking if she could crash at her and Kyle's place for the night.

On the train into the city, the other passengers' faces were drawn, their eyes on their electronics. Wasn't it spring? Olivia didn't see a sign of the season anywhere—not out the window, where they passed industrial wreckage in the fading light, nor among her fellow passengers, who were clad in the dark colors of business.

The train deposited Olivia in Penn Station, the unofficial armpit of Manhattan, in the middle of evening rush hour. Yet compared to New Delhi, the station felt almost deserted, the overhead lighting oddly dim, the corridors too wide for the commuters who hustled past.

Bridget had texted to say Olivia could spend the night. It was three more trains to their place, and then finally, nearly four hours after landing, she was outdoors. Bridget and Kyle lived near the water. It was almost dark, and the air was damp and chilly, but, Olivia thought, discernably spring.

Bridget and Kyle occupied a large loft on the third floor of a converted warehouse. It had tall ceilings and gleaming wood floors and was decorated in a rather civilized fashion for people their age, which was to say, there was evidence of some intentionality behind the selection of the furniture. Bright throw pillows adorned the gray couch, and the dining table, where Olivia had brunched on New Year's, could seat eight. From the windows, you could see the tops of some Manhattan landmarks peeking above the building next door.

After she greeted her friends, Olivia accepted the offer of a shower. She emerged in borrowed pajamas to find Bridget making up the couch with sheets Olivia remembered from college—ancient pink and white stripes with a ruffle at the top.

They sat down and Bridget and Kyle asked Olivia about the trip. They had never been to India, or anywhere in Asia, and their questions were mostly about the food: what had she eaten, had she gotten sick, and if so, what had made her sick.

"Weren't you there last summer?" Kyle said.

"With my family," Olivia said. "And my father's girlfriend was there. I couldn't really focus on—what I needed to focus on."

They nodded, polite and distant. It wasn't just that they didn't understand what the past year had been for her, she saw, but that they didn't want to try to understand. Loss, grief—her friends insulated their youth against such things, as if to even truly acknowledge them was an invitation.

In the morning, fueled by two cups of Bridget's strong coffee, Olivia began looking online for sublets. She was hoping she could find someplace to move into immediately, but as the morning wore on, that began to seem less realistic. Everyone looking for a roommate wanted to meet in person, and no one responded to her queries right away, other than one guy who asked her to send a picture of herself. She wasn't, she recognized, that desirable of a roommate. She had no job, and only wanted to stay a few months, until summer school began.

The apartment was sunny and pleasant, but by midday Olivia grew restless. She began looking for a yoga studio in the area, wondering if she could find an inexpensive class, but stopped when she realized she didn't have a key to get back in. Bridget had told her the door would lock behind her when she left, assuming Olivia would be gone by the time she returned from work. She rummaged in the fridge and debated frying eggs, but there were only two left in the carton. She made toast instead.

She messaged Ty, telling him she was home. It was the middle of the night in India and jetlag overcame her. When she awoke, the light had changed, and she'd received no response from Ty. She'd heard back from a few potential roommates, though, who could meet her the next day.

She stood by the windows. The sun was still high, moving west over Manhattan. The trees on the sidewalk, whose branches reached just below Bridget and Kyle's windows, were on the verge of blossoming, their swollen buds dancing in the breeze. She opened a window and spring flew in, colder than she expected and with the sour tang of the river.

Around four o'clock, she called Ty. He sounded gruff when he answered—he was probably busy at work.

"Did you see my text?" Olivia demanded.

Ty said he had, and then Olivia felt foolish, because all the text had said was that she was back in town. She had been hoping he would invite her to stay with them without her having to ask.

"Could I stay at your place?" she said. "Just for a night or two. I'm looking for a sublet but I don't have one yet."

There was a pause before Ty responded. "I have to check with Christina. But I'm sure it will be fine."

Ty said he would let her know when he was leaving work. His standoffishness removed any doubt in her mind that he was mad at her. She didn't want to accept a favor given so grudgingly. She wondered if Bridget would mind if she stayed another night.

Kyle got back from work at five thirty—it hadn't occurred to her that anyone would be home so early, but his office was in Williamsburg, walking distance.

"I didn't think you'd still be here," Kyle said when he saw Olivia, but he didn't sound displeased.

Olivia sometimes felt a little weird around Kyle because he was friends with Pat. She felt the need to impress him, so that whatever news of her got back to Pat would make him realize his grievous error.

But a few beers dispensed with any awkwardness. They began reminiscing about college. Olivia had actually met Kyle before Bridget—they'd been in the same freshman orientation group. They were laughing about how some of the other kids in that group had turned out to be very different from how they'd seemed that first day.

"You were the only normal one," Kyle was saying to Olivia, after reminding her of a girl who arrived at orientation carrying a ratty stuffed dragon.

"And look at me now," Olivia said.

The door opened and Bridget came in. Olivia and Kyle stopped talking and greeted her. Kyle got up to give her a kiss.

"Kyle, I thought you were going to do laundry tonight," Bridget said. Shooting Olivia an apologetic look, Kyle got to his feet and began stripping the bed. That was Bridget. It was seven on a Thursday night and she had Kyle—one of the most desirable guys in their class—changing her sheets. Olivia smiled at Bridget, hoping for a hint of collusion, but Bridget went to the fridge and began pulling out salad stuff.

"No luck with a sublet?" she said over her shoulder.

"You can't get a sublet in one day. I emailed a bunch of places, and I'll see a couple tomorrow."

"There are hostels," Bridget offered. Seeing Olivia's face, she added, "Just kidding. Of course you're welcome to stay—"

"Of course she can stay," Kyle called over his shoulder. The door slammed behind him as he left the apartment with a Santa-like sack of laundry.

"I get it," Olivia said. "Your place is small. No wait, it's not small—it's a giant loft, bigger than my brother's apartment, bigger than anyone else's apartment we know."

Bridget ripped leaves off a head of lettuce and tossed them into a salad spinner. It wasn't even the prewashed stuff that everybody used—it was probably from the farmers market. Olivia sat on the couch disconcerted, her beer buzz no longer fun.

"Ugh, Olivia, it's not all about you," Bridget said. She jerked the cord of the salad spinner and it skittered across the counter. "We have jobs. I had a long day. Call me selfish but I just wanted to come home and eat dinner and hang out with my boyfriend for a couple of hours, maybe watch some TV, pedestrian as that probably sounds."

"I love watching TV," Olivia protested. But Kyle and Bridget didn't even have a TV, Olivia realized. They probably watched shows on a laptop in bed.

Bridget sank onto the couch next to Olivia. "Now I feel like a bitch," she said. She picked up Olivia's beer, but it was empty. She'd gained some weight in the last year, Olivia thought—her face had always been round, but there was a fullness in her hips and thighs that hadn't been there in college.

"I'm going to Ty's," she told Bridget. "I just couldn't get in until he got home from work."

Bridget's face relaxed. Olivia stood to gather her things.

"I don't know why we're fighting," Bridget said. "You're one of my best friends."

Olivia could think of a few responses to that, but she was also aware that she couldn't afford to lose anyone else. So she thanked Bridget, and promised to call soon.

AS OLIVIA WALKED to the train, her low-grade headache was transitioning into a regular-grade headache. She'd spent twenty-four hours indoors, emerging after sunset for the second day in a row. She was starving and regretted the two beers. At least her backpack protected half her body from the damp breeze coming off the river.

To get to Ty's, she had to transfer at West Fourteenth Street, but he was probably still at work and not eager to see her anyway. So she came aboveground to a cacophonous blur of cabs and buses. She would find something to eat, she told herself, maybe a slice of pizza, but the first place she saw was a bar so she went in there instead.

The bar was modern and minimalist, made of curving pale green glass. She sat on a high white stool and ordered a vodka martini without consulting the menu the bartender placed in front of her. She figured she couldn't undo the beers, so she might as well re-up.

Everything on the short food menu was expensive. She ordered chicken skewers. The martini was very cold and initially clarifying. She'd fucked up by not making any plans for her return, by just expecting everyone to know she was coming and welcome her. Well, what was done was done. She'd find an apartment in a day or two. She didn't need to feel bad about staying with Ty—he was her brother, for God's sake! If anyone knew what she'd learned about Franco and her mother, what she was (she couldn't help thinking of it this way) selflessly enduring, without burdening her family, they'd understand her flakiness—in fact, they'd marvel that she was functioning as well as she was. Maybe this was why people went to therapists: because they had secrets they didn't want to ruin anyone else's life with.

The bartender set the chicken skewers in front of her. He was only a little older than she, she thought, tall and thin with sweeping bangs that nearly hid his light brown eyes.

The skewers were chewy and tasteless, but she ate them anyway.

"Refill?" The bartender asked. He was definitely good-looking. But there was no way she could have more to drink.

"I shouldn't," she said.

He raised his eyebrows. "You don't look old enough to have *shouldn'ts*." He took her glass away. She finished the chicken. A sort of woozy numbness was descending. If she went home with the bartender, she thought, she wouldn't have to stay with Ty. But he probably didn't get off work for hours.

The bartender set down a short glass, half full with an olive. "Here are some dregs," he said.

Olivia gulped her water instead. She'd barely eaten all day and was starting to forget basic sorts of things, like Ty and Christina's address. She could contemplate her mother's death, and the upcoming one-year anniversary, with a degree of distance that didn't seem quite natural. Everyone's parents die, she thought, and maybe it didn't have to be this defining thing about her. Everyone's parents die, and a lot of them probably have affairs too.

The bartender had said something to her, but she hadn't heard him. "Can I get you anything else?" he repeated. His tone was less friendly than before. Maybe it was because she was staring into space, occupying valuable real estate as the bar filled up. It was, after all, a Thursday night. To her left, two women ten years older than she kissed hello, while a man to her right studied his phone, perhaps waiting for his date to show up. There was house music on that seemed a bit aggressive, but that was New York, always reminding you to hurry up, hurry up, so you didn't miss out.

Olivia looked at her phone. Ty had called, and he'd texted a while ago saying he was on his way home, they were going to order food, had she eaten. The bartender brought her the check. How much did you tip on a martini, she wondered. She tipped some amount that probably wasn't enough, and got to her feet. She felt wobbly—she was in trouble. She almost left without her backpack, and then turned back, momentarily frantic, but it was propped below the bar where it had been all along.

She was near her old territory, just a few blocks west of the Likely offices and close to Michel's place as well. She was going to walk to Ty's, hoping to sober up before she arrived, but after walking a block in the wrong direction, she hailed a cab.

The driver was curly haired and looked Indian or maybe Pakistani. He was listening to the evening news, and Olivia momentarily felt soothed to be out of the bar and on her way to a place that felt more like home. But when the cab made a sharp left on Hudson, she realized driving had not been a good idea. She felt dizzy, then hot, then quickly nauseated. She tried to roll the window down but it was locked. "Please, the window," she said, and the driver put it down only a crack.

She held her nose up like a dog, and then she opened her mouth to tell him she needed him to open it more, much more, all the way. Then the cab hit a pothole and she threw up in her lap. The driver slammed on the breaks, cursing, and pulled over to the curb. She threw up again, because by that point the damage was done.

"Why you not open the door, lady?" the driver shouted.

"I'm sorry," Olivia said feebly. The interior of the cab was spinning.

"You have to pay fifty dollars extra," the cab driver said.

"I don't have it," she said. The vomit, anyway, was largely on her, though there was some on the windowsill and the door handle and the floor. Just the smell of it was going to make her sick again. "Do you have any paper towels?" she said.

"You pay fifty dollars and you get out," the driver said again, his tone calmer.

Olivia slid across the bench seat toward the curbside. "I only have twenty," she said, holding out a crumbled bill. It was more than double what was on the meter. She noticed, and hoped the driver didn't, that there was now a smear of her vomit across the seat.

He was reaching into the glove box for something, which she dimly hoped was not a weapon. Her fingers were on the door handle but some perverse notion of manners kept her from fleeing. He pulled out a manual, which he waved in the air. "It's the law, you puke in cab, you pay fifty dollars." His voice had risen again.

Olivia opened the door. She dropped the twenty-dollar bill on the seat. "I'm sorry," she said again. "Have a nice night." She climbed out of the cab and moved away from it as fast as she could.

She turned right on the first side street. Whatever adrenaline had allowed her to escape quickly subsided. She was sick again—she put her hands on someone's gate and heaved into their garbage can. A man walking by made a noise of disgust. Wasn't there anywhere in this city it was okay to throw up?

She stood. Her jacket and jeans had puke on them but at least, she thought, she had a change of clothes with her.

That was when she realized she'd left her backpack, as well as the bag of souvenirs, in the trunk of the cab.

She sank to the street. All her clothes, her camera and footage, her passport, the silver bangles she'd bought Kelsey—they were all gone, in the hands of a New York City cab driver who had every reason to hate her. Her phone and her wallet were in her pocket, but this was a bare consolation.

The panic, and fury at herself, that coursed through her were instantly sobering. She felt electrified with worry, alert enough to run ten miles, to lift something three times her own weight, if that were required. But there wasn't anything she could do.

She pulled her phone out of her pocket. She had three missed calls from Ty and a series of increasingly irritated text messages. It was almost nine o'clock. Her mind instinctively flicked to that scab—*what would Mom think*—her most reliable source of self-flagellation for the last year. But it didn't matter what her mother would have thought.

Feet stopped in front of her. "Do you need help?" a man said. She looked up at his face. He was about Michel's age, dressed in a suit. She tried to gauge how he was looking at her—like she had looked at beggars on the street in India? She couldn't tell, and it didn't matter anyway. She told him she was okay.

She got to her feet. There was a bodega on the corner she'd passed, and she went in. Keeping her head down, she got a bottle of water out of the fridge, and grabbed a roll of paper towels from a high shelf. At the register, she chose a pack of gum.

"Someone threw up on me on the train," she told the clerk. He looked at her with indifference. She chugged water and paid with a credit card. She emerged from the bodega. She opened the roll of paper towels and began to clean herself off.

Something made her glance at the curb. It could have been any cab, pulled over with the flashers on—but no, that was her driver, leaning into the back seat through one of the rear doors.

She walked toward him. He emerged, holding a spray cleaning product and a rag. He was cleaning up her puke.

Olivia cleared her throat.

The driver turned. When he saw her he smiled. "You remember your bags," he said. "I thought you're not stupid."

Wobbly kneed, Olivia exhaled.

"I figure, if you remember it's better for both of us," he said, shrugging. "I thought you might come back."

"I can go to an ATM," she said.

"Credit card okay," he said. He held open the back door for her. She slid in. It smelled like disinfectant. He got back in and did something with the meter, and $75.00 appeared on the screen.

He turned back to her. "I checked online," he said brightly. "The price went up." She swiped her credit card, thinking about the twenty dollars she'd already given him but terrified to say anything.

Her credit card was authorizing, and then it went through. She heard the driver pop the trunk and then he got out to help her with her luggage.

He held her tote bag while she put on her backpack and then handed it to her. "You're not so stupid," he said again.

She shook her head at him. "You saved my life," she said.

He laughed. He had a round face and thick, dark hair. "Two bags is your life?" he said. "I think not. You save your own life."

She wasn't sure if it was a proclamation or an order. He drove away. On the corner, she took off her mother's sweater and wadded it up and threw it away. And then she pulled it back out of the trash, from amid the bags of dog shit and Styrofoam food containers, because she still couldn't throw anything of her mother's away, and that was when she began to cry. She carried the bundled sweater in her arms and she walked slowly to Ty's.

THE DOORMAN IN Ty and Christina's brightly lit, climate-controlled lobby greeted Olivia, calling her Miss Harris. If he was startled by her disheveled appearance, he didn't let on. Olivia almost wished he would call up to give Ty and Christina more of a warning, but he only waved her through, and then she was riding up to the eighth floor, feeling her stomach churn again.

It was Christina who opened the door. "Olivia!" she said, and then her smile faded and she actually took a step back.

Ty appeared over her shoulder. "Jesus Christ," he said. "What happened to you?"

There was a moment when Olivia wasn't sure they were going to let her in. Then Christina remembered herself.

"Come in, come in," she said, moving Ty out of the way. "Are you okay?"

"I got sick."

Christina made sympathetic noises. Olivia was helped out of her backpack, and the jacket was taken from her. She was given a glass of ginger ale and led to the bathroom, where Christina even turned on the water, and gave her fresh towels and a bathrobe. The kindness of it made Olivia fight back tears, though she knew that once she got out of the shower, she was going to have to explain herself, if not to Christina then to her brother.

She lingered in the heat and steam, wrapped her hair in a towel, brushed her teeth with a fresh toothbrush Christina had laid out. She wondered if she'd ever be the sort of person who stocked extra toothbrushes. It seemed unlikely, but life was long.

Finally she went out into the living room, where Ty and Christina were eating fragrant Thai takeout. The apartment, which had always been tidy when she was there, felt more cluttered, with full paper shopping bags sitting along the floor near the wall. She joined them at the table, where a place had been set for her. Christina pointed around the table, naming the dishes—papaya salad, coconut curry, stir-fried chicken with basil.

Ty lifted his hand, cutting her off. "What the hell happened to you?" he said. "I thought you would be here hours ago. I left work early, and I called you, and we waited to order food—"

"Ty, she got sick."

"I'm sorry," Olivia said. She wanted, badly, to eat. The food smelled insanely good. She reached for the rice, the nearest thing to her, and Ty lifted it up out of her reach.

"This is our home," he said. "Not a hotel."

Christina put her hand on his arm and he turned to her fiercely. "And can you be on my side for once?"

Christina dropped her hand into her lap and looked down. She was very thin, Olivia thought, and her skin looked pale and fragile after a winter in the city.

"I had a couple of drinks, okay?" Olivia said. Though Ty had every right to be mad at her, after the near luggage disaster, being scolded by her brother felt like an extremely manageable problem. "I didn't drink much on my trip and I miscalculated."

"You miss Christina's bachelorette and barely even bother letting us know. Then you need a place to crash again, fine, but you show up here literally looking like a homeless person—"

Christina opened her mouth, and then closed it again.

"You can't just do whatever you want all the time."

"I'm sorry," Olivia said. "I'm really sorry."

Ty and Christina's faces both relaxed a little.

"I had the dates mixed up when I changed my ticket. Which I did," she added, "because I hadn't gotten as far as I needed to on my thesis. I should have changed the ticket back, but—"

"Really, it's okay," Christina cut in, in a tone that indicated she was going to persist whatever Ty said. "I didn't want Ty to make such a big deal out of it. It was supposed to be fun, not an obligation."

"It would have been fun," Olivia said. "I'm sure it was."

"Okay, okay," Ty said. "Enough excuses. I'll drop it."

As Olivia gulped ginger ale and filled her plate with food, Ty and Christina asked her about her trip. Between bites of cooling curry, she answered as well as she could: the yoga had been good, interesting, though she wasn't about to become a devout yogi. Goa was beautiful, and it was there that she'd been able to shoot more of her thesis, because she'd felt more comfortable using her camera.

She turned the conversation to the wedding, which was a little more than two months away, as quickly as she could. It sounded like pretty much everything was taken care of: they'd hired a local caterer and signed a contract with a florist. There were two bands— one that played rock and Motown for the reception, and a string quartet for the ceremony. A tent was reserved for the yard. The bridesmaids, including Olivia, had ordered their dresses months before and Christina was about to start a series of fittings for her dress. She pointed to the paper bags Olivia had noticed on the floor— those were the invitations, back from the calligrapher and addressed, ready to go out on Monday. Olivia guessed they'd decided not to postpone because of Holly's pregnancy—no one had mentioned it since Christmas.

Ty looked bored, but Christina didn't seem to notice. Eventually he cut in to ask Olivia more about India. She was gratified that he didn't seem upset with her anymore, but it was hard to talk about the trip without mentioning Franco, and she didn't much feel like talking about Will either. She told him about the people she'd befriended at the ashram, and the girls' school, and she presented them with a small Buddha statue which, truthfully, she hadn't bought for anyone in particular. By the time she'd finished eating she could barely keep her eyes open.

★ ★ ★

SUNDAY MORNING, TY helped Olivia move into the sublet she'd found in Brooklyn. They took a cab from his apartment, her suitcases in the trunk. It was a frigid day, with rain coming sideways in gusts. When Olivia tried to open the cab door outside her new home, it blew shut in her face.

Ty dragged Olivia's suitcases up the stairs to the third floor and surveyed the small apartment. "Not bad."

Olivia suspected Ty was secretly appalled. But the apartment, whose official tenants were a gay couple in their thirties, Charles and Duane, wasn't bad at all. It had a pleasant smell, as though candles or some non-cloying potpourri had been used recently, and was full of plants—a tree in the living room, planters hanging from above all the windows, and herbs on the kitchen windowsill. Olivia's bedroom was tiny and separated from the living room by French doors, over which someone, perhaps the last roommate, had hung a tapestry.

"You can replace this," Duane had said two days earlier when Olivia came to see the room, fingering the colorful batik fabric. "I can't explain why we own it."

When she'd told him and Charles she'd take the room, they'd gone into the kitchen to confer.

Charles stuck his head around the corner. "What did you say you do?"

"I'm a student. My father can cosign." Max was helping her with rent until summer school started.

But there'd been nothing to cosign. She'd paid the deposit and first month's rent in cash, and they'd given her a set of keys and the combination that would open the door to the building.

The room came with a double mattress and box spring, which looked clean, and a night table with a lamp. There wasn't room for much else, but there was a small closet with hangers. Anyway, it would only be for a few months—in June she would return to Vassar for summer session. The same day she'd come to see the apartment, she'd secured part-time employment at a coffee shop a few blocks over.

It felt like Olivia's whole life was on the slanted floor of that bedroom, but it was really only the clothes she'd had with her in India, plus a few colder-weather things she'd stashed at Ty and Christina's before her trip. She'd brought everything back to Rye when she'd moved out of the Upper East Side apartment at the end of January.

Though it was Sunday, Ty had to go into the office. Olivia hung up a few things in the closet. She didn't have a set of sheets. She needed some kind of cheap set of drawers to put her clothes in.

That afternoon, Olivia worked her first shift at the coffee shop that had hired her. She'd claimed some understanding of how to make espresso drinks (she knew, after all, that there was espresso in them, and usually milk as well), but Vic, the manager on duty, explained everything to her from scratch, for which she was immensely grateful. Really, that afternoon, he and another girl made all the lattes, while Olivia ground beans, wiped counters, and refilled jugs of cream and house-made almond milk. The clientele were bona fide hipsters, heavily tattooed, in tight ripped jeans and motorcycle jackets.

After her shift, Olivia took one train west and another south to Red Hook, where IKEA was located. Doing her best to ignore the swarms of weekend shoppers (mostly couples a little older than she, the women manic, the men nervous), she found the things she needed: sheets and pillows, a chest of drawers, a wastebasket. She stood in one line to pay and another line to arrange for delivery, which cost nearly as much as her items had. But she left IKEA quietly victorious.

Back at the apartment, Charles and Duane were listening to *The White Album* and chopping vegetables for a stir-fry. They invited her to eat with them later. The delivery arrived right on time and Olivia put her clothes away, made the bed, and bought a light bulb at the corner store.

THE FAMILY GATHERING the following weekend cast a shadow over the coming week. Sunday would mark a year since Eleanor's death. Olivia and her brothers would arrive in Rye Friday night and some relatives and friends—Olivia didn't know exactly who—would come over on Saturday.

Kelsey hadn't been there for the funeral—she'd been studying abroad in Ghana. So even though Olivia hadn't invited her, she'd announced months earlier that she'd be flying in for the anniversary weekend, just a few weeks before her own college graduation.

Olivia didn't think she could tell Kelsey about finding Franco. She couldn't tell Kelsey about the affair without revealing the bigger secret, and as much as she wanted a confidant, it felt too disloyal to air her family's dirty laundry. Knowing that she would have to keep the only things that mattered hidden made the prospect of Kelsey's visit not very relaxing.

But however she felt about it, Kelsey was coming. Her flight landed Thursday night, and she was at Olivia's new apartment by a little after nine.

Kelsey had dark circles under her eyes and looked thinner than she had at Christmas. She said her parents had told her to treat Olivia to dinner, so they went to a restaurant in the neighborhood Olivia had heard was good.

Kelsey was wearing a fleece. "You look like a New Yorker now," she said, touching Olivia's wool coat.

It was a cool, damp spring night. It had rained all day but it wasn't raining anymore, and the streets were saturated and dark.

Kelsey was chattering—about the flight, about how much she had to do before graduation—with a kind of pent-up, nervous energy, but just being near her made Olivia feel better.

The restaurant, though barely findable from the street, was packed. Olivia loved that about New York: walking through an unassuming doorway and being hit by a wall of noise, as though the establishment were something hidden she'd found.

The mustached bartender delivered them menus and tiny glasses of room-temperature water. Olivia ordered for them: bacon-wrapped dates, kale Caesar, shrimp and grits.

Wine arrived, along with a mug of popcorn. "That's weird," Kelsey said. They devoured it. The bartender refilled it, smiling for the first time.

"You look thin," Olivia told Kelsey.

Kelsey beamed, but her face changed quickly. "Liv, it's been so stressful," she said. Her newly prominent cheekbones caught the warm yellow light at the bar.

Kelsey launched into the drama of trying to figure out what to do after graduation. Olivia was glad Kelsey was talking about herself—it meant she, Olivia, wouldn't have to. But she couldn't focus. She was distracted by a couple on the other side of the L-shaped bar. The man had arrived with flowers for the woman. They were kissing passionately, as if they hadn't seen each other in weeks. They looked out of place, too conservative, she with a sleek blond bob, he in a suit.

"Enough about me," Kelsey said. "I want to hear about India. You haven't told me anything. Did you find that man? Francis?"

"Franco," Olivia said. "He wasn't at the ashram when I got there."

Kelsey looked crestfallen. "You must have been so disappointed."

"I was at first." She told Kelsey about the ashram, about Brandon and the other friends she'd made, about the girls' school, and the week in Goa. Talking about Will—who actually had emailed her once—was the best way to make Kelsey forget about Franco.

"Was the sex that good?" Kelsey said, hearing about the hours spent in bed.

"It was kind of revolutionary," Olivia said truthfully. "Once you let go of these college guys, there's a whole world out there."

"You were already with someone older," Kelsey pointed out.

The time with Michel felt so long ago, so irrelevant, despite the misery it had caused. "I'm not saying older," Olivia said. "I'm saying grown-up." She paused—Will hadn't been grown-up, exactly. "I'm saying nicer."

Their wineglasses were empty and then they were full. The food arrived all at once, the bacon-wrapped dates nearly caramelized inside, the kale nothing more than an unwieldy vehicle for cheese. Olivia studied her friend's face, serious as she asked questions about Olivia's film, as she dipped bites of shrimp in the buttery puddle of grits. Even without talking about Franco and what she'd learned, it was nice to have Kelsey there.

It was raining when they left the restaurant and they jogged back to the apartment, warm from wine and food. They hadn't brought umbrellas—they hadn't even checked the weather. They slept next to each other in Olivia's bed, their arms just touching.

THE NEXT MORNING, Olivia worked on her film in the living room while Kelsey slept. In the afternoon they walked around the neighborhood, which Olivia was still getting to know.

They met Ty at Grand Central in time to catch the five fifteen out to Rye. Alec and Holly, who was six months pregnant, had landed at JFK about an hour before, she from London and he from LA.

"Where's Christina?" Olivia asked, after Kelsey and Ty had hugged hello.

"She's coming out in the morning. She had stuff to do, and I thought it might be cool for it to be just family tonight."

Weird, Olivia thought, since Christina was to become family in less than two months. "What are we doing tonight, anyway?"

Ty didn't know. "Holly will be jetlagged, I'm sure. I wonder if June will be there."

Olivia found that she didn't care whether June was there. The commemorative weekend felt unreal to her, and her father might as well do whatever made him happy.

Olivia got the window seat, with Ty on the aisle and Kelsey in between. It was a Friday night and the train was crowded. Men stood near the doors drinking tallboys in paper bags.

Olivia loved the rhythm of the train (not so different from the Indian trains), the long tunnel that carried them uptown before they emerged in Harlem. The days were growing long again and the sunlight was diffuse after the rain, which had continued into the early afternoon. She rested her head against the window and dozed.

She woke when the train got to Harrison, one stop before Rye. Kelsey and Ty were speaking in their low, familiar voices. Olivia kept her eyes closed, listening. Kelsey was telling Ty what she had told Olivia the night before—how stressed she was about her relationship and what would happen after graduation. Olivia smiled to herself, wondering how Ty was containing his boredom.

"What do you want to do, really?" That was Ty, not sounding bored at all.

"God. No one's asked me that."

Olivia felt remorseful. She was one of the people, apparently, who'd failed to ask Kelsey that question—who'd half listened without even really trying to help. But the problem with Kelsey was that she was too determined to figure things out—she believed things *could* be figured out, and she got bogged down. Other people, more effective people, just picked something.

"He must be crazy," Ty said, and Olivia sat up in surprise. His voice was soft, and even—she really did think—flirtatious. They were facing each other but Ty sank back in his seat when he saw Olivia was awake.

"What are we talking about?" Olivia said.

"Oh, just my mess of a life."

"Your life isn't a mess." Olivia wasn't sure whether she was being loyal to her friend or trying to put an end to Kelsey's damsel-in-distress act.

"Maybe I could be a paralegal at your law firm." Kelsey said, looking back at Ty. She spoke in a silly, desperate tone, as though being a paralegal were the worst thing she could think of.

Ty laughed. "You'd bring the average intelligence up by fifty percent."

"Is there only one paralegal at your firm?" Olivia said.

"There's like forty," Ty said.

"Then there's no way Kelsey could bring the average up fifty percent."

"Okay, so I was exaggerating." Ty gestured at Olivia and told Kelsey, "She's the one who should have gone to law school."

Kelsey stayed on the train when Olivia and Ty got off—with all the Harris kids home, it would be a full house, so she would stay with her parents and all three Grants would come over the next day.

Olivia was expecting to find Max waiting at the Rye station, maybe with Alec, but there was no sign of his car. She and Ty both checked their phones—nothing.

"You told him the time, right?" Olivia said.

"I emailed him this morning."

They waited for ten minutes, and then called Max, who didn't answer, so they took a cab the short distance to the house.

IN THE KITCHEN, there was evidence of sandwich eating. They found Alec outside on the phone, pacing the lawn with a cigarette. An empty plate and a beer sat in the grass nearby.

"I only smoke when I come back here," Alec said accusatorily after he hung up.

It was in the high fifties, but Alec was wearing an old jacket of Max's and a scarf, while Ty and Olivia were comfortable in sweaters. They teased him about his Californian softness.

Alec told them Max hadn't been there when he'd arrived an hour before. "I let myself in. The key is still in the same spot."

"Do you think he's okay?" Olivia said.

"Yeah. He texted me saying he was with June and he'd be home later. Some reception," he added, though he didn't sound as though he really cared. He put out his cigarette on the bottom of his shoe and dropped it on the empty plate. Olivia remembered Michel at Thanksgiving, tossing a butt into the water, and was viscerally angry at him as she hadn't been in weeks.

Holly was already asleep, as they'd predicted. Olivia hadn't seen her since she'd been pregnant. "God, I bet she looks gorgeous."

"Holly's always gorgeous," Alec said loyally. "But she doesn't see it that way." He dropped his voice. "She's gained—she won't even tell me how much, but I bet at least forty pounds so far."

"She was so skinny to begin with, she probably had to," Olivia said.

"She hates it," Alec said. He was now whispering, though the bedroom where Holly slept was on the other side of the house. "She eats so much. All this cheese. Red meat. Stuff she wouldn't touch before. It's bizarre. And I'm going to have to shower before I get into bed with her. A cigarette would make her file for divorce."

"But doesn't Holly smoke sometimes?" Ty said.

"Well, obviously not now."

THEY WENT INSIDE in search of drinks. There was a bottle of bourbon in the bar, along with Max's staple scotch and some ancient gin. It was increasingly weird that Max wasn't there. Olivia had thought there would be some forcedly jovial welcome dinner with him and June. The sky was pink and they took the bourbon outside and dragged chairs from the patio onto the grass, where Alec had already set up camp, to be closer to the water. Ty called Max again while Olivia poured the bourbon over ice.

"It's spring," she told her brothers. "Take off your shoes." Her brothers obeyed, grumbling about the cold, wet grass.

After inquiring about Christina, Alec asked how the wedding planning was going. "Is she a closet bridezilla?"

"It's actually been really easy so far," Ty said flatly.

"You make it sound like that's a bad thing," Alec said.

"When did I decide to do this?"

Alec laughed. "Wait until she's pregnant."

Unlike Ty and Christina, who had dated for almost three years before getting engaged, Alec and Holly had moved fast—Alec proposed less than a year after they'd met, so quickly that Max had wondered if Holly were pregnant. Eleanor had known better: *He's not going to let that one get away.*

"But seriously," Ty said. His voice was a note louder than usual— it sounded as if he were already feeling the whiskey. "When did I decide to have this entire life?"

"What are you talking about?" Olivia said, although she thought she knew what he meant. She'd just never heard Ty question his extreme normalcy before.

Ty drained his bourbon. The ice rattled in the glass, and Alec reached forward to pour him more, topping up his own as well.

"To get married. To have a job like Dad's." He sipped. "Christina wants to move to the suburbs."

"Now, or eventually?" Olivia asked.

"She actually asked me if we could buy this house."

Olivia recoiled at the thought. The only thing worse than the Rye house being gone would be Ty and Christina presiding over it, playing the role of the parents.

"Relax," said Ty. "She's insane to think we could afford it, which is what I told her."

Alec dismissed this. "I bet she just didn't think it through. Women—no offense, Liv—can go a little nuts with the nesting stuff. The second she got pregnant, Holly wanted us to look at bigger houses."

"You live in a three bedroom." Olivia was outraged.

"Exactly. And Holly was like, 'Yeah, but I want to have two kids, and we need a guest room and a playroom.'"

Olivia knew she couldn't be certain, but she didn't think she'd ever be like that, crazed about weddings or babies. She didn't want kids. The most she hoped for was some sort of reputable boyfriend.

"But you love it," Ty was saying. "You're probably already house hunting."

"I love Holly, sure," Alec said. "You love Christina."

"You do, right?" Olivia said. Ty wasn't getting to say what he wanted to, but they were all so unused to any kind of existential crisis from Ty that it was hard to know how to proceed.

"Tyler Harris, you were destined for this path," Alec intoned.

"Shut up."

Ty was the one who'd done things right, according to Max. Dartmouth followed by Columbia Law School. Max had always said Ty should have tried for Yale (Max himself had gone to Columbia), but Ty had wanted to be in the city.

"You did it, buddy," Alec said. "I haven't said it enough, but I am so proud of you. You're smart, you're ambitious—maybe you'll be president someday."

"Zero is the right number of times to say that," Olivia informed him. Her hair was piled into a high, messy bun and she sat on a lawn chair in her newly erect meditation posture, feet tucked under her. She sipped at her whiskey, enjoying watching her brothers get drunk, enjoying being the self-contained one, enjoying being home. The constant gnawing truth of her mother's betrayal hadn't gone away but it hadn't worsened either. It was just the same reality in a new environment.

"I never really decided I wanted to get married," Ty was saying.

"Does any guy?" Alec said.

"You wanted to marry Holly."

"I wanted to *possess* Holly. I wanted to make it hard for Holly to ever leave me."

"You wanted to marry her," Ty insisted.

"It wasn't about the institution of marriage, though, or anything abstract. I just knew I wanted to be with her."

"And you were ready," Ty said.

Olivia knew what he meant. After college, Alec had moved to LA with grandiose plans and no job. Five years later, he'd made his way into a fairly legitimate career as an agent, and he met Holly at exactly the moment he was ready to become serious about someone—at least that was the way it had seemed to his family, tracking his progress from across the country. Alec and Holly had married two years later, when he was twenty-nine and she was twenty-four. His execution couldn't have been smoother, complete with a picturesque wedding in the English countryside of Surrey, attended by B-list celebrities and fledgling paparazzi.

Alec threw up his hands in happy defeat. "Meeting Holly made me ready."

"You're having doubts?" Olivia asked Ty.

"Christina's awesome," Alec said. "I mean, Christina's one of those do-it-all people. She's got a great career, but she's also going to be a *wife*."

"You're not letting Ty talk."

"I'm not really saying anything," Ty said.

"I don't think Holly has ever made me dinner."

"Who cares?" Ty said. "That's not the point of marriage."

The whiskey glasses were empty and Olivia refilled them, though the ice had melted to wisps. It was almost entirely dark, but the lights on inside the house cast enough of a glow to see by.

"We don't get cold feet," Olivia said. "We're not that kind of people." It came out sounding prim, harsh, as though she were telling Ty to get his act together. Really what she'd meant was, if he was having doubts, they were probably real. In her family, undue process was not a virtue. Her parents had always been decisive and confident—at least they'd seemed to be—and Olivia had seen this as a strength.

But knowing what she'd learned from Franco, she wondered. What had her parents' marriage really been like? They'd married young, less than a year after they'd met. Olivia, too, jumped into things—refusing to go back to Vassar the previous fall, Michel. Even letting herself be forced out of her job at Likely, which she maybe should have thought about for more than eight seconds. There might have been options. She'd always acted on impulse. Her parents had sometimes been annoyed—when they'd thought she had made the wrong decision. But the refrain when she was a child was always *Hurry up.*

"Where the hell is Max?" Ty was saying. "I'm starving."

"We can order pizza," Olivia pointed out. Her brothers were amazed by the brilliance of the suggestion.

Olivia made the call. "Two pizzas." She cupped her hand over her mouth. "What do we want on them?"

She ordered one pepperoni and one plain cheese and hung up.

She sipped her drink. Alec had gone inside to check on Holly. Ty looked sad. Olivia watched him, trying to think of what to say.

But he spoke first. "It's not cold feet exactly. It's more like this feeling that the rest of my life is already decided."

Olivia couldn't imagine that feeling. "Do you think Mom and Dad should have gotten married?"

Ty looked offended by the question. "Of course."

"You think they were happy?"

"They liked hanging out with each other."

It had certainly seemed that way, Olivia had to admit. Max and Eleanor weren't demonstrative but their time with each other had been a priority, even with three kids. For as long as Olivia could remember, Friday had been date night, with her brothers or some local teenager babysitting when Olivia was a child. Her parents had made a habit of taking an annual winter trip without the kids, to Mexico or the Caribbean.

But maybe something had been missing. Or if it hadn't always been missing, it had gone missing in the last few years.

Alec came back into the yard. A few minutes later, just as he was asking Olivia about India, Max showed up.

As they greeted him, Olivia's phone rang. It was the pizza place—someone was outside the house but no one had answered the door, because they couldn't hear the bell.

Olivia kissed her father's cheek and extracted his wallet from his back pocket.

"A classic maneuver," he called behind her, as she ran into the house to open the door for the teenage pizza bearer.

OLIVIA DROPPED THE pizza boxes on the grass. "Peee-za."

Her brothers lunged at the pizza. Max dragged a chair over for himself, a slice in one hand. Olivia took a too-hot bite, burning the roof of her mouth. She chewed with her mouth open to cool the pizza. "Where were you?" she asked her father after she had swallowed.

Max sipped bourbon out of someone's glass. "I was with June. I lost track of time."

His children exchanged glances, Alec's eyebrows wiggling suggestively.

"Oh, come on," Max said. "I don't mean anything racy." He paused. "As a matter of fact, we got into a quarrel."

"About what?" Ty asked.

A breeze was coming off the water. It was becoming more difficult to ignore how cold it was. Olivia was the only one who was still barefoot, and she had goose bumps.

Max looked sad when he finally answered. "It was about this weekend. She asked me if I thought she should come tomorrow. To the event."

"I thought she was coming," Alec said. Olivia and Ty nodded—they'd assumed this as well.

"As did I," Max said.

They waited.

"She asked, and—I suppose I didn't give the answer she was looking for." He set his partially eaten slice down carefully on the lid of one of the boxes.

"What did you say?" Olivia prompted.

"She said—or she asked—whether it should really be just for our family. And I said maybe she was right, and that she shouldn't come if it made her uncomfortable."

"Well, she is right, don't you think?" Ty said. "It should be just us."

It would be weird to have June there the next day, and yet it might be even weirder to not have her. A year after Eleanor's death hardly seemed the time to begin excluding June from family events.

"I hadn't thought it through," Max said unhappily. "But my response upset her."

Obviously, Olivia thought.

"How did you leave it?" Alec asked.

"She wanted to know my plans, in terms of our relationship. And I said I didn't have a plan."

"You can never say that to a woman," Ty said. He sounded drunk.

"You could call her," Alec said. "Or go over in the morning with flowers. Tell her this weekend is emotional and you were confused."

"Which probably has the advantage of being true," Olivia added.

"Dating advice from my kids." Max smiled weakly. "Where's Holly? It's freezing."

"I was afraid Olivia was going to make us sleep out here if you didn't rescue us," Alec said.

"You're a California wimp now," Olivia told him, though her teeth were beginning to chatter.

They took the pizzas inside and settled around the kitchen table. Max got out plates but everyone was already full.

They asked who was coming the next day, and Max named a few close family friends, two teachers Eleanor had been close with, Eleanor's sister, Vera, and her husband, Lake, and Lake's daughter from his first marriage, Maris, who always wangled her way into things.

Apparently, these people had been instructed to come over around three or four—Max would have to check his email to remember—and there was no particular program or plan for what to feed them.

"We'll pick up stuff tomorrow," Alec said. "Chips and salsa. It'll be fine."

Olivia wondered why Max had set up this whole event and invited people besides immediate family, when he was clearly approaching the whole thing with a mixture of indifference and dread.

Whatever momentum the evening had had faded. Max announced that he was turning in, though it wasn't even nine. Ty had a headache. Olivia sat on the kitchen floor.

"What would Mom have wanted us to be doing?" Ty asked generally.

Nobody knew, but they didn't think this was it.

"Would she want us to go to the cemetery?" Olivia said doubtfully.

Her brothers didn't think so.

"Maybe the beach?" Eleanor had loved the beach—they all knew that.

"We'll be on the water," Alec said. "She loved it here. It's probably close enough."

They went into the den, which smelled like Max, and turned on the TV. They flipped through the channels. Alec left and returned with a slice of cold pizza. Ty was doing work emails.

Eleanor's study and Max's den, on opposite ends of the house, were the only rooms that could reasonably be described as cozy. Both were furnished with rejects and leftovers—the couch in the den had been their living room couch when Olivia was very young, and was boxy, out of style, and much more comfortable than the living room furniture. The carpet was nubby and brown.

When Olivia was young, her brothers claimed the space—it was the only room in the house with a TV and they played video games and watched shows she didn't understand. But once her brothers moved out, and especially once Olivia went to college, it became Max's room.

Her brothers were talking about a new show—had she seen it? There was a baseball game on somewhere and they navigated to that, and watched for a while, but soon everyone peeled off to their own rooms, professing sleepiness.

WHEN OLIVIA WOKE, it wasn't yet eight. The air coming through her bedroom window was cool and damp. She dressed to go running—a new habit she'd resumed after India—and went into the kitchen.

Max was awake, leaning against the counter and reading the newspaper. "I didn't know you ran," he said.

"I don't, usually." She didn't want her father to get too invested. Max had always been a runner, and Ty ran too; when the whole family was together, sometimes Alec would join in.

Max squinted at her from across the "Week in Review." "How far you going?"

"How far is it to the beach?"

"A little under a mile. The whole loop is three miles. Three point two."

Olivia held on to the edge of the kitchen counter and bent forward, stretching the backs of her legs.

"Maybe I'll join you," Max said. "If you don't mind."

"What about Ty?" Olivia didn't want company. Her father was a good runner, a real runner. She didn't want him egging her on, saying her form was bad or her form was good or that she could go faster.

"Ty can go later." Max hesitated. "Unless you'd prefer to be alone."

She told him she didn't prefer it, that it was fine for him to come. She drank a glass of orange juice while he changed.

Max didn't stretch. He broke into a trot as soon as they got to the mailbox and she followed him. It was the week of daffodils, and they were everywhere—outside everyone's fences and shrubs, jubilant. It was that perfect running weather: cool and damp, still a little cloudy over the water.

Olivia was relieved that Max didn't seem to want to talk much. It was best to run single file anyway; the roads that led to the beach were narrow and had no shoulder. She found that it was easy to keep up with him. The smooth macadam was like nothing in the city and her feet sprang off it.

When they got to the beach path, Max dropped back beside her. "Go ahead, sweetie, if you want. I'm getting old."

She shook her head. She couldn't stand the thought of being a faster runner than her father.

"Did you talk to June?"

Max hadn't. Their sneakers snuffled on the dirt as they ran past the nearly empty beach parking lot. On the beach, a man was throwing a tennis ball for a big white dog. "I feel bad," Max admitted. "She's right. I hadn't been thinking about the weekend—I wanted her here for me, but it didn't really make sense."

But none of this made sense, Olivia thought. They were all still experiencing the whiplash of Eleanor's death. And in a world in which her mother had hidden her cancer from her family and had had an affair months before she died, Max inviting his girlfriend to a haphazard day of commemoration was as reasonable as anything else.

"I know you can't understand why I would want June to be here," Max said.

"I can," Olivia said, and Max looked at her, surprised.

Before she could say anything else, he stumbled forward and cried out. He caught himself before falling—he'd tripped over a root—but he was doubled over, clutching the back of his right thigh.

"What happened?"

"My hamstring. Shit. Sorry, sweetie."

"Didn't you hurt your hamstring before?" A memory was surfacing: Max not running last summer because of a hamstring tear.

He sank onto the grass beside the path.

"Does it hurt a lot?"

"Not unless I move," Max said.

Neither of them had brought phones, so Olivia jogged through the parking lot and down to the beach. The man and dog had disappeared, but there was a woman running on the sand, wearing those thin amphibian running shoes. She took off her headphones when Olivia waved at her.

"My father hurt himself," Olivia said, pointing up toward the path, where Max was a small T-shirted blob. The woman let Olivia use her phone. But there was no reception on the beach.

The woman, who was blond and thin, a kind of suburban Christina, emitted waves of resentment as she followed Olivia up to the parking lot, searching for a signal. Olivia called the house and then her brothers' cell phones to no avail. Between each call, the woman's phone locked and Olivia had to hand it back to her to reenter the code.

"Why don't you just call an ambulance?" the woman asked, jogging in place.

Finally Olivia got Holly. "He isn't supposed to be running!" Holly said, before she handed the phone to Alec.

When Olivia returned the phone, its owner sprinted toward the beach as if she were being chased.

Alec and Holly arrived in Max's car a few minutes later. Alec groaned in sympathy when Max told them what had happened and Holly fussed over him sweetly as they helped him into the front seat.

"Should we take you to the hospital?" she asked.

Max said no, although he didn't look certain. He mentioned his physical therapist, Vanessa: maybe she could be prevailed upon to make a house call.

"Didn't Vanessa tell you not to run?" Alec said. "Because your hamstring was still weird?"

"Sort of," Max admitted.

Olivia struggled not to be annoyed at the ridiculous turn of events: she, a non-runner, had inadvertently motivated Max to go running against doctor's orders. What had started out as her wanting to clear her head for half an hour before the day began had turned into a family fiasco, for which she felt responsible.

They settled Max on the couch with a bag of ice. It was still only nine in the morning and there was no sign of Ty, though Olivia thought of him as an early riser.

"Sweetie, go finish your run," Max said, when he saw Olivia pacing.

Gratefully, she set out again, this time with headphones on and running fast.

WHEN OLIVIA RETURNED, Max was on the couch with his eyes closed, alone, but by the time she'd stretched and showered, Holly was sitting on the floor next to him, painting her fingernails with light pink polish.

Ty and Alec were in the kitchen. Alec presided over a pan of scrambled eggs. "Want some?" he asked. When she said yes, he cracked two more eggs into the already cooking eggs.

Ty was about to pick Christina up at the station when the doorbell rang.

"You think she caught an earlier train?" Alec said.

Ty answered the door. Olivia was picking at Alec's eggs, trying to eat only the parts that looked cooked.

"Hey, Kelsey," they heard Ty say.

Kelsey came down the hall, her wooden clogs slapping and echoing. Olivia got up to greet her. Kelsey was slightly breathless, carrying two bags from the gourmet store.

"Oh thank God," Alec said, giving Kelsey a hug and taking one of the bags from her.

"Give me that baguette," said Holly, getting slowly but gracefully to her feet.

There was tapenade and heirloom tomatoes, smoked salmon, bagels, cream cheese with chives, prosciutto, fresh mozzarella, a whole bunch of other cheeses, a loaf of homemade sandwich bread that Kelsey said was reserved for making her mother's famous grilled cheese sandwiches, and a pound of bacon, "in case of emergency."

Alec dumped the rest of his eggs into the sink, and Olivia did the same.

Ty lingered. "Should we make mimosas?"

"This isn't a party," Olivia told him. But she was the one arranging things on little plates.

Ty left to get Christina. Kelsey trimmed a bouquet of lilies she'd brought, arranging them in Eleanor's favorite vase, which she'd found somewhere. She moved efficiently, as though the kitchen were hers: replacing the trash bag, brewing a fresh pot of coffee.

Speaking in a low voice, Olivia told Kelsey about Max's hamstring, and the fight he'd gotten in with June. "Also Ty's being weird about his wedding," she said, though as soon as she spoke, she regretted it.

"Weird how?"

"I don't know. Nervous."

Kelsey popped an olive in her mouth thoughtfully. She licked her fingers and then began to slice the tomatoes. She arranged them on a plate and liberally applied olive oil and sea salt.

They took the food into the living room, where Alec and Max were watching golf. They sat on the floor and everyone made sandwiches. Holly emerged from her bath, wearing a long black dress that hugged her stately bump, around the time Ty and Christina returned from the station. Christina inquired about Max's injury while Ty went to fetch him a new ice pack. Olivia and Kelsey held on to each other's arms and took turns stretching each other's backs. At moments, everything seemed so normal that Eleanor could just be in the other room, getting dressed or grading a few tests, which she would often slip away to do in small batches. Then Olivia would remember. Her mother was not there. She had chosen not to be there, Olivia couldn't help but think, though she knew it wasn't as simple as that.

Christina fussed over Holly's baby bump and answered Holly's questions about the wedding.

"I'm so sorry I won't be there," Holly said, her hands on her belly. She looked sincere, sort of, but also serene. Whatever Alec thought, Holly seemed to Olivia to be at least as beautiful six months pregnant as she'd been before, and probably more so.

Time went slowly until it was suddenly three o'clock and people were coming in an hour. It emerged that Max had ordered some food from a caterer in town, which he claimed to have forgotten the night before, though they all guessed the truth: June had ordered the food, and Max only remembered when the caterer called saying it was ready for pickup.

Alec was deployed to get the food while Ty and Christina made a drinks run. When Olivia went to shower, Kelsey followed her and sprawled on the bed, flipping through an ancient magazine.

Olivia emerged in a steam cloud, one towel around her body and another wrapping her hair. Things she never knew to appreciate until she left home: luscious water pressure, an abundance of clean, fluffy towels.

She put on an old sundress she found in her closet, a bit summery for April but somehow more right than dark winter clothes. Kelsey combed and French braided Olivia's hair, a skill she'd mastered effortlessly as a child.

They took a walk through the neighborhood, cutting daffodils from the unstewarded strips of land between people's border shrubs and fences and the street. They weren't sure they should be cutting the flowers, which had probably been planted by someone at some point, but daffodils had such a short season and no one else was cutting them.

Back at the house, Holly and Christina were unpacking the catered food, putting things that needed to be reheated on baking sheets. Max, dressed in khakis and a button-down, was filling a bucket with ice. He began to carry it outside, walking with a pronounced limp, but he refused to let Olivia take it, so she settled for gripping the other side of it. They put it in the grass beside the house, where Ty and Alec had dragged a table.

Eleanor's sister, Vera, and her husband, Lake, were the first to arrive. Vera was five years older than Eleanor, though it had always seemed like a bigger age difference than that: her entire style was of another era. Her hair had never been darker than platinum blond, and it was cut short and blown out carefully. Vera was very tall—even taller than Eleanor, who had been five foot nine—but she wore heels, which Olivia admired. Lake was mousy beside her, a pastel cashmere sweater pulled tight over his soft belly.

Cousin Maris accompanied them. Maris was in her midthirties, a few years older than Alec, and the Harrises had always found her to be a bit of a sad case: she'd launched and abandoned several careers and tended to be overeager about other people's lives. Eleanor had had no patience for her.

It was declared warm enough to go outside. Olivia and Christina located the cushions for the outdoor furniture; Kelsey carried around a tray of stuffed mushrooms, warning people that they weren't very good. Others arrived—the Milligans, the Vincents, Kate Beckerman and Martha Jacobs from Eleanor's school. Olivia wished she'd thought to invite Suzanne from the yoga studio.

"I can't believe it's been a year," Vera murmured.

"What's a year supposed to mean, anyway?" Max said.

Vera's teeth clinked the edge of her wineglass. She was silent for a moment. "Where's your friend?" she asked Max.

"She's not coming today."

"She seems very nice." Vera smiled diplomatically, as though speaking of someone about whom she'd heard a bad piece of gossip.

"She is nice," Olivia said, surprising herself as much as her father and aunt. She didn't even know when Vera and June would have met—Vera had spent the holidays skiing in Switzerland with Lake's family, as she did every year. Vera hadn't made any particular effort, at least not as far as Olivia knew, to see the Harrises in the year since Eleanor's death, though she lived half an hour away.

Ignoring Max and Vera's inquisitive glances, Olivia escaped to the drinks table, where Alec was opening more wine.

"Who put that in there?" Alec said, gesturing to a bottle of champagne in the ice bucket.

Olivia didn't know, but the champagne seemed in keeping with the general weirdness of the day. Part of her wanted to drink it, and part of her wanted to throw the bottle at the side of the house.

"Mom loved champagne," Alec said. He handed it to Olivia. "Want to do the honors?"

She removed the foil and the wire cage around the cork.

Maris made her way over. She was wearing a long purple skirt and a beaded top, and looked like she'd ambled in from a music festival. "I hear Uncle Max is selling the house," she said by way of greeting.

Alec glanced at Olivia, probably afraid she'd freak out. "I don't think he's rushing into anything. Ty—" He stopped, perhaps realizing that Maris might not have been invited to the wedding.

"I know all about the wedding," Maris said, not quite managing to sound nonchalant. In one hand she held a crumpled napkin, out of which tumbled a partially eaten stuffed mushroom. Olivia watched it fall to the grass.

"Is he working with a broker yet?" Maris asked.

Olivia had a vague recollection that Maris might be in real estate. She was about to respond, with an appropriate amount of hostility, when there was a loud *pop* right by her ear and something flew past her face, skyward. Alec was laughing, a deep, full laugh that she hadn't heard in a while, a laugh that made her think of her mother, and her hand was covered in champagne, which continued to flow from the now-open bottle she was holding.

She and Alec stood there on the grass, barely able to contain themselves, while their guests looked on.

"You can't," Alec said, when he'd caught his breath. "You can't take off the wire or it just blows."

"Apparently." The fountain had subsided.

Holly came over to take the bottle away, shaking her head at them. "You two can't be trusted."

Olivia sought refuge in the kitchen from the disapproving looks, where Kelsey was assembling grilled cheese sandwiches, slathering one side of bread slices with butter and the other with a white substance from a jar she'd brought with her.

"Bacon fat," she told Olivia proudly.

"Gross."

"Trust me. You know how addictive my mom's grilled cheese is. It's the taste of bacon without actual bacon—it drives people crazy."

Several cheeses were grated in piles on waxed paper. The griddle and another large frying pan were on, butter sizzling.

"Where are your parents, anyway?"

Kelsey nibbled some Gouda. "Running late, of course. They'll be here soon."

Ty emerged from somewhere in the house. He leaned against the counter and sipped from a juice glass. They watched Kelsey prepare the sandwiches, lightly frying the lard-covered sides of the bread first, then removing the slices from the stove to heap on cheese. She put the assembled sandwiches back on the stove, to brown the exteriors and melt the cheese.

She took the sandwiches off one at a time, cut them into quarters and then diagonally into eighths, put the triangles on a platter, and stuck in toothpicks. It was rare to see Kelsey so focused and precise. Olivia and Ty each took a triangle, and then another. They were impossibly rich and gooey, the bread seeming to dissolve in Olivia's mouth.

"You witch," Olivia said. "You're right—it *is* the bacon fat." It was a fact that Kelsey's mom's grilled cheeses were the best, but she'd never stopped to consider why.

Kelsey smiled, proud. "Take them outside."

OLIVIA OBEYED, CIRCULATING the sandwiches on the lawn. Soon Kelsey's parents arrived. Nina gave Olivia a long hug. As Olivia answered their questions about her summer plans and the trip to India, she glanced inside—Kelsey and Ty were still in the kitchen. Kelsey was sitting on the edge of the counter, her legs crossed, her expression serious. Ty's back was to Olivia.

Everyone wanted to greet Olivia. She spoke to Kate Beckerman and Martha Jacobs. Both were a bit younger than her mother, in their late forties, Olivia guessed. In high school, they had been Mrs. Beckerman and Ms. Jacobs—Olivia had been in Ms. Jacobs's trigonometry class junior year—but now they were Kate and Martha, or so they insisted.

Olivia had been dreading having to fake a whole range of normal-seeming emotions while everyone talked about her mother in hushed tones. But after the obligatory pleasantries, Kate and Martha launched straight into high school gossip. Another old math teacher of Olivia's, Mr. Rick, had quit abruptly that spring after rumors spread that he'd been sleeping with a student.

"No one even believed it had happened, until he essentially left town in the middle of the night," Kate said.

Martha was shaking her head. "I still don't believe he really did it," she said. "He must have just been so embarrassed—he was always a shy, awkward man—but God, it made him look guilty."

Martha mentioned that her girlfriend was out of town. Noticing Olivia's surprise, she said, "It's nobody's business at school. But I assumed your mom would have told you. She met Ruth many times."

"My mother was big on privacy," Olivia said. Kate and Martha exchanged quizzical glances.

Across the lawn, Kelsey's parents were with Holly and Alec. Everyone was laughing. Holly's hands were clasped around her belly. She was wearing some sort of tasseled shawl over her shoulders that Olivia coveted. Olivia began to make her way over to them.

"I can't believe how old we're all getting," Nina was saying to Alec. "I can remember the first time I met you, when you and your mom came to pick Olivia up at our house. You couldn't have been twelve. And you"—she said, turning to Olivia—"you're going to be an aunt."

"Liv will be the fun aunt," Alec said. "She'll be the one with candy, who lets her watch TV—"

Holly nudged Alec sharply in the rib cage.

"You're having a girl?" Olivia said. They'd said they weren't finding out the sex. A lump materialized in her throat.

"I was being politically correct," said Alec, glancing between her, the Grants, and Holly.

"It was supposed to be a surprise," Holly said crossly.

Nina laughed. "The baby's going to be enough of a surprise. Trust me." She put her arm around Kelsey, who had just joined them.

The light was turning golden, and Max murmured, "I guess I'd better say something."

Holly settled into a chaise lounge and Olivia perched on the edge.

Max stood with the house behind him, holding his drink. He cleared his throat and tapped his fingers against his glass until everyone looked at him.

"Thank you all for coming today," he said. He was holding a few leaves of paper from a yellow legal pad. Olivia hadn't realized he'd prepared a speech.

She glanced back at the house. Ty wasn't in the kitchen anymore, but he hadn't come outside.

"I didn't speak at Eleanor's funeral," Max said. A few people nodded. No one had really been able to do it. Alec had said a few words on behalf of the family, but they had mostly let other people do the talking—Eleanor's principal, one of her former students, and her best friends from college, who lived in Boston.

Max gazed out at the assembled group, his eyes clear, his posture excellent in spite of the morning's injury. "I thought a year later, I'd be able to say something. Maybe that's why I invited you here—to pay a tribute to my wife, to give her some fraction of what she deserves." He looked down at the notes in his hand and there was another long pause.

"They say losing a spouse is like losing a limb. But that doesn't begin to cover it." His voice cracked and he raised his eyebrows, surprised at himself. He sipped from the glass of wine he was clutching.

"Losing Eleanor has been like losing half of everything. Half my brain, half my heart, half my liver." He laughed abruptly and was met with silence.

No one had heard him talk this way before, Olivia thought. No one knew what to do. Vera and Lake were exchanging meaningful glances. Olivia wondered if June was why they'd kept their distance over the last year. She went to stand beside her father and took his hand. He squeezed hers. Still, nobody spoke. Olivia glanced at the papers her father was holding, which were slashed with his illegible scrawl in black ink.

Then Alec joined them, putting his arm around Olivia's shoulder. "We miss her so much," he said. "We know you do too."

There were murmurs of assent, or maybe relief.

"There's more food inside," Max called, as people began to stir. Holly and Christina circled with bottles of wine, refilling glasses.

"Where's Ty?" Olivia asked Christina. Christina didn't know, but her face betrayed none of the annoyance that Olivia felt.

Olivia went inside, through the kitchen and into the living room. Ty was on the couch, looking at his phone.

"What are you doing?" Olivia demanded.

Her brother looked up, startled. "I had a few emails."

"You missed Dad's speech."

Ty set down his phone. "Did he announce his engagement to June?"

"He was actually really nice."

"I would think you of all people would see today as a charade," Ty said, ignoring the tremor in her voice.

"I'm not sure," Olivia said. Maybe Ty was the one she could tell what she'd found out, the one she had to tell. Maybe he could help her make sense of it. "There's something I found out about Mom," she began.

"Kids." Max was behind them, his hands on their shoulders. "What's going on?"

They were both quiet.

"People are taking off," Max said. "Come say goodbye."

"Olivia was—" Ty began.

Olivia shook her head quickly. She walked toward the kitchen, and her father and brother followed her.

IT WAS TRUE that the guests were leaving. Some were in the kitchen, quietly stacking plates and scraping food into the trash.

As people began their prolonged goodbyes, Alec and Holly were the only ones still outside. Olivia was about to join them but she stopped in front of the sliding door. The sky over the Sound was streaked with pink, and Alec stood at the edge of the lawn, close to the water. As Olivia watched, Holly pushed herself to her feet and walked barefoot through the grass to stand beside him. He put his arm around her and kissed the top of her head.

Kelsey and her parents left. Silently, the Harrises finished putting away the food and tidying up the kitchen. Olivia wiped the countertop with a ragged sponge that badly needed replacing. The image of Max living there alone with a filthy sponge was almost too much for her. Had no one told him sponges needed to be replaced? The cleaning lady came twice a week—why didn't she buy one?

Alec and Holly retreated into their room, and Ty and Christina were debating what to do. "Maybe we should just go home," Olivia heard Ty say, although everyone had been planning to spend the night.

She was about to object when Max said to her, "Let's go to Eddie's."

Eddie's was the divey bar the next town over where Max played pool. It was a habit Eleanor had laughed about—*Dad's going to hustle some teenagers.* Though Max claimed he never played for money, he also boasted about putting himself through law school playing pool.

They didn't speak on the drive. Eddie's was ten minutes away, on a side street. A neon sign announced the presence of Budweiser.

Olivia had been there before—when she was underage, hitching a ride on someone's fake ID—but never with Max. It was the kind of place that smelled like beer when you walked in, and it was mostly deserted at that early hour, with a few old men and three thuggish-looking boys who barely looked out of high school, crowding around the shuffleboard table.

Max strode to the bar. "Want a beer?" he asked Olivia, as the bartender exchanged his singles for quarters.

She couldn't remember the last time she'd seen Max drink a beer, but he bought them two lagers. He fed quarters into the table, racked, and handed her the cue to break, but she barely disturbed the neat triangle of balls so he did it for her, landing two solids and a stripe. She was glad—in her limited experience, it was easier to hit the striped balls in the right place.

Max sank another solid and used his next turn to break up the remaining balls. He handed her a lighter cue, then leaned against the wall, sipping his beer and watching her line up her shot.

Olivia sank the blue and missed the red, aware of her father's gaze and the advice he was struggling not to dispense.

He made a long shot and paused. "Is something wrong? Besides missing Mommy?"

Mommy. No one had called Eleanor that in fifteen years. Olivia couldn't look at him. She shook her head no.

Max aimed for the orange. The angle looked impossible from where Olivia stood, and he had an easier choice, but though he didn't quite make it, he left the ball at the lip of a side pocket.

Olivia scratched on her next shot. Max fished the balls out, putting the purple striped one back where it was and handing the cue ball back to her. "You have to hit it really low down to get back-spin. Try again."

She made the shot, and the one after it. They both had three balls left. Max circled the table, assessing his options. He stopped and stood his cue on the ground. "I miss her too. Probably more than you think."

Olivia wished everyone would stop assuming that she was upset because they didn't miss Eleanor enough. The summer before she *had* felt that way—but at the bar, her anger about June felt indistinct and distant. For her, the past year had been a series of varyingly successful distractions, with all the logic and profundity of a dream sequence. How could it have been otherwise for her father?

"I rushed things," Max was saying. "I shouldn't have made you guys deal with me dating someone else so soon." He moved back toward the table and lined up his next shot.

"It's not about anything you've done wrong," Olivia said, after he'd sunk the orange and another ball.

Max made a face, like he didn't believe her. He missed his next shot and turned back to her.

She sank the yellow and missed the green. The jukebox was playing one of those classic rock songs she knew by heart without knowing its name or who the band was, the kind of song that made her nostalgic for things she had never experienced. "Mom lied to us," she said.

Max was rubbing chalk on the tip of his cue. He raised his eyebrows.

"She knew she was sick. A long time before we found out."

Max said nothing. Olivia drank her beer, and he set down the chalk and moved back toward the table. He tapped his last ball in so gently. "Where did you acquire this piece of information?"

"I found some papers in her study. I traced them—" She stopped, taking a breath and giving her heart a moment to slow its ricochet.

She'd considered telling Kelsey, or Alec, or even Holly—she'd come close to telling Ty an hour ago. She'd never imagined the scenario in which she told her father. "An old friend of hers," she continued. "A yoga teacher. Apparently this person knew."

"Marco?"

"Franco." She said it automatically.

"That's right." He bent and squinted and sank the eight ball in the side pocket, the cue ball hovering at the lip, a victim of his perfected backspin. "We'll play again," he said consolingly.

They sat down in an empty booth. Olivia rested her hands on the edge of the wooden table. It had a greasy, waxy feeling, like if you stuck in your fingernail, it would leave a mark.

"What did Franco have to say?" Max asked.

"How did you know about him?"

Max waved his hand dismissively. "Mom had all these yoga friends."

"But you knew that she told him? Or did she tell you too?" Why hadn't it occurred to her before, that Max might have known all along? It was tangled in her head—what Franco had told her and what she had inferred.

"Around the time we got the official diagnosis—in January— and told you kids, she told me." He pinched the bridge of his nose and closed his eyes. Then he dropped his hand back to the table and looked at Olivia.

"Told you what, exactly?"

"That she had known she was sick. That she knew chemo wouldn't work, so she'd decided to try alternative treatments."

"She was having a shaman treat her for brain cancer." She wanted to be kind, to be gentle, but she couldn't let Max get away with making this insanity sound reasonable.

Max actually laughed. "I think you're exaggerating, sweetie."

"I'm not."

He turned his palms—*What can you do?*

"Weren't you mad?" She couldn't say what she meant: *devastated, broken-hearted.*

Max's eyes were closed again. A year ago, Olivia's mother had been alive and asking for Orangina. Her father had gone out and bought a case. They'd used at least one bottle just pouring cold glasses and throwing them away. "Mommy didn't want us to be sad for a year."

It had been a year—they were still sad.

"You know how she hated wallowing. She couldn't stand everyone worrying when it wouldn't have done any good."

Excuse me, Olivia thought, *if our being upset would have gotten on her nerves.*

"She wanted you to finish college. She didn't want it to be like when her dad died, false hope compounding misery." Max smiled, making his appeal. "She didn't want casseroles and people talking about her behind her back."

"She made fools of us," Olivia said. The words sounded overly dramatic, but that was what it felt like.

"She was trying to protect us," Max said. "She may not have thought it through perfectly."

They sipped their beers. Olivia tried to breathe, to calm down. There was plenty of time for this inquisition, she told herself. But after a moment, she persisted, hating herself for asking questions that could only make Max feel worse: "But there was some chance she would have survived."

"She would have needed surgery. It was risky. You remember Grandpa."

Olivia nodded, though Eleanor's father had died fifteen years before she was born.

"She never forgave the doctors for that. Or her mother, for pushing him to have the surgery. He would have had—oh, I don't know—at least another six months."

"She thought we would have forced her to have a pointless surgery?" Why hadn't she given them more credit?

"The tumor—I'm sure you remember—they would have had to cut into parts of the brain that control speech and movement."

"I know. But—"

"She thought she could beat the odds doing it her own way. And she was right. She slowed the tumor down through sheer force of will." Max actually sounded proud.

The bar was slowly filling up, people clustered around the TV at the bar, watching a game. Olivia and Max had to speak loudly to be heard over the music.

"She told you about some of the other ways she tried to treat it?" She couldn't imagine this: her mother explaining, with a straight face, these treatments to her father.

"Yes, with Marcus. The trip to Mexico."

She wondered if he was getting Franco's name wrong on purpose.

"It sounded like it was worth a try," Max said.

She stared at him in mute amazement.

"Some of it seemed to help her feel better. Yoga, breathing, all that. She said acupuncture helped the most, with the headaches. I've been meaning to go, for my hamstring."

Olivia just looked at him.

Max looked to the side, as if trying to remember something from long ago. "It's funny, I don't even remember how I felt when I found out. The main thing was just—"

"What?"

"The main thing was the main thing."

"That she was dying."

He nodded. Two heavy, tattooed men had taken over the pool table. They joked loudly. It was time to go.

THE DRIVE HOME was quiet. Olivia wondered if her dad knew about the affair, too, but she wasn't about to ask. And Max didn't say anything about her brothers, but she knew she wouldn't tell them. She didn't regret knowing everything—it was impossible, she found, to imagine a state of not knowing it. But it wasn't helpful, and she didn't wish it on Ty or Alec.

Maybe Eleanor's decision would have been the right one, if she could have prevented them from ever finding out. *But you're not here anymore*, Olivia said to Eleanor. *You can't control anything that happens to us.* It didn't feel like anyone was out there—it just felt like she was talking to herself.

"Try not to let this become the most important part," Max said to Olivia as they pulled into the driveway.

Everyone was in the den watching a movie. Ty and Christina hadn't left. Olivia settled in the corner of the couch.

"I'll join you in a minute," Max said. Olivia wondered if he was going to call June.

6.

They were at dinner in Brooklyn when Ty made the announcement: his firm was opening a small office in the Bay Area, and he would be one of the associates to transfer.

"I've always wanted to live in San Francisco," he said, as though this were a known thing. He sipped his beer while they all struggled to respond appropriately.

"How exciting!" June exclaimed, while Max let out an ambiguous "Wow."

Olivia had never imagined Ty living anywhere outside the city—he hadn't even wanted to consider Chicago or California for law school. But the year, not yet halfway through, had been one of surprises, and this could be a happy one. It was clear Ty needed a change.

It was mid-May, and the dinner was to celebrate Olivia's thesis, which had passed a few days before. Max told her to pick the restaurant, so she had chosen a new place in Williamsburg, but she was already regretting it. The menu was appealing but their server was too cool, responding with sarcasm to Max's admittedly unnecessary admonishment not to overcook his steak. Still, Max and June liked the place or at least pretended to, praising the industrial decor and stylish patrons. Antique bronze light fixtures hung over the large, gleaming U-shaped bar, where couples Ty's age sipped cocktails served in champagne saucers.

"What about Christina?" June asked as Olivia took her first bite of salad. It was what they were all thinking.

"Her job is here," Ty said.

Less than two weeks after the Harrises had gathered in Rye to commemorate Eleanor, Max had phoned Olivia to report that Ty had postponed the wedding.

"Did he say why?" Olivia had asked. She felt a rush of relief—and then guilt, for feeling that way. She'd liked Christina more as she'd gotten to know her, though that hadn't diminished the feeling that something was off.

Ty hadn't told Max much. "He said they were putting it off for a few months to figure some things out. Maybe you can get more out of him than I could."

He and Christina were still living together, Ty said when Olivia called him—they just needed some time. He sounded calm and assured, much more so than he had a few weeks before, when discussing the upcoming wedding. But it was clear that he wasn't going to say more. And when Olivia had emailed to confirm that Christina would be joining them for dinner in Brooklyn, he said no.

Slowly, Ty revealed his plans. He would be moving in just a few weeks, he told them—he'd been looking for a new apartment anyway (*Was Christina keeping their old place?* Olivia wondered. *Could she afford it by herself?*) and the firm was giving him several weeks off, paid, to relocate.

"It was hinted that transferring might shave a year off the partnership track," Ty said. "But who knows if I'll even go in that direction."

Max looked more surprised by this than he had by the move. "What other direction are you considering?" he said. It had long been assumed that Ty would follow his footsteps, at a smaller but equally prestigious firm.

Ty didn't know. He was interested, he said, in environmental law, perhaps in consulting.

"You're so young," June said, before Max could register his opinion. "What a great idea to consider your options." She smiled reassuringly at all of them, and though she wouldn't have admitted it, Olivia was glad June was there.

Olivia had ordered trout, but she ended up stealing a couple of slices of her father's steak, which was perfectly cooked—if anything, a little bloody, but they both liked it that way. Reluctantly, they stopped questioning Ty, and conversation turned briefly to Olivia's plans: summer school began in a month.

In the past, Max had urged Olivia too to consider law school, but though she wasn't quite sure why, her four-month sojourn at Likely had convinced him that film editing was a legitimate career.

"You should talk to Alec," he said between bites. "He probably knows people in New York."

Alec did know people in New York—he was the reason she'd gotten the job at Likely, though Olivia didn't want to remind her father that. Thinking about what she would do after graduation took her appetite away. It wasn't that she wanted to be a student for any longer. But the hiatus from college, the whole last year and a half, had been a kind of suspended state in which the rules of regular life hadn't fully applied. With graduation, she suspected the bubble would burst, and she'd be just another twenty-three-year-old trying to cobble together a life.

In the end, her thesis had been a sweet nothing, a thirty-minute non-narrative film. Officially, she'd gone with the idea she'd had in Goa: a portrait of the country for her mother, who hadn't been able to see it (never minding that her mother was no more able to watch Olivia's film than she was to visit India).

What she would return to was not the film itself, but a handful of still images from the footage. A man smoking a betel-leaf cigarette in front of a fabric stall. Brandon in a handstand. The sadhu by the door of the Kali temple, hard to make out in the dim light. Franco on the ride back to the ashram, his drawn face against the lush green background. A blurred shot of the same wet greenery she took on the train. Will in bed with the sheet all the way around his face (she hadn't included this shot in her thesis, as it wasn't credible that she would have shown this man in bed to her mother). From the first trip to India, the fountain outside the store where they had bought their Indian clothes in the rain their first day—there was one frame that was everything she'd wanted it to be, the dark cars framing the children at the fountain whose arms were lifted in play, the light ethereal in the rain. A similar image from the Taj: the forms of other tourists crowding the arched entrance, framing a first glimpse of the unearthly mausoleum.

The film wasn't really a film at all—it was a collage of beautiful stills. If she could have, she would have turned the whole thing into a photography exhibit. But it was too late for that, so she strung the footage together as best she could, and the faculty said she had a good eye and let her pass.

It was during dessert (olive oil cake and pistachio ice cream) that Olivia noticed June was wearing a rather large and sparkly ring on the fourth finger of her left hand. The center stone was square and yellow—maybe a yellow diamond—surrounded by tiny white diamonds, on a platinum band.

June's head was tilted toward Max. She was asking when his tee time was the next day.

"Nine twenty," he said. "If it's not rained out."

"I didn't know it was going to rain," June said.

"How would you? You never check the weather."

Olivia opened her mouth to say something about the ring, and then closed it. Max was smiling at June. She'd never heard how they patched things up after that weekend in Rye. She didn't even know whether wearing a ring on that finger always meant what she thought it did.

IT WAS FRIDAY night. Max and June wanted to give her a ride home after dinner, but she wasn't going home—she was meeting Brian at a party nearby. She'd been seeing a lot of him since she came back from India. He'd helped her with her thesis, even sneaking her into the Likely office at night a few times to use software. Her nascent crush on him had been flourishing; the fact that he was friendly but not flirtatious only egged her on.

Her father settled for dropping her off at the party, which was only a few blocks away. If he didn't like the idea of her walking around Williamsburg alone on a mild spring night, she wanted to tell him, he wouldn't think much of the neighborhood farther east where she actually lived.

Before she got out of the car, something made her put her arms around his neck from the back seat. She thanked him for dinner. June leaned over to kiss her cheek. Ty had grabbed a cab back to the city, unencumbered by parental safety worries.

The party was at the top of a fifth-floor walkup occupied by friends of Brian's. Olivia barely met the host before she and Brian took beers and went up a rickety ladder in the hallway that led to the roof.

From up there, you could see slivers of Manhattan between the taller buildings closer to the water. It felt cooler than it had on the street, and Olivia crossed her legs for warmth. Brian asked about dinner.

"I think my dad might be engaged," she told him. It sounded ridiculous to her out loud, not so much the prospect of a union as the word *engaged*, which conjured up cheesy romance, and which, until recently, had been used about Ty and Christina.

"You think?"

She told him about the ring June had been wearing, and how no one had mentioned it.

Brian asked if she liked June, a question which seemed strangely beside the point. Brian knew about Olivia's mom, but they hadn't talked about it much. It was the idea of a wedding, she told Brian— of her father's wedding—that was the most upsetting, not Max being married to June. As it was, they operated like a married couple. Max hadn't mentioned selling the house again since the winter, but the threat loomed.

She wondered if the ring had something to do with how they'd made up after their fight the month before.

Brian was telling Olivia stories about the assistant they'd hired to replace her, whom he swore was mentally impaired. They'd somehow switched from beer to punch, a cough-syrup-sweet, boozy potion she was already regretting. But there was a giddiness to the night, the feeling of deepening the friendship with every story exchanged.

"I bet you could get your job back in the fall," Brian said. "I really think so. Or maybe even a second assistant editor. We could use one."

There was a pause, which Brian misinterpreted. "I'm sure you've got better options," he added.

"It's not that," Olivia said. The giddiness, the drunkenness— they were making her want to be truthful. "They didn't really make me leave because I lied about graduating from college."

"No?"

"It was much worse." She took a deep breath. "Remember that guy Michel Zahavi?"

"Yeah. I think he fired us."

That Michel had dropped Likely anyway was unexpectedly painful. Olivia regretted invoking Michel's name—even the thought of him seemed capable of ruining the evening. "I was involved with him," she said, because Brian was waiting for her to continue.

"I sort of figured," Brian said. "It was weird that time he accosted us on the street." He didn't sound judgmental. But he also didn't sound as though he wanted to know more.

"Let's just say—" Olivia began. She stopped talking. People on the roof were singing the chorus of a song that had been playing constantly on the radio last summer, and for the first time, she understood the words. She was too cold in her cotton sweater.

"It's okay," Brian said gently. "They're all assholes anyway."

She'd thought it might be the night that something happened between them, but it wasn't. They left the party soon after. Brian walked her to the train, and then continued on to a different train. On her way home, she worried their conversation like a loose tooth: Why hadn't Brian wanted to know—insisted on knowing—what happened with Michel? It didn't occur to her then that his lack of appetite for humiliating stories about her past was a desirable quality.

MIRACULOUSLY, OLIVIA HAD managed to keep her job at the coffee shop, and she picked up more shifts there after she'd finished her thesis. She saw friends and she went to help Ty, who was packing and sorting for his imminent departure to the West Coast, but she couldn't shake the restless, suspended feeling. She had turbulent, unsettling dreams: in one, she screamed at her mother until she went hoarse and couldn't make a sound. When she woke, she couldn't remember what she'd been angry about. In another, she was in Rye, driving her parents' car, but the brakes weren't working. She woke as she was coasting down the backyard toward the water, unable to stop.

It was a cool, rainy May but the temperature rose in time for Memorial Day weekend. The city cleared out. Sunday she would go to Rye for a family barbecue before Ty left town. Ty leaving would mean one less of the handful of people she saw in New York. She dreaded the possible announcement of Max and June's engagement.

So Friday night she did the only reasonable thing: squeeze into a too-tight dress she'd had since high school, drag Brian to a roof party in the Village, drink too much vodka, and throw herself at him.

When she woke up in her apartment, alone, with a trashcan beside her bed, she remembered snippets of the night before, like footage on rewind—her face close to Brian's, running into high school friends and thinking it was the funniest thing in the world that she couldn't remember their names, insisting on smoking a cigarette on the balcony which resulted in—*ick*—nausea, leaning into Brian in the cab, expecting them to kiss, and him pulling away.

She was mortified, by her failed seduction more than her drunkenness. Maybe Brian was gay, she thought. He was no more attracted to her than her roommates, who looked on with a mixture of amusement and disapproval while she groped around the kitchen for water and Advil.

But Brian called, and when Olivia didn't answer—she had decided on a strategy of permanently hiding—he called a second time.

"You're meeting me for brunch," he informed her, and named a place halfway between their apartments.

The one good thing about her hangover was that it put her in survival mode, keeping embarrassment partially at bay. She brushed her teeth, wrangled her hair, long overdue for a trim, into a bun, threw on shorts, and got to the restaurant first. She sat in the backyard, which was charmingly overgrown, wildflowers and weeds and rusted machine parts that lent a country air. Fresh-squeezed orange juice was served in mason jars.

In this bucolic garden, Brian explained to Olivia that he did not intend to fall for her shit. "Enough of that," he said. "I'm twenty-eight." He pointed out that she was about to leave the city for two months, he hinted that she might not know what she wanted, and he said that he wanted an actual girlfriend.

Olivia didn't see why any of this would have prevented him from wanting to at least make out with her the night before. Perhaps, she thought, embarrassment tightening her solar plexus, he'd been afraid she would throw up on him.

And yet he smiled at her as though he already loved her a little. "Am I the first person who's rejected you?"

She could feel herself blushing. Her hangover swelled and pitched in her stomach.

"I'm not rejecting you." Brian held out his big palms, as if to say everything were hers for the taking. "I just don't want to be the next ball of yarn you bat around." He dropped his hands to the table and looked at Olivia earnestly. "Be my friend."

After brunch, Olivia called Kelsey.

"Girls tell guys they just want to be friends when they don't like them," Kelsey said after she'd been apprised. "But I don't think he would have wanted to see you today if he didn't like you."

Olivia considered this.

"Besides," Kelsey said. "Maybe being friends isn't so bad." There were plenty of guys Olivia could sleep with, she pointed out, but not that many she'd want to have brunch with.

Since graduation, Kelsey had found a yearlong volunteer position with a women's organization in Ghana. She was at home in

Katonah, getting ready to leave. "You have to come visit me," she begged, and Olivia promised to try.

IN THE THREE weeks that remained before summer school, Olivia saw Brian nearly every day. She'd thought they were already friends, but what Brian meant was something more: Saturday jogs over the Williamsburg Bridge and late, confessional nights on the couch. It was the kind of friendship she'd only had with girls before, but in one way it was even better: it lacked the vein of competition that ran through many female friendships. Kelsey was right—it was much easier to find someone to hook up with than it was to make a new friend. Perhaps because they'd worked together, Olivia felt more in sync with Brian than she did with the people she'd gone to college with.

At Ty's going-away barbecue, Max and June announced their engagement. They would get married Labor Day weekend, and they were thinking of a small wedding in California, so that Holly and Alec and the baby, who was due in July, wouldn't have to travel. It was a muted celebration, perhaps because Ty should have been the one about to be married, or perhaps because they all feared Olivia's reaction. June was wearing a turquoise silk dress that complemented her eyes. June's daughter, Liza, who had apparently found an apartment with friends in Park Slope, arrived just in time for dinner. She didn't look particularly overjoyed by the engagement, and no one uttered the word *step-sister*, for which Olivia was grateful.

"Are you okay?" Ty asked her, when they were alone together in the kitchen.

Olivia didn't know how to answer. It was true that the balloon of righteousness she'd been carrying around since her mother's death was mostly deflated after India. But that didn't mean she had to be happy about Max and June getting married.

"It doesn't feel real yet," she told Ty, and that was partially true, in the way that September always felt implausible in May.

"They could have waited longer."

"Is it really over with Christina?"

Ty looked instantly miserable, and Olivia wished she hadn't been so blunt.

"Maybe I can't be the one who has it all together anymore," he said.

"You're fine the way you are," Olivia said protectively. She wanted to tell him she thought he was brave to call off a wedding he knew wasn't right rather than stifle his doubts. Brave to shake off everyone's expectations, to move across the country. "You're perfect."

Ty gave her an odd look.

"What?"

"You sounded like Mom there, for a second."

They stood in the kitchen, both a little embarrassed but pleased, looking out the window where, over the water, they could see shades of pink and orange beginning to streak the sky.

OLIVIA WAS AT summer school when her niece, Sadie, was born. A week later she flew out for a weekend to visit. Alec picked her up in his convertible and they drove west to Santa Monica. It had been sweltering outside the airport, but the temperature dropped as they neared the ocean, even on the freeway. The Friday-afternoon traffic was bumper to bumper, but Alec couldn't stop grinning, as though he were on drugs.

"I think she already knows us," he said about the baby.

The youngest child, Olivia hadn't had much experience with babies and hadn't formed a strong opinion pro or con. But sitting in Alec and Holly's backyard, holding tiny Sadie, who resembled a kitten as much as a human, Olivia too fell in love. It was an idyllic weekend—Ty flew down from San Francisco and they took walks on the beach and ate healthy takeout and napped when the baby napped. Holly was exhausted but happy and calm, and Ty was brimming with energy. He looked healthier somehow after less than two months in California.

There was a moment Saturday night after dinner, after Holly had taken the baby inside for a fresh diaper, when Alec's eyes filled with tears. "I can't believe Mom will never meet her."

Mom would have loved Sadie, Ty and Olivia murmured—as though Alec needed their assurance that Eleanor, mother of three and career teacher, would have delighted in meeting her first grandchild. They were sincere, and yet, Olivia saw, they couldn't understand Alec's particular grief: to have a child and not a mother. They were outsiders, and could only offer kind, useless words.

That night, not for the first time, Olivia was tempted tell her brothers what she'd learned in India. Maybe they would understand it better than she did—maybe telling them would make her feel less alone. But she was the one who had found the letters and gone looking for something—a story, an explanation. It wasn't fair to foist a secret on her brothers that they'd never asked for. So she settled for sitting beside them, watching Holly watch Alec as she carried the baby back out into the yard. Watching Ty's face flicker with everything he wasn't saying. They didn't fully know each other. But that had nothing to do with love.

Sunday they had an early dinner in the backyard before Olivia and Ty left. There were citrus trees—lemon and lime, the fruits all green and more than halfway ripened. In a basket on a chair between Alec and Holly, Sadie slept, her face free of complications. Alec and Ty were talking about golf: Would they be able to fit one round or two over Labor Day, when everyone would be together again for Max and June's wedding? No one was saying much about the wedding itself—Olivia knew only that rooms had been booked at a hotel on the beach.

It was then that the idea began to form in Olivia's mind: *Why not move out to LA, at least for a year?* There was nothing holding her in New York—maybe, at least for now, one year had been enough. Her mind flickered to Brian, but the moment she thought of him, he became a reason not to stay. She was twenty-three, and she would not be the person who made choices based on some guy (especially some guy she wasn't even dating). She was in film, and film was in LA. Besides, the majority of her family was now in California.

Summer school wasn't as bad as Olivia had anticipated. She was taking two classes—Terrance's History of Italian Film, and a Spanish class she needed to fulfill the language requirement. She hadn't taken Spanish since freshman year, so the intermediate course ended up being a stretch, but it wasn't the worst way to spend her time: afternoons lying out in the quad listening to Spanish conversation through earbuds, and evenings watching old movies.

She hadn't expected anyone she knew to still be on campus, but there were a few familiar faces from the class below her, other people who hadn't managed to graduate in time, and kids even younger who recognized her and said hello (because it was always the case in school that younger students paid more attention to older ones than the other way round).

One night, after her visit to LA, she went out for a beer with Sammy and Efron, two guys who had been in the class below her. Like Olivia, they would be receiving their diplomas after completing summer session. Their future plans sounded romantic and improbable: Sammy, a skinny pothead from DC, wanted to become an Outward Bound instructor, and Efron was moving to Germany to be a DJ.

"Do you speak German?" Olivia asked.

Efron looked affronted. "Everyone there speaks English."

Olivia walked home alone. It was a warm night and stars tacked the sky. She felt nostalgic, and also free. Alec had found a few people for her to speak with in LA about jobs. Nothing was certain yet, but she knew at that moment she wouldn't move back to New York in the fall. It was a mesmerizing city—it was *her* city—but there was so much she hadn't seen. New York had a way of making you forget about the rest of the world, and she wasn't ready to do that.

IT WAS THURSDAY night before Labor Day weekend, and Olivia was in Rye. The next morning she would fly to LA for the wedding. The following week, she'd start her job as a production assistant. It would likely be more coffee runs and cheese plates, but it was at a big studio—it would open a lot of doors, if she didn't screw up.

Max had wanted her to come out with him and June earlier in the week so they could help her find an apartment. But Alec and Holly had said she could stay with them while she looked for a place, and she'd wanted a few days alone at the house, to sort of commune with it before she left. Max still hadn't put it on the market. But June's house had sold, and he and June were spending some of their time in Manhattan, in an apartment they rented near Central Park. Either way, nothing was going to stay the same—if they didn't sell the house, they'd probably gut the kitchen.

In the past three days she'd sorted through her bedroom, setting aside garbage bags of clothes for Goodwill. There was little she wanted to take to LA—two suitcases of clothes and shoes, light without winter wear. She'd snagged an old, soft set of sheets from the linen closet and her mother's ancient and well-seasoned cast-iron skillet, which wouldn't be missed among June's shiny copper pots.

She'd leave behind boxes of books and papers from college, winter jackets and boots. It made her life feel small, having so little she wanted to take with her, the way her mother's life had felt small when Olivia went through her study and sorted the scant collection of papers and trinkets Eleanor had deemed worth saving. But she was never going to want the detritus her bedroom had been housing: hair clips, birthday cards, dusty ends of scented candles and faded receipts from the drugstore. No one had asked her to do this. But she didn't want someone else doing it later.

For all of her life, this place had belonged to her. All day she'd been walking through the rooms, trailing her fingers on the walls and feeling the cool wood floors beneath her feet, snooping on their lives. She pawed through the empty drawers in her brothers' rooms. She found yellowed paperbacks under the beds, ratty old clothing in addition to a few newer items forgotten or abandoned on visits home. In Alec's room, there were fluffy bathrobes her mother had bought for guests, particularly Holly, who had been known to spend much of the day in a good robe.

In Ty's desk drawer: chemistry flashcards, dried-out highlighters. A postcard from Budapest signed *Love, Emily*, which Olivia had scrutinized but could not date. She didn't remember there ever being an Emily, though she remembered many girlfriends her brothers had over the years.

Now, on her last night, she ventured into her parents' room. It was the only one of the four bedrooms that faced the backyard and the water. It was also the only room that had been redecorated in the last ten years: custom built-ins and California closets, all the lights on dimmers, a spa-like bathroom with stone floors and a huge tub, in which Olivia had sometimes been allowed a soak.

Max's wardrobe looked scant and tired—if he'd acquired any new clothes since Eleanor died, he must have already moved them into the city. But he'd always had a thing for soft sweaters and Olivia recognized them all. There were ties with animals on them she'd chosen for him as a child, and those ubiquitous gray New Balance sneakers he'd always worn.

Last summer, during those blurry weeks after her mother died, there had been a rush of dividing belongings. As the only daughter, Olivia had first dibs on pretty much everything. But she'd found her father's impulse to clear out the closet distasteful. At Holly's urging, she'd taken some clothes, though nowhere near all of them. Later, there were the sweaters June gave her, the ones that had been at the dry cleaner when Eleanor died.

As it turned out, Olivia had worn anything that had been her mother's obsessively, compulsively. She'd regretted any scrap of clothing that had gone to charity. She'd insisted that they leave the jewelry for later, and now she saw that her mother's jewelry box was there in her closet, where it had always been. Everything was there: the gold wedding band and the sapphire engagement ring Eleanor wore only on special occasions, two watches, a jade bracelet bought on a family vacation out west, various pairs of earrings and necklaces, a cloth-covered button that had been there for as long as Olivia remembered, and a handful of someone's baby teeth.

Olivia took a pair of gold knotted earrings that were a staple of her mother's into the bathroom. She flicked on the lights and tried them on in the mirror. They looked entirely wrong on her, as though she were playing dress up, which, in fact, she was. It didn't help that all she was wearing was a T-shirt of Brian's.

Brian had taken the train out that afternoon, taking a rare half day off work to spend time with her before she left for LA. They'd slept together for the first time a few hours ago. When he'd fallen asleep in her bed, Olivia had resumed her inventory. It was late, after three, and Olivia's eyes had that dry, tired feeling. But all week she'd had insomnia, and she'd been postponing getting into bed.

She put the earrings back in her mother's jewelry box, which, she'd decided, needed to stay exactly where it was, on the closet shelf, in this house, forever. She left her parents' room and walked down the hallway, her bare footsteps the only sound in the quiet house. She slid open the glass doors in the kitchen and walked outside. She was surprised by how fresh the air felt—it had been hot and oppressive all week. The sky was overcast, obscuring the stars, but in the diffuse light she could see well enough to make her way down the lawn to the water.

After she'd returned from summer school, she and Brian had resumed their pseudo-couple routine. But Olivia hadn't thought anything more would happen between them, especially once she knew she would be moving to LA. Brian took her out for celebratory drinks when the job came through a few weeks before—he had not behaved like someone who was upset that she was about to move across the country.

So what had that been earlier, she wondered, as she neared the water's edge. She and Brian had grilled shrimp they picked up on the way home from the station. Maybe the domesticity of the evening— cooking at a house in the suburbs—had been an aphrodisiac. Or maybe it was that they didn't know when they'd next see each other.

When he'd kissed her in the kitchen, she'd laughed in surprise. He'd pulled away and looked at her, his expression serious, as though to be sure he hadn't made a mistake. To clear things up, she kissed him back.

It was only when he unzipped her shorts—a ratty pair of cutoffs she'd had since high school—that he paused again to ask, "Is this okay?"

"You're asking me?" she said.

At the water, she stripped off his T-shirt. It was high tide and the water was only a foot below the retaining wall. Part of her had hoped something would happen with Brian, and part of her had been afraid it would: she hadn't wanted leaving town to feel complicated.

But it had happened, and it didn't feel that complicated. She didn't know what would come next, but nobody did. Things would get better and then they'd get worse, and better again, and worse again. Things she was excited about would amount to nothing and things she dreaded might not be so bad. She didn't have to decide how to feel about Brian or Max and June or even her mother. She didn't have to know how long she'd want to live in California.

She reached her arms over her head, squeezed her legs together, and dove into the Sound. The water was warm, the same temperature as the air and her skin. Here was all she needed to know: Was she tired enough to sleep. What time should she leave for the airport.

ACKNOWLEDGMENTS

I am so grateful to the many generous and brilliant people who helped, supported, and hung out with me while I was writing.

From our first conversations, PJ Mark and Liese Mayer felt like the absolute dream agent and editor for this novel. Thank you, PJ, for your early belief in *Alternative Remedies* and for helping it, and me, find our way. Thank you, Liese, for your sensitivity, insight, and dedication. This book is better because of you both.

Thank you to Ian Bonaparte, Michael Steger, and the rest of the Janklow & Nesbit team. Thank you to Grace McNamee, Jenna Dutton, and Sarah New for taking such good care of me, and to the many others at Bloomsbury who worked on this project, including Tree Abraham, Marie Coolman, Cristina Gilbert, Nicole Jarvis, Laura Keefe, Natasha Qureshi, Patti Ratchford, and Ellen Whitaker. Bringing this novel into the world together has been a privilege and a huge pleasure.

To my first reader and dear friend Lindsay Whalen—I am the luckiest to have had such a gifted and intuitive editor and writer in my corner from the earliest drafts. And to Genevieve Lowe, Lindsay Pharmer, Katie Ries, Madeleine Sackler, and Caroline Trefler, all of whose thoughtful input was a big help.

To Maggie Shipstead for her advice and generosity. To Joanna Hershon, Rebecca Dinerstein, and Molly Prentiss for their kind words.

To Josh Henkin for his counsel and encouragement over the years. To Ellen Tremper, Amy Hempel, Jenny Offill, and my classmates at Brooklyn College. To David Mason and Jane Hilberry at Colorado College. To Luis Jaramillo, Chrissy Heyworth, Anna Fels, and Jane Fransson. To the late Jack Rosenthal, who was very kind to me when I was Olivia's age. To Annie Piper, for her friendship and guidance. To Vermont Studio Center for giving me time and space to complete the first draft.

To my family, the Gablers, Cantors, and Piekarskis, who have given me more love and support than any person could possibly expect. Thank you, Mom, for reading to me endlessly—that must be at least partially why I prize story above pretty much anything. I'm so happy to be sharing this with you. Thank you, Dad, for sustaining the somewhat clinical belief that I could do anything I wanted to (and only telling me once that I should have gone to law school). I only wish you could be here to meet this book. To Matt and Doug, Brandy, Danielle, Jackson, Dylan, Jack, and Lily—I am so thankful for your unconditional love, encouragement, and friendship. To Dick and Pam, for your wisdom and grit, which inspire me, and for the use of the Tinker Hill Writing Retreat at a couple of critical moments. To Leo, for insisting that we leave the house, and sweeping me up in your boundless joy.

And to Mendy, my best friend, most trusted advisor, and tireless cheerleader. Your love makes everything possible.

A Note on the Author

JOANNA CANTOR holds an MFA from Brooklyn College and a BA from Colorado College. She was the 2014 recipient of a Vermont Studio Center Fellowship. She lives in Brooklyn with her husband and dog.